WAYFINDER

REPUBLIC OF STEAM CHRONICLES

WAYFINDER

REPUBLIC OF STEAM CHRONICLES

◆ Book Two ◆

CRAIG & JALEESA SNOW

WAYFINDER

ISBN 979-8-9876866-1-4 (pbk)
ISBN 979-8-9876866-3-8 (eBook)

Follow us at:
www.craigandjaleesasnow.com
Instagram: @authorcraigjaleesasnow

Library of Congress Control Number: 2025906780

Dedication

To my parents, who were always my biggest cheerleaders and
helped me see that I could do anything I put my mind to.
JAS

To my mother, who taught me creativity
and the importance of standing up for what is right.
CRS

SADRIA

SADRIA

NARDOOWE
TRIBE

EVERSTORM

TRANQUILITY

SHAOGUAN

SHAOG

camilla nelson

NORTHERN SADRIAN RANGE

HIDDEN COVE

BAHRI

VASHI

TURNA

ABYSSAL RIFT

DERVIS

IAN SANDS
DUNE SEA"

DUSTFALL PLATEAU

HAVVA

SADRIA

PLANTATION
PLAINS

SADRIA

AZURE RIVER

SABAN

VERITAS

KUSTAPATA

VECDI

SEVKI

FERHAT

TOROS

LEGACY: SCHEMATICS

LEVEL 1: HOLD

SUPPLIES

PROPELLER

COAL CRATES

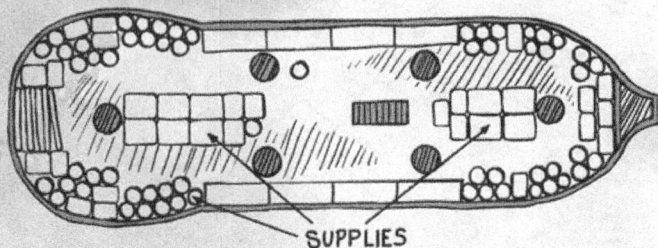

LEVEL 2: ENGINE DECK

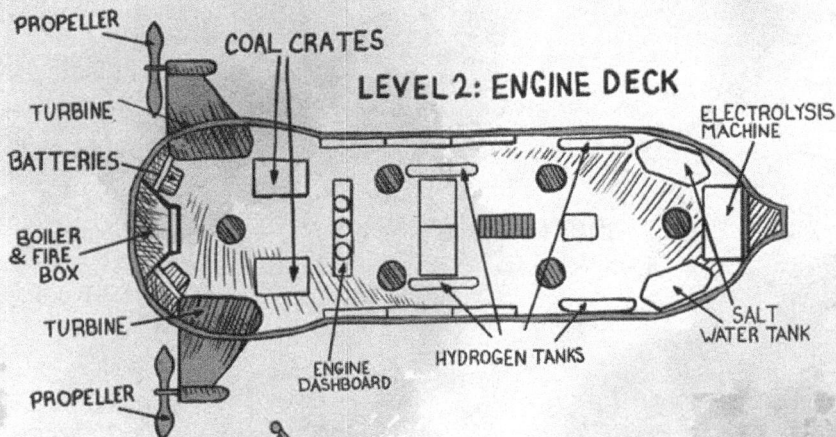

TURBINE

ELECTROLYSIS MACHINE

BATTERIES

BOILER & FIRE BOX

TURBINE

PROPELLER

ENGINE DASHBOARD

HYDROGEN TANKS

SALT WATER TANK

WING

LEVEL 3: LOWER DECK

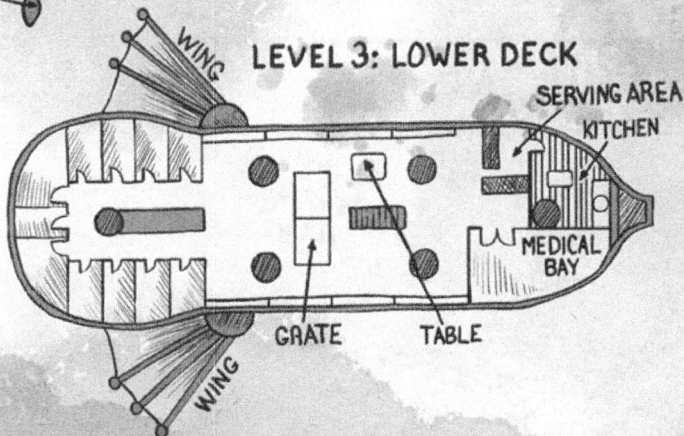

SERVING AREA

KITCHEN

MEDICAL BAY

WING

GRATE

TABLE

LEVEL 4: MAIN DECK

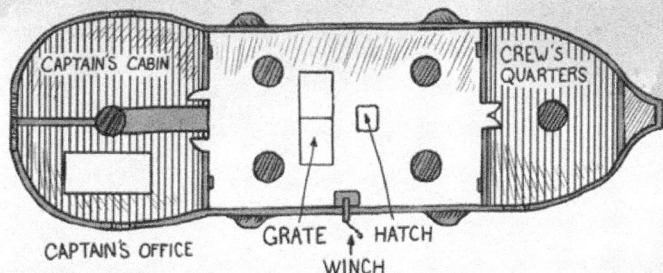

CAPTAIN'S CABIN

CREW'S QUARTERS

CAPTAIN'S OFFICE

GRATE   HATCH

WINCH

LEVEL 5: QUARTER DECK

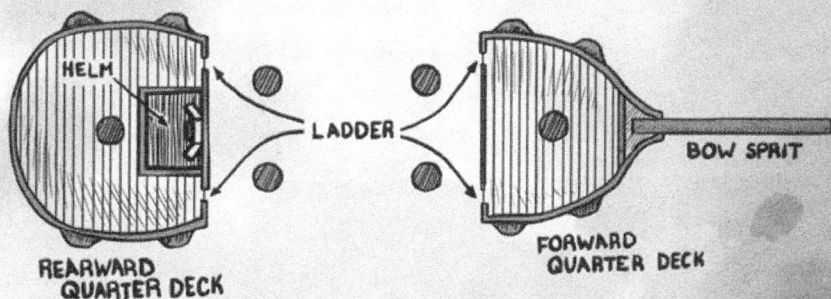

HELM

LADDER

BOW SPRIT

REARWARD
QUARTER DECK

FORWARD
QUARTER DECK

LEVEL 6: ENVELOPE

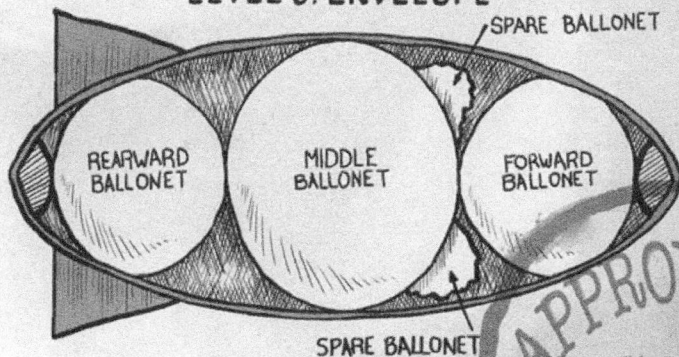

SPARE BALLONET

REARWARD
BALLONET

MIDDLE
BALLONET

FORWARD
BALLONET

SPARE BALLONET

APPROVED
Steam
Engineering
Corps.

Table of Contents

Prologue

Daken Morecraft

Cold fog blew across the airship's deck, thickening the already dark shadows of the night. Daken Morecraft soundlessly closed the hatch and glided past the armed Steam soldiers on watch. Never once did their gazes pass over Daken. Even if they had, it wouldn't matter. They'd see someone else entirely—someone he'd killed weeks ago.

The elaborate deception should have filled him with satisfaction. Instead, anger smoldered within him. He was long overdue for a visit to his *apprentice*.

He reached the airship's bow and stretched a hand into the night. Slowly, he pulled backward, drawing the darkness of the mist around him until even the crescent moon was snuffed out.

There, he thought. *Much better.* He closed his eyes and pushed his power outward. Tendrils of shadow leached from his fingertips and over the airship's railing into the empty night air toward the Nardoowe jungle below.

Despite his eyes being closed, Daken could see through the tendrils as they continued to stretch downward through the dark canopy. Once there, the darkness slithered silently through the branches, searching.

The tendrils passed bats, snakes, tarantulas, and other creatures before finding a sleeping falcon hidden in a thick nest.

Daken commanded the darkness, and it responded like a viper, latching onto the bird and ripping it through the canopy back to the airship. Daken opened his eyes as the dark tendrils drew the falcon into his hands.

He ran a hand down the falcon's back, holding it close as he inspected it. The bird trembled in his hand as he looked it over. He inspected its black wings, the talons, the beak.

This will do. Darkness grew again from Daken's hands and wrapped around the bird. Then it sank into the bird's mouth and eyes, like a sponge sucking in water from a puddle. The bird writhed in his hands, letting out one soundless squawk before growing still.

Without a second look, Daken threw the carcass over the edge of the airship and put his hands together. Again, the darkness flowed out from his fingers, but this time it wrapped around his own body and dissolved it into darkness. He reformed again, much smaller, with inky black wings, razor sharp talons, and a thick beak.

He launched into the night sky, leaving the airship behind in the swirling mist. His wings sliced easily through the humid air, turning the dense canopy below into a blur. The raucous jungle grew deathly silent with his passing, more keenly aware of the danger Daken posed than the foolish Steam soldiers behind him.

Miles passed before he caught the sight of his destination: a scorched airship grounded below. He circled above before dropping into a predatory dive. He zipped past the legionnaires on patrol and landed on the edge of an open porthole.

The room inside was sparsely furnished with a cot and shelf. Daken waited on his perch, letting the ledge cloak him in shadows. The moon outside crossed over a quarter of the night sky before a woman with jet black hair, smooth features, and an athletic physique glided into the cabin and kicked the door shut. She took a glance around the room before taking off her black boots and setting them next to a small, utilitarian shelf. Then she picked a mirror off the shelf and studied herself.

She smiled at her reflection, turning her face in front of the glass until it revealed the long white scar across her cheekbone. Then her smile transformed into rage, and she threw the mirror at the wall. The glass shattered into pieces.

She stared at the wall, panting. Then she screamed.

Despite all the noise she made, no one came pounding to her door. They were afraid of her, but Daken was not. He slipped through the porthole into the room. The Huntress wheeled around and threw a knife in the same movement. The blade passed harmlessly through Daken as he reformed into a man.

Her face turned pale, but that didn't stop her from feigning cool confidence when she whispered, "Hello, Master."

"You disobeyed me, Viviette," Daken said with a dangerous calm. "At the cave, I told you to keep the Steam girl alive. Instead, you let Honorhorn nearly burn her alive."

"So, what if I did?" she spat back. "What does it matter?"

Daken took a step toward her. Her face grew more pale, but she held her ground.

"I do not accept failure, or disobedience, Viviette," he warned. He took another step.

She swallowed.

"You are fortunate she survived," said Daken. "If she hadn't, you would have suffered even more."

"More?" The word barely escaped her lips before Daken grabbed her arm and sent tendrils of darkness into her body. She gasped for air before crashing against the shelf and collapsing to the floor.

"The girl must be kept alive," continued Daken as he looked down on the Huntress writhing at his feet. "I need her to unravel the safeguards her wretched grandfather left behind."

Her mouth was locked in a silent scream as her veins turned black across her whole body. The sight made her ugly beyond belief. His lips turned upward into a cruel smile. How the proud could fall. His magic had done its work.

He yanked his hands backward, and the tendrils retreated into his hands. The Huntress's flailing limbs slapped the floor with dull thuds. She gasped for breath, her exhales blowing sweaty hair from her face.

Daken knelt down and leaned over her face. "Do you understand me now?"

She gave a weak nod.

"Good." He stood and watched her lean up against the wall and wipe black spittle from her mouth. She froze as her eyes locked onto the inky black veins running up her arms. Blood drained from her face.

"What did you do to me?!" she rasped. She snatched a shard of glass and lifted it up to see her reflection. Her mouth dropped open.

"My face...!" She ran her fingers across the ugly blackened veins across her face.

Daken leaned in close and whispered into her ear. "I can do *far worse.*"

Tears streamed down her face. "Change me back," she begged. "DO IT NOW!"

Daken tsked. "I only reward those who do my will and succeed."

"Please!" she sobbed. "Send me right now. I'll do anything!"

"No." He pulled away from her and straightened his cloak.

"You promised me power!" she gasped. "You promised me an empire! You promised me beauty beyond imagining! Instead, you made me... HIDEOUS!"

He took a small bow. "All will be yours *if* you help me succeed. Otherwise, I'll twist you into a *nightmare!*"

It was time to go. The sun would come soon, and he needed to be back on the *Legacy.* He turned his back on her and stretched his hands out.

"WAIT!" she gasped.

He paused.

"What about the Steam soldier with the Everblade? Let me kill him! Let me redeem myself!"

He turned around slowly, calculating his response carefully. "He is of no significance."

"But he killed the Nardoowe beast!" she replied frantically. "He used the sword!"

"He is no threat!" Daken replied vehemently. "Without me, he'll *never* have power over that sword. Once he and the Steam girl give me the Wayfinder, they'll both die."

He turned his back for a last time and stretched out his hands.

CRAIG & JALEESA SNOW

Tendrils wrapped around his body, transforming him back into the bird of prey.

"Don't leave me like this, Master!" Her voice was growing more and more frantic. "Take me with you! I'll do anything you ask! Anything!"

Her desperation was like honey to his ears, but he needed to do this next part alone.

"I'll tell you what to do when I'm ready." He exited through the porthole and disappeared into the deep fog. Uncontrolled screams echoed after him, slowly dying in the distance.

Chapter 1: Sadrian Range

Amelia

"Cap, ya sure about this?" Veronica shouted over the roar of the airship propellers. Colossal peaks materialized across the horizon, appearing through gaps in the misty cloud layer of the Nardoowe jungle. The peaks made the mountains they'd been passing over for the last couple of days look like hills.

Amelia Steam only grinned in response. She gripped the helm and felt nervous excitement race through her. No one had ever attempted to pass over something so high before. This was a challenge worthy of a Steam.

"I need more hydrogen," Amelia said through the horn, a brass contraption that carried her voice to the engine deck. Hydrogen pipes hissed in response and the airship rose.

They entered thick clouds. The deck bounced and shook with turbulence, making her teeth vibrate. When they broke through the layer of clouds, she looked back and took a deep breath. For the first time in weeks, she could see miles all around.

The sight was freeing. So much had happened in the jungle behind them. They'd crashed the *Legacy*, survived attacks, entered a deadly labyrinth, killed an otherworldly beast, and lost friends... all to get the Everblade.

The blade was more powerful than she ever imagined. Seeing Ander wield it had terrified her. He had moved like lightning while the blade burned with searing fire. He even slayed a dark beast that had savagely ripped apart Gifted legionnaires—arguably the most powerful soldiers in the world.

They'd lost the sword to the Enchantrans and barely recovered it back. She didn't want to think about the devastation the Enchantrans could have caused on the Republic of Steam with the blade, if they had failed.

Of course, the sword also had a second perilous purpose. The Everblade was one of the four talismans required to access the Source of all magical power. If the Enchantrans got ahold of the Source—which was their eventual goal—they'd have the ability to destroy the Republic and reshape the world according to their desire.

That wasn't an option.

"Captain?"

Amelia focused her attention on a Steam soldier climbing up a ladder to where she stood at the helm. Second Lieutenant Charles Rig came to stand beside her. His armor was freshly oiled, and he wore his standard-issued helmet—even though no other soldier was wearing theirs.

Great. Just who she needed to see, Amelia thought, as she turned to face the stuffy soldier. The feeling of levity she felt before disappeared with a wave of annoyance. "What do you want, Charles?"

"Miss Steam, I insist we turn around!" He withdrew a pocket version of the military code of regulations and flipped to a page. "I found in section 4, article 6, paragraph 3...."

Amelia groaned. "Charles, get to the point. I'm busy."

He cleared his throat and read faster. "Airborne military airships shall operate no higher than 10,000 feet above sea level, given the stress it creates on the human body."

Really? she thought. Now that Bragg was locked up below, everyone seemed to want to share their opinion *all* the time. "We've been over this already. We *know* the dangers of extreme altitudes." She sighed as she repeated the list she'd already discussed at length with the officers. "Changing air pressures, less oxygen, and stronger air currents—that's why we just spent days making oxygen lines out of bamboo and filling the electrolysis machine with oxygen."

"But—"

She shook her head. "We have to cross over those peaks, Charles. The decision's already been made."

"Those behemoths are far above 10,000 feet!" he said, pointing. "We'd *severely* breach regulations to get over them!"

She cocked an eyebrow. "If we can get over those mountains, we'll reach Sadria months before the Enchantrans. That's precious time we can't afford to lose."

"But it's against the regulations!" said Charles, as if that explained everything.

She pinched the bridge of her nose. How could she re-explain to this thick-headed, by-the-book idiot that the Enchantrans were likely going after the Wayfinder next, which was rumored to be in Sadria?

If the Enchantran got to it first, they'd be able to use its power to find *anything*. That included wherever they safeguarded the Everblade and the other two talismans to the Source.

No, there was too much at stake. They had to succeed. *She* had to succeed. Going after the Wayfinder was more than just the right thing to do for her. Nothing short of saving the Republic would be enough for her to belong with her people again, to find home again. If the Enchantrans found the Wayfinder before they did, she'd lose everything she had worked for.

"You're more than welcome to walk to Sadria," she said. "I'm sure that would be well within the bounds of the regulations."

"But for military airships, the regulations say...."

"Ah!" she said with a smile. "For *military* airships. *My* airship isn't owned by the military. Is it?"

"Uh." Charles scrunched his eyebrows. "But... it's chartered by the military, which section 2, article 10 states that—"

The hatch swung open. A grizzled soldier appeared and blinked in the bright sunlight.

Relief filled Amelia. "Garret!" she called out. "Could you help Charles take his station?" She raised her eyebrows meaningfully.

He glanced between the two before understanding dawned in his expression. "Charles," he said, "Ander needs you to monitor the telegraph. Once we pass through those mountains, we'll need to get word to a relay station as soon as possible."

"But those peaks, the regulations..."

"Ah, Charles. You see, those regulations...." Garret put his arm around the soldier and led him below the hatch.

Amelia let out a sigh. *Finally!*

She manipulated the controls until the airship settled at 8,000 feet. Brass dials told her that the temperature was 43°F now, which she calculated was 31°F less than the jungle below. Mountainous foothills passed only hundreds of feet beneath the airship, and still the range rose. She buttoned up her pilot overcoat, knowing that from here forward, the air would only get colder.

The hatch opened again, and this time Ander emerged. Like the other soldiers, he was in his tactical gear, with a steam crossbow strapped to his magpack and a longsword at his side. He held a second magpack in his right hand and moved with athletic grace despite the heavy gear.

She realized she was staring and quickly fixed her gaze on the airship gauges as he climbed up next to her.

"Emmett got that leak fixed up," he said, holding up the magpack. A large tank was attached to the pack, equipped with a hose and a breathing apparatus. "He said you've got about 30 minutes of oxygen, so you need to use it when it counts."

"Oh, good." She flashed him a smile and slipped the pack on. It was heavy, but that seemed to be the trend with military gear. "This will work great." She tugged the straps, making the magpack fit her slight form better.

"Perfect." He looked out at the approaching peaks and ran a hand through his hair. When he moved, the hilt of his sword flashed in the sunlight.

That's the Everblade! she realized. She eyed the wide, V-shaped crossguard, leather-wrapped handle, and a circular pommel embossed with an emblem of fire.

It's amazing how simple it looks, she thought. *Only the pommel gives any sign that it's unique.*

Unanswered questions exploded through her mind. How had he

used the sword back in the vault? He wasn't Gifted—or at least she didn't think he was. There was no way he would be in the Steam military or even a citizen if he were. Still, how did he power it if he was a Commonborn?

Amelia opened her mouth to ask, but then closed it. There were too many people on the deck. Only she and Ander's team knew what had happened in the vault, and all of them had silently agreed to not speak of it to the rest of the crew. If the crew found out, she knew Ander would be accused of being Gifted and get locked up with Bragg. That was the last thing they needed.

"How's Axe doing?" she asked instead, choosing a safer but equally pressing topic.

Ander leaned against the railing and sighed. "We got him settled. Eugene says he's stable, but...." He grimaced. "He isn't looking too good."

She shivered, thinking of the grisly procedure Axel had gone through. It had only been a week since they fought the beast. Axel's hand had been mutilated after an explosion had gone off in his hand while in the monster's mouth. It was a miracle that he was still alive, considering the damage done. Eugene and James, the airship's combat medics, had to amputate Axel's hand at the wrist. Since then, they'd been working day and night to keep him alive.

"I hope he pulls through," Amelia said.

"Me too...."

They stayed silent for a moment before Amelia glanced at Ander. He was staring at her. "What?"

Ander looked away.

"*What?*"

"A week ago, I thought you were dead," he whispered. He looked at her with an intensity she'd never seen before. Then it was gone in a flash. He stiffened up soldier-like. "Anyway, everyone below deck is at their breathing line now, including Charles. They're ready for you to give the order."

"Okay," she said, studying his impassive expression. She hesitated before adding, "You realize it's going to take a lot more than an oversized cat to kill me?" She raised a mocking eyebrow.

He looked unconvinced, so she continued. "Besides," she lowered her voice, "now that you have that sword, we don't have to worry about any more beasts."

Doubt flashed across his face. Then his expression turned more uncomfortable, reminding her of the masquerade ball. "Anything else you need from me?" he asked stiffly.

She sighed. "No, I'm good."

He nodded and left. As soon as he disappeared below decks, she leaned over the wheel and pulled at her hair. Why did she have to say what she did? *It's going to take more than an oversized cat to kill me.* He had literally seen her get carried off the airship by an unearthly beast! Of course that would affect him! He had thought she had died!

She gave a long exhale. *Well, I'll add that to the list of epic Amelia Steam blunders..., next to 'almost got his friend electrocuted.' Mental note: Next time, close your mouth.*

A sudden wind rattled the airship. Amelia snapped her head up and saw steep slopes approaching. *That's the valley updraft.* She shoved the conversation into the back of her mind and focused on the wall of impassive mountains.

"Everard," she said through the horn. "Let's start pumping hydrogen again."

Steep slopes closed around them as she guided the airship into a climbing pass. The jungle peninsula disappeared behind them, now obscured by craggy foothills.

They punctured through a thin cloud layer before they topped off at 11,687 feet. It was higher than she had ever taken the *Legacy*, which was designed to top off at 11,000 feet when fully loaded. But they still had much higher to go. The mountains were covered with snow now, and frost crept over the brass and steel parts of the airship.

"Veronica. Let the spare ballonets fly." Her words came out with small puffs of white in the cold air. Her first mate repeated the command to the half dozen sailors on duty, and the crew went to work, closing the main hydrogen valves and opening ancillary valves. They filled two ballonets and strapped them onto either side of the envelope with netting. It wasn't a pretty job, but the airship resumed rising.

"Amelia," came Everard's voice from the horn. "I need you to monitor those ballonets. Since they're outside the envelope, they're more susceptible to the air pressure changes—"

She rolled her eyes. "I know." Goodness. Sometimes Everard worried too much. If a ballonet did rupture and deflate, they still had an emergency ballonet deflated as a backup. They were fine.

"Okay," he said, sounding a little miffed. "It doesn't hurt to be cautious."

Amelia called Veronica and gave orders for sailors to monitor the ballonets. As soon as people were in place, she let Everard know to ease his concerns.

The wind grew in strength, still pushing from behind. She pulled her overcoat closer around her shoulders and checked the thermometer. The gauge was so blurry she had to squint to make out

29 °F.

The pass grew narrower and narrower, and still the mountains rose. At 14,101 feet, they passed the tree line where sparse vegetation gave way to snow and rock.

"Oi, point of no return," said Veronica from the main deck. Amelia nodded. If something went wrong past this point, they wouldn't have access to wood for fuel or repairs. But instead of feeling worried, Amelia felt excited. Besides, everything was going exactly as she had planned.

"Steady ahead," she replied. The pass wound back and forth, and morning sunlight glowed at them with each break in the lower peaks. The raw, rugged terrain was beautiful despite the growing cold.

Soon the mountain pass veered to the right, so she led them up and out of it. The white puffs of air she expelled kept getting into her eyes, making it hard to see. A thrumming headache formed, and she shook her head to clear it. They were 16,526 feet high now, twice standard airship height. Still, the mountains climbed.

The headache worsened, and her left wrist joined the chorus of pain. She rubbed her former injury with her other hand and exhaled a cloud of steam into the frosty air.

She wasn't the only one struggling. Sailors left and right were shifting uncomfortably at their stations. Two had sat down, clutching their heads. Another fell over and vomited across the deck.

Altitude sickness, she thought. She had hoped they could get more height before the crew experienced symptoms.

"Veronica, begin running the oxygen lines to the crew."

"Aye Cap." Veronica stumbled as she ordered the crew to their stations at the bamboo shafts.

Amelia repeated the same order down the horn, and soon the

hissing of oxygen running down lines joined the hum of mechanical noises from the airship. She rubbed her forehead and glanced longingly at the magpack oxygen tank Ander had brought her.

Not yet, she told herself. As tempting as the tank was, it didn't have nearly the same capacity as the crew's tank. She needed to endure as long as she could before using it. The altitude sickness would only get worse the higher they got, and she did not know how deep the range was. The last thing she wanted was to run out too early. If they crashed here, they would never get off the mountains alive.

She glanced again at the altimeter. Frost slowly crept across the gauge, but she scrubbed it away with the pad of her thumb until she could make out the reading of 17,001 feet.

A rogue gale rammed into the airship, sending the deck rocking. She stumbled before pulling the wheel to realign their heading. The airship was slow to respond. She gritted her teeth, realizing the extra ballonets strapped to the sides made the envelope less aerodynamic.

The gales grew stronger and her steering grew less wieldy. Cliff walls closed in on either side, and for the first time, worry crept up her spine. She needed to get more speed, or she'd lose steering control with the wind.

She grabbed the horn and shouted. "Everard! I need more thrust!"

"What was that?" came his reply.

She gripped the horn harder and repeated each word louder. "I. Need. More. Thrust!" She had to take a deep breath after repeating the order.

"Amelia, can you repeat?"

What was his problem? Did she need to spell it out for him? She put a hand to her pounding head, and turned to Veronica.

"Tighten the sheets!"

"Oi! What was that, Cap?" asked Veronica.

What was wrong with everyone? Didn't they notice the gust growing stronger around them? The pounding in her head grew ferocious.

"I need more SPEED!" she shouted to everyone at once.

"What?!" said Veronica at the same time Everard said, "You aren't making any sense!"

Anger burned up her throat like bile, consuming so much of her attention she barely registered sailors shouting at her. An outcrop of cliffs appeared out of nowhere, and they were heading straight toward it.

Her body jolted into action, swinging the airship into a hard banking maneuver. Sailors crashed to the deck as the *Legacy* barely slipped past the protrusion. She sighed, but her relief was cut short as the airship overcorrected and headed straight toward the opposite side of the skinny, craggy pass. She swung the wheel again and was met with muffled shouts. Veronica yelled something, but she couldn't register the words. It felt like her ears were filled with cotton. Then the world around her blurred into vague shapes and colors before it went black.

She jolted awake and realized she was lying on her back. Veronica knelt over her and held a mask over her nose and mouth. Her first mate held the wheel with a free hand.

"Stay with me, Cap," Veronica said, her eyes intense.

Amelia took greedy gulps of air and closed her eyes, trying to calm her racing heartbeat. Once her pulse calmed down and her head cleared, Veronica helped her stand and take stock of the situation.

Loud hissing came from the ballonet strapped to the port side of the envelope. Crew members scrambled along it, applying tar patches to repair the tear. Fortunately, they were hovering safely over a valley, but the next band of mountains loomed menacingly ahead.

Amelia glanced at the altimeter and cursed. They had lost elevation, and the needle was still slowly dropping. The crew also seemed to be struggling, wearing pained expressions at their breathing line. A couple shot her furtive glares.

Doubt crept across her mind. Was she pushing them too hard? They still had further to go, and the way forward only rose higher. It would get worse before it got better.

Still, she knew they couldn't go back. The Republic depended on them.

She slipped off her mask and shouted down the horn. "Everard! I need more lift!"

"I'm getting high pressure readings for the ballonets!" came a reply. "Any more and we'll get into the red!"

"Just do it!"

We don't have a choice.

Slowly, they rose.

17,336 feet.

She saw a few more of her crew drop to the deck as the air thinned even more. Another vomited and then held his head.

18,102 feet.

The temperature dropped even further as the soaring, barren mountains turned white with snow. Amelia scraped the frost off the gauges again.

19,687 feet.

A gap grew in the pass a mile ahead, and beyond it was nothing but blue sky.

The end! She broke into a wide grin. They had done it! They had reached the crest of the pass!

Violent wind ripped past them, sending turbulent shudders through the deck. She held tight to the helm and steadied her feet.

They were *so* close!

Everard's voice sounded through the horn, but another rogue gust of wind garbled his voice.

She took the horn in one hand and shouted into it. "Repeat, please."

"The oxygen lines are leaking!" said Everard.

"*What*?!" she replied.

"We don't know how long we've been leaking, but we're down to 27% of oxygen."

"Twenty-seven?!" She bit her lip. "Get a patch on that ASAP!"

"Sexton and Bell are on it, but we've lost a lot."

A lot was underselling it. They should have had twice that amount.

"How close are we?" Everard asked.

"I can see the crest to the pass. We're almost through, but we still need to rise higher."

There was a pause before he replied. "Keep going. I'll keep you updated on the oxygen levels."

Amelia was shaking now, but whether it was from the low temperature or the stress of getting over these mountains, she didn't know. The wind grew more and more turbulent, but fortunately the pass opened wider as they rose higher.

She tapped the altimeter. The gauge was barely rising. "Everard? If you want to get over these mountains, I need my hydrogen!"

"We're topped out!" he replied. "There's no more capacity."

No more capacity, she silently scoffed. *We'll make capacity.* She tugged off her mask and yelled to Veronica, who was one of the few still on her feet.

"Fill the emergency ballonet!"

Veronica repeated the order, sending sailors scrambling to deploy the last ballonet through a hatch at the top of the envelope. Amelia tapped her fingers against the wheel as this all happened, anxiously glancing between the crew and peaks ahead. Every second counted.

"C'mon, c'mon!" she urged.

"It's set!" came a voice from above.

Amelia grabbed the horn. "More hydrogen!" The airship rose once more, barely keeping above the rising landscape. She slipped her mask back on and sighed.

"21% oxygen," said Everard.

She swallowed and felt her ears pop from the lessened air pressure. Overhead, the ballonets creaked as well, the fabric straining underneath the expanding hydrogen. As they rose, every jolt of the airship in the wind made her wince as she heard more groaning from up above.

21,257 feet.

They were so close.

21,379 feet.

"18% oxygen," Everard said.

Keep going, she urged the *Legacy.*

Just as she was sure they were going to top out again, they cleared through the pass. Ahead the mountains sloped downward to a blinding desert as far as she could see.

"Sadria!" She pumped a fist in the air.

BOOM! The patch on the port side ballonet blew off. The airship cantered to an angle and dropped. Her stomach plunged with it. The mountains that had seemed small now grew quickly. Soon, she was weaving around peaks, dodging cliffs, and diving through barren valleys. The wind screamed past her ears as her mind worked in double time.

Last time she had flown like this was in the Nardoowe jungle.

Last time, they crashed.

She shoved the fear down and bit her tongue as pure adrenaline poured through her. They were *not* going to crash. Not this time.

She checked the altimeter and cursed. They were losing height too quickly. At this rate, they'd level out by the time they hit the desert—if they even reached the desert. She glanced up at the envelope. *Were there more leaks?* There was no way to tell without sending the crew up, and given their current state, that would not happen.

She yanked on the horn and shouted, "Everard! I need more hydrogen!"

Seconds passed without a reply.

"Everard?"

"He's out cold!" stammered Sexton, the younger of the two inventors on board. "Th–there was nothing I could do."

"Sexton! I need the hydrogen pumping now!"

"I–I'm getting mixed readings. I think we have a couple have holes!"

"I don't care! Keep it pumping or we'll—" Her words cut off as the way ahead narrowed abruptly. She managed to tuck in the wings before the cliff face ripped through the extra ballonet on the starboard side. The deck rocked hard to port before dropping violently. The entire crew screamed as the bow angled downward. Amelia white-knuckled the helm and held her breath as her ears popped with vengeance.

One second passed. Two. Three. The pass opened up, and she yanked the levers that controlled the wings. *WHOMP!* Scrambling, she rotated the wings and slowly the airship pitched upward.

Sexton's voice echoed through the horn, both an octave higher and twice its normal speed. "Cap, I got hydrogen pumping to the emergency ballonet. The other two are already at capacity, and I figured you didn't want the other two reading zero since, hypothetically, they were probably—."

She cut him off. "That's great!" She steadied the airship until finally it leveled out at 4,474 feet. The tallest mountains were now behind them. Ahead, the range transformed into craggy foothills, mesas, and tablelands. Beyond that were rust-colored sand dunes as far as she could see.

The sight contrasted sharply with the jungles on the opposite side of the range. Instead of layers of clouds and dense foliage, here the few clouds were wispy and the landscape was barren.

Still, they had made it through the range!

Moaning sailors snapped Amelia's attention back to the airship. Several, including Veronica, held their hands over their ears. When Veronica pulled her hand away, blood covered her hand.

"Get the medics!" Amelia called. Soon James Cole appeared above deck and began moving from person to person.

Meanwhile, Amelia called through the horn. "Can I get a status report?" Instead of a reply, the hatch opened and Everard climbed out. Relief filled her, but as he grew closer, she saw a welt on his head.

He noticed her looking and waved it off. "Just a minor bump from my fall. Nothing to worry about." He climbed up onto the helm and threw his arms around her. "I'm glad you're okay."

She squeezed him back.

When he pulled away, his expression was serious. "What we *do* need to worry about is the hydrogen and fuel situation."

Amelia furrowed her brows. "What's wrong?"

"We're dangerously low," he said with a grimace, "and we aren't in the best environment to fix that problem."

She stared at the barren landscape, feeling her stomach sink. If they were low on both hydrogen and fuel, that meant their shortcut to Sadria might strand them in the middle of nowhere.

"Maybe Sadria City isn't far away," she said. "We should be just fine." She glanced again at the horizon and the sinking feeling grew worse.

Ander climbed out on deck. "Millie?" His face was pale.

"What's wrong?" she asked him.

"It's Axe," he whispered.

She felt as if ice gripped her heart. She didn't breathe for a second before she asked, "Is he...."

"He's alive," he said quickly, "but he's in critical condition. Eugene needs to talk to you."

"Okay." She handed the helm to a sailor and followed him down the hatch. As soon as they got to the med bay, she wanted to step back out. Axel was thrashing around on his bed. His skin was red and his breathing was labored. His bandaged stump was bloodied, and the surrounding skin was red and pulled tight. Blood crusted around his ears, and she guessed he experienced the same thing as Veronica.

Blaze and James were trying to hold Axel down as Eugene drew a glass syringe from a red vial.

"His pulse is at 160," James said to Eugene.

Eugene looked up and noticed Amelia. He handed the syringe to James and pulled her just outside the med bay.

"How is he?" she asked quietly.

"Not good," Eugene said grimly. "He has a severe infection, and the trip over the mountains didn't help. His fever alone is enough to worry me, and his wound is festering. I'll spare you details, but it's not pretty." His voice turned quiet. "It's bad, Amelia. I don't have the medications to help him through this."

She glanced back into the room at Axel, still thrashing in his cot. Guilt stabbed into her chest and twisted painfully. She had done this to him, hadn't she? If she hadn't been so ambitious, if she hadn't wanted to get to Sadria so quickly, Axel might not be in as bad of a state. This was her fault.

"What do we do?" she asked, fearing the answer.

Eugene sighed. "The only place that would have the medicines we need is the Republic. Honestly, our best shot is to find the closest warship and hope they have the stock we don't have."

"He doesn't have much time," Ander added.

She took a steading breath. "Okay, we do everything we can to get Axe help. We'll start heading east right now. There'll be plenty of warships over the sea—"

A throat cleared behind Amelia. She turned around to Everard.

"What is it?" she asked.

"With the state we're in, we don't have enough fuel for a sustained burn. We aren't going anywhere fast."

She cocked her head and then narrowed her eyes.

Everard quickly put his hands up. "Look, don't shoot the

messenger. But we are in a desert. We don't have the resources to get anywhere quickly. I'm sorry."

She took a deep breath and glanced back at Axel. His life was on the line. She couldn't accept no for an answer.

"Okay," she said with a heavy breath. "We'll figure this out." At least, she hoped.

Chapter 2: Scorching Sands

Ander

T hree days passed with blistering waves of heat and slow progress. Given the limited amount of fuel left on the airship, the crew flew with only the sails, tacking against the wind in a zigzag pattern toward the east. As they flew, the landscape changed from crumbling tablelands and cracked valleys to rusty dunes and hazy mesas.

Vegetation was sparse and scraggly, appearing only on the tops of mesas. Ander led a brief expedition on one, looking for water and fuel. He found neither, but discovered the place teemed with hidden life. Large birds called desert sprinters scattered at the approach of the airship, leaping off the mesa, down the steep sides, and sprinting away on the sands. As his team searched, they discovered camouflaged geckos, metallic beetles, horned scarabs, red ants, and rattlesnakes. Despite all the life, no water existed on the mesa and the brush they found wouldn't burn easily.

After the expedition, the crew continued on with no additional stops. As each day passed, the effects of the heat intensified. Every metal surface of the airship became as hot as frying pans, and the inside of the airship grew suffocating. Soon, the only bearable places on the airship were the crew's quarters and serving area where the portholes were greatest. The only relief came when the sun dropped below the horizon. But then the temperature swung to the opposite extreme, becoming as frigid as winter.

Whenever Ander had an opportunity, he visited Axel and took a turn fanning the soldier until his arms burned with exertion.

Axel remained unconscious during each visit. His amputated forearm had swollen and was splotched with deep reds. The heat it radiated was beyond the sweltering desert outside, and the wet rags the medics used to cool it did little to help. Every few minutes, his body would shake with a tremor and the medics would jump up to keep him from thrashing his bandage loose.

Each visit filled Ander with more anxiety and helplessness. His friend was progressively getting worse, and there was nothing he could do about it.

As each day passed, the airship dropped lower and lower to the ground. Their water also declined with their increased need to stay hydrated. As it did, the crew became more sluggish and irritable. Conflicts broke out, one of which required Ander to physically extract the parties from each other. By the afternoon of the fourth day, Ander decided it was time for an officers' meeting.

He looked out at the group assembled around the table: Amelia at the opposite head of the table, with Veronica, Everard, Emmett, Charles, Garret, and Eugene around the sides. Freya leaned against a corner next to the door. All the men were scraggly because of the need to ration water. The only exception was Charles, who had somehow still shaved according to military standards without water. All of them were visibly worn as they looked at Ander now.

He took a deep breath and stood. "I know many of you are aware of the state we are in, but I want to go over it again because we are going to make some important decisions. Amelia, could you give a status update on our progress?"

"Sure, let me get my map." She stood, walked around the table, and opened the door.

Blaze stood there with a hand cupped around one ear. He jumped and threw his hands behind his back. "Oh! Hi, Millie. Fancy seeing you here!"

Ander ran a hand down his face. "Blaze, why are you at the door?"

Guilt passed quickly over Blaze's face before he took on an innocent expression. "Oh, me?" He put a hand on his heart. "I wasn't listening in, if that's what you think. That would be against the rules. Am I right, Charlie?" He gave Charles a wink.

Garret let out an irritable groan.

"No, I–I was guarding," Blaze continued. "Yep. You should have seen all the other people trying to listen in." He pointed out at the mostly empty deck.

Amelia put her hands on her hips.

"Oh, excuse my manners. Millie, I'll get that map for you. It's what a charming gentleman would do."

She raised an eyebrow. "And *how* do you know I need a map?"

"Uh?" he scrambled away before anyone could say anything more.

Ander shook his head. "Garret, could you handle Blaze after the meeting?"

Garret cracked his knuckles. "Yep, I've got some ideas."

Ander turned to Amelia. "While he's fetching the map, could you continue with your update?"

She nodded. "I know everyone is anxious to get out of this desert, and we need to find another Republic airship so we can get Axe the medicines he needs. Our challenge with both is speed and distance."

Blaze returned and handed her the map. She unrolled it onto the table and pointed at the southwestern corner of Sadria. "I believe we exited the range somewhere around here. Which, under *normal* flight conditions, would get us to Sadria in about a week and a half. But we aren't operating under normal conditions. With our current wind speed and rigging configurations, we are going half as fast. So if you take ten days and times that—"

"Twenty days then," said Emmett, the older of the two airship inventors. His counterpart, Archibald Sexton, was covering in the engine room.

"Precisely," she replied. "Unless we find more fuel, this is our first complication."

"How much fuel do we have?" asked Ander.

Everard cleared his throat. "We only have enough for about an hour of operation. We've been conserving this in case of an emergency—which, I might add, happens around here."

Blaze threw an arm around Ander's shoulder and said, "If only there was a way to create fire without fuel. Am I right?"

Ander's shoulders knotted up as unease crept up his spine. All the officers, except Amelia and Garret, believed Ander only found the sword. They didn't know he actually used it as well.

"Blaze, you are excused." Ander met Garret's eyes and understanding passed between them. Garret rose and escorted Blaze out the door.

Thoughts whirred through Ander's head as he waited for Garret to return. The Everblade had created a difficult situation for him—one he honestly didn't know how to handle. On one side, he had spent his entire life training for one sole purpose: to become a Steam soldier and make a difference. This mission, securing the talismans to the Source, was *exactly* what he had prepared himself to do. Yet, everything changed for him as soon as he held the Everblade—as soon as it caught on fire.

Those who manifest Gifted power were enemies of the Republic. It was even written in the Soldier's Code of Regulations. Yet Ander's blood status was Commonborn. It shouldn't be possible. Unless his blood status was a lie.

The fact he was adopted left room for doubt, and the truth terrified him. If he was Gifted, he would be cast out from the Republic or imprisoned. If he wasn't, he'd never be able to use the blade again.

You must be wary, echoed the dying words of the Warden in his head. *The sword may be needed again to... save the peace."*

Charles cleared his throat, snapping Ander to the present. "What did he mean by creating fire without fuel?"

Ander opened his mouth, but no words came to his mouth. He wasn't one to lie, but he also couldn't tell Charles the truth. Charles lived by the Soldiers Code of Regulations, which did *not* have a good answer for Ander's situation.

"Half of the things Blaze says makes little sense," said Amelia, rescuing him from a response. "Back to our discussion. Everard, could you explain our hydrogen situation?"

"Sure." The airship engineer cleared his dry throat. "Our hydrogen tanks are depleted, and what hydrogen we have is already in the ballonets. You may have noticed that we've been losing elevation every day. That's because our hydrogen is losing purity. If we don't generate more, I'm expecting by tomorrow evening we will be stuck on the sand."

Several people in the group swallowed hard.

Ander ran a hand through his hair. "I didn't realize it was that bad."

Amelia nodded grimly. "We recently calculated it out."

"Now," continued Everard, "If we could tap into our spare drinking water, we could expand that time—"

"Are yeh daft?" said Veronica with a hand cupped over her still recovering ear. "Ya asked this mornin', n' yesterday, n' the day before. The answer is the same! We will *not* be usin' our drinkin' water."

"The airship won't be sailing if we don't!" Everard shot back. "Does being stuck on the sand sound attractive to you?"

"That's enough," said Ander, coming to a rise. "Let's hear everyone out. Then we'll decide which ideas are good and bad. Everard, is that all?"

The engineer glared at Veronica and said, "No. I was going to say if we could replace our hydrogen, we could get back to higher altitudes. Which would mean faster wind currents and lower temperatures. We could get to more water faster."

"We could help Axe sooner," Amelia added quietly.

Veronica folded her arms.

"We need a lot of water to refill the ballonets with hydrogen," said Emmet, with a calculating expression. "How much do we have?"

"Veronica?" asked Ander. "Could you explain our status for

supplies and crew?"

"Yes, sir. We 'ave two n' half barrels. Barely enough ta make the journey if we can keep the airship goin'. We've already been rationin', we 'ave, n' the crew are strugglin'."

"Going over the range was a mistake," muttered Charles.

"Oi! I'll not 'ave ya questionin' the cap's decisions," said Veronica, rising in her chair. "She's the best cap you'll ever 'ave!"

Charles threw his hands up. "Standard airship regulations state we should never voyage without more cargo than the trip warrants. That's what we broke when we set out over those mountains. AND you and others got injured because we pushed past the regulatory height!"

Amelia exploded. "OH, and would YOU have rather gone back through the Everstorm? Since that went so well last time? Does that meet your standard of regulations?"

A chuckle escaped from Garret's lips. Everyone in the group turned to look at him. "Sorry!" he said, wiping the corner of an eye. "Has anything about this trip been standard?"

The look both Amelia and Charles gave him would have melted a boiler.

"Alright," said Ander, "so we are low on water and morale is strained. What else is wrong?"

"Half the crew is still recovering from the battle with the *Firelancer*," said Eugene.

Veronica's face grew dark. "Oi, next Gifteds comin' my way, there'll be a reckonin'."

People throughout the room grumbled in assent.

Sweat trickled down Ander's neck, sending cold chills throughout his body. His mind drifted to the sword strapped to his hip. What would happen to him if they found out his secret?

"There's more," said Eugene. "James and I have exhausted everything we know to help Axe. I don't think he has twenty days in him."

The room grew somber.

Ander let out a long sigh. "Alright, so we know what we are up against. Now for ideas."

Amelia pointed to the map at a broad river in the southeastern part of the desert. "My plan so far has been to find this river, since that would solve some of our problems. But, as you've noticed, this desert keeps going and going. My only landmark for finding said river is to watch the Sadrian mountain range. Once it veers south, it's about a three-day flight, assuming my map is to scale."

"And we don't have three days of hydrogen," said Everard quietly.

"So, we might need to make some sacrifices?" Ander surmised.

Amelia nodded.

"What if we siphoned water from the boiler?" asked Emmett. "Could that be a workaround?

Everard paused and scratched his chin. "We could extract some, but we'd need to run the engine to keep the batteries charged. That only works if there's water *in* the boiler—"

Shouts rang from outside the office. The group immediately stood up. Freya opened the door, sending Blaze stumbling back through the doorway.

"What's wrong?" asked Ander.

"We've got an incoming rainstorm!" Blaze replied with wild delight.

Ander pushed past Blaze onto the deck. All around, the crew

whooped and hollered. He made his way to the railing and looked out. To the east was a long line of thick storm clouds.

Garret slapped Ander on the back. "Well, it looks like we might have a solution to our predicament."

Amelia appeared on his other side and frowned. "I'm not so sure." She withdrew a spyglass. Curious, Ander followed suit.

Billowing dark clouds grew from the ground and extended several thousands of feet into the sky. Lightning flickered and cast an otherworldly orange glow. The sight sent prickles down his spine.

"Those don't look like normal rain clouds," he said.

"They aren't," Amelia said. "It's a dust storm. A massive one, and it's heading right for us!"

Chapter 3: Sandstorm

Ander

The noise and excitement died quickly as word spread around. Ander let out a long sigh. This was the last thing they needed. Another complication.

He turned to Amelia, choosing to defer to her authority as captain. "What're your orders?"

"Here we go for another crazy, hair-brained idea," muttered Charles. "What's a few more broken regulations?"

A few others around him with injuries grumbled in agreement. Amelia's face fell.

Ander clenched his fist, feeling anger rise in him. He narrowed his eyes at Charles and with a piercing calm voice said, "Charles, you are dismissed from the main deck. That's an order."

No one breathed. Charles' back went stiff. A heavy pause hung in the air before he disappeared down the hatch. Freya and a few

CRAIG & JALEESA SNOW

others followed him.

Ander watched them go with disgust. Weeks ago, they had all supported him and Amelia. They even helped him replace Bragg as the mission commander. Now, that support was deteriorating.

We need to get out of this desert, he thought.

He turned back to Amelia. "We're ready for your orders."

"Millie," said Everard. "You realize if we get caught up in that storm, it'll wreak havoc on our systems. It'll be weeks of cleaning and servicing. We'd be lucky to start our engines again in a month!"

"Oi, why not take the wind across our beam 'n 'ead south?" asked Veronica. "We'd be at our fastest point of sailin' 'n could shelter in the foot'ills before the storm hits."

"What about Axe?" said Eugene. "We'd be losing time."

Amelia bit her lip and looked up at Ander. Her face was tight, but he had spent enough time with her to read her thoughts. Charles' comments had struck her hard.

He put a hand on her shoulder and said, "We're all behind you. You've got this."

"Thanks," she said. She looked out at the storm and tapped her chin. Then her eyes lit up, bringing with it a breathtaking smile. Ander was so caught off guard that he barely heard Everard speak.

"Oh no, I know that look. You realize how treacherous it would be if we got caught in that storm?"

"Everard, the *winds*." She pointed at the storm. "If we could get above the storm, those winds would drive us far, fast. This could be exactly what Axe needs."

There it is, Ander thought. *The solution we need to get out of the desert and help Axel!*

Garret clapped Amelia on the back. "Leave it up to you to turn a problem into an opportunity."

She smiled, determined now. "We are *going* to save Axe. Veronica, rig the sails for 45° northeast. Everard, siphon as much water as you can from the boiler and start the electrolysis going. Ander, get the soldiers to close the portholes and batten the grates."

"On it!" Ander rallied the soldiers and together they stretched canvas over the loading grates and nailed strips of wood to keep it in place. Then they systematically ran through the airship, latching each porthole and strapping down the mess area's table and chairs. Once they finished, he sent soldiers to help secure the kitchen, clean the inventor's mess of half-finished gadgets and parts, and lock down the opened crates in the hold.

As Ander was climbing up the stairs from the hold, Everard called out. "Ander! Help me transfer this water!"

"Yes, sir!" He and the soldiers with him stepped off the stairs and trotted to where Everard stood at the boiler. Three barrels were filled to the brim with water.

"Pray this is enough," Everard said. "It's all we have left."

They clamped lids on the barrels and moved them to the opposite side of the airship. Then, Everard opened the tops of the salt water tanks and guided the crew in dumping the barrels into the tanks.

Sweat ran down Ander's temples in rivulets, though that was less because of the exertion and more because of the heat. Now that the grates and portholes were sealed, the engine deck became as suffocating as an oven.

Once the barrels were emptied, they closed the tanks up and started up the electrolysis machine. It purred with a mechanical hum and began pumping water from the tanks.

Everard wiped his face with his sleeve. "Thanks!"

"Of course," said Ander. "Mind if we check in with Millie?"

The engineer nodded, leading Ander to the engine dashboard. There, Everard leaned into the receiving side of the horn and said, "Amelia, status report from the engine deck."

"Go ahead," came her reply.

"We've finished siphoning the boiler and have started the electrolysis machine."

"Perfect. I want that hydrogen pumped ASAP!"

"I'm sure you would," Everard muttered low enough that only Ander could hear.

Ander smiled and shook his head. He leaned into the horn. "Millie, this is Ander. We've gotten everything closed up and strapped down."

"Perfect. I need all members of the crew to their stations. Get ready for a bumpy ride."

Ander clapped a hand on Everard's shoulder. "That's our cue to go." He jogged to the lower deck and gathered the soldiers into two lines. Garret led a quick roll call. Even Cid was there, though the stowaway hugged the very back of the lower deck.

Ander faced the group and cleared his throat. "Captain says this'll be a bumpy ride, so strap in and hang tight." He nodded to Garret, who reached up to the ceiling and pulled a latch. Leather loops dropped above the soldiers' heads, and each stuck a hand through one and held on tight.

Ander reached for his loop and paused. Last time he stood here was when they were flying over the range. He remembered when the crew cried out for Amelia right before she passed out.

Worry grew inside his chest, squeezing his lungs. Thoughts of worst-case scenarios flashed through his mind. He grabbed onto his loop and closed his eyes. *This is different,* he told himself. *She's not going to extreme heights. Everything will be fine!*

The feeling continued to build, bringing with it flashing images of the nightmarish Nardoowe beast on the main deck. Suddenly he was back in that moment, lying on his back. The team had formed around him. Then the beast leapt over them all, aiming toward the lone figure at the helm: Amelia.

A hand grabbed Ander's shoulder and jolted him back to the present. Garret stood next to him with eyebrows drawn together. "You alright?"

Ander shook his head. "I need some air. Keep an eye on the soldiers."

He left Garret and climbed the stairs. As soon as he pushed through the hatch into the fresh hot air, he immediately felt the pressure in his chest subside. He took in a few deep breaths before stepping all the way out and climbing up the helm.

Amelia had her pilot goggles pulled over her eyes and stood in a power stance before the wheel. Seeing her there, he suddenly felt foolish for worrying at all. She looked ready for anything.

She eyed him quizzically as he came to a stand next to her. "Is everything all right?"

He nodded. "The crew below deck are at their stations and strapped in."

"Everyone except for you," she added with a mocking eyebrow.

He raised his hands up. "Guilty, I know. I needed a breath of fresh air."

She nodded and let out a sigh. "Thanks for standing up for me."

"Of course." He ran a hand through his hair.

"This trip has been wearing, to say the least." She leaned on the wheel and steered with her elbows. "It's hard to know if I'm making the right decisions."

It was his turn to raise an eyebrow. "If you're thinking about the trip over the pass, you did the right thing. Going through the Everstorm again would've been much worse."

"But Axel–"

"Would have been thousands of miles farther from help if you took the other path," he finished for her. "Don't blame yourself for this one."

She let out a sigh. "Thanks, I guess I needed to hear that." Silence fell between them before she added. "You know, you're a good friend." She gave him a smile that sent tingles from his head to his toes.

The airship shuttered as gusts of hot air slammed the deck at an angle. The orange cloud wall was coming at them quickly. Thankfully, it didn't look like the Everstorm, but unlike the Everstorm, it was hurtling toward them with astonishing speed. He watched as the clouds engulfed a sizable mesa in seconds.

"Lifelines everyone," Amelia called. She leaned into the horn. "I could use that hydrogen now!"

"We're about ready," said Everard. "You'll feel a dip in altitude before we rise. We need to cycle out some of the old hydrogen before pumping in the new."

"Alright, make it quick because this storm is minutes away from impact!" She turned back to Ander and gave him a wry smile. "Not to cut this short, but I need you to take your station."

He hesitated, unsure about leaving her. Then a smile crossed his face. "You know, I could take a page from your book, ignore your request, and help you from right here?"

She rolled her eyes and bumped him with her shoulder. "Don't make me turn that into an order." She said mockingly. "Plus, I don't have an extra lifeline."

"Yes, ma'am." He gave her a mock salute, earning a final eye roll before he finally left the helm. He climbed down the stairs and took up his position next to Garret.

"Was that a good breath of fresh air?" Garret asked with a raised eyebrow.

"Yeah, actually. Why do you ask?"

"You've got a big smile plastered across your face," Garret said with a grin.

Ander frowned. "What?" Then the airship began to sink, causing his stomach to dip.

"Uh, is that supposed to happen?" asked Blaze nervously.

"Don't worry," said Ander. "This is part of the plan. Everard is cycling out the old hydrogen. Hang tight."

The airship continued to shake as it dropped. Along with it came a rumbling that grew louder with each passing second. It grew to a roar before the airship stopped sinking and began to rise.

Sweat trickled down Ander's neck. Since the portholes were shut, he couldn't see what was happening. He had no idea how close the storm was, but it sounded like it was about to collapse on them.

Tingles of pressure grew in his chest, and he quickly took deep breaths. They would get through this. Everything would be fine. They were probably just climbing over the storm.

"Brace for impact!" said Emmett through the grate below their feet. Ander gripped his strap tight as the world exploded.

SLAM! Ander was thrown swinging forward as the world around him changed from shaking to full turbulence. His stomach rolled and sank as he sought to maintain a steady footing on the ground. The strap bounced in his hand like a jarring pneumatic steam drill.

"Is this part of the plan, too?" Blaze shouted.

No. Something was wrong. They were supposed to fly over the storm, not through it.

Maybe I should have stayed above with Millie? He shook the thought quickly. It would've been a suicide mission without a lifeline. Still—

Abruptly, the turbulence subsided and was met with cheers on the engine deck. "We're above the storm now!" said Emmett. "Everard just got confirmation from Miss St—"

A horrifying *CRACK* above their heads drowned his words out. Everard's voice boomed from below, "WE'RE LOSING PRESSURE IN THE BAL—"

The engineer's voice disappeared as the airship suddenly sank. The room shook violently and whipped into a turbulent spin. Ander's feet lost contact with the floor as the entire airship tilted at an extreme angle, filling the room with screams and shouts. The swinging lantern above their heads broke free from its mooring and crashed to the floor, throwing the room into darkness.

Ander held onto the strap with all his strength as he was flung around like a rag doll caught in a wolf's mouth. Then the airship slammed into an abrupt stop.

The strap broke from the ceiling with a shoulder-wrenching jolt, and he crashed to the floor. All the air in his lungs exited in a rush. He gasped for breath, but his lungs refused to expand. The world stopped spinning, but the world outside the airship still rumbled.

Seconds passed before he could breathe. He gasped in large

gulps of air as he processed what just happened.

They had crashed!

He rolled onto his hands and knees. The moans from all around were barely audible over the raging storm. His mind cleared as his training took over.

"Garret! Head check!"

Garret groaned before calling out names. A light appeared, raised by Freya. All across the floor were soldiers, slowly picking themselves up. A quick scan of the room verified they had narrowly survived any major injuries. Of course, they were fortunate to have been in the central most deck in the whole airship. If they had been on the main deck—

Millie! "Garret, take charge here," he blurted. "Hammer and Blaze, I need you with me." He rose to his feet, ignoring the throbbing pain he felt in his shoulder and back, and stumbled to the railing. He pulled himself up the angled stairway and kicked the hatch open.

Sand pelted him with sharp needles and stung his eyes as he stepped out into the storm. He squinted and shielded his face as he rushed to the helm. Battered sailors groaned left and right around him. He moved past them, rushing up the helm.

Amelia hung limply in the air—suspended by her lifeline, which was tangled in the wheel itself. Her auburn hair whipped about wildly, and one side of her face glistened with gritty blood.

No. No. NO. He drew his knife and sliced through her lifeline. She crumpled into his arms, limp and lifeless. He set her legs onto the floor, but the deck was too angled to set her fully down without her sliding. So he cradled her upper body with one arm while, with the other, he checked her neck for a pulse.

Tense seconds passed. *Come on, come on!* The pounding of his own heart beat so loudly it was hard to recognize anything else.

Please! No! Not Millie!

There it was. A soft regular beat.

The tense knot in his shoulders loosened. She was alive. He brushed a hand across her hair to look at the wound across her temple. The cut was shallow and already dried.

"Thank goodness," he whispered. A warmth blossomed in his chest as he became aware of their closeness, her soft hair, the freckles sprinkled across her nose—

"Ander?" Her voice was feeble in the howling wind.

"Ah!" He startled and let go. Her limp body slapped the ground and slid down to the railing. He cursed and rushed to her. She was out cold.

He gingerly picked her up and prayed she wouldn't remember anything when she woke up. She was light in his arms, and when he adjusted her weight, her head rolled to rest on his shoulder. The movement set his heart pounding, muddling his concentration. He shook his head and forced his mind to think straight. He needed to get her to the medical bay.

He took a step toward the hatch and froze. A sixth sense flared inside him and sent cold prickles up his spine. Slowly, he rotated until he was looking off the airship into the blurred dark. The swirling sand and dust obscured everything from view, yet his intuition warned him that something was out there in the haze.

Red lightning flashed, silhouetting large dunes in the distance. The image was gone as quickly as it came, yet he stared into the dark, searching for more. Coldness grew inside him, despite the hot wind and sand pelting him. Something was out there. He knew it.

"You're lucky she's out cold," mocked a ragged voice. Ander

nearly dropped Amelia again as Cid materialized next to him and bent over to pick up Amelia's airship flying goggles.

"She'll want these," he said before setting them on her stomach.

Ander wanted to punch Cid for sneaking up on him, but the warning sense in his gut took precedence. "Did you see anything?" he asked quickly.

"See what?"

"Out there?" He pointed to the distance. Lightning flashed again, revealing a flat expanse. He blinked. Was he imagining things? The icy feeling was gone, yet a warning buzzed at the edge of his consciousness.

Cid raised a cynical eyebrow before wordlessly leaving him.

Ander stayed there a few seconds longer until better sense caught up to him. He rushed Amelia inside the airship and to the medical bay. A crowd of injured people swarmed outside the door. James was hurrying through the crowd, triaging people left and right. One look from the medic and Ander was immediately ushered into the room.

He set Amelia down on a tilted cot and stepped back. She looked peaceful now, and a strong part of him wanted to stay by her. He couldn't, of course. He needed to reinstate order with the airship, and he wasn't looking forward to it.

Chapter 4: Hopeless

Amelia

Amelia opened her eyes, and slowly the world came into focus. Yellow and orange light spilled across the wooden planked ceiling above her. She blinked in the light, unsure where she was. The ceiling of her cabin was usually dark, and she couldn't remember going to sleep. Last she remembered, she was at the helm when a spar broke loose.

She reached up to her left temple and felt a large bandage covering where the spar had struck her. The area throbbed with a dull ache. She let her hand drop and groaned.

What happened? She surveyed the room and realized she was in a tilted version of the medical bay. Every cot was filled with injured sailors, and a light layer of sand coated the floor. Eugene was slumped in a chair just underneath an open porthole. Blinding light spilled through the porthole. Next to Eugene was Axel, breathing shallow and irregular. Axel's complexion looked too white to be healthy. Much too white.

Dread surged through her, propelling her straight up to a sitting position. Light-headedness and nauseousness slammed into her, and she doubled over with a groan.

Eugene woke at the sound and rose. "You're awake?"

The discomfort dissipated, but was replaced by urgency. "What happened? Why are we not flying? Why is the airship tilted?"

Eugene walked to the cot nearest to her and sat on its edge. He gestured with his palms downward. "You need to calm down and take a breath."

"Calm down?!" She glanced back at Axel and shivered.

Ander appeared in the doorway, slightly out of breath. "Oh good, you're awake." Dark circles surrounded his eyes, but he gave her a tired smile.

"What happened?" Amelia asked again, this time to Ander.

Ander ran a hand through his hair, dusting off sand in the process. "We crashed."

"Crashed?!" Alarm blared through her mind. She spotted where her boots sat and grabbed them.

"Whoa! Where do you think you are going?" asked Eugene.

"I need to get out there!" She slipped on a boot.

"Not in this condition, you aren't!"

"Watch me." She laced up the boot and began putting on the other one.

"Are you insane? You have a concussion and four stitches. You need rest!"

"I feel fine!" she said. "We need to get airborne! We have to keep moving for Axe!"

Eugene exhaled heavily and looked away.

"What?" She paused and looked from the medic to Ander. Both of them avoided her eyes.

"Eugene?" Ander prodded.

Eugene gave Ander a look before saying, "She needs to rest."

Worry built inside her. "What's wrong? What aren't you telling me?"

Ander raised an eyebrow at Eugene. "Do you really think she's going to rest until she knows?"

The medic gave a frustrated sigh and turned to Amelia. "After the crash, Axe began deteriorating quickly. He's got maybe today and tomorrow left at best. Probably less."

The words hit her like a blow. "No... he can't just...." She couldn't say the word. Couldn't accept what they were saying.

"You should get some sleep," added Ander. "The rest of us can get the airship back into the air."

"So, we're just giving up on him?" She glared at the two of them. "I can't accept that."

"I'm not saying we give up," said Eugene with a huff. "What do you think I've been doing this whole time? I've literally been doing all I know to stabilize him, and it's not enough. He needs advanced medicines and it might even be too late for that. Amelia, I'm sorry. I truly am."

Tears rolled down her face, but she refused to wipe them. Doing so felt like admitting the situation was real. That Axel really was about to die.

She resumed tying her boots with a vengeance.

"Millie?" Ander's voice was quiet. "I don't think we are going to make it to the Republic in two days."

"I know that!" Her voice was full of emotion, and her eyes were clouding over with tears. Even if they were operating at full power and had ideal wind conditions, they still wouldn't make it.

She finished her knot and stared at her boots. Helplessness and grief poured through her, filling her whole body. Nothing they had done was enough. They had failed Axel. She had failed Axel.

"All we can do is pray for a miracle at this point," said Eugene.

A miracle.

She slapped her forehead. "I'm so stupid!"

Ander sat down next to her. "Don't blame yourself for this."

"No, Ander, we need a miracle." She pointed at her right leg, the same leg that had been sliced open by the Nardoowe beast.

"I'm not following—" said Ander.

She rolled her eyes. "Maybe we don't need Republic medicine. She dropped her voice to a whisper. "Maybe what we need is—magic."

Ander's eyes went wide.

"Have you lost your mind?" asked Eugene.

Amelia balled her hands into fists and narrowed her eyes. "Really, Eugene? I thought you said you were doing all you could?"

Eugene ran a hand down his face. "Look, I need some fresh air." He pointed at Amelia. "You're going to take a sedative when I come back." He disappeared out the door.

"I'm not taking a sedative," she said through clenched teeth. She rose to her feet and felt her head swim.

"Whoa, there." Ander steadied her with a hand on her back. "You're still recovering."

"I'm not giving up on Axe." Her voice was raw and she knew she should be lying down. But urgency pounded in her chest. She had to do something to help.

Ander pinched the bridge of his nose. "Okay. What's your plan?"

She was trying to figure that out, and the throb in her head wasn't helping. "Just help me get this airship running."

"Wait. You aren't going out there, are you?"

Amelia ignored the question and exited the medical bay. The floor of the lower deck was slippery given the angle of the airship and the sand everywhere, and she stumbled a few times before reaching the stairs. Ander caught her arm.

"How are we going to find a Gifted healer in the middle of the desert?"

She'd been thinking about the same question, but it wasn't until that moment that she had an answer. "We'll find a village. There's bound to be one somewhere out here."

He processed that for a second before saying, "Okay. I can get behind you on that. The crew will be another matter. You know how they feel toward Gifteds."

She let out a short exhale. "Then we won't tell them everything. But we *will* find a village, and we *will* save Axe."

She exited through the hatch and surveyed the scene. Sailors were taking down ripped sails and broken spars while soldiers shoveled at dunes that had grown around them during the storm. She avoided the disapproving look Eugene gave her and circled the airship.

The integrity of the hull was intact, along with the wings, but the crash had mangled and buried the rudder. She met with Everard to assess the damage inside the airship. The storm had blown enough sand into the airship to coat every greasy surface. The worst, however, was the hydrogen. Most of the hydrogen in the ballonets was gone. Only a fraction of it remained because Everard had pumped it back into the tanks after the crash.

After making her assessment, she shouted at soldiers and sailors alike, directing sailors to replace the broken spars and torn sails while the soldiers strapped ropes to latch points and heaved the airship into a level position.

After filling the emergency ballonet with their feeble amount of hydrogen—only enough to lift the airship a few feet off the ground— Amelia beckoned to Ander and Hammer.

"The rudder is bent and won't do any good hanging below us now. I need you to raise it." The two soldiers barely had enough time to hoist it from the sand before the airship was underway.

The airship creaked and groaned as it glided forward. Since the rudder was out of commission, she and the few uninjured sailors had to steer with only the sails. Now and then, the airship crashed and broke through dunes like waves. One large dune stopped the airship entirely, so Ander and the soldiers hauled lines and use shovels to get the airship over.

Throughout the morning, news about Axel spread through the airship like wildfire—which fueled everyone to work faster. Even many of the injured assisted in duties. But as the unforgiving sun rose to its peak and the expanse of sandy dunes remained the same as far as the eye could see, that motivation tapered.

Amelia was checking some lines when she caught two sailors speaking in hushed tones behind the steam cannon.

"This is all hopeless," one said. "There's no way we'll get anywhere near the Republic in time to save Axe."

"We'll be lucky to get out of this desert," said the other.

Fiery words came to Amelia's mind, but she bit her tongue. She couldn't tell them her actual plan. Ander was right. The crew would

CRAIG & JALEESA SNOW

not approve, and she needed all the support she could get. It didn't stop her, though, from assigning them both to sweep sand out from the lower deck. It was a Bragg-like thing to do, but she didn't care.

The order didn't stop the feeling of hopelessness from spreading across the deck. Over the next hours, others peeled off one-by-one to tend to injuries or other "important" duties. Eventually, only Ander and a core few remained.

The heat grew more intense as the landscape turned into an oven. Sweat dripped down Amelia's face, forcing her to replace her bandage twice. The bleeding was gone, but Eugene insisted she keep the area dry so it wouldn't get infected. She had agreed only to appease him, but now the bandages irritated her scalp.

By mid-afternoon, the heat had grown to sweltering. Heat waves rippled across the dunes, making everything distant look blurry. Hot wind made it worse, blowing coarse sand into her eyes and teeth. In the heat, the airship sank low enough to scrape the sand. Soon, she asked Everard to begin converting their drinking water into hydrogen.

Word about the order spread through the airship like wildfire. Sailors and soldiers shot her dirty looks whenever she passed below decks for supplies. One group finally confronted her and asked why. When she asked them if they'd rather walk or fly out of the desert, they fell silent. The answer did little to lift morale.

The numbers on the main deck shrunk again, leaving only Amelia, Veronica, Ander, and two sailors. The work became too much for their small group, and they were beyond exhausted.

Amelia wiped her brow. "Veronica, will you round up a relief shift of sailors?"

"Aye, cap," Veronica said before disappearing into the crew's quarters.

Amelia waited several long minutes for Veronica to return. When her first mate didn't, she frowned, handed control of the helm to Ander, and approached the doors to the crew's quarters. She paused at the threshold at the sound of hushed voices.

"Oi, I'll 'ave none of that," said Veronica. "Cap's orders are cap's orders."

"But you 'ave to admit," someone said, "she's sacrificin' our water to save an already dead man."

Were they complaining about her? She clenched her teeth and leaned in closer.

"She cares more about her airship than us," said another. "Who's to say she won't start throwing us off as dead weight next?"

Voices chorused in agreement while Veronica protested. "She'd never do that, I'll 'ave you know."

Maybe not before, Amelia thought. *It's tempting now.*

"Yer dehydration is talkin'," Veronica said. "The cap is very loyal to 'er crew."

"She's insane that she is! Look at the crash, the mountain range, the jungle, even the Everstorm! She's crazy and runnin' us to the ground! We'll all be buried by the time everythin's through!"

Agreement surged again with the group.

"She's not insane!" Veronica's voice rose.

They think I'm insane?! Indignity burned through Amelia. She reached for the door handle.

"What about the fire?" asked a sailor.

Her hand froze around the handle, and her heart stopped.

"We never talk about that! And maybe it's time we did!" The room chorused in agreement so loud, the sailors on duty behind her looked in her direction.

"Oi! Those people died because of *her* poor judgment!"

Her chest grew tight. *No! They have it wrong! It wasn't her fault! It couldn't have been!*

"She didn't care about 'em!" said the first voice. "Not. One. Bit!"

Each emphasized word was like a stake being pounded in her heart.

"Those workers burned alive because of *her!*"

I cared about them all! Tears sprang to her eyes and ran down her sunburned cheeks. *It was an accident!*

"THAT'S ENOUGH!" Veronica's voice pierced through the hubbub. "OTTO NEVER PERMITTED THIS DISCUSSION AND NEITHER WILL I!"

"We trusted her because Otto trusted her! And look where that got him!"

Amelia couldn't stand there any longer. She let go of the handle and shuffled back to the helm with her eyes cast downward.

"What's going on in there?" Ander asked, pointing to the crew's quarters. "I heard shouting."

She wiped underneath her eyes with her forefingers. "They aren't going to help."

She looked up at him, and his eyes widened. Then his entire demeanor transformed from concerned to terrifying calmness in an instant.

"I'll handle it." He climbed down from the helm and seemed to grow bigger as he crossed the main deck to the crew's quarters. Then, with both hands, he shoved the doors crashing open.

"GET TO YOUR STATIONS NOW!" His voice boomed out of the open doorway so loudly the deck seemed to shake. Sailors tripped over themselves as they scrambled out in haste. They each stopped at their station and stood at attention.

Ander walked out across the middle of the deck slowly and eyed all of them. Then he continued in the same voice. "If ANY of you disobey an order from your captain again, I will personally throw you off this airship. Is that clear?"

"Yes, sir," responded the crew in unison.

"I SAID, IS THAT CLEAR?"

"YES, SIR!"

"Good! Current shift, you're relieved. Lookout, you are watching for any signs of civilization. Civilization means water. You two with the sour faces! I want every inch of this airship swept and mopped until I can see my reflection! Everyone else, you're on duty. MOVE!"

Sailors scrambled to their tasks, and the deck became a flurry of activity. Amelia gave Ander a watery smile, and he nodded his head. He climbed up next to her.

"I'm sorry they were giving you trouble," he said.

She shrugged. "I should have suspected it would happen, eventually."

He raised an eyebrow. "I can't see any reason why they wouldn't follow you. It's the shortage of water and heat talking."

She frowned. She knew of a very *large* and valid reason why the crew could never follow her—at least not 100%.

"For what it's worth, I trust you completely." He gave her a smile and left. She watched him go and felt pressure grow again in her chest. Did he know about her history? Or did he trust her completely because he *didn't* know?

Chapter 5: Mesa Village

Ander

Ander assigned a night watch before crashing to bed. His stiff cot was a luxury after working straight through the previous night. The rocking and creaking of the airship didn't wake him once until morning sunlight peered through his porthole. He rose and began the day with a check on Axel.

The large soldier's pale complexion had a bluish hue, and his forehead was cold to the touch. Only the weak rise and fall of his chest indicated he was still alive.

"He's not swallowing water anymore," said Eugene, his face grim. "Same with broth."

Ander ran a hand through his hair. "How long do you think he's got?"

"Not long." He wouldn't look at Ander's eyes.

Ander let out a heavy sigh. "I guess all we can do is pray for a miracle and hope we find civilization soon." Ander squeezed Axel's shoulder. "We're trying, Axe," he whispered, before leaving.

He emerged onto the main deck and found Amelia already at the helm. She held a wide stance, and her gaze was fixed on the horizon. The bandage on her head was gone, revealing black stitches at the corner of her hairline.

"Any news?" Ander asked.

She nodded. "Only an hour ago, we found camel droppings and those." She pointed off the starboard side at a string of tracks they were following.

He blinked. "That's great news!"

She nodded and pointed to Freya patrolling around the edge of the main deck with a steam crossbow in hand. "Freya guesses the droppings are about a day old, so we aren't too far behind."

Freya looked up at the sound of her name and frowned at Ander before resuming her patrol.

"Okay." Ander scratched his head. He had no idea what Freya's expression was about.

"So now," Amelia continued, "we just have to hope we'll find a village soon. And hopefully, it has a healer. And most hopefully, Axe holds out till then."

He sighed. "At least there's hope we'll find a healer." His eyes rested on her stitches. "Speaking of healers, how are *you* doing?"

She shrugged. "My forehead feels a lot better, though somehow there's a big bump on the back of my head." She pointed at the spot Ander had dropped her. "I must've hit my head twice in the crash."

"Oh?" Heat rose to his cheeks. "Um, that's weird."

She eyed him, almost like she knew *exactly* where it had come from.

He swallowed, suddenly wishing he could dive off the airship rather than stand here. He cleared his throat. "Well, um, what can I do to help around here?"

She eyed him a second longer before spouting off a list of tasks he could organize around the airship. As soon as she was done, he left the deck in a hurry.

Activity around the airship increased as the sun rose. When the sun reached its apex, the crew had caught up to a small caravan of camels. The riders gawked at the airship, but they provided directions to the nearest village. It was a two-day journey west by camel, which Ander knew would take a half-day at their current speed.

Around the same time, Axel deteriorated more. Several times, he stopped breathing entirely, only to resume seconds later. Tension built around the airship with each hour that passed. The race between the airship and Axe put knots into Ander's neck and shoulders.

As the sun neared the horizon, a wide mesa materialized into view. Smoke spiraled out from the tops of simple adobe buildings. Palm trees, fronds, and other vegetation grew all alongside the homes, along with rows of plants. They had found what they were looking for. Now he hoped they had a healer.

. . . .

"Whatcha mean you're lookin' for a Gifted 'ealer?!" Veronica shook with anger. Ander ran a hand through his hair as he looked out at the entire crew assembled around him. This was not how he wanted to open this conversation, and he didn't have time for an argument.

He put his hands out to calm her. "Veronica, this is the only way to save Axe."

"Gifted are the enemy!" said Charles, pointing out to the mesa village in the distance. "We can't work with them!"

Amelia appeared from her cabin with an armful of Sadrian clothing. She shoved a pile into Ander's and Hammer's arms. "I only have enough for two. Put the robes on first." She was already dressed in a light-colored dress with a wide leather belt. Blue beaded earrings dangled from each of her ears.

Ander groaned. "Millie, we're losing time!"

"We don't want to look threatening. Otherwise, they won't help!"

"Fine." He unbuckled his sword and magpack and threw a light-colored robe over his armor.

"Cap, you aren' agreein' with this?" asked Veronica.

"Would you rather we let Axe die?" Amelia asked, donning a yellow headscarf.

Ander finished putting on his robe and began strapping his gear back on.

"Oi, but Otto? 'E was killed by Gifted." There was a note of pain in the first mate's voice.

Amelia paused. "Otto was a hero, and my goal is to prevent another tragedy from happening."

Ander picked up a hooded cloak with more folds than he could count. He frowned at it until Amelia grabbed it and threw the folds this way and that over his shoulders. By the time she was done, the cloak covered his magpack entirely, and he looked distinctly Sadrian.

"I don't like this," piped in Charles. "Nothing good comes from Gifted magic!"

Ander felt the words like a punch to the gut. Magic kept them alive on Tranquility, guided them to the Everblade, healed Amelia after being attacked, and destroyed the Nardoowe beast. But there wasn't time to push the point. Axel was on his deathbed.

"This isn't open for debate!" he said. "Amelia, Hammer, and I *will* enter that village and look for a healer."

The deck grew awkwardly silent. The scene reminded him of when Bragg was in charge. He sighed and continued with orders.

"Eugene and James, I need you to prepare a stretcher for Axe. Garret, I need the soldiers on standby in case trouble arises. Veronica, we need the water casks hauled to the main deck, ready to fill."

The last statement broke the awkward tension in the air. Whispers of *water* rippled through the group, sending everyone moving.

Maybe I should have opened with that? Ander threw a rope ladder over the railing of the airship and climbed down. Amelia and Hammer followed. Once down, they jogged across the rusty sands toward the mesa village.

The mesa grew upward as they ran, and its shadow stretched out at least a mile in the dying light. They reached its bottom and circled around it until they found a path. Then they rushed up it as quickly as they could. Only when they reached the top did they pause to take a breath.

Wind swirled dust through streets of quiet adobe homes. Nothing moved except for billowing lines of clothes hung between buildings.

Ander glanced at his two companions and frowned. "Where are the people?" His hand drifted down to the pommel of the Everblade.

"I'm not sure," Amelia answered.

"People here," said Hammer in his deep voice. He pointed up to a solitary watchtower where red smoke spiraled upward into the dying light.

That's a warning fire, Ander realized from his academy training days. He reexamined the empty village with new eyes, searching for threats. Any number of alleys, buildings, or outcrops could hide Sadrian warriors.

"Feels like a trap," he breathed.

"If we don't find a healer," said Amelia, "we're going to lose Axel."

Ander swallowed. It felt like a tactical mistake, but what choice did they have?

He led the way forward, keeping a hand on his sword. He scanned the buildings, and realized with a start that eyes were watching them through shuttered windows.

"How are we going to find a healer if everyone's shut inside?" he whispered.

"Healers are expensive," said Amelia. "It'll be a more prominent home."

They continued farther, looking for a home that might belong to a healer. The dwellings were simpler than what he recalled in Sadria, only single story and more weathered.

When they reached a simple central square, the scene transformed. The buildings there wore long cracks and blackened scorch marks like scars. *This place had seen battle,* he realized.

"There," said Amelia, gesturing to a home that looked no different than the others.

Ander raised an eyebrow. "How do you know?"

"There's a eucalyptus leaf carved at the top of the door," she said, as if it was obvious. When the other two just stared at her, she added, "It's the Sadrian symbol of healing."

They approached the door and knocked. Long silence passed. They knocked harder.

"Not welcome," came a muffled old woman's voice. Her speech was in the common tongue and heavily accented.

Amelia moved closer to the door and replied in fluent Sadrian.

The old woman cut her off brusquely. "You from dat Republic of Steam. You are *not* welcome."

"We have injured," said Ander in an equally unfriendly tone.

Amelia glared at him and said, "We can pay you well for your services."

The door opened a crack, revealing a sliver of a wrinkled face. The old woman looked them up and down with suspicious eyes. Then her gaze transfixed on the Everblade hanging on Ander's hip. The look sent a shiver down his spine.

The old, shawled woman opened the door slowly, revealing a dark room lit by only a clay oil lamp. She shuffled away from them and disappeared behind a beaded curtain at the end of the room.

Ander hesitated. Were they supposed to follow?

Pungent aromas drifted from the house, stinging his eyes. It smelled like a suffocating mix of old person, burned incense, and dead animals. He gagged and took a step backward.

Amelia pushed him forward. "Go on, don't be rude." He swallowed, took a deep breath, and stepped in.

As his eyes adjusted to the dim light, he saw haphazard shelves lined four walls and were covered by a chaotic assortment of yellowed glass jars, bleached bones, dried plants, and clay censers. Sun-bleached curtains covered the only window in the room. The furnishings were composed of a wooden table, a desk, and a few chairs, all of which looked heavily weathered.

"Sit down," said Amelia, insistent. Hammer gave one look to the heavily weathered, wooden chairs and moved to stand in a corner.

Ander stood there longer until Amelia gave him a withering look. He shook his head and glanced at the beaded curtain. Who knew what she was doing behind there? All of this could be a trap.

A foot tapped against the back of his calf. He turned and saw Amelia glaring with the heat of a thousand suns. Her arms were folded and her lips were stretched tight. He gave way, sitting down next to her, but he kept a hand ready by his sword.

Minutes passed in silence before the old woman reemerged through the curtain with a burning oil lamp in hand. She sat down behind her withered desk.

The light illuminated her grouchy face, which was so creased that her wrinkles seemed to have wrinkles as well. Her wild hair was white, and some even sprouted from her chin and curled off her eyebrows. Her intense brown eyes burned into the trio, full of life and intelligence.

"I let you in," the healer croaked. "What is it dat you want?"

"We have a friend who's injured and has a severe infection," said Amelia quickly. "He isn't with us right now, but we can bring him later."

"How bad?" The healer's tone was disinterested, but her eyes told a different story. Her eyes gleamed in the lamplight as they drifted to the Everblade.

"Very bad," answered Amelia.

The healer's lips parted into a subtle smirk that sent spiders crawling up Ander's spine. He shifted his cloak to cover the blade, but the healer's eyes stayed locked on where it was hidden.

"What offer you in payment?" asked the healer.

"We have plenty of money to cover the cost," said Amelia.

The old woman held her hand up. "Money is little value here.

Only supplies. And if dis is bad as you say, I need *plenty* payment. It will take toll to heal your friend."

Ander eyed Amelia warily. He didn't trust this healer, and they were already limited in their supplies as it was.

"Millie," he warned.

"We need to help Axe," she said from the corner of her mouth.

She was right, but he didn't like it. He clenched his teeth.

"What supplies do you need?" Amelia asked.

The healer leaned forward and circled a finger around a hair on her chin. "Here is offer. I want dat slave." She gestured to Hammer. Then she turned to Ander. "And I want dat sword."

Alarm surged through Ander. Instinctively, he gripped the handle tightly.

Amelia grabbed his arm. "Hammer's not a slave," she said calmly, "and the sword is not for sale."

The healer's eyes flicked again to the sword, the greed in her eyes unmistakable. "Dat is fair trade," she croaked. "*Mirabetal.* Life for life and sword for compensation."

"Hammer is a friend, not a slave," Amelia repeated.

She frowned. "Fine. I want dat sword den. Dat's my offer."

The muscles in Ander's neck tightened. "Why do you want my sword?" His tone carried all the suspicion he felt.

The healer clasped her hands and gave a wide smile. As she did, a simple tattoo on the inside of her forearm caught the light. Two dunes were drawn with squiggly horizontal lines just above. "For my own purposes," she said simply. "Do we have deal or is dis waste of time?"

"It's because of the slavers, isn't it?" said Amelia with a note of concern in her voice. "Your village has been hit recently, hasn't it?"

The old woman sighed and leaned back in her chair, which creaked from the movement. "Tree times dis year. Lost apprentice, I did." She swallowed hard and looked away. The gesture was full of emotion, but Ander wasn't buying it.

"That's awful," said Amelia. "If it's weapons you want, we can supply you with swords."

"Just not mine," added Ander.

The healer thought for a moment before sighing. "What your bargain?"

. . . .

The sun was gone by the time they returned to the village. This time, Eugene and James joined them, carrying Axel between them on a stretcher. A stiff wind blew sand in their faces as they hurried toward the healer's clinic. Axel was deathly pale and horribly still.

When the old woman let them in, Eugene and James laid the stretch on the table and took a step back. No one spoke as the healer walked around the table, feeling Axel's head and gently touching the red and purple streaks that ran up from his heavily wrapped stump. She frowned before disappearing through the beaded curtain.

"Are you sure we can trust her?" asked Eugene quietly.

No, Ander thought, but trustworthy or not, this healer was Axel's last option.

Eugene shook his head and inspected the room. "Do you see these jars?" he whispered. "This seems less like a medical clinic and more like a witch doctor's hut!"

"If you look by her desk," said Amelia, her voice hushed as well, "she has bandages, antiseptics, and other normal tools."

Eugene snorted quietly. "Normal?" He pointed to a jar of a murky brown liquid labeled *Memory Restorative.* "Really? We're going to trust Axel to a Gifted who uses nonsense like memory restoring mud water?"

The old woman burst through curtain, making them all jump. She dropped an armful of supplies next to Axel's head with a loud clatter.

"Mud water?" the healer repeated. "If dis is how you feel, den you can leave!"

Amelia stepped in front. "Please ignore him. He's only here to transport our friend."

"I'm his medical provider," Eugene snapped. "And it's my responsibility to ensure he receives optimal, reputable care."

The healer shuffled past Amelia and stopped when she stood eye to eye with Eugene. "Magic is more powerful den Commonborn treatment. Dis is why you, medical provider, need *me*. Magic can knit skin, kill infection, and fuse bone. It can even restore memory, so long as you have part to recall."

The healer turned back to Ander and Amelia and put her hand out. "Payment?"

Ander felt the knots in his shoulders loosen slightly. He motioned to Hammer, who set down a clanking canvas bundle on the desk. The healer shuffled over, unrolled the bundle, and inspected the gleaming assortment of swords and knives.

"Dis will work. Stand back."

The group moved to the edges of the room as the healer began working. After filling a stone basin with a sour smelling fluid, she removed Axel's bandages and dabbed it on the swollen, puss-filled stump. Then she emptied a jar of herbs into a mortar and began crushing them with a pestle, pausing now and then to add more ingredients from her array of jars. Once the mortar was full, she held a hand over it and poured energy into the concoction.

Whomp! The mixture burst into flames, causing everyone except for the healer to jump. Blue-green smoke floated up and filled the room with a foreign, spicy aroma. The healer weaved her hands around it, and the smoke drew itself together into a thick spiral. She continued gesticulating with her hands and directed the smoke toward Axel's head. It entered his nose, filled his lungs, and exited through his mouth.

"How is this—" James started, but the woman held up a hand. She continued guiding the smoke in and out of Axel's head, sometimes redirecting the smoke out his ears instead of his mouth. After a couple minutes, his pale complexion pinkened and his breathing grew more regular.

The healer disappeared into the back room again and returned with large, green leaves. She clutched them in one hand and put her other hand on Axel's injury. She closed her eyes and a wave of energy rippled through the room. Axel's streaked and pussy stump glowed blue. New skin grew across the long incision and knitted itself back together. Ander stared at the injury unblinkingly as the process continued, shrinking down the swelling, evaporating the puss, and leaving behind smooth, pink skin.

Once done, the old woman let go of Axel and opened her other hand. A handful of ash remained from what was once green leaves, and this she let fall to the floor. Her face was gray and covered in sweat.

"It is done," she said, out of breath. "I should have asked more in payment. No matter. Dat infection is gone and dis wound is healed. But keep it wrapped for more days till skin gets stronger."

Ander ran a hand through his hair, not believing what he was seeing. Axel's stump was fully healed, and his chest rose and fell regularly. It seemed impossible. Only moments ago, Axel had been knocking on death's door.

Both Eugene and James stared, shocked. They approached Axel and checked his vitals and injury. Then Eugene shook his head in amazement.

"Thank you so much!" said Amelia. Her eyes shined with unshed tears. "We—we couldn't have—"

"No. You couldn't," the old woman said. "I have set healing in motion, but he need time to fully recover. Now, go. I need rest."

Ander opened the door for the stretcher. Gratitude filled him as a much healthier Axel was carried out into the night. Amelia and Hammer followed after. As Ander pulled the door shut, he once again caught the healer eyeing his sword just before the latch clicked shut.

He shook the image out of his head. Their arrangement with her was done. Axel was healed. This was the last they'd see of the healer.

Exhaustion hit him like a ton of bricks as they walked back to the airship. They'd been through so much the last few weeks, and now that Axel had been treated, he wanted nothing more than to sleep.

Sailors and soldiers thronged them when they reached the airship, asking a thousand questions. He ignored them all and cleared a path for the medics to take Axel to the medical bay. Once the recovering soldier was settled, Ander headed straight for his cabin.

His cot was a welcome relief after the long day, and sleep quickly took over. Dreams filled his head with visions of swirling blue-green smoke and the healer's intense interest in the Everblade. *Something isn't right*, his dreams warned.

A sixth sense woke him up in the middle of the night. He stared about his room blearily. The porthole was unlatched and knocked gently in the night wind. His thoughts scrambled as he reached for his sword.

He grasped at empty air. Panic surged through him as he looked all around.

The Everblade was gone.

Chapter 6: Stolen

Ander

Ander bolted out of his cabin and up the stairs. As soon as he reached the main deck, the night watch sounded the alarm. Just off the bow a hooded figure sprinted toward the village. Moonlight glinted off a metal blade in the figure's hands.

The Everblade! Ander grabbed a rappelling line and dropped over the side of the *Legacy*. As soon as he hit the ground, he bolted after the figure.

His heart pounded in his chest, matching the rhythm of the fury burning through his veins. How did this happen? He had the blade next to him the whole night.

The thief caught sight of Ander and increased his pace.

Not happening! Ander gritted his teeth and pushed his legs to move faster. They reached the winding path to the village and raced up it. His heart pounded from more than just the exertion. If he lost the Everblade, everything they had gone through to get it would be for nothing.

As soon as they reached the top, Ander finally caught up. Throwing his whole weight, he leapt onto the thief and slammed him to the ground. The force sent the blade flying out of the thief's hands, sending it skittering feet ahead.

The thief tried to wriggle away, but Ander held firm, pinning his arms back. Pounding footsteps echoed from the path behind. A pack of Steam soldiers were incoming, with Cid trailing not far behind.

"I've got him!" Ander shouted. It wasn't until this moment that he noticed a tattoo on the back of the thief's wrist: two dunes with squiggly horizontal lines just above.

His eyes narrowed. It was similar to the healer's.

The thief contorted his fingers and sand exploded underneath them. The blast lifted Ander off his feet and threw him backward onto his back. He gasped and rolled to his feet as the thief began running away again. This time, the thief was just a vague figure in the cloud of dust.

"NO!" Ander ran after the figure, chasing him as he continued to throw up more sand. As Ander drew close, the man abruptly split into two, and then split again into four.

What? He tackled the closest and flew straight through it. The figure dissolved as the remaining figures multiplied again before splitting into six different directions.

Ander shook the sand out of his eyes and cursed. The Steam soldiers trailing him caught up and split different ways, following after the fleeing figures. He watched them go and slammed a fist into the ground.

"You've been duped," said Cid behind him.

He glared at the stowaway. "What are *you* doing here?"

Cid shrugged. "Looked more entertaining than sweeping the deck."

Ander shook his head. He wasn't in the mood for a conversation, especially with Cid. They needed to find the thief as soon as possible.

He took off at a jog. Cid followed a few steps behind, keeping pace.

"You're running the wrong way."

"Not now, Cid."

"There's no footprints in this direction."

Ander paused and looked down. Unfortunately, Cid was right.

"It's a classic misdirection," Cid rasped, "and you fell right for it. I bet that thief is long gone now."

Ander clenched his jaw, trying to keep his anger in check as he retraced his steps. Cid continued to follow, seeming to grow smugger as Ander grew more frustrated.

"All that work to get the blade," Cid mocked, "and you lost it to the first common thief you encountered."

Ander wheeled on him. "Look. If you know *so much*, how about *you* find the thief?"

Cid glared. "Fine. But if I do, I'm done cleaning the decks."

"Fine."

Cid turned and disappeared into the village, following none of the directions the thief took. Ander shook his head. He had as much confidence in Cid finding the thief as he did in Bragg's leadership.

He retraced his steps back to where he had tackled the thief and found Freya there. She studied the ground, following a series of faint depressions. After a couple minutes, they disappeared entirely.

"I'm not sure where he went," said Freya with an exasperated sigh. "He covered his trail like he knew what he was doing."

Ander groaned and ran a hand through his hair. "We can't lose that blade. Keep looking for signs. I'm going to go back and bring the rest of the soldiers. Nothing gets in or out of this village until we find the Everblade."

He rushed back to the *Legacy* and rallied the rest of the Steam soldiers. Then they reentered the village dressed in their tactical gear and fully armed. He sent a group to secure the entrance while he led another to the healer's home. When they reached there, they kicked the door down and entered with their weapons drawn. The healer was gone, and they made quick work of searching the house. The Everblade was nowhere to be found.

As the morning sun rose, Ander widened the search, sending two-person teams from home to home, searching each and asking questions. The people offered little resistance and huddled in corners when their homes had been searched. He hated the looks of fear they gave them, but he *had* to find the Everblade for the safety of the Republic.

While the soldiers searched the village, a team of sailors found an underground cistern filled with thousands of gallons of water. They used this to fill up casks of water and brought it back to the airship. By lunch, the *Legacy* hovered overhead the village, adding another layer of security to the search.

As each hour passed, uncertainty grew inside him. What if they never found the sword again? What if the thief had hidden it so well, it was gone for good? Losing the Everblade was more than just a loss for the Republic. It was a loss to him as well. The blade was *his* charge from the Warden. *He* was the new Warden of the blade. And only weeks after getting it, he had already lost it.

The feeling grew worse as evening came. By that point, the soldiers had searched every home in the village twice and came out empty-handed. They even sent Blaze down into the village's cistern to make sure the blade hadn't been tossed down it.

He couldn't shake the feeling that they were missing something. There wasn't any sign of the weapons they had paid the healer, nor any sign of the healer herself. All of it had gone into hiding. The villagers had offered no help either, the majority staying silent when questioned.

He returned to the *Legacy*, knowing he wouldn't be able to fully think through their predicament without a hot meal and a break. He had been awake since the thief had come in the night and had only eaten a small ration at midday.

He made his way to the mess hall, passing a stream of sailors bringing in dried desert brush and breaking it down into fuel for the engine deck. Amelia had been overseeing the resupplying of the airship through the day, and she had given the crew specific instructions on what they should collect and what they shouldn't. Their goal was to resupply enough so they could make it to Sadria, not to strip the land of resources the villagers would need.

As he entered the mess hall, he could see Amelia now, sitting at a table, talking to Eugene and Garret. A small smile appeared on her face when he entered, and she scooted over to make room for him. He grabbed a bowl of stew and took the open seat.

"Hey," she said softly. "I heard you couldn't find anything."

He sighed into his bowl. "We searched every house, every outbuilding, even the cistern. Nothing."

"Could you sense the sword?" she asked, even quieter. "Like in the Everblade vault?"

He shook his head. "I tried. If they somehow got off the mesa, they could have hidden it anywhere, and we'd never be able to find it."

Garret leaned forward. "What stumps me is the healer. She's disappeared as well. None of the villagers knew where she was. The only thing we got out of them was that she was a recluse. They only saw her if she was going out for herbs or someone needed healing."

"She's definitely the key," Ander said. "She had the same tattoo as the thief."

"We shouldn't have trusted her in the first place." All eyes turned to Charles, who was grabbing a bowl. Freya was a step behind him. "I told you, nothing good comes from Gifted magic."

Tension filled the room like steam building up in an old brass boiler. Ander measured his tone carefully so as not to release the pressure in a raging torrent.

"Charles, now isn't the time," he said.

"Of course it's not!" Charles pulled a chair at the head of the table while Freya leaned against the wall nearby. "The time to talk was *before* this whole situation happened. If you had listened to us and not gone to that healer, none of this would have happened."

Ander narrowed his eyes. "Does the handbook tell you this is a democracy?"

Charles' face went red. "Well... no!"

"Charles," said Eugene. "I also had my own reservations about visiting a Gifted healer. But I followed orders, and do you know what happened? That healer *saved* Axe's life."

Charles folded his arms. "Fine. But at what cost? Think of what we all went through to get the Everblade! How many lives did we lose for that?"

Ander smacked the table with both hands and rose to his feet. "Do you think I don't know what it cost to get the Everblade? You think I forgot Axe lost his hand, Eugene almost drowned, Amelia was almost killed by the beast, Hammer was struck by lightning—not to mention the crew and soldiers we lost to the Enchantrans? You *really* want to remind me what it cost, Charles?"

The room fell silent. Everyone watched Ander and Charles stare each other down. Charles finally looked away.

Ander sat back down and raised a spoonful of stew to his mouth.

"You know," said Freya in a low voice, "the healer wouldn't have known about the sword if you hadn't worn it to her home in the first place." She eyed Ander. "You may have found the sword, but that doesn't mean it's *yours*."

Ander set the spoon back down, appetite gone. Mixed emotions flooded through him: indignation at the accusation Freya clearly didn't understand, and frustration that she had a good point. If he hadn't worn the Everblade to the healer's clinic, none of this would have happened.

Still, Freya, Charles, and everyone else didn't understand the Everblade. Yes, it was their charge to secure and take back to the Republic. Yes, it was a key to the Source of all magical power. Yes, it could be a devastating weapon in the wrong hands. Yet, it held a purpose that Ander felt more than understood.

The last words of the Warden of Tranquility stirred in his memory.

"I sense... dark powers stirring again... Shadows that have remained hidden... are taking on new faces. You must be wary.... The sword may be needed again to... save the peace."

How could he explain to her that he had proven himself worthy of the blade? That, in a sense, it was his to protect and to wield? That it was his charge now?

A raspy voice interrupted his musings. "When you're all done arguing with each other, I'd like to tell our *leader* where the sword is located." All eyes turned to Cid, who was leaning against the wall.

Great. Just who I need. Ander leaned back and folded his arms. "You've got my attention."

A wide smile spread across Cid's mouth. "I first need a drink."

Ander stared at Cid for a few seconds before waving a hand to Garvin. The cook brought a jug of water and filled a cup. Cid took it and frowned at it.

"You've got your drink," said Ander. "Tell us what you know."

Cid ignored him and took a sip. After a long pause, he said, "While you were playing soldier and making people too afraid to open their mouths, I looked for signs of a thieves' network."

He took another sip. Ander felt his patience growing thin.

"The signs were all there," said Cid, taking a seat. "So I did some digging and found a group that call themselves the Mirage."

Mirage. The word sparked a distant memory from Ander's days at the Forge Military Academy. The Mirage was a ruthless desert tribe committed to overthrowing the Sadrian throne. Ander had learned about them in his studies, though the details were fuzzy.

"How did you find that out?" asked Amelia, unconvinced.

"I listened," said Cid evenly. "People are more willing to share their secrets when they believe they won't be overheard." He turned to Ander and added, "Or interrogated."

Cid finished his drink and wiped his face with his sleeve. The muscles in Ander's neck tightened.

"Right," said Amelia. "Because they were sharing their secrets in the common tongue?"

Cid glared at the airship captain and spoke a phrase in the desert tongue. Ander didn't recognize the words, his own Sadrian language training being limited to military applications. The disrespectful tone, however, was crystal clear.

Amelia's face turned red. "HOW DARE YOU!"

Cid smugly leaned back.

"That's enough!" Ander stood up and grabbed Cid's cloak and yanked him so they were eye to eye. Cid squirmed, but Ander's grip was firm. "Unless you have anything *useful* to offer, you're going straight to the main deck to mop, and we both know how much you *love* doing that."

Cid glared at Ander. "Fine. I know where their hideout is."

Ander let go of Cid's cloak, and the stowaway crashed back to the bench.

"Their hideout?" Ander repeated. "How do I know you're telling the truth?"

Cid withdrew a sword from his cloak and dropped it on the table. All eyes went to the blade.

Amelia leaned forward. "That's one we sold to the healer."

"I can lead you to the hideout," said Cid, "but we need to leave now."

"Alright," said Ander. "I'll get a team ready."

"No." Cid's tone was firm. "Only you can come. Otherwise, it won't work."

Amelia grabbed Ander's arm. "This feels a little too convenient."

Ander pursed his lips. It *was* suspicious, but this was his *only* lead, and it wasn't like Cid to make friends with anyone—even with a band of thieves. Still....

"Garret's coming too," Ander said with finality.

"Fine, but both of you need to be silent. No tromping around like you normally do." Cid turned and left for the hatch.

Garret shrugged. "I guess that's our cue to go."

"I don't trust him," said Amelia. "I'll get the airship ready, just in case you need it."

. . . .

Ander and Garret followed Cid through the village to a rocky outcropping on the edge of the mesa. Here, Cid pulled away thick brush to reveal a cave entrance.

"This is how your thief and healer escaped," Cid announced. "It's an alternative exit from the mesa."

They followed the cave's sloping path downward until they exited through another obscured entrance at the base of the mesa. Then they walked out into the desert.

The wind on the desert was stiff now that the sun had dropped below the horizon. The sand, however, still radiated heat from the long day. That would change soon, he knew.

After several minutes of walking, several more mesas appeared on the horizon. They started as dark spots, but grew with each step they took. Soon, their sheer rocky slopes and barren tops became clear.

"Down!" said Cid. He pulled them down into the sand and pointed. A plume of dust rose from the distance, heading toward the mesa nearest to them.

Ander pulled out his spyglass and peered at the shape hurtling through the sand. It was a wooden skiff-like craft with sponsons stretched on either side. It slid over the sand like a sled, propelled by large sails on the top.

Sand sailor, he realized. He'd read about these crafts that Gifteds used to travel through the Sadrian deserts. The sponsons were used for travel over sandy dunes and added stability to the craft. Wagon wheels could also be installed for usage on desolate, flat terrains. Typically, they were propelled by Gifted wind magic, which was used to fill the sails and propel the craft forward.

"I wonder what that's doing out here," Garret said.

"That's the reason we need to move quickly," Cid said.

Ander frowned. "Explain."

Cid groaned impatiently. "Those sailors move wicked fast, faster than your airship. That's why we've got to be discreet. We have to get the blade out before they do."

"Before they do?" Ander a raised eyebrow.

Cid let out a painful exhale. "Think about it. You supplied weapons to the Mirage. Does the village we just left look like their headquarters?"

Ander knew the answer was "no," but the tone of Cid's voice made him not want to state the obvious answer. Instead of responding, Ander lifted the spyglass and watched the sand sailor come to a stop in front of the mesa at another cave. Two hooded, cloaked figures exited the cave and approached the craft. Both wore cloth coverings over their mouth and nose. On their chests were mismatched armor from animal hides, and across their backs were spears tipped with long fangs.

Ander shivered at the sight of the spear tips. Whatever animal those came from must have been big.

"So, this is a holding place for the Everblade until the Mirage can get it to their headquarters?" Garret asked. Cid gave them another irritable look, and that was all the answer they needed.

"How do you know all of this?" asked Ander.

"Where do you think I've been all day?" said Cid with exasperation. "Sunbathing?"

"Fair point," said Garret. "Do you have a way in?"

Cid nodded. He rose to a crouch and skittered forward, keeping to the shadowed sections of the dunes. Ander and Garret activated their steam crossbows and followed. They took a wide arc around the mesa until they were out of view of the cave entrance. Then they moved close to the mesa's craggy walls.

Ander trained his crossbow ahead as they crept around the mesa. His pulse beat faster.

Cid stopped them before they made it all the way around. He put a finger to his lips and pointed to a narrow crack in the wall.

Ander and Garret glanced at each other before peering into the crack. It was barely wide enough to squeeze through but continued on, widening into a dark tunnel.

Ander felt his respect growing for Cid. While Cid's personality was intolerable, Ander had to admit Cid was good at what he did.

Cid and Garret squeezed through. Ander stepped toward the gap and froze. Tingles ran up his spine and sent his heart pounding. Fear spread through him as he recognized the feeling. It was the same feeling he felt when he first encountered the Nardoowe beast.

Slowly, he looked out at the desert and scrutinized it. Nothing but sand and dunes met his eyes. Still, he felt something was out there. Something dangerous.

He shook his head. Was he losing it? He knew soldiers sometimes reexperienced traumatic events at unexpected moments. Was this happening to him?

Cid grabbed his arm. "Do you want to get the Everblade or not?"

Cid was right. They were losing time. He slipped through into a natural cave. Only a sliver of moonlight poured through behind them. Beyond that was impenetrable darkness.

Garret shifted his magpack off. "I'll get us a light."

"And get us caught?" hissed Cid. "No light." He disappeared into the dark without waiting.

Garret muttered something under his breath that included the words *kicking* and *long drop off the airship*. Ander smiled as he waited for the grizzled soldier to sling his magpack back on. Then they followed the direction Cid had left.

The passage tilted downward and angled deeper into the mesa. Ander kept a hand on a wall, using that to guide his footsteps in the deep darkness. After a minute, his hand fell away into a rough crevice.

"You took your time," said an irritable voice from the opening. "It's this way now."

He felt the crack and realized it was an offshoot from the tunnel. The opening was so thin, he had to take off his magpack and squeeze through. Sharp rocks scraped at him. He bumped his head twice. Both times took willpower not to say anything. The way angled and grew even tighter. He pushed his way through, feeling the stone grate against his armor before he broke free into a dimly lit tunnel.

Ander took several steadying breaths as he gathered his bearings. The floor was flat, and the walls were roughly carved out. Thick beams spanned up the walls and overhead, spaced at regular intervals. Light glowed from somewhere ahead where they could hear muffled voices.

Cid leaned against a wall with his arms folded. Garret appeared behind Ander, covered in dust. Silently, Ander drew his sword while

Garret shouldered his crossbow. They followed Cid down the tunnel, toward the light and voices.

The passage ended in a T. A clay oil lamp burned nearby, casting an orange glow in what was definitely a major tunnel. The passage was wider, and the ground was well worn by foot traffic.

Voices approached from the right. The trio took a few paces back and hid behind wooden beams. Several heartbeats passed before two desert warriors passed with large wicker baskets in their arms.

"They're taking those to the sailors," Cid said in a hurried whisper. "Quick."

They came to the intersection and turned right. They followed the passageway until a new set of voices became audible. Cid slowed down and shrunk into a crouch. They moved forward until they reached a hard turn. The voices were clear now, but they were speaking in the desert tongue. Cid mouthed the word *here.*

Ander moved to the front and peered around the corner. Ahead was a rounded room filled with baskets and clay pots full of supplies. A burly desert warrior sat on the edge of a table with his arms folded. Power radiated from the man, who seemed to be in a conversation with someone just outside Ander's line of sight. On the table behind the soldier was the canvas roll of swords they had paid to the healer.

"*This* is what you brought me out for?" The warrior said in Sadrian with a cynical tone.

"It has power!" An old woman stepped into Ander's line of vision. *The healer!* She spoke in fluent Sadrian and held out the Everblade by the sheath so that the warrior could draw the blade.

Anger poured through Ander's veins. She *had* been behind this after all! Even after they had haggled other forms of payment, she still had taken the Everblade from him through other means. The anger turned into steely resolve. He was going to get it back. He just had to figure out how they'd take down two Gifteds in the close confines of the caves.

The warrior drew the blade, held it up, and frowned. "I don't sense any power."

The healer cracked the sheath over his head. "Not with your eyes. Use your senses."

The warrior narrowed his eyes. "My senses tell me that this was a waste of my time."

Strange, Ander thought. When he closed his eyes, he could sense the Everblade clearly. Was that not normal?

Garret put a hand on Ander's shoulder. *Plan?* He mouthed.

Ander put a finger up and mouthed, *One moment.* He was curious to see if the healer and warrior could get the blade to work. Maybe the two of them could solve what Ander couldn't for the last month.

The healer grew more impatient in her words. "It has power in it," she said. "It's nothing like I've ever seen. Connect to it with your magic."

The warrior focused his gaze on the blade and poured power. Energy filled the room with a hazy aura and ran down the hall, sending waves of static past where the trio hid. Ander watched, expecting fire to burst forth from the length of the blade. Instead, the sword remained the same.

The warrior growled and shoved the sword back into the healer's hands. "Is this a trick? Or has age finally taken your sanity, Grezlgra?"

The healer sheathed the blade angrily. "I am not wrong. I would demonstrate myself if it was not locked from me somehow. I assumed this was because I am not a warrior, and this holds a warrior's magic."

Locked.... Ander almost slapped his forehead. Of course, it was locked to them. What had the Warden of Tranquility said to him?

The right to the sword comes from the bloodline.... Chills ran up his spine, taking him back to the dimly lit room where she had spoken inside his head. He remembered the disappointment he felt when he found out that only a specific ancient bloodline could use the blade. He had gotten that same right to use the blade by complete accident. That meant neither of these two Gifted could ever wield the blade, no matter how hard they tried.

The memory continued as more words from the Warden rushed into his head. *You do not have the power to wield the sword,* she said to Ander. *You are like a lantern with no oil, full of potential, but no fuel for the spark.*

The words felt like a chained anvil to his soul, dragging him down into the depths of a bottomless ocean. Why did it matter to him that he be able to use the sword again? Why did it feel discouraging to think that the Everblade might never work for him again?

"Time's running out," Cid hissed into Ander's ear, snapping him back to the moment. Footsteps echoed down the tunnel, heading their direction.

Ander swallowed. They needed to incapacitate the two Gifteds quickly. Still, the healer was powerful, and the warrior looked formidable. He wished he hadn't listened to Cid and brought his entire team. With only him and Garret, they'd be hard pressed to survive without an advantage.

An advantage.... An idea grew in his mind. He pulled away from the edge and whispered to Garret. "Use a blunt to knock out the healer. Then cover our rear." Garret nodded and shouldered his crossbow. Cid stared at them both like they were insane. Maybe they were.

Ander removed a canister from his belt and took a deep breath. Then he nodded to Garret.

They broke around the corner. Ander threw the canister while Garret fired. The bolt flew true and dropped the healer where she stood. The Everblade clattered to the ground at her feet while the warrior drew his saber and disappeared behind cover.

Boom! The room filled with smoke, and Ander charged in with his sword drawn. As soon as he passed through the doorway, he immediately ducked under a swing. More strikes followed, all with lightning-fast speed.

Ander blocked, ducked, and weaved. The Gifted's energy blazed bright in his mind, painting a clear picture of the warrior's movements. Dispersed energy also filled the room, giving Ander a vague outline of the environment. The warrior, on the other hand, was striking aimlessly into the dark and screaming for reinforcements.

The plan was working!

Ander pressed his advantage, pulling away from the warrior's reach, then rotated to the warrior's side. Then he reached for his knife and threw it so it clattered to the opposite side of the room.

The warrior launched at the sound, leaving his entire back exposed. Ander raised his sword and twisted it to strike with the flat side. But as Ander moved in, his right foot crashed through a clay pot that was invisible to his senses. The warrior wheeled around in a heartbeat and rammed into him.

Ander's feet left the ground as he crashed through pots and baskets before stopping against a wall. He gasped in pain and realized his sword was gone, lost in the piles of supplies. He looked frantically left and right, but all he could sense was the power of the warrior and the aura of energy hovering at the ceiling. His weapon was gone.

The warrior charged. Ander leapt aside and scrambled over unseen objects as the warrior crashed after him, swinging his weapon left and right. It was all Ander could do to keep a few feet ahead of that blade. He needed to find a weapon. He needed—

The Everblade glowed faintly in the center of the floor. It called to him like a lighthouse in a stormy sea.

He rushed for the blade, heedless of the crazed warrior behind. Again, supplies claimed his footing as he reached close. He crawled the last couple of feet and wrenched the blade from the ground.

Whoosh! The smoke rushed out of the room in a gust.

"You are persistent," groaned an unsteady and hunched over healer, "but you will die!"

The warrior leapt on top of Ander and locked blades. Inch by inch, the warrior pushed their blades closer and closer to Ander's throat.

Ander knew he couldn't win against this warrior in a contest of brute strength. Within the next few seconds, he'd lose this battle. Unless....

Come on! Ander urged the Everblade, hoping against hope. *Light!*

The blades crept closer to his throat.

Light, you stupid thing! LIGHT!

The voice of the Warden entered his head with a mocking tone. *You are like a lantern with no oil, full of potential, but no fuel for the spark.*

Ander shoved the voice out. *I COMMAND YOU TO LIGHT!*

Energy rushed into the sword, running down its length before entering into him and coalescing inside his chest. Then, that energy ignited inside his core. Power coursed through his body, sharpening his senses and filling his limbs with strength. Then it connected to the sword.

In a heartbeat, he shoved the warrior's blade back with incredible might. Then he slammed his pommel into the warrior's temple. The force lifted the warrior off Ander and sent him crashing to the ground, where he remained unmoving.

Ander rose to his feet and stumbled, the energy and power gone in an instant. Filling its void was extreme exhaustion. His arms ached as if he had done pushups for the last twenty minutes.

"H-h-how?" stammered the healer. She took several steps backward.

Ander wondered about the same question. He looked at the blade with shock and wonder. It actually worked for him!

"Dat impossible," said the healer. "Not unless...."

CRASH! A pot exploded over her head, and she crumpled to the floor. Cid stood just behind her, holding another pot ready. Ander and Cid stared at each other for a second. Then Cid broke the silence.

"What took you so long? I thought you were special forces!"

Ander blinked. Did Cid see what he just did? *No, he couldn't have.* Cid had been behind the healer and besides, the sword never burned with fire. It had, however, given him strength somehow. Despite everything, it had worked for him.

Ander looked again from the sword to the unconscious healer. What was she about to say? Did she know how he had gotten the blade to work?

"Your blundering here made a lot of noise," said Cid, bringing him back to the moment. "We need to go."

Right, Ander thought. *Leave now, figure out what just happened later.* He exited the room, going back down the passage he came from.

Blam. Blam. Blam. The passage echoed with the sound of Garret's semi-automatic steam crossbow, firing again and again. He was hunkered down and using the corner for cover.

"I've got the blade!" Ander shouted.

"Good!" grunted Garret. "Because this place is a beehive. We've got twenty, *at least!*"

Twenty?! The way they came was blocked by Mirage warriors. "Cid, we need a way out!" He rushed back to the room and found it empty. "Cid?" Cid was already gone. A rug had been pulled off the floor and a wooden trapdoor was hanging open.

"Garret! We've got our way out."

"Good," Garret replied. Garret sprinted from his position and dropped through the trapdoor. Ander paused before following. Pounding boots were heading their way. Lots of boots.

Ander threw a canister behind him before dropping after Garret into the tunnel below.

"Run!"

Boom! The earth rocked. Dust and debris fell from the ceiling. More rumbling followed in a continuous round.

Garret broke a flare and held it up to light their way. They sprinted down the passageway as it twisted and turned. Then it ended at a door that was already agape. A rusty iron bar lay on the floor.

They pushed their way out into the cold desert wind. Cid's footsteps were clear in the sand, heading back toward the airship. Nearby, men screamed in the desert tongue. Along with it came the clanking of armor and weapons.

Yep. Time to run. The two sprinted as hard as they could, following Cid, who was already far ahead of them. Sand kicked up behind them as they bolted. Shouts followed them.

"Hope the *Legacy* is ready to go," said Garret between breaths. "I don't think we'll want to stick around."

Ander set off a signal flare. Red light shot up into the sky and broke in a burst.

Garret looked back and cursed. "They've got the sand sailor mobilized!"

"Already?" The sand sailor began pulling away from the mesa and turned in their direction. "Great."

The *Legacy* rose in the distance. Sails began dropping on either side. Without engines, it'd be a moment before the airship picked up speed. The sand sailor, however, did not have that problem. A cloud of dust blew up behind it, and the low rumble it gave shook the sand all the way to Ander and Garret. Mirage warriors hung off the sides of the craft, holding their long spears ready.

Gifted power rippled past Ander, laced with a familiar cold, dark sensation. Chills ran up his body and filled him with unexplainable fear.

Not now! he thought. This was the worst timing to experience any post-traumatic stress. Dread fueled his already leaden legs to push faster, but he could feel his strength diminishing quickly.

The rumbling increased to a roar. Shouts rose in unnaturally high pitches from the Mirage warriors. If Ander didn't know better, he would have thought they sounded like fear rather than battle cries.

He measured the distance between them and the *Legacy* and compared that to the sand sailor.

"We're not going to outrun them," he gasped. "We need to make a stand."

They stopped and turned. Ander reached for his crossbow and hesitated. If he could get the Everblade to work, he could finish this fight quickly. He could give them a chance. He drew the blade and willed it to come to life.

Nothing happened.

The rumbling became deafening, setting his eardrums vibrating. Sand all around bounced and kicked up dust. Behind the sailors, a shower of sand shot high into the air.

He tried the sword again and experienced the same result. He gulped and prepared himself to jump out of the way of the hurtling sand sailor. As the craft drew within twenty feet, the sand exploded underneath it.

Rock and sand exploded outward as rows of long, jagged teeth snapped shut around the sand sailor in a horrible shrieking crunch. The creature continued to rise from the ground, trailing clouds of dust from its body.

Ander stumbled backward and gaped. The creature's snout was long and reptilian, with amber eyes glowing from sunken sockets. Its black-scaled, sand-encrusted body ascended out of the ground, long and circular like a snake. Its body was half as wide as an airship deck. Rows of curved spikes ran down the length of its body. Cold, dark power radiated from it with terrifying intensity.

The creature reached its apex three stories high before arcing down and crashing back into the sand. *WHOOMP!* Dust billowed outward as the sand rippled outward in a wave.

Ander turned to Garret. "WHAT in the world was THAT?"

Garret looked as shocked as he felt. "I think that was a

sadriconda."

"What? I thought sadricondas were a myth."

The ground continued to rumble, and they could see where the sadriconda was moving underground as the earth above it shot up in a long spray. It now took a long turn around.

Dread tingled up Ander's spine. "Um... is that thing coming back?"

"Uh." The two shared a look and took off running toward the approaching airship. Cid stood on top of a large dune and was waving his hands at the approaching airship, which was still a quarter mile away.

Vibrations shook the ground again, and the rumbling grew louder.

"Drop the rope!" Garret screamed, pulling ahead of Ander. "DROP THE ROPE!"

Ander pushed himself as hard as he could, but he felt strength fading. His brief use of the Everblade had sapped more energy than he realized. Still, fear nipped at his heels, and dread built with the growing rumble of the sadriconda.

The Everblade was still in his hand. Could he use it to go faster?

The rumbling grew to a roar. Ropes dropped from the airship ahead. Cid grabbed one and started climbing.

Ander gripped the sword tighter and willed it to come to life. *Come on!* He could use a burst of speed right now. Ahead of him, Garret reached the rope and was now climbing.

Come on! COME ON! The Everblade refused to ignite. He could feel nothing, no connection to it. The rumbling ground grew earsplitting.

At last, the rope drew close. Ander stretched forward still

gripping the Everblade. He lunged and managed to get a fumbling grasp on the rope. "GET US UP!" he screamed. He could feel the spray of sand from the sadriconda approaching from only dozens of feet away. His heart pounded out of his chest.

The airship rose quickly, and he gripped tightly. Then the ground exploded from underneath. Jaws opened wide below him, revealing rows of sharp teeth. He pulled his legs up and closed his eyes.

CLAMP! He felt the force of the jaws snapping shut within inches of his feet. Rock and debris crashed into him, but he held on for his life. Tense seconds passed before the sadriconda crashed back into the ground in a violent eruption.

He let out a long breath. His whole body was shaking with adrenaline. The crew pulled his line until he could climb over the railing.

He sank to the deck and ran a hand over his face. Clutched in his other was still the Everblade. The sword that was his to wield and protect. The sword he had lost but now had recovered.

"Ander!" Charles and Freya approached him now.

"We can't go through that again," said Charles.

"We?" asked Garret sarcastically nearby. "I didn't see *you* out there."

Charles ignored him. "We need to lock up the Everblade so it gets back to the Republic safely."

Was this really happening? Ander thought. *Right now?*

Amelia stepped in between. "Give him a breath. Did you see what just happened?"

Freya folded her arms. "I agree with Charles. It's not safe for him to wear it around like a trophy."

Ander stared at them with his mouth open. He had just recovered the blade! Now they wanted to take it from him again?

Amelia gave him a pitying look. "Ander?"

He couldn't just give it over. The Warden of Tranquility had chosen him to find it. He had proven himself worthy of it. It was *his* to protect.

He looked into all of their faces and let out a sigh. *They were right*, he realized. They couldn't lose the Everblade again. Not after they all sacrificed so much. The sword was bigger than him. It was one of four keys to the Source. He couldn't just wear it on his hip. Besides, did he really want Gifted power? Each time he used it, he risked losing his standing with the Republic. Did he really want that?

Everyone stared at him. His muscles fought against him as he lifted it up and held it out. Amelia had to pry it from his fingers to get it from his grasp. She turned around. Charles reached out for it, but she sidestepped away.

"We can store it in the captain's lockbox," she said. "It's the most secure place on the airship."

Ander watched her leave and felt a part of him leave with her. Why did he feel such a strong connection to the blade? Why did he *want* to use it when it only threatened his standing with the Republic? And *why* did it work for him inside the Mirage hideout and not outside? He wasn't Gifted, was he?

These were all questions he didn't have answers for. Questions that would burn in his mind for weeks.

Chapter 7: Hidden Pasts

Amelia

The desert passed by in a blur. A couple of weeks had passed since their encounter with the Mirage. Since then, the *Legacy* had been flying at a comfortable elevation of 4,000 feet, relying on the stronger air currents to drive them toward the city of Sadria.

The winds grew colder as the light disappeared over the horizon. Amelia finished her evening meal and was on her way to her quarters when she saw a silhouetted figure standing at the bow of the airship.

Ander. He was leaned over the railing with bunched shoulders— the way he usually looked when he had something on his mind. His brown hair had grown longer in the last months and now blew with the wind. The look contrasted with his close-cropped appearance from before.

He's changed from when we first met, she thought, though she couldn't quite pinpoint how. He was still the same stiff soldier as before—only now he needed a haircut. She gave a wry smile, realizing that wasn't quite true. She had seen that stiff exterior dissolve. Underneath, he was kind and caring. Odder still was that, somehow, they had become close friends, despite how much he infuriated her only months ago.

She found herself automatically walking over to him. As she neared, he looked up and tucked his hands underneath his arms.

"You know," she said, "you don't need to assign yourself night watch to compensate for Bragg being gone." She raised an eyebrow and took a spot next to him.

He smiled, but his eyes were loosely focused on her. She waved a hand in front of him and said, "Hey? You there?"

He blinked. "Sorry. You caught me lost in thought."

"Clearly." She bumped his shoulder with her own and he smiled in return.

They looked back out across the dark landscape, which looked dark blue under the crescent moon above. Silence grew between them, but it was strangely comfortable despite the chilly wind. Far below, a flock of desert sprinters raced over dunes while two sadricondas chased after them.

After a moment, she said, "What's on your mind?"

He sighed and glanced backward. She followed his gaze to the few sailors in the background. He withdrew a rod-like device from underneath his arm—an electrodetectualizer, a meter designed to detect if someone had Gifted power.

"Look at this." He put both of his hands on the meter and showed her the gauge reading. The needle stayed at zero. *Magicless.*

She tilted her head. "How is that possible? I've seen you use magic. The meter should pick that up."

"I know." He gave a heavy sigh.

"I've never heard of an electrodetectualizer giving a false negative. Unless it's broken?" She took the meter from him and turned the device over in her hands. Aside from some scuff marks, it appeared intact. "I'm not seeing anything wrong."

"I've never registered on one of these before."

"If that's the case, how could you have used the sword back at the vault?" She looked into his eyes and saw the same confusion as her own.

"The only thing I can think of is at the vault. The Nardoowe guide Kadesh put a hand on my shoulder and I felt a spark of power. After that, I could connect to the sword. At least, temporarily."

She frowned. "Kadesh had power?"

Ander nodded.

She tapped a finger on her lips. "I thought he said he didn't like people who were Gifted?"

Ander shrugged.

"The spark of power thing doesn't make sense either. You can't give someone Gifted power. That's not possible. Otherwise, more people would manifest power."

He gave a heavy sigh and ran a hand through his hair. She noticed the movement and recognized it as a trademark quirk of his anytime he was stressed.

"Yeah... I guess that makes sense." He didn't sound convinced. "Well, I suppose I should be grateful it's reading zero. But...." He opened his mouth to say more and hesitated.

She raised an eyebrow. "What?"

He glanced over his shoulder again. Then, in a whisper, he said, "When I was at the Mirage outpost, for a moment, I could connect to the sword again. I honestly don't know how."

She frowned. "Explain."

He shared the whole adventure with her, omitting nothing. He finished by saying, "I don't know who I am anymore, Millie." His expression was intense. "The Everblade says I'm Gifted. This device says I'm not. How can they both be right and wrong?"

She fumbled for the right words to say, and all she could come up with was, "I don't know."

He gripped the railing harder and took a deep breath. "All my life, I've wanted to be a soldier. To protect others. To fight for the freedom of the Republic. Now... I might be the very thing that I've been protecting the Republic from."

"I don't believe that for a second." She held his worried gaze. Her mind flashed back to everything they had been through together. She had seen those eyes be determined like steel and soft like clouds, with smile lines around the edges....

Heat rose to her cheeks as she realized she was staring. She looked away and cleared her throat. "You know, there are a couple tests we can run that might help us understand why you can use the blade, even though you are registering zero power."

"Yeah?" He raised his eyebrows.

She nodded. "Follow me." She led him away from the bow and down the hatch. They passed the lower deck and engine deck before stepping down into the hold. Then she led him to the stern and opened a hidden locker with a key. Inside was the Everblade.

"You ready?"

He took a deep breath and nodded.

"Alright." She took out the Everblade and connected it to the electrodetectualizer. The meter lit up with power.

"Ah!" She pointed to the meter. "You see that. You don't register as having power, but the sword does."

"So, what does that mean?" he asked.

"We're not done yet." She handed him the Everblade in one hand and the meter in the other. The meter remained at zero.

"Huh," she tapped a finger against her lips. "I thought we'd register something. I guess it's not like an electrical current. Do you usually do something to turn the blade on?"

He raised a quizzical eyebrow at her. "You realize this is just a sword, right? There's no switch to turn it on and off."

"Right, but we can both agree that you've essentially turned it on and off. So, how do you do *that*?"

"The first time was with Kadesh–"

"But not the second time," she finished. "What did you do that time?"

"I–" he looked down at the blade. "I told it to light."

"Then do that. Try it now."

He stared at the sword awkwardly. "I command you to light!"

Nothing happened.

"Hmm."

"This is how it normally is," he explained. "I've tried a hundred times. It doesn't respond."

She frowned. "Maybe it only works when you are in danger?"

He shook his head. "I tried to make it work after the vault when the Huntress attacked. It didn't work then. I also tried when the sadriconda attacked. Both times I was in danger."

She scratched her head. "Yeah, I'm stumped." She took the Everblade and locked it back up in the panel.

He sat down on a barrel and sighed. "I don't know. I can't help but wonder if it has something to do with my blood status. I mean, I can sense Gifted power."

"You're adopted, right?" She took a seat on the barrel next to him. "Do you know who your birth parents were?"

He shook his head. "There's no way I could figure that out unless I could remember back when I was a little boy."

If he could remember... An idea shot through her mind like lightning. "Wait. What if you *could* remember back then?"

He looked at her like she was crazy.

"Go with me on this. That Sadrian healer had an elixir that could restore memory. A memory restorative. You know the one Eugene insulted her about?"

He straightened. "If we could find another healer in Sadria, that could work." Light filled his eyes. "Millie, that's brilliant!"

She beamed and shrugged modestly. "Well, you know. I have my moments."

"Do you think it would work?"

"No idea. I'm not convinced the lady wasn't 95% insane, and she did say that the memory had to be—"

"One you could partially recall," he finished for her. The light in his eyes dimmed and his expression turned hesitant.

She furrowed her brows. "What's wrong?"

"I only have one memory of my parents. That was the day they died."

"Oh...." Her expression fell.

He rubbed his fingers down his face. "I don't know. I'm not sure I'd want to remember the day my parents died? Would you?"

The question caught her off guard, and guilt surged through her with an unexpected heat. Memories of flames, falling timbers, and screams appeared before her. She was fourteen again, wearing a white dress smudged with ash, staring at her father's factory in flames. Ash dropped from the sky like dark snowfall. Hot tears streamed down her face as she screamed for help. Inside her was a maelstrom of shock, fear, disbelief, and guilt. She didn't intend for this to happen. It wasn't her fault. But... it was.

She shoved the memory far to the back of her mind. *No,* she didn't need an elixir to remember. She'd never be able to forget that night, no matter how hard she tried.

Ander stared at her. His eyes were full of concern. "I'm sorry," he said. "I didn't mean to–"

"It's fine." She waved a hand as if to brush it off. But she could never brush off her past. Her mistakes were blackened spots on a white dress, never to come out.

Ander's expression softened. "I heard about the factory fire. I was overseas in Brinkerhoff, taking part in a training drill for the academy. It sounded horrible."

She swallowed and nodded.

"Were you at home when you found out?" he asked.

She stared at him. *He didn't know?! Was this a joke?*

No. He wasn't the kind of person to joke like this. He *really* had no idea about her role in that fire. Which made a horrible kind of sense. He was her first close friend in years and had shown her so much kindness. She was even an honorary member of his squad and had a nickname. How could that have happened if he knew she was responsible for one of the Republic's most tragic events?

Her heart pounded as a horrible thought rose in her mind. What would happen if he found out? Would he reject her, too? Like everyone else?

No, he can't find out.

She stood up and clasped her trembling hands together. Words fell from her lips in a rush. "I need to go. We're going to reach Sadria soon, and I need to give the navigator directions on where to land."

"Okay," he said. His face fell, and so did her heart.

She gave him a tight smile and left before he could say more. Her feet couldn't have moved faster up the stairs. Inside, her stomach was twisting into knots, and her head felt like she had spun too many times in a circle. She pushed through the hatch into the cold desert wind.

"Hey Millie?" A gentle hand caught her arm. She stopped and turned to face Ander. His expression was soft and the intensity of his gaze rooted her to the spot.

"Thanks for talking to me," he said. "I don't know what I'd do without you."

The words washed over her like warm sunshine, overpowering the chilly wind gusting past her. How long had it been since she'd heard words like those? How long had it been since she felt like she belonged and mattered?

"Same here," she said quietly, surprised at the depth she felt while saying it.

He let her go and returned to his watch at the bow of the airship. She lingered by the hatch, watching him go. Thousands of thoughts and feelings swirled inside her. The fire took everything from her. And now, for the first time since, she felt happy.

The warmth began to dissipate as the chilly wind took over. She wrapped her arms around herself and let out a puff of steam.

She didn't want this to change. If he found out the truth, she was afraid of what would happen. Would he reject her? If he did, she was sure it would break her.

No, she thought. She wouldn't let her past take this away from her, too. Ander could never find out the truth. She'd make sure of it.

Chapter 8: Serenity Pools

Amelia

A melia rose in the morning and opened the curtains to her cabin windows. The airship was grounded, offering her a panoramic view of the sprawling landscape. Orange light reflected off yellowed scrub grasses and cracked earth. The dunes from the night before were gone, now that they were near the coastal city of Sadria.

She made her way to her vanity and paused before it. The dresser was broken and scored with long claw marks. A mirror was anchored on top of it; although the glass was missing except for two jagged shards. It was once a beautiful piece of furniture, but their encounter with the Nardoowe beast had ruined it. Since then, she hadn't had time to fix it.

She washed her face using a bent tin basin of water. Then she dried off and looked into the mirror. Her reflection was jagged and broken.

Pain lanced through her heart at the sight. Her life felt broken, held together only by sheer determination. Anytime it seemed to get better, the fire always came back to haunt her. She could never escape it.

She wished she could turn back the clock and change what had happened. That was impossible, of course. Unlike Ander, there was no restorative that could bring back what she lost. She would always carry her past with her. Her only hope was to redeem herself and her family name.

She pulled her hair back into her usual bun and cinched her tool belt around her hips. Then she took a deep breath and exited her cabin.

Humid, salty air filled her lungs as she took in her surroundings. Ahead of her, Veronica and the night crew were tying up the last of the sails. To her left was a cracked plain of scrub grasses, and to her right was a large mesa that blocked all view of the east.

"Oi, mornin' Cap!" said Veronica.

"Morning, Veronica," she replied. "How did the night go?"

"Found a hidin' place for the airship, I did. Several miles from Sadria City n' nowhere near major roads. Winds were frustratin' but we managed to settle 'im down jus' fine."

Amelia nodded her approval. The extra distance to the city would make travel to Sadria a hassle, but it was better than being out in the open. Last time she checked, relations between Sadria and the Republic were strained, to say the least.

A Steam soldier climbed over the port side railing, and for a second, she thought it was Ander until she saw Garret's gray-streaked hair.

"Morning, Millie," he greeted. "Just finished organizing the sentries. No one will be approaching without our knowing."

"Oh, good," she replied. She looked over his shoulder, looking to see if Ander was there.

"He went down to rest a few hours ago," he replied, answering her unspoken question.

"Oh, right. Night shift. Makes sense." She cleared her throat. "Could you ask Charles to telegraph that contact Secretary Drake gave us? I'd love to start searching for the Wayfinder as soon as possible."

"Will do. I'll ask him to send a telegraph every hour. Hopefully, we get a response soon."

"Excellent."

"One more thing," he glanced at Veronica. "No offense, but we're going to stand out like a signal beacon as soon as the sun crosses over to the west. Every brass and metal part of this airship will reflect light for miles."

Veronica folded her arms, but said nothing.

"Hmm." Amelia surveyed the west. "You're right. That's going to be a problem."

"We could stake n' stretch out canvas if we 'ad enough," said Veronica.

"True," said Amelia. "Alright, we'll add canvas to our list of needs when we make our trip into Sadria. Until then, let's use what we've got."

The crew got to work staking canvas sheets into the cracked earth and stretching it up to the canvas envelope above. As the sun continued to rise, more sailors joined to shovel mounds of dirt and help obscure the lower half of the hull. Everard appeared a few hours into the work and gave Amelia a long list of items that needed repaired and replaced. The sand had done a number on the systems, so it was his goal to service every major system on the engine deck.

She reviewed the list and sighed. Materials like engine parts and coal would need to be shipped to them from the Republic somehow. Maybe Secretary Drake could pull some strings. Otherwise, the *Legacy* wouldn't be traveling anywhere quickly. That would be problematic when the *Firelancer* reappeared.

She sought Charles and handed him Everard's list. "Are we in range to the nearest Republic telegraph relay station? We need to send in a supplies request to Secretary Drake."

"I'll check." He took the list and began composing a reply with quill and parchment.

Amelia turned to leave right as the telegraph began clicking. She paused and waited for the entire message to pass through. Then they quickly translated it.

MEET CONTACT AT 14:00 TODAY. LOCATION: SADRIA, SOUTHWESTERN MARKET, SERENITY POOLS.

"This is only a few hours away!" Amelia gasped, grasping the parchment. "We have to leave now to make it!"

. . . .

Amelia, Ander, and Blaze trekked south through dusty scrub grass, cutting a path to the nearest highway to Sadria. The sun burned high overhead, and the humidity was suffocating. Thankfully, their light-colored Sadrian disguises blocked the worst of the sun's rays.

Amelia was dressed in her yellow headscarf and Sadrian dress again, though this time she adjusted her yellow headscarf so it covered all of her face except for her eyes. A leather satchel hung over her side. She had disguised Ander and Blaze as well, though it had taken convincing to keep them from wearing their Steam armor. That hadn't, however, stopped them both from strapping knives and canisters underneath their clothing. They were hidden, at least, which was what Amelia cared about most. Their best protection, she explained, was to blend in.

They reached a dusty highway and turned southeast. The road twisted and turned until it came to a rise. As they crested the rise, their view of the region expanded. To the south gleamed the Azure River, the only major river in all of Sadria. Plantations grew all along its edge, featuring dusty rows of barley, red spice fields, and date palm orchards. Raggedly dressed slaves worked the plantations while taskmasters watched over them.

Directly to the east rose the sandstone walls of Sadria City. The walls were three stories high and were scored from generations of conflict. Square towers grew out of the fortifications, and together they continued in an unbroken line as far as they could see. Beyond the walls and to the north rose the golden domes of the sultan's palace, which were surrounded by an even taller set of walls than the outer walls.

The trio continued down the highway toward an arched gate. As the walls grew closer, so did the number of people on the highway until it became a procession. Many carried wicker baskets on their shoulders while others pulled carts laden with simple goods.

Guards materialized on top of the walls and more stood by the gate entrance. They wore iron helmets with wide brims. Cloth draped down from the sides of their helmets and obscured the lower half of their faces. Across their chests was banded iron armor, and at their hips sat wide, curved sabers. Each of them scanned the crowd with wary eyes.

"Keep your head low," she whispered to the others. They complied as they passed beneath the gates. She could feel the gazes of the guards pass over her, like hawks searching for prey. The feeling sent a chill down her spine, despite the intensifying heat of the morning sun.

After the gates, two guardhouses rose on either side of the sandy road. Yellowed wanted posters rustled along the sides of the buildings, the most prominent featuring a scarred, fierce looking man named *Abdulmalik, the Insurrector*. Fresh posters had been added to the bunch, and these in particular caught her eye.

Wanted: The Desert Steam Soldier. The headline stretched across the top of seven or eight posters. A cloaked figure in Steam armor accompanied the words, sometimes with more similarly cloaked figures behind. None of the posters had a face, and each listed a different series of crimes ranging from mass theft, destruction of property, and sabotage. The sum at the bottom of the posters was enough to make her eyes pop.

Who was the Desert Steam Soldier? Whoever it was, she doubted their actions were sanctioned by the Republic.

The next poster made her heart turn to ice. *Reward: Capture of Anyone from the Republic of Steam.* She pulled her scarf tighter around her face and quickened her pace.

Just beyond the guard houses was an open space before the city proper began. Bordering the sides of the road were javelins embedded into the ground, each topped with skulls in various states of decay. Some wore Steam soldier helmets. A sign read, *Here's what happens to those who defy the might of Sadria.* Amelia grimaced. She'd never seen anything so barbaric before.

This could be us if we aren't careful.

"Phillip?" whispered Blaze. "No, definitely a Bartholomew. Greggory, keep hanging in there. Jessica, sorry it never worked out between us. Elfonzo, keep your head held high. Sadie, sorry my looks knocked you dead."

Both Amelia and Ander looked sidelong at Blaze.

"Are you sure it was a good idea to bring him?" Amelia whispered through clenched teeth.

"I've been having second thoughts since we left the airship," said Ander, trying not to laugh.

She gave him a stern look. "This is serious. He's going to draw attention."

"Blaze, shut up!" hissed Ander. "That's an order."

Blaze looked like he was about to reply when Amelia gave him her classic glare. His mouth shut tight, and he turned his gaze forward.

As they stepped into the city proper, tall adobe buildings rose on either side of the sandy street. With it came a tumult of noise. Vendors shouted over each other from either side, showing off wares from cracked barley, dates, spices, clay pots, homespun cloth, and more. Many were using magic to draw a crowd, whether by dispersing the scent of their wares, levitating products in the wind, or even making their goods appear more radiant in the sunlight. Others had slaves manning their booths while they sat off to the sides, barking orders.

Amelia took a deep breath and composed herself. *My name is Auria,* she thought, rehearsing the role she prepared earlier. *I'm from a small village along the edge of the Azure River. I'm no one special, no one to notice.* Her shoulders relaxed, and she felt herself blend with the shuffle of the crowd.

She checked her companions and groaned inwardly. Ander's eyes darted left and right, scanning every person they passed. He had the look of someone trying to avoid trouble, the exact look that would alert the guard. Blaze, on the other hand, stared at the wares they passed with gleeful eyes. It looked like his whole body itched to break off and explore.

She pinched the bridge of her nose. *This* is why she preferred to work alone. But that was a foreign concept to these soldiers. For them, no one ever worked without backup.

She was so lost in her thoughts that she didn't see a vendor thrust something toward her.

In a flash, Ander stepped in front of Amelia, snagged the vendor's wrist, and twisted it around. The woman yelped and opened her palm. Inside was a seashell necklace.

Amelia groaned. This was *exactly* the kind of scene she was trying to avoid. She stepped around Ander before he could make things worse.

"I'm so sorry," she said in Sadrian, while giving Ander a glare that could have melted steel. "My companions are jumpy after the road." She gave the woman a tight smile and pointed to the necklace. "This is beautiful."

"Thought the shells would complement your complexion," said the woman apologetically. "Are you from overseas?"

She opened her eyes wide. Was it that obvious? She knew her skin tone was lighter than the locals, but she hoped that the months she'd spent piloting an airship in the sun would have compensated for that difference. And she'd hidden her auburn hair, which would stand out amongst the dark hair color of the locals. Her disguise should have been enough to get by. Apparently, she had been wrong.

"Married into a trader's family, thank you," she said quickly.

"Where's your accent from?" the woman asked.

Accent? Apparently, that was obvious, too. "Shaoguan." She patted the woman's hand and left before the woman could ask more.

Well, this complicates things, she thought as they pressed on down the busy road. She needed to be careful whom she interacted with. But she could figure that out in a moment. First, she had unfinished business to attend to.

As soon as they turned around a corner, she pulled both Steam soldiers into an empty alley.

"What were you thinking?" she hissed at Ander. "You're lucky there weren't any guards who could have seen you!"

"It looked like she was about to stab you," Ander replied without making eye contact. His gaze was focused away on the crowd outside the alley.

Is he taking this seriously? She grabbed his collar and yanked him so they were eye to eye. "Stabbed? It was only a necklace! I'm more worried about the fact that you keep staring down every person like they could be a threat. You're going to give us away and bring down the entire guard."

"Yeah, Ander," said Blaze mockingly. "Why do you have to be such a scrap head?"

"Don't get me started on you," Amelia snapped. Blaze took a few steps back. She directed her attention back to Ander. "You need to stop acting like a soldier. You are a common citizen from one of the Azure River villages. You've been here a *thousand* times, so much so that you don't even notice the crowd or the sand in your boots anymore. You got that?"

She was almost nose to nose with Ander, and he shifted uncomfortably from the proximity. Despite that, his jaw was set in place and there was a stubbornness in his expression.

"I'm *not* going to let you get hurt," he said. "I can handle the guards if I have to."

Handle the guards? He wouldn't have to handle the guards if he just blended in!

She opened her mouth and felt the words slip out of her mind. Something about the intensity of his gaze set her heart beating faster. She tried again to recall what she was going to say, but it was gone.

Blaze coughed. "You know Millie, I could use a talking-to myself." He wiggled his eyebrow.

Her cheeks flushed, and she pushed Ander away. "Just follow my lead," she said with exasperation, "and keep your head down." She marched out of the alley, not bothering to see if they followed.

It took her a few minutes to compose herself enough to ask a shopkeeper for directions to the Serenity Pools. They followed the directions, turning down multiple streets before reaching a large square.

Inns and shops bordered the edges of the square. In the center, light glowed off shallow stone pools of water where children splashed and shouted with wild glee, and adults stopped at their edges to wash the dust from their feet.

Yep, this is the place, she thought. Their contact hadn't left them with any instructions about how they'd meet, only the location and time. They were a little early, based on the height of the sun, which was just fine with her. She had a list of supplies to purchase.

She traveled from shop to shop with the two soldiers in tow. Both remained silent the whole time. The feat was especially impressive for Blaze, though his usually mischievous grin was replaced with a sour scowl. Something seemed to be bothering him, especially by the way he kept glancing between her and Ander. She didn't care enough to ask what.

Again, the shop owners seemed to pick up that they were foreigners. Some eyed them closely, while others seemed uncomfortable. One even doubled their price right there in the moment. Each encounter added another layer of worry inside Amelia. How long would it be before someone linked them back to the Republic?

After an hour of shopping, they had a couple bushels of barley and a sack of sand sailor canvas. The food wouldn't last long given the size of their crew, but it was the best she could manage without arousing suspicion. She handed it all to Blaze and asked him to haul it back to the airship. He looked at them both suspiciously and left without making a wisecrack.

"You think he'll make it back safely?" Amelia asked, while watching him go.

"He can be reliable."

She raised an eyebrow.

"When it's important."

She raised her eyebrow higher.

"Most of the time," he added.

She smiled. That was certainly true.

"What I want to know," he said, "is how you got him to be silent for so long. That was great!"

They both laughed.

"Yeah, he certainly was quiet," she said. She checked the position of the sun. "Well, let's find some shade until our friend finds us."

They found an awning next to a restaurant called the Scorched Scorpion. A cool breeze blew from a window of the restaurant, bringing with it the smell of cooked fish and foreign spices.

Her stomach grumbled. "That smells good. I wonder how they get the temperature so comfortable."

"Gifted magic."

His answer was so confident that she cocked her head. "How do you know?"

He gave a tight smile. "I can feel the ripples of power. Same as over there." He pointed to the middle of the square where a woman gesticulated with her fingers by a well. Water shot up and landed in the pools, which sent the kids roaring in delight.

"You can sense all of that?"

He nodded.

"Wow." She leaned back into the building and watched the woman pull water out of the well again. The fact he could sense the power so clearly was incredible and strange. She'd never heard of any Commonborn having the ability. In fact, she hadn't heard of Gifted having it either.

He leaned next to her. His arm brushed hers in the process and sent unexpected tingles through her whole body. She shifted to make room, consciously aware of how warm she felt with him right there. The feeling was strange and yet comfortable at the same time.

Comfortable, she thought. That was a good way to describe how she felt around Ander. While the rest of the world seemed intent on pushing her out, Ander made her feel like she belonged.

It's all a lie, a voice said inside her. *He doesn't know the truth about you. What will happen if he finds out what you've been hiding?*

The warmth faded as quickly as it came, leaving a void in its wake. *Was this really all a lie? Would everything change if he found out?*

She glanced at him, wondering the answer. He was focused on the crowd again, looking back and forth for threats. He caught her gaze and grinned. "I'm trying to be subtle about it."

She nodded appreciatively while her mind continued to spin. Was it wrong to hide her past, to not want this to end? It wasn't like he needed to know everything about her to be a friend.

He stiffened and pushed off the wall. The movement happened so quickly, she jumped in surprise.

"We need to go," he said brusquely. He grabbed her hand and pulled her deeper into the square.

"What's wrong?" Did something show in her expression? Did he know she was hiding something?

Ander shoved their way through the crowd.

"Ander!" she gasped, worried they'd draw attention. "What are you doing?"

A horn blared from the main entrance behind them, followed by rippling gasps through the crowd. Sadrian guards poured into the square with curved blades drawn. A beat later, sand rose into a wall, cutting off the entire front entrance.

Fear wrapped around her insides like a snake coiling around its prey. Were they here for them? She tried to keep her expression calm, but she knew she was losing that battle. This was a nightmare!

She looked around and realized the square had no alleyways.

They were trapped.

Chapter 9: Mirabetal

Ander

A nder pushed his way through the now frenzied crowd, pulling Amelia with him. Teams of guards shoved through the crowd, ripping off head coverings left and right. Others moved from business to business, ordering the people to exit to the main square.

"Where are we going?" Amelia hissed. "They've got the entrance blocked!"

"Through that building." Ander pointed to a large inn labeled the Sleepy Sands. "I haven't noticed any supplies going through the front, which means they have backdoors."

They reached the front steps of the Sleepy Sands when the doors slammed open. Occupants spilled out, forcing them to step out of the way. Shouts echoed from within the building—more guards from the sounds of it.

How had they gotten there so quickly?

Amelia squeezed his hand and pointed up. "They're on the roofs too!"

Ander cursed. Whoever planned this Sadrian operation had thought of everything. He swallowed. "We need to break through before they close this noose."

Her eyes grew wide. "What about the guards inside?"

His expression was grim. "Ready?"

She took a deep breath. "Ready."

A hand grabbed Ander's shoulder. He reacted instantly, wrenching the person's arm and slamming them against the wall of the inn. The figure was a bald, older Sadrian with a potbelly.

"Legacy, legacy!" said the man. "Don't go in there or death will be your legacy."

"He's the contact," Amelia said.

Ander let the man go.

"Go with the crowd," said the man quickly. "You're not who they're after."

"Go back?!" Ander grabbed Amelia's hand again and pulled her toward the door.

She yanked her hand out of his grasp. "Ander, I think we should listen to him!"

He growled. The stream of people from the inn was lessening, which meant the guards would be out soon. They needed to leave now.

The contact was gone, having disappeared with the crowd. Of course, he had nothing to fear. He was Sadrian.

Amelia grabbed his arm and looked into his eyes. "You promised after the library that you'd listen to me."

He gritted his teeth. "Fine. Lead the way."

She took his hand and pulled him back into the crowd. He followed, despite the fact that every one of his instincts screamed for them to run. Soon they were buried in the midst of the crowd.

Horns blew again, and the crowd grew silent. "On your knees!" bellowed a grating, commanding voice.

A *familiar* voice.

Ander cursed. He knew that voice from a mission that seemed like an eternity ago: Khaldun Abdi. No wonder these guards were so well organized. Amelia had to yank his arm before he went down to his knees and set his head on the sandy ground like the others.

Ander peeked up from his submissive position. Khaldun sat astride a battle horse. He wore the same armor and uniform as the rest of the guard, but he carried himself with a distinct air of command. He was tall, lean, and middle-aged.

Whispers rippled through the crowd.

"Silence," shouted Khaldun. "I am looking for Anwar Degamb, a fugitive from the law and a member of that pathetic group, the Mirage. He was seen at the Sleepy Sands collaborating with a foreigner. Someone from the Republic of Steam." He spoke the words in the common tongue with clipped precision.

Murmurs rippled amongst the crowd, along with a palpable sense of fear. Ander pulled his hood lower over his face.

"I said silence!"

A door slammed from the inn behind them. Boots stomped out, but Ander didn't dare look back. Guards materialized in his line of sight, holding a struggling man. The man's lighter complexion was clear, even from where Ander kneeled. The guards escorted him to Khaldun.

"Hasaan Shahan, is it?" asked Khaldun. "Or would you rather go

CRAIG & JALEESA SNOW

by Edward Hart?"

"You've got the wrong man," the captive gasped. "I'm just a simple laborer—" The captive's speech was cut short as guards punched him in the gut.

"Do you know who I am?" asked the rider. He leaned over his saddle. "My name is Khaldun Abdi, the Sadhdron. I am the high commander, the keeper of the peace, the balancer of the scales of justice."

The crowd was deathly silent. No murmurings followed this declaration. Ander knew firsthand how dangerous Khaldun was. The last time he saw Khaldun, the Sadhdron had trapped Ander's team on top of a lighthouse and set it on fire. He had no doubt Khaldun was the most dangerous man in all of Sadria and would apply any means necessary to execute the law.

"Where is Anwar Degamb?" commanded the Sadhdron. Edward stayed silent. Khaldun growled and addressed the crowd. "Where is Anwar Degamb?"

The crowd remained silent.

The Sadhdron growled and gestured to his guards. A detachment broke away and crashed their way back into the Sleepy Sands.

Khaldun turned back to Edward. "For your crime coming here from the Republic, thirty lashes and a life sentence in prison, as stated by the law."

The guards ripped Edward's robe down the back. They stretched his arms out and held him there as a muscled guard approached with a whip.

"For your crime as an agent, mirabetal. You will be tortured until you reveal *your* secrets."

Crack! Edward howled and the crowd gasped. Ander cringed and clenched his fingers. He wished he could do something to save the man. He couldn't, of course. There were too many guards, not to mention Khaldun, who probably had a vendetta toward him after the bombing.

"For killing one of my warriors, Nadir Taha," Khaldun continued. *Crack!* "Mirabetal. A life for a life. After five years of imprisonment, you will be sentenced to die. That is all."

The whipping continued while Khaldun waited. A few minutes later, guards reported back from the Sleepy Sands. Their exchange was quiet and ended with Khaldun growling with anger.

"Search the people!" Khaldun roared. Guards roved the crowd, ripping off hoods and headscarves alike. Sweat ran down Ander's neck. He and Amelia were near the back of the crowd, which gave them only a little time before the guards reached them. When the guards did, he knew they'd be identified as foreigners—especially Amelia. Her auburn hair would stand out like a beacon in this crowd.

They couldn't get caught. Too much was riding on them finding the Wayfinder. At the same time, attempting an escape wasn't a great alternative either. Guards loosely ringed the perimeter of the crowd and archers also stood at the ready on the rooftops. If they ran, they'd have to get past the guards without being shot.

He cursed. They should have made a break for it when they had a chance. Now the job was a thousand times harder.

He bumped Amelia's arm and whispered with the barest of noise. "Get ready to make a break for it."

"Don't!" she breathed.

His shoulders tightened. They were running out of time. "Millie, if they see your hair—"

"They're looking for a man," she said quickly. "Besides, I can fake an Enchantran accent if I have to."

She sounded confident, but he could still detect a slight quiver in her voice.

He opened his mouth to say *Khaldun knows me*, but the guards were now too close. He let out a slow, tight breath and moved his hands closer to his weapons. He prayed it wouldn't come to that. Maybe if he kept his head low enough, he could get by too.

A guard stepped next to Amelia and reached down. Before his fingers could grasp her headscarf, Edward screamed.

"Anwar Degamb is gone! He slipped out the back!"

Ander's heart pounded out of his chest as the guard held his position, hand hovering just over Amelia's head.

"Where did he go?" asked the Sadhdron.

"I–I don't know!"

"LIAR. Increase his lashes!"

"He went south! He didn't tell me the destination."

"Sargeant!"

The guard next to Amelia straightened up and put a fist to his chest. "Yes, High Commander?"

"Send a platoon south. If we don't find Degamb, increase the lashes!"

"Yes, sir!" The guard waved to several others and hustled away. Ander let out a pent-up breath as relief poured over him.

That was close, he thought. *Too close.*

Khaldun clenched his fists and then relaxed his grip slowly. "The scales of justice must be balanced. That is why I will invoke ulesibli mirabetal."

Gasps broke through the crowd and immediately people scooted away from the Sadhdron.

"One of you will take Degamb's place. If the criminal is not found within thirty-days, this person will suffer the price of his crimes in his place."

All sense of relief fled Ander in a rush as his mind turned to the worst possible scenario.

Not Millie. Don't take Millie.

Khaldun trotted his horse deeper into the crowd. People parted before him as if repulsed by a magnetic force.

"Which of you will it be?" Khaldun asked.

Not Millie!

The Sadhdron reached the middle of the crowd and stopped. "How about the young woman with the yellow headscarf." He pointed a finger toward Amelia.

Ander's heart stopped.

"Take her."

Ander's mind processed Khaldun's words as if in slow motion. *They were taking Millie!* Cold sweat broke out across his whole body. He couldn't let them take her. Every fiber of his being knew that wasn't an option.

He grabbed her hand and tried to yank her up. "Millie," he breathed frantically. "We need to run!"

She remained frozen to the spot with her mouth agape. Guards appeared and ripped her from the ground. As her hand slipped from his grasp, something broke inside him.

"Not happening!" he said as protective determination poured through him like molten steel. He stood and punched the nearest guard straight in the chin. As that guard crashed backward, Ander pivoted, grabbed a second guard's arm, and threw him over his

123

shoulder. Both guards crashed to the ground within a second of each other.

The quick movements threw Ander's hood back.

Khaldun's eyes popped. "YOU!"

Ander dropped a smoke canister, grabbed Amelia's hand, and ran.

BOOSH! Smoke exploded and sent the crowd screaming in panic. Chaos broke forth as people scrambled to their feet and ran over each other in their haste to get away. Khaldun's shouts for order were barely audible over the mass panic.

Ander and Amelia broke through the perimeter of the crowd and slammed through the doors of a restaurant. Arrows whistled through the open door and shattered the surrounding windows, slamming into the vacant tables and chairs of the dining room.

They kept their heads low as they dodged around fallen chairs, past a stairwell, toward a door next to the serving bar. Ander rammed into the door and broke it off its hinges.

His momentum shot them through the kitchen. Four guards stood on the other side, blocking the exit to the street outside.

"Ander!" Amelia warned. They backpedaled into the dining room right as more guards crashed through the front doors and windows.

"This is why I hate your plans," she muttered. She took point, pulling him up the stairs. Guards rushed after them like a swarm of angry bees.

"My plan was to leave earlier!" He ripped a canister pin with his teeth and dropped the rest behind him. "Staying was *your* idea!"

"Which almost avoided THIS exact scene!"

BOOM! The stairwell exploded behind them, sending them

tumbling forward into a hallway. Guards screamed behind them, but Ander and Amelia didn't waste any time looking back. They picked themselves up and sprinted down the hallway toward a shuttered window.

Amelia slowed down as they neared the window, fiddling inside her satchel.

"What are you doing?!" Ander asked, throwing the shutters open to the busy street below.

"Give me a second!" she replied.

CRASH! A hulking guard rose from a crouch at the top of the shattered stairway. Power radiated from the man as he cracked his neck and drew a saber.

"Gifted!" Ander grabbed Amelia's elbow and pulled her to the window, but she resisted.

"Just one more second!"

Stress seeped through every muscle in Ander's body. "We're out of time!"

The hulking guard grinned and charged. He held the saber against the sandstone wall as he ran, leaving a trail of sparks behind him.

"Got it!" She threw her whole satchel at the guard, grabbed Ander's hand, and jumped. They tumbled out of the window and hit the sandy street hard. Stabbing pains lanced through Ander's legs while Amelia yelped and crumpled.

"HALT!" shouted one of the guards posted at the back door of the building. Whatever else the guard had to say was drown out by an earsplitting blast.

Ander dropped protectively over Amelia as the top level of the building exploded. Sandstone debris crashed down around them as dust billowed outward.

MOVE! His mind screamed at him. Once the dust cleared, the guards would be on them in seconds.

He pulled Amelia up and felt her stagger into him.

"My ankle!" she gasped.

Worry burned through Ander's chest, but there wasn't time to ask questions. He threw an arm around her waist and supported her as they ran.

They emerged from the dust into a panicked crowd. Hysteria reigned as people scrambled to get away from the rising cloud of dust. People jostled them left and right, but Ander held on tight to Amelia.

They raced around a corner and continued down the block. The crowd slowed down, staring and pointing at the plume of dust that rose in the sky.

"Did we lose them?" Amelia gasped between breaths.

Ander glanced behind. "No guards so far. What in the world was in your bag?"

She gave him a wry smile before wincing. "That was *my* backup plan in case we needed to make a classic Ander escape."

He rolled his eyes and caught movement racing into the crowd. He cursed. "We've got pursuit. Four guards and all of them Gifted."

"Keep your head down and your pace slow," said Amelia quickly. "They'll be looking for people escaping. Only the guilty run."

Ander did as she asked, pulling the hood of his cloak lower and moving them to the side of the street.

"OUT OF THE WAY!" shouted the guards. One of them threw their hands up and pushed outward. Waves of sand grew from the street and parted the crowd. The guards raced through the cleared path, scanning the crowd as they ran.

Ander held his breath until the guards passed by. Then he let it out slowly.

"There!" shouted an unseen fifth guard, trailing after the others. "In the yellow headscarf!"

It was Amelia's turn to curse. They broke from the crowd and turned down an alleyway. The crowd screamed behind them as the guards used magic again to push them aside.

Ander continued to support Amelia as they ran, but with every step she took with her injured leg, she winced and staggered. It was slowing them down, and they needed every ounce of speed if they wanted any hope of escape.

He swallowed. "Sorry!"

"For wha–"

He threw her over his shoulder and picked up the pace.

"Really, Ander?!" she yelled, before blurting, "Dodge!"

He weaved to the side as a blast of molten sand hit the building next to them, leaving a long score mark. Ander glanced back to see all five guards hot on their tail.

"Left! Move left!" Amelia said.

Searing heat passed inches from his face and burned a hole straight through a clothesline hanging above.

"Ugh, my left, not yours! They're picking up speed!" The end of the alley was only seconds away. Beyond was a thick sea of people they could lose themselves in.

Ander groaned as he kicked up his pace. He leaned forward as all his muscles screamed for him to stop.

WHOOSH! A wall of hardened sand rose before them. Ander slammed into it, sending both of them crashing to the ground. He immediately flipped around and drew his knives.

The Sadrian guards slowed to a stop ten feet away. One stepped forward. "Put the weapons down, or we'll take them."

Ander's mind raced. This was a Steam soldier's worst nightmare—to face off against more than one Gifted. This was a fight he'd lose five times over, but he couldn't bear the thought of them taking Amelia.

Ander took a deep breath. "Millie, climb the wall. Get out of here. That's an order!"

He charged into the guards with a battle cry. They converged on him like vipers, striking from all directions. He allowed his instincts to take over, blocking, weaving, and adjusting to each strike. The guards' explosive use of magic telegraphed every movement to his mind a millisecond before it happened. But it was barely enough to help him hold his ground as each successive strike seemed to come faster and faster.

After a few seconds of pure, sweat-dripping concentration, he lost his footing. The guards were on him in an instant, slamming him to the ground hard enough to rattle his entire body. He struggled as they wrenched his hands behind his back and shackled his wrists and ankles. Something slammed the side of his head, making his vision swim.

Somewhere beyond him, he heard a wild cry. Then a blurry Amelia crashed into the guards.

"Amelia!" he screamed. Just as quickly, she too was slammed to the ground next to him and shackled.

No, no, no, he wanted to scream. She hadn't gotten away. After everything they had just experienced, Khaldun would still capture her.

Chapter 10: Tipping Tavern

Amelia

Amelia gasped for breath underneath the crushing weight of the guard's knee on her back. She could see Ander next to her, looking terrible. Sand coated a cut on his temple and his lower lip was swollen. Worse still—she'd never seen him look so defeated.

"You didn't run," he croaked.

The desperation in the words sent pain lancing through her heart. Maybe she should have. She *had* climbed the sand-hardened wall. There was plenty of time to escape when she reached the top, but for some reason, she hesitated at the thought of abandoning him. Everything about the thought felt wrong. Even then, she didn't quite understand why she leapt off the wall onto the nearest guard. It was certainly the stupidest impulse she had ever followed, considering they were now both captured.

"I guess I'm no good at following orders," she said.

Their conversation was cut short as they were abruptly yanked to their feet.

"You should have stayed in the Republic," warned a guard in a deep bass. "Now, you'll pay the price."

Ander struggled against his captors and was rewarded by a meaty thump across his head. His head rolled forward and his whole body went limp.

Amelia gasped. "Ander!" She moved toward him and was yanked away.

"We'll take them straight to Khaldun," ordered the guard. He slung Ander's limp form over his shoulder.

Guards grabbed Amelia on either side and forced her to limp as they retraced their steps back down the alleyway. Amelia stared at Ander. He had willingly sacrificed himself for her. If it wasn't for her insisting that they stay at the Serenity Pools, none of this would have happened.

Guilt rose up her throat like acid reflux. This was *her* fault. It was all her fault. If only she had listened to Ander at the start, maybe they would have made a cleaner getaway. Or if she paid more attention at the square and kept a lower profile. Or if she hadn't twisted her ankle. If it wasn't for her, they wouldn't be captured. They wouldn't be heading toward—

Blam blam blam! Crossbow bolts slammed into the guards' helmets with loud, ringing peals. Amelia gasped and dropped her head down. In a heartbeat, every guard around her crashed unmoving to the ground, leaving her completely exposed. Only the guard carrying Ander remained standing. The powerful brute had somehow caught the heavy, blunt-tipped bolt aimed for his own head.

High above the alleyway stood a lone figure at the edge of a rooftop. The figure's cloak billowed in the hot wind, revealing sandy-brown Steam armor that was flecked with orange rust and covered with bolt magazines. Steam curled out their crossbow.

"The Desert Steam Soldier," cursed the last remaining guard.

"That's as far as you'll take them," commanded the figure in a woman's voice. Shutters crashed open along the balconies of the alleyway. Semi-automatic crossbows appeared from at least ten of them, held by similarly dressed Steam soldiers.

Steam soldiers? Amelia processed everything as if in slow motion. Was this a rescue?

The wind howled as the guard and the soldiers stared each other down. Amelia's eyes bounced between the two sides, finally landing on Ander's limp form on the guard's shoulder.

If the Steam soldiers fired, Ander would be in the crossfire.

"Don't shoot!" she screamed. Gazes swiveled to her. Then the world erupted into chaos.

The guard bolted toward the alleyway exit with blinding speed. Bolts fired after him, barely missing as he weaved back and forth in an erratic pattern.

"Ander!" She chased after the guard, heedless of the burning pain in her ankle and the manacles that shortened her stride. It was hopeless, she knew. The guard was moving too fast, even when Steam soldiers dropped to the ground to block his way. He simply kicked off the walls over them and used sand magic to blast them to the ground.

Despair tore through her chest, its depths widening as the guard grew smaller and smaller. He was nearing the exit now. Once he disappeared through there, Ander would be gone forever. Khaldun would kill him.

She pushed herself to run faster and succeeded in tripping face first into the sand.

"No!" she screamed through sand-coated hair. Groaning, she struggled to her feet and tripped again.

"No!" she repeated, feebler this time. "Ander!" Her strength faded as the guard reached the exit and disappeared.

Tears welled in her eyes. He was gone. Ander really was gone.

Crash! The guard tumbled back into view and slammed into the alleyway wall. Ander slipped off his shoulder and crumpled to the ground. The Desert Steam Soldier from the roof appeared next with her crossbow trained on the guard.

Hope surged through Amelia's veins. She rose to her feet and rushed toward Ander, pushing past the rising Steam soldiers in her way.

Ahead, the guard and the soldier fought. Molten sand blasted left and right, with the soldier dodging each maneuver. Then the guard grabbed the soldier in a chokehold. In a flash, the soldier flipped the guard over her shoulder and slammed the stock of her crossbow into the guard's temple. Only then did the guard crumple.

The fight was finally over.

Relief bloomed through Amelia as she reached Ander and knelt next to him.

"Ander?" she whispered.

Ander groaned as his eyes flickered open.

"Move aside," ordered the Desert Steam Soldier, pushing Amelia away.

Unable to catch herself, Amelia fell backward into the sand again. "Ugh!" She clenched her teeth and bit back a retort as she awkwardly used her hands behind her back to prop herself back up.

The Desert Steam Soldier grabbed a key ring from the crumpled guard and unlocked Ander's hands and legs. As she did, Steam soldiers closed in around them.

Amelia studied the soldiers, appreciating for the first time how their sandy-rusted armor blended well with the surroundings. Yet, it also gave the group a defiant, non-regulation look. Most were storing their crossbows behind their cloaks before pulling everything over so that their armor and gear were obscured. By the time they finished adjusting their cloaks, they looked like ordinary Sadrians.

Ander groaned and propped himself up. He blinked before squinting at the Desert Steam Soldier. "What happened?"

"I just saved your life, *Blackwell*," replied the Desert Steam Solder. She reached a hand toward Ander. As she did, a lock of wavy, blonde hair fell out from her hooded cowl.

Amelia stared at the figure with a growing sense of unease. That unease grew when Ander's face broke into an enormous smile.

"Olivia Fonte?" He clasped the soldier's arm and allowed her to pull him up.

"It's been a few years since the academy, Blackwell," the so-called Olivia replied lightly.

Amelia frowned at the congenial exchange. She would have folded her arms too if they weren't still chained behind her back. Ander and Olivia embraced as if they were long-time friends, but Amelia knew that couldn't be true. She had never heard Ander talk about an *Olivia* before.

She cleared her throat loud enough to cause both of them to look at her.

"Who's the civilian?" asked Olivia.

"This is Miss Amelia Steam," Ander replied.

"Ah," said Olivia with a guarded tone. "I thought I recognized your handiwork." She tilted her head toward the plume of smoke rising in the sky behind her.

Amelia narrowed her eyes and met none in return. The depth of the Desert Steam Soldier's hood cast enough shadow that all she could see was the vague outline of the soldier's face, covered with cloth. She would be surprised if the soldier had a soul at all.

"We need tae get a move on afore mair guards show up," spoke one soldier in a deep, Brinkerhoff accent.

Olivia nodded. "Get us a handcart and quick. You four, I need you to scout the surrounding area. Go!"

Amelia waited for an order to unshackle her, but it never came. Instead, Olivia's attention stayed focused on Ander as they waited in the alleyway for the soldiers to return.

After a full minute of waiting, Amelia finally said, "Do you mind unshackling me?" She shook her chains meaningfully.

Olivia only glanced at her before throwing the keys at her. "Make it quick."

The keys hit her face and slapped the ground.

Really? Anger surged inside her. She knelt down and twisted so she could pick up the keys behind her back.

"Here," said Ander, "I can help." He took the keys from her and unlocked her hands and wrists. "How's your ankle?"

"It's FINE!" she said through gritted teeth.

"Oh," he took a few steps away from her. "Okay."

I didn't mean it like that. She closed her eyes and pinched the bridge of her nose. "We appreciate the help, *Olivia,* but Ander and I need to be going."

Olivia whipped around. "That's Lieutenant Colonel Fonte to you, civilian."

Yeah, I'm not calling you that.

"Besides," Olivia continued, "I thought you needed to meet with one of our intelligence operatives. Or is that not the case?"

Amelia clenched her fists.

"Millie," said Ander, "it'll be alright. I've known Olivia for a long time."

She didn't like the way he said *long.*

A soldier reappeared in a rush, stopping before Olivia. "Khaldun's locking down this part of the city! It's a hornet's nest out there!"

A handcart pulled in front of the alleyway, filled with wicker baskets and a canvas stretched over top. At its front was another soldier Olivia had sent off before.

"Quick," said Olivia, pushing Ander and Amelia forward. "Get in. We'll smuggle you out."

Ander and Amelia climbed into the handcart, squeezing between the baskets until the world was obscured by nothing but wicker. Someone rapped on the back of the cart and it began to move.

Amelia stilled her body and quieted her breath. Her heart still continued to pound in her ears, and her mind raced.

I thought I recognized your handiwork. She squeezed her eyes tight as pressure built in her head. She hadn't intended to create so much destruction. Civilians were out of the way, and she was just trying to escape. Still, there were guards who were in that building, guards who would have had no way out as the building collapsed.

Memories of screaming voices filled her head—voices caught in a fire from which they couldn't escape.

She shook her head. *You can't think like that! What I did was an*

act of self-defense. Khaldun tried to imprison me. He would have killed
Ander! The rationalization only made her feel slightly better.

She let out a slow, heavy breath. This mission was quickly
becoming a string of messes. First it was crashing the airship, then
almost losing Axel, then escaping Khaldun, and now getting stuck
with the Desert Steam Soldier. How much more would she have to go
through to finally clear her name?

The handcart hit a bump and halted. Seconds later, a knock
rapped on the back of the handcart.

"Quick," said the soldier in his Brinkerhoff accent. "Get oot afore
ye're seen."

Amelia and Ander wriggled out and emerged into a dark
alleyway. The Brink waved them over to a stack of barrels. Waiting
behind was the bald, pot-bellied contact from the square.

"This here is Amir," said the soldier. "He'll be takin' yeu frae
here." The soldier nodded to the three of them before slipping past
the handcart and disappearing into the streets.

Amir eyed the two of them with a frown. "Follow me at a
distance. Don't draw attention." He directed the second statement to
Amelia before turning and disappearing into the crowd.

Really? Amelia thought. Was everyone against her?

Amir took off in a hurried walk back into the streets. They
followed, with Amelia limping every other step. After crossing
through the next street and entering another alleyway, Ander put an
arm around Amelia to support her.

"Thanks," she whispered.

He nodded.

They moved in and out of alleyways and crowds, so often she
wondered if Amir was trying to lose them as well. At one point, they

even followed him into the front door of a flatbread bakery and out the back door. The whole time, the contact maintained a steady distance from them.

After almost an hour, they slowed down in a derelict part of the city. The buildings were three stories tall and looked as if they had been finely crafted at one time. Now, however, the buildings were cracked and crumbling. Shutters hung at odd angles and the whole environment stank of refuse. The contact stopped before a tavern with a sandstone tower leaning at a precarious angle. It wasn't until this point that he allowed Ander and Amelia to catch up.

"Welcome to the Tilted Tavern," Amir announced. He led them around the building to a side door. Then he knocked in a unique pattern.

A shutter screeched open above them, and a burly, shawled woman appeared through it. "Amir, who are these vagrants dirtying my alleyway?" Her voice was gruff, and in her hands was a heavy wooden crossbow.

Ander stepped in front of Amelia as Amir raised his hands in a placating gesture. "These are refugees from Kustapata, and only need a little help before they are on their way."

The large woman frowned. "I'm not in the mood, Amir. Send them away."

"But the lady," Amir gestured to Amelia. "She's sick with child and has been walking all day."

Amelia kicked him in the leg with her good foot as hard as she could.

Amir howled.

"Sick with child?" Amelia repeated through clenched teeth. "Do I look pregnant to you?"

The large woman chuckled and shut the shutter. A few seconds later, she opened the side door wide.

"Anyone who'd kick my brother is a friend of mine. Come on in."

Amir glared at Amelia before leading them into a dimly lit kitchen. Wooden preparation tables lined the edges of the room and were covered with spices, vegetables, and clean dishes. Sacks of barley were stacked in a corner while dried onions and pans hung from racks above. A stone cooking fireplace was built into one wall and was large enough to roast a whole hog.

The large woman bowed slightly and said, "I am Adeena Azzam. Welcome to my tavern. Who are you?"

"You never met them," Amir replied shortly.

Adeena put her hands on her hips and frowned. "Yet you bring them here, risking *my* home." She looked behind them. "Where's Hasaan? He was at least nice to me."

Amir grimaced, and her expression fell.

"He said he was close." She pinched the bridge of her nose and turned away.

Amir sighed. "I need to borrow your kitchen."

"I'm sure you do." Her tone was harsh. She gave Ander and Amelia each a sad look and left the room. Amir walked to the stone fireplace, reached into the back, and pushed.

The back of the fireplace hinged open into darkness. Amir gestured to the opening with one hand and said, "After you."

They climbed through the opening into a dimly lit room. The walls were stone and circular and had a faint sparkle in the low light. Along its edge were crates, magpacks, and other gear. A telegraph sat on the edge of one crate, with a chair next to it. A table occupied the center of the room, covered with faded maps and Steam crossbow magazines. Chairs circled around its edges.

"Are we at the bottom of the tower?" Amelia asked.

Amir nodded. "In a room that doesn't exist. Wait here." He disappeared back through the entrance without waiting for a reply.

They waited there for only a moment before the fireplace opened again. This time, Olivia appeared with Amir and several soldiers in tow. The soldiers scattered, one to the telegraph while the rest pulled a ladder from the ceiling and climbed up to a next level through a trapdoor.

Olivia stopped before Ander and Amelia and gestured to the chairs at the table. "Take a seat."

Ander and Amelia took their spots. Olivia hung her cloak on the back of a chair opposite them before sitting.

Amelia studied the Desert Steam Soldier's features for the first time. She had expected the woman to have ratty hair, harsh features, and perhaps a wart on the end of her nose. Instead, her face was heart-shaped, and her wavy blond hair was cut in a stylish bob. Her bright eyes were laced with long eyelashes, and her lips cocked to one side when she smiled. Add in her athletic physique, and she was the type of woman that would turn heads.

I've seen barking, corroded exhaust pipes turn heads too, Amelia thought.

The insult wasn't creative enough. So, she imagined the grimiest exhaust pipe she could, with cracked joints that leaked chunky burnt oil. When that image wasn't good enough, she added herself lighting it on fire and throwing it over the side of her airship. Only then did she smile.

"... already met Amir Azam," said Olivia, gesturing to Amir.

Amir nodded and took a seat at the side of the table.

"Amir, this is Lieutenant Ander Blackwell and his associate, Miss Amelia Steam."

Amir's eyes narrowed at Amelia. "Steam? Any relation to Nicholas Steam?"

Amelia raised an eyebrow. "Yes. He's my grandfather."

Amir frowned.

Amelia cocked her head. "Why?"

"Did you get to Edward?" Olivia asked Amir, interrupting the exchange.

Amir sighed and shook his head. "Khaldun got to him first. Declared mirabetal."

Olivia cursed.

Ander furrowed his brows. "Could you explain what mirabetal means? I'm not familiar with that term."

Olivia gave a tight expression. "It's not something they teach at the academy."

"Mirabetal is our way of life," explained Amir. "When the Creator, Soleth, constructed our lands, he formed everything with balance and instituted it as our highest law. Mirabetal is the declaration of setting into balance. Left and right. Up and down. Light and dark. Value paid with equal value. In this case, a crime must be paid equally in justice."

"Edward killed one of Khaldun's guards," said Olivia. "Mirabetal means Edward will receive the same fate."

"Could we rescue him?" asked Ander.

Olivia shook her head. "The Sadrian prison is located in the heart of the military district. We'd lose more people than save."

Ander grimaced. He glanced at Amelia and asked, "What about that other phrase Khaldun said? The one before he chose a victim at random?"

"Ulesibli mirabetal," Amelia answered. "It means to substitute another to meet the demands of mirabetal. At least, that's what my tutors taught me."

"Yes. Because balance is our highest law," explained Amir, "The Sadhdron's job as high commander and balancer of the scales is to ensure every imbalance is addressed. If someone commits a crime and the criminal cannot be brought to justice, then he will select a substitute."

Ander's eyes opened wider. "So Khaldun could punish anyone for a crime?"

Amir nodded. "If he does not, then the gods will strike our lands again and send us into another thousand years of hardship. The scales must be balanced."

"This is why with our operations, we try to do as little harm as possible," explained Olivia. "Every action we take against Khaldun will be measured back out. If we kill someone, he will kill someone. If not us, then someone else—likely one of the citizens here in Sadria."

Amelia put a hand over her mouth as cold realization poured through her. What would Khaldun do after her explosion? Would he find a Republic target? Or would he find civilians to punish?

Ander ran a hand through his hair. "I don't mean to be insensitive, Amir, but that's a horrible philosophy."

Olivia gave a tight smile. "In an effort to restore mirabetal, Khaldun's been targeting agents, immigrants, diplomats—anyone he can get from the Republic."

"And those in the crossfire," Amir added grimly.

"Which is why my operations only employ the best." Olivia's

eyes settled on Ander with a piercing intensity.

Amelia shifted uncomfortably in her seat, understanding where this conversation was going.

"I saw your fight against those Gifted," Olivia continued. "You held your own against all of them for longer than I've seen anyone do."

Amelia cleared her throat and scooted closer to Ander. "Yes, Ander is very talented. But—"

Olivia talked over Amelia as if she wasn't there. "We could use someone like you to help us take down the slave trade."

"We already have our own mission," Amelia said before Ander could respond.

Olivia waved her hand dismissively. "I'm aware of Secretary Drake's desire to get you into the Sadrian Archives to find *information*. What I'm offering is the chance to rescue *people*."

"I can't, Olivia," Ander replied.

Relief filled Amelia.

Olivia frowned. "Before you decide, let me update you on current events. After your bombing raid, the value and demand for slaves exploded overnight. Slavers started to bring in Brinkerhoffs by the cargo hold since buyers were afraid the enterprise would close soon."

Ander's mouth fell open. "How is that possible? We took out their headquarters."

Olivia shook her head. "They moved operations to the military sector of the city."

"I thought the Sultan didn't employ the slavers," said Amelia, "which is why we are at war against slavery and not Sadria directly."

Amir leaned forward, resting his elbows on the table. "Officially he doesn't. That's been his outward political stance, and it's kept him safe from open war. But he receives a heavy tax from every sale."

"We told parliament as much," said Olivia with a sigh. "It's done nothing to change their stance."

"They probably want to avoid war as well," said Amelia, thinking back to the council meeting she attended months ago. "Especially with the looming Enchantran threat."

Olivia nodded. "Regardless, the shift in location makes it impossible to strike at their headquarters again without risking open war. So, we altered tactics. Major General Hawke's been leading the fleet, canvasing the ocean, and seizing slaving ships along the Brinkerhoff-Sadrian shipping routes. My mission here is rescue and recovery of those taken."

"What about protecting the shores of Southern Brinkerhoff?" Amelia asked.

Both Ander and Olivia turned to look at her.

"Southern Brinkerhoff is under the Shaoguan Dynasty occupation," explained Ander. "It's part of the reason why they are so vulnerable right now."

"It's a war zone," continued Olivia, "and the Republic isn't interested in joining that fight either at this time, no matter how badly our Brinkerhoff allies wish for it. So we are making the best we can with what we have."

"Well," interjected Amelia, "it seems you have things handled. Ander and I need to—"

"Blackwell," Olivia's gaze grew intense, "I need your help. We've nearly destroyed their entire shipping enterprise and yet slaves are still flowing in by the masses."

"Even with the oversea patrols?" Ander asked. "How's that

possible?"

"We don't know," answered Olivia, "but we have to find out how and bring the operation down. That's why I need your help and any troops you can spare."

Impatience flooded into Amelia. She stood and slapped her palms on the table. "He's already given you an answer, Lieutenant Colonel! We're looking for information vital to the safety and security of the Republic. We were promised that someone here could help us, but so far no one has. If you can't help us like we were promised, then we'll move along until we find someone else who does."

Olivia's expression grew dark. She leaned back and addressed Amir without taking her eyes off Amelia. "Tell them your experience at the archives."

Amir paused a beat before clearing his throat. "A little over fourteen years ago, I worked at the archives as a scholar. Ancient Sahadrian was my specialty, and I thoroughly enjoyed it until your grandfather visited, Miss Steam." His expression soured.

"Helping him was my hardest and last assignment at the archives. He was obsessed with finding answers to long-lost secrets— so much so he barely ate and slept. Thought someone was out to kill him and was suspicious that it could be anyone. He carried his bad luck with him because only a month later, Sultan Aramah was assassinated in his own palace."

Amelia cocked her head. From the few memories she had of her grandfather, he wasn't paranoid or mad. He had wrinkled smile lines, and his bushy white mustache tickled when he kissed her on the cheek. The person Amir described wasn't him.

Amir continued his story. "Sultan Aramah's son, Salim, took power and worried he'd die next. So, he cast out everyone who worked within the palace and replaced them. That was the last time I walked the archives.

"What made you come back to Sadria?" asked Amelia, genuinely curious.

Amir's expression turned dark. "I came back when the sultan made things personal."

Amelia had no idea what that meant, and Amir didn't elaborate.

"Point is," Olivia cut in, "Amir knows the archives well, enough to get what *you* need and what *we* need."

Amelia raised an eyebrow. "What *we* need?"

Amir nodded. "The archives are where the sultan keeps tax records of every slave sold."

"With that information," said Olivia, "We could understand who's funding the slaving operations and how it's being hidden. It would be a major step toward ending this conflict."

Ander cleared his throat. "Then it looks like our interests are aligned."

"They are," Olivia agreed.

"So, what are we dealing with?" Ander asked.

"The archives are behind the palace walls. With Sultan Salim's paranoia, only guards and members of the embassy pass through its gates."

Ander blew out. "That complicates things."

"It's taken work, but we concocted a way in. Two weeks ago, the fleet captured an Enchantran corsair called the *EveningGale*. A delegate from the Arcanum, Lady Tornala, was on board, heading on an official visit to the Sadrian embassy. We believe we could get someone in by impersonating the delegation. Perhaps we can make up an identity for an Arcanum apprentice—pretend they and their servants are the only survivors. Secretary Drake said your team has a specialized operative in Enchantran Gifted covers. Someone quite talented?"

Amelia nodded. "That would be me."

Olivia raised an eyebrow and turned to Ander. "Do you vouch for Miss Steam's capabilities?"

Ander nodded. "Amelia is one of the best I've seen."

Amelia beamed at the praise.

"Good," Olivia leaned back, looking relieved. Amir, on the other hand, sat up straight.

"Wait! YOU are the Enchantran operative that'd get us in?!"

Amelia folded her arms. "Do you have a problem with that?"

Amir ran both of his hands over his bald head. "You don't understand! The Sadrian elite guard the palace. One slip up, and we'll both be DEAD."

"That's usually how these undercover missions work," said Amelia with a raised eyebrow.

"May Sarlketh help us all!" He turned to Olivia. "You expect me to trust *her* with my life?"

Olivia put a hand on the scholar's shoulder. "Relax. She just has to get you through the front gate."

"Wait." Amir narrowed his eyes. "What information are you looking for?"

Amelia glanced at Ander.

Ander cleared his throat. "We're looking for an artifact called the Wayfinder—"

"Nope!" Amir stood to his feet. "I'm not doing it. I'm not going through this again."

"Again?" Amelia said.

"Amir!" Olivia stood and grabbed the scholar before he could walk away. "With Edward gone, those slave records are your only chance of finding your niece."

Amir only shook his head.

"Think of your sister running this tavern alone!" Olivia continued. "Think of the countless others who've lost family. If you can get into those archives, you actually have a chance.

Amir tightened his lips. Conflict warred in his eyes.

Amelia studied Amir, confused by his reaction. This wasn't about her. It wasn't about the fire. No, this was something about her grandfather's visit. What happened? Did the Wayfinder have something to do with it?

After a long pause, Amir let out a pent-up breath. "Fine. I'll do it for my niece."

"There you go." Oliva patted his shoulder and sat back down. "It's decided then. All that needs to be worked out are details."

Olivia paused as the telegraph nearby began click-clacking. Once it finished, a soldier handed Olivia the message. She silently read the message and frowned. "Is your airship the *Legacy?*"

"Yes," said Amelia.

"Your supply request has been denied." Olivia handed the message to Ander. Amelia snatched it and scanned the words.

LEGACY SUPPLY REQUEST DENIED. ALL RESOURCES ARE BEING CONSERVED FOR THE SADRIAN-REPUBLIC SLAVE CONFLICT.

Amelia put a hand to her forehead as her mind raced. Without coal and essential airship parts, the *Legacy* was crippled. They'd have to limp all the way back to the Republic to get what they need. They'd waste months!

Ander took the parchment from her hand and ran a hand through his hair. "I don't understand."

"I'm sorry for your predicament," Olivia said. "I would offer to help but my resources are limited, and I don't have authority to override directives from high command.

"However," she leaned forward and spoke directly to Ander, "if you were to join my operations, I could get your request approved since your efforts would be supporting the Sadrian-Republic Slave Conflict."

Amelia's jaw dropped. *Does this woman stop at nothing to get what she wants?*

Ander stood up. "Give Amelia and I a moment to talk this through."

Olivia nodded and leaned back.

Amelia followed Ander to the kitchen entry. Once they got there, she spoke first.

"Ander, you can't be considering this. She just wants you to join her group of *rusty rebels* so she has more fodder to throw at Khaldun. Besides, I need you."

Ander gave her a sad smile. "I can't go with you to the archives."

Her stomach sank. "Why not?" Unease filled her with anxious energy as her mind flashed through all the possible reasons for why. *Is it something I said? Is it because he'd rather work with Olivia?* The last thought hit harder than the rest. *Does he suspect I'm hiding my past from him?*

"Khaldun knows my face," he said. "If I accompanied you to those gates, you'd be apprehended on sight."

She let out a stressed breath and pinched the bridge of her nose. *I suppose that makes sense.* She didn't voice the words, however, for fear it'd make Ander's statement true.

"Besides," he continued, "we need those supplies and repairs if we're to keep ahead of the Enchantrans."

She glanced back at Olivia. The woman's attention was turned to a stack of reports.

Why does she want Ander so badly? She didn't like the way the lieutenant colonel's eyes seemed to linger longer on Ander than anyone else in the room, nor the woman's relentless interest in recruiting him. If he got captured, there's be no rescue. Olivia made that clear with Edward's case.

What if Olivia tells him about my past? Amelia put a hand to her head as dizziness washed over her. Ander put a hand on her shoulder to steady her.

"Millie?" When she didn't look at him, he put his hand on her other shoulder and pivoted her so they were speaking eye to eye. "I know it's not what you were expecting. But it'll be okay. I've known Olivia for a long time."

That was the problem, she thought. She could only imagine what Olivia would say about her.

She couldn't let that happen. If Ander were to find out about her past, she wanted it to be from her own lips.

"It'll be okay," he repeated. "Maybe we can enlist Hammer or one of the others on the team to accompany you."

Her mouth felt dry and swallowing felt like a chore. "Fine," she breathed. "I guess we can do it."

Ander nodded and led the way back. She followed him numbly and sat down. Olivia looked up from her reports.

"Did you make a decision?" Olivia asked.

Ander nodded. "I'll join your command, along with my soldiers on these conditions. You'll help Amelia, Amir, and one of my soldiers get into the archives, you'll approve our supply request, and as soon as Amelia's mission is completed, we're free to leave."

A large smile spread across Olivia's face. "Deal." Amelia watched the two of them stand and shake hands, solidifying an arrangement she already hated.

Amir sighed. "When do we start?"

"The Sadrians expected the *EveningGale* to port two days ago," Olivia explained. "If we wait too long, our window of opportunity will pass. We need to move tonight."

Amelia's stomach dropped. "Tonight?"

Olivia nodded.

Amelia's heart raced as stress washed over her. That was only hours away, and she had to prepare for what would undoubtedly be one of the hardest roles of her life. If she was going to tell Ander about her past, it was going to have to happen soon.

Chapter 11: Parting Ways

Amelia

The meeting ended in a flurry of activity. Olivia called in soldiers and sent them this way and that to begin preparations for the operation. The commotion seemed to blur around Amelia as her thoughts raced. She needed to get back to the *Legacy*. Her Enchantran trunk was in her cabin, and she needed to talk to Everard about repairs while she was gone. On top of that, she needed to talk to Ander, and she didn't want to do it here with Olivia.

She took a deep breath to clear her head, but it didn't feel like enough. The enclosed room felt more and more suffocating by the second, and she longed for the freeing feel of the breeze on her face.

Ander put a hand on her shoulder. "What do you need to get ready?"

The contact seemed to ground her, and her vision became more focused. *I can do this*, she thought. *I'm Amelia Steam, and Steams accomplish the impossible.* She cleared her throat and met his eyes.

"We need to get back to the airship. That's where my supplies are." *And perhaps we can talk on the way,* she mentally added. Heaviness settled over her at the thought, but she was committed now.

"What gate did you come through?" Olivia asked, jutting herself into the conversation.

"The southwestern gate," Ander answered.

Amelia rubbed her head to stem a building headache. She was beyond ready to be done with Olivia. Didn't the woman have an operation to get ready?

"We can take ourselves out," added Amelia. "Just let me know where I need to be to start the operation."

Olivia shook her head. "You don't know the city like I do, nor the beachhead we'll launch the mission from. I'll escort you out. It'll give me an opportunity to inspect Ander's command anyway."

"But—" Amelia started, but Olivia was already throwing her hood on and leading the way out of the secret room. Amelia balled her fists before following with Ander.

They exited the building into the side alley. The sun was descending, but the cooler temperatures of the evening hadn't yet set in. Olivia paused long enough for Ander to catch up by her side before setting a quick, hard pace southwest.

Amelia limped a few steps behind them. Thankfully, the pain in her ankle had lessened into a dull throb, but the sight of Olivia and Ander talking to each other in hushed tones more than compensated for the lessened pain. How was she supposed to talk to Ander now? The woman was like a blood-seeking leech!

They cut through streets and alleys in a zigzag pattern toward the southwest. Amelia's temperament only soured more with each successive step. She should have been thinking about her upcoming mission, or even what she'd say to Ander when she could finally get him alone. Instead, she burned over the fact that Olivia had taken her spot next to Ander. It was like the woman knew Amelia was about to tell Ander something that could destroy their friendship and had already swooped in to replace her.

Several times, Ander looked over his shoulder to check on Amelia with concerned eyes. She looked away each time, disappointed he'd stoop so low as to make friends with this *hag*.

Time dragged before they were finally passing through the gates to the dusty highway beyond. By that point, the sun had dropped significantly and shone directly in their eyes. Only hours were left before nightfall.

I don't have much time to get ready or talk to Ander. She didn't feel like talking to Ander at the moment. Her neck and shoulders ached, and she was looking forward to being alone in her cabin. Plus, she had so much to do before tonight— talking to Ander would have to wait until she was ready. That way she could get her mind into the right place.

The group quickened their pace, following the highway until it wound out of sight from the walls. Then they broke off from the path and trekked through the desert wilderness.

The *Legacy* finally came into view, though now it looked more like a gigantic canvas rock rather than an airship. Garret hailed them and began to give Ander a report. Amelia didn't stop to converse. Instead, she bumped past Ander and continued on.

"What has her upset?" she heard Garret ask Ander.

She didn't look back or attempt to listen. Instead, she ducked under the canvas tarps, climbed into the *Legacy*, and went straight to her cabin. Only then did she take a deep breath.

"Come on, Amelia," she said to herself. "You can do this." She opened her trunk and pulled out a long sapphire blue dress and a dark, long-sleeved overcoat with silver buttons and black lace. Next came out ivory gloves, stylistic boots, and other accessories.

As she changed, footsteps pounded from all directions toward the main deck. Then Olivia's muffled voice filtered through the door.

Great! she thought. She mostly tuned out the Lieutenant Colonel's voice, catching only the gist. Apparently, the woman was wasting no time asserting authoring and taking command.

Her thoughts turned again toward Ander. It felt strange that he wouldn't be with her on this mission, especially after all they had been through over the last few months. Granted, his undercover skills were as subtle as a bent crankshaft. Still, she'd miss his steady presence and level head. She'd miss the way he made her feel—like she belonged and mattered.

A knock sounded on the door.

"One moment," she replied. She finished pulling on her gloves and opened the door. Everard stood there, looking as exhausted as ever. Relief filled her. "Oh good. You're just who I needed to see. Are you okay if I keep getting ready as we talk?"

"Of course." He sat down on her bed as she turned to her broken vanity to apply makeup.

"I've made arrangements for those supplies and parts we need," she explained. "I won't be here to help install them, so I need you to make sure it all happens correctly."

She turned to Everard. "Could you light that candle and heat my curling iron over it?"

He nodded and retrieved the candle.

She continued. "Also, I need you to keep an eye on Emmett and Archibald. They keep showing me designs for modifying the rudder, and I trust them as far as I can throw Bragg. Oh! The bearings on the right wing keep sticking, so you probably need to regrease it. But make sure to clean out the sand before, otherwise—"

"Amelia," he cut her off. "What's happening? What's this mission you're going on?" His eyebrows were furrowed, and his hair looked more gray than normal in the dim lamplight.

She gave him a soft smile before explaining the mission. He listened quietly and didn't speak until she finished.

He let out a tired breath. "It's a big risk. Are you sure it's worth it? Are you sure *any* of this is worth it?"

She didn't answer immediately. Truthfully, she *hoped* it was all worth it. There was no place for her in the Republic if she didn't succeed.

"I have to do it," she replied. She took the hot iron from him and began curling her hair.

Everard let out a heavy sigh. "You're so much like your grandfather. Determined. Passionate. Willing to do anything for others. But you look so much like my sister."

His voice hitched, and he looked away. Amelia set the iron down and wrapped him in a tight hug. She'd never heard him talk about her mother, not since the fire. But he never blamed her for it either.

"I'll be okay," she whispered.

"I hope so," he said with emotion.

He pulled away and dabbed his eyes with a greasy handkerchief. "Sorry, this probably isn't helping. What can I do to help?"

She gave him another soft smile. Just his presence had melted so

CRAIG & JALEESA SNOW

much of the weight of the day. She couldn't ask for a better uncle.

"What you are doing now is perfect." Then she thought about Ander. "Actually, there is one thing you could do. Could you send for Ander?"

He raised an eyebrow.

"Don't you give me that," she said, pointing the iron at him.

He chuckled. "I'll go get him now." He got up and left.

She rolled her eyes. Sometimes Everard was like a father to her. Other times, he was too much like a father.

She pinned her curls up and stuck in a jeweled comb. Everything was now complete. Now she just needed to talk to Ander.

A knock sounded on the door. Her stomach tingled with anxious anticipation. She took a deep breath. This was it. This was really it. She was going to tell him. She rose and opened the door.

Olivia stood on the other side. "It's time to go, Miss Steam."

Her shoulders fell.

. . . .

Amelia pulled her overcoat closer around her as the secluded beach came into view. The breeze that blew in from the ocean was lukewarm and saturated with the scent of salt and seaweed. Waves crashed against the shore in continuous rhythms, competing against the volume of her heart.

Here we are, she thought. Nerves tingled throughout her body as Olivia and her soldiers moved past her to secure the beachhead. Soon, only Amir and Hammer stood next to her.

"Are you ready?" she asked.

Amir only grumbled in response. She frowned at him. He was dressed as finely as an Enchantran servant, but his attitude needed work.

"Ready," Hammer replied. The large man was dressed even simpler than Amir, with his old slave tattoo clearly visible in the crescent moon light. His role was to be her personal slave, adding credibility to her position as a Sadrian sympathizer.

"I'm sorry you have to dress like this," she said.

Hammer shook his head. "Ander orders. Protect Millie." Amelia put a hand on his arm with a grateful smile.

Speaking of Ander, she hadn't seen him since first arriving at the *Legacy*. His missing presence was palpable. She expected him to be here when she left. Instead, he was gone.

Is he already pulling away from me? She shook her head to clear the thought, but it didn't go away. Why hadn't he come with them? Did he care? Or was she just a coworker to him and not a friend?

A sailboat appeared on approach to their location. Amelia recognized it immediately as one used to scout ahead of important convoys: an Enchantran forerunner. Its hull was pocked with scorch marks, and it leaned at an odd angle.

"We're going in *that*?" Amir asked skeptically.

"Don't worry," said Amelia, "if it starts to take in water, I'll just order my servant to bail."

He glared at her. "I'm regretting this mission already. Nothing good happens with Steams."

She turned away so he couldn't see how the words hit her like a slap. She'd prove him wrong.

The sailboat slid to a stop. Desert Steam soldiers piled out, holding mooring lines.

"Steam, Azam, Hammer," Olivia called, "time to leave."

"Wait!" shouted Everard.

Amelia whipped around in surprise. Everard was running

toward her, and—

"Ander?" Butterflies fluttered in her stomach. She ran toward them. Her uncle reached her first.

Everard wrapped her in a tight hug. "I'm sorry we're so late. By the time we got to your cabin, you were already gone."

She squeezed him back. "I'm glad you found me."

He pulled away. "Stay safe, kiddo."

She nodded, not trusting her voice with a reply. She turned to Ander next.

He stood there, scratching the back of his head awkwardly. Then he met her eyes. "I know why you wanted to see me."

Her stomach did a somersault. "You do?"

He swallowed. "I know you're mad at me for this whole arrangement."

"Oh...."

"I've been regretting it since and—"

She wrapped him into a tight hug, and his words fell. Warmth filled her as his strong arms wrapped around her.

"I thought you weren't coming," she whispered. She closed her mouth quickly, surprised the words spilled out of their own accord.

"I wanted to be here," he whispered back. "Olivia assigned me to sentry duty. I had no idea when you were all leaving until you were already gone. If it wasn't for Everard, I would have missed you."

"Wait," she pulled away. "You left your post?"

He shifted from one foot to the other.

Her mouth dropped open. "You broke the rules just to see me? You rebel!" She punched him in the arm.

"I found a replacement," he clarified. "I'm not that irresponsible, unlike someone else I know."

She grinned from ear to ear. "Oh, of course not." She shook her head in amusement and bit her lip.

"Miss Steam!" shouted Olivia. "We need to get going!"

Amelia ignored the command. She liked this moment, being right here. Once she got on that ship, she'd be saying goodbye. She'd be leaving all of this for who knows how long.

Her smile fell with the thought. She needed to tell Ander about her past. It had to be now.

She tucked a curl behind her ear. "Hey, I need to tell you something."

"Yeah?" He frowned. "Is something wrong?"

She looked up at his soft eyes and felt her resolve falter.

I can't do this, she thought.

You're living a lie if you don't.

"Steam!" shouted Olivia more insistently. "I need you on that ship now!"

She swallowed hard. "I...." She looked down. "Be safe out there, mophead."

"You too."

She gave him a sad smile before turning away. Regret filled her with each successive step toward the ship. She barely noticed Olivia's glare as she passed and barely felt Hammer's hand as he helped her climb into the ship.

As the ship pulled away, Amelia moved to the stern and looked back to shore. Ander and Everard stood next to each other and waved. Then they faded into the dark.

Why didn't I tell him? Her stomach roiled, but it wasn't because of the waves. *What will happen when he finds out? What will he think about me?*

It was out of her control now. The beach was gone, and there was no turning back.

She sighed and shifted her gaze forward. Her past would continue to haunt her until she made up for her mistakes. Her only choice was to succeed in this new mission. If she did, they'd know where to find the Wayfinder. She'd be one step closer to redemption.

Chapter 12: Ambassador

Amelia

Thick fog blew across the dark Sadrian harbor, blurring the distant city lights into ethereal splotches of yellow and orange. Imposing sea towers materialized in the gloom, spaced across the harbor entrance waters like giant wards to the underworld. Waves crashed around their rocky bases, sending spray tens of feet into the air. Not even the highest crash came close to the tops of the towers, which were equipped with imposing catapults large enough to bring down castles, let alone ships.

Waves clawed at the limping Enchantran forerunner, tugging it toward the otherworldly scene. As it neared the towers, a bell tolled shrilly across the waves. In reply, a ghostly shape emerged from behind the towers and turned toward the limping craft.

A wooden sea dragon's head materialized, teeth bared and eyes unblinking. Then the massive hull appeared, with red sails and five rows of sloshing oars on either side. White foam peeled off to either side of the warship, parted by a heavy ram that cut through the waves just below the waterline.

A shiver went down Amelia's spine. As a girl, she had heard stories of red-sailed ships raiding the coasts of Brinkerhoff and setting villages to flame. Valuables were taken while the young women and men were sold into slavery. The sight set her pulse racing.

The warship crashed through the waves toward them, propelled by hundreds of synchronized oars. Slaves would be behind those oars, she knew. Along with their Sadrian task masters.

"I didn't expect we'd be greeted by the Sadrian navy," Amir whispered.

Amelia didn't respond, but waited for the warship to grow closer and closer. Soon, she could see the individual barnacles crusting the sides of the hull.

"You there!" shouted an officer just off from the sea dragon's head. "State your business!"

"You there?" Amelia replied in a sharp, haughty tone. "Who are you 'you there'-ing at? Is this how Sadria treats all of its diplomatic guests?"

The warship now leveled with them, giving them a clear view of the guards along the fighter ports on the side. She swallowed hard.

"These waters are restricted at night," said the officer with irritation. "State your business!"

She was committed to her role now. "Do you have sand in your ears? I said I'm a diplomat from Enchantra. My business is with the embassy."

Amir's face turned white. In a hushed tone, he said, "Are you trying to get us killed?"

No, she wasn't, but his concern wasn't helping. Staying in role, she snapped on Amir. "How *dare* you interrupt me, servant! Speak again out of turn and you'll regret it."

"You sailed from Enchantra in that?" asked the officer in a flat, skeptical tone.

"No, you idiot! I was part of the *EveningGale* before it was attacked by those infernal Republic airships! Now, unless you wish to insult me and the Arcanum further, you will point me where to dock."

The officer gave a heavy sigh and turned to his crew. "Signal the Sironjian." A ball of blue fire roared up ten feet from the back of the ship and dissipated. The officer turned around and pointed toward the shore. "Docks for the embassy are located in the northern end, fourth pier from the harbor station. Move along."

"Move along?" Amelia repeated with disdain. "Slave, take us forward. Hopefully, the reception there will be warmer after what we've been through."

Hammer angled the forerunner in the direction the officer pointed, and they sailed on. When the warship disappeared behind them, Amir exploded.

"What was that back there?! They could have boarded us and taken us prisoner. Did that ever cross your mind?"

Anger surged through Amelia, and she put her hands on her hips. "Have you ever met an Enchantran before? I was in character. How about you, Amir? Was 'terrified bystander' your character?"

Amir's face grew red. "You're just as insane as your grandfather!"

Amelia glared at Amir, but the man turned away, refusing to meet her gaze. That was fine with her. She didn't want to see his face anyway.

The fog lessened as they approached the shore lights. Hundreds of piers grew into view, with more ships docked next to them. Hammer guided the forerunner to the fourth pier, past a large building that must have been the harbor station.

As they approached the dock, a group of well-dressed Sadrians and a few guards were already waiting at the pier.

Amir cleared his throat. "Those are officials from the embassy. Don't blow it. We've got only one shot at convincing them we're authentic."

She glared at him again. It was easy for him to say. All he had to do was pretend to be her servant. He didn't even have to pretend to be Sadrian. She, on the other hand, had to do the real convincing.

She closed her eyes and took a deep breath. Their lives really were depending on her acting. Unlike the day before, her goal here wasn't to blend in with the crowd. This time, she purposely stood out in her long-sleeved overcoat and sapphire blue gown. One slip up, and they'd add their skulls to the gate entrances of Sadria.

She smoothed down her gown and took another deep breath. *I can do this.* This was just another role—one she was already familiar with. As long as she wasn't asked to perform magic, all would be fine.

As soon as the forerunner bumped into the dock, servants grabbed ropes and secured the boat. Then a tall man with green robes and a long nose stepped out from the group and held out a hand to Amelia. She took it and let him pull her onto the dock. The man took a deep bow.

"Welcome to port, Lady...." he left the words hanging.

"Lady Canterloch," she replied, keeping her head high. Only servants bowed in Enchantra.

"Lady Canterloch," the Sadrian repeated with a smooth voice. He rose back up and gave a smile that looked shallow.

"My name is Mazin Harron, the Sironjian, Keeper of the Embassy." His gaze flicked to the forerunner. "Where's Lady Tornala and the *EveningGale*?"

Amelia huffed. "Sunk by one of those infernal airships. Lady Tornala, my master, didn't make it. We're all that survived."

"You made it here in that?" The Keeper gestured to the forerunner with his lips.

"Yes, and I'm beyond ready to get out of this cold. Could your servants prepare a hot meal for when we get to the embassy?"

She swallowed quickly, realizing her slip up. She shouldn't have said 'we.' A real noble would have never noticed the servant and slave. Luckily, the Keeper simply waved a hand and said, "Let's get you out of the cold."

She nodded gratefully. "Slave, bring my trunk." She followed the Keeper without sparing a glance at Hammer. Hammer hoisted the chest and followed without a word.

His silent obedience pained her soul. *How could people actually live this way?*

They reached the end of the dock and proceeded toward the large adobe harbor station. The building itself was dark, but a fire burned just outside. The Keeper continued walking before stopping at the fire.

Amelia moved quickly to the fire's warmth, grateful for the heat after the cold spray of the waves.

"Forgive me," said the Keeper. "Before I can take you to the Embassy, I must verify you are who you say you are."

A cold bead of sweat ran down her back. "Of course," she said with a tight smile.

"Did you bring any papers of identification?"

She gestured to Hammer, who opened her trunk and handed the man several papers that were water damaged beyond comprehension.

The Keeper frowned. "I see the Enchantran seal, but the rest is incomprehensible. Do you have any other forms of identification?"

She put her hands on her hips. "I wasn't planning on the *EveningGale* being attacked. I'm fortunate to have escaped at all."

His frown deepened. "Your master was a member of the Arcanum. Are you one too?"

"Not yet, but I will be."

"Then surely an aspiring member of the Arcanum has ways to vouch for her identity." He looked at her with a knowing expression.

Amelia swallowed. He wanted her to do magic. "Surely the Enchantran seal on my papers is enough to vouch for my identity."

The Keeper sighed. "It's not. Seals are all too easy to fake. I'm afraid if you can't show me another form of identification, we won't be able to host you. Security's important to my guests, especially with the slave conflict on hand. I'm sure you understand."

No, she didn't understand—couldn't understand. They had to get into the embassy at any cost. If they didn't, they wouldn't get access to the archives. They'd lose any leads to finding the Wayfinder. Worse still, she'd lose her chance at redeeming herself. Her family name would remain ruined, and she'd have no home in the Republic. She'd continue to live her life alone with this horrible weight on her chest. That couldn't happen.

Emotion clawed up her throat. "My master was told that we'd be hosted. It's not my fault we were attacked!"

"That is indeed regrettable. Fortunately, there are many inns nearby. You could stay the night and then book passage back to

Enchantra in the morning."

"Please," she grabbed his arm, and he pulled it away. She gritted her teeth and felt anger surge through her veins. "Fine. I'll vouch for my identity. But I warn you, I've had a very long four days since the attack."

She marched to the fire and picked up a burning tree limb. While she was turned from the others, she reached into her overcoat, found the small gas cylinder sewn into its lining, and turned the knob. Immediately, compressed gas traveled through a tube down her right sleeve.

She turned around and held the flaming tree limb up while gesticulating dramatically with the other hand.

Nothing happened.

Her heart skipped a beat. She waved the brand again, hoping it'd catch the quickly depleting gas. Still, nothing happened.

The Keeper stared at her unamused.

"Hang on." She grabbed the limb with her left hand and moved her right hand closer to the flame.

With a loud *whomp*, the flames exploded into a full flamethrower. The Sadrians stumbled backward; their mouths wide open. Even the Keeper eyes went wide.

Amelia smiled and readjusted her grip so she could reach into her overcoat and turn the cylinder off. As she twisted, the knob broke from the cylinder.

Her eyes widened as pure dread washed over her like a tidal wave. She couldn't stop the gas! The flames grew larger and larger until it jumped to her sleeve.

Panic overtook her. She screamed and ripped her coat off as quickly as she could. Then she raised her skirts and stomped on the coat until it went out.

Silence fell across the group. She leaned over and sucked in rapid breaths of air. Her heart pounded out of her chest and her hands trembled.

That was less of a demonstration and more of a disaster!

The Keeper slowly walked toward her with narrowed eyes. Cold sweat broke across her whole body underneath his scrutinizing gaze.

"That was quite the demonstration of power." He kicked over her overcoat. "But you have no control." He picked up the extinguished tree limb with one hand and gesticulated his fingers with the other. The top reignited into flames. He gesticulated again, and the flames went out.

"Your finger technique is atrocious. Clearly, you are early in your training." He dropped the tree limb into the fire. "We'll prepare a room for you at the embassy." He pointed to a servant. "Fetch a carriage."

Relief poured over Amelia. It worked! They had an invitation in!

Amir's face was ashen, and when she caught his eye, he frowned and crossed his arms.

Well, someone's hard to please! she thought. She mentally noted to make Amir do the next magical demonstration in a gown. His opinion of her might change after that.

A servant moved toward her discarded cloak, but she waved her off dismissively. "My slave can take care of that." She gestured to Hammer.

Hammer did as she asked, storing it into the trunk. Once it was out of sight, she breathed a sigh of relief.

A moment passed before a luxurious covered carriage appeared, pulled by two elegant horses with braided hair. Amelia blinked at the sight. She hadn't seen a single carriage yesterday.

The Keeper took her hand and helped her climb in. Then he sat down on the side opposite from her and waved the driver on. The carriage jolted and pulled them away from the docks.

So far everything has worked out according to plan, she thought. Hoping to push her luck further, she cleared her throat. "When can I visit the Sadrian Archives?"

The Keeper yawned. "Is it still your intent to pursue your master's mission?"

"No. I've found a new one," she said launching into her rehearsed cover story. "After the attack, I realized there is no safety for us Gifted while the Republic commands the skies. That's why I will find a way we can use magic to make ships fly."

"A fantastical notion," he replied. "Ships have too much weight. The power required is too great."

"Perhaps," she countered, "but I will make the Republic regret the day they took away my master."

He waved a dismissive hand. "It's not my call who can go into the archives or not, but shall I submit your request?"

She smiled her first real smile of the evening. "Yes. That would be wonderful."

He nodded. "I will reach out to set up a meeting with the Sadhdron."

"The Sadhdron?" Alarms pealed through her mind.

"Yes, Khaldun interviews all who are admitted within the palace walls. I'll organize a meeting for his earliest convenience. It might not be for a couple weeks."

"Thank you." She said the words, but they felt hollow. She'd have to meet with Khaldun, the most dangerous man in all of Sadria! Only the day before, he was trying to capture her. What had she gotten herself into?

It was too late to turn back now. She was committed.

Chapter 13: Abilities

Ander

A nder moved through the dark spice fields in a low crouch. His eyes roved back and forth through the sights of his steam crossbow. Garret and Blaze flanked either side of him, with weapons trained out to the sides. The red spice stalks whispered around them as they brushed past, filling the air with pungent aroma.

In the distance loomed the dark silhouettes of a plantation manor and a crumbling outbuilding. Orange pinpricks of light roved around their edges, casting shadows up their adobe walls. Those would be the sentries, Ander knew.

Blink blink. Metal flashed at them in quick succession from a nearby ditch to their left. Ander slowed to a stop. He gave a subtle hand gesture, and they pivoted toward the light.

They trained their weapons forward as they crept toward the ditch, careful to not make a sound. As they neared it, a Desert Steam

Soldier materialized before them. He gave Ander a nod and gestured behind him. They complied, moving to the bank and dropping over into its sandy depths. Crouched low in the depression were more Desert Steam Soldiers, huddled in a circle around Olivia. They turned as Ander, Blaze, and Garret approached.

The closest soldier smiled and nodded his head toward Ander. "Oi, now we're ready," he whispered.

As they joined their ranks, another soldier clapped Ander on the back. "What surprises do you have up your sleeve this time, Blackwell?"

Ander gave them all a tight smile. It had been a couple weeks since parting ways with Amelia. He'd been on four missions since then, and each one had brought encounters with Gifted guards. Each one had required him to secretly use his abilities to help them succeed—especially on the last mission.

They had broken into a wealthy government official's home and reached the slaves' quarters. Inside were Khaldun and twelve Gifted guards disguised as slaves, all waiting for them. If Ander hadn't recognized their Gifted auras and pulled them out, the entire platoon would have been taken out.

"I still can't believe the last mission," said another guard. "How did you know it was a trap?"

Ander swallowed. "Something didn't seem right." It was the best answer he could give without telling the truth.

"Surely there must have been something that tipped you off?" asked another.

Ander hesitated under the pressure of so many eyes. What could he say to them? "They didn't have slave tattoos," he said finally. The lie tasted bitter in his mouth.

Freya frowned. "How did you spot that? The room was dark."

"Alright, fall in line," ordered Olivia, saving Ander from answering more.

He breathed a sigh of relief as the group reassembled into a circle. His abilities were getting him noticed, which wasn't good. One slip up and he'd be locked up as a Gifted spy. He needed to avoid using his abilities entirely, at least until he could figure out what was happening to him. Why was he manifesting Gifted-like abilities when he was Commonborn?

Olivia interrupted his thoughts. "There are six guards on patrol, with another ten in the manor. Thanks to Khaldun, none of them are Gifted."

The soldiers chuckled and elbowed each other.

Apparently Khaldun had been conscripting anyone Gifted that could fight and sending them northwest to Vashi to fight the Mirage. The Sadhdron himself left only a week ago with a host of cavalry to settle Mirage uprisings happening in Havva. His absence had created a convenient opportunity for the Desert Steam Soldiers.

"This particular target is vital to our operations," Oliva continued. "On the premise are two recently acquired slaves from Brinkerhoff. If we can liberate them, we may discover how these infernal Sadrians are transferring slaves under the fleet's nose."

She pulled her hood up and shouldered her crossbow. Her voice was muffled from the heavy fabric. "Sergeant Allred's team is already in position to strike. Blackwell, Mills, and Attwell, you're with me on infiltration. Harper, you've got perimeter with the rest. Make sure no one escapes to alert guards from the city. You have your orders. Move out."

The soldiers slipped out of the ditch one by one until only the infiltration team remained. They waited there a moment longer before Olivia led them out.

They glided through the spice fields, adjusting their positions so there was always a hill or bluff between them and the roving lights around the manor. When they neared the manor, they lowered to the earth and crawled the rest of the way to the edge of the field.

Two guards conversed in front of the outbuilding's doors while others patrolled lazily around the manor's perimeter. Unlike city guards, they were lightly armored and less disciplined.

If they had to engage, Ander didn't doubt they could take out all the guards with their team alone. The plan, however, was to minimize violence as much as possible. Any injury they inflicted would be repeated again by Khaldun in the name of mirabetal.

They waited there in the field, timing the gaps between patrols. When they found the pattern, they broke across the yard and scrambled up the manor walls. They slipped over the edge of the upper balcony before the next patrol appeared.

Ander's heart pounded as they waited for the patrol to pass by again. When they were in the clear again, the infiltration team stacked up along the balcony's door and waited for the signal.

Noise exploded from the field they had just come from, followed by shouts of "HURRAH!" That was Sergeant Allard's team from the Brinkerhoff Royal Marines, who could only be described in one word—insane. But their job *was* to draw attention. And not die.

Olivia squeezed Ander's shoulder. He kicked the balcony door open and burst into the master bedroom. The plantation owners jolted awake from bed. The woman screamed while the man reached for a saber leaning against a dresser.

Thwack! Garret's bolt knocked the weapon away. The woman

screamed harder. Her husband looked at the saber now lying across the room and turned back to Ander. Ander sensed power rising in the man.

"Don't even think about it!" he said.

Olivia glanced at him, and he mentally chided himself.

"Get up and put your hands behind your head." He sensed power in the woman, although it felt almost blocked. *No, that isn't right,* he thought. *More like dormant.* "Both of you," he added.

Ander could see the frustration burning in the man's face and the fear in the woman's eyes. Olivia roughly shoved them out onto the cold balcony.

"Order your guards to stand down," said Olivia, her voice steel.

In the yard below, a dozen of the plantation's guards fought against four Brinkerhoff soldiers, who were each dodging and blocking their strikes easily. The Brinks' only weapons were round metal shields with fixed blades that jutted out beyond their fists. They fought dauntlessly against the Sadrians, striking their shield blades against the sabers, almost as if they were in a fistfight. Four guards already laid on the ground unconscious.

"Yeu call this fightin' mate?" shouted Sergeant Allard, who, like his compatriots, was short, broad shouldered, and red-haired. "I'm not en' breakin' a sweat."

"I know," replied another soldier. "It's like fightin' me grandam, except they got more teeth!" A couple of the Brinkerhoffs laughed at that.

A powerful swing sliced right where Sergeant Allard's head had just been. Another two followed, and he blocked both with his shield blades.

"What you want from us?" the plantation owner asked in broken common tongue.

"For you to order your men off!" Olivia repeated. "NOW!"

The man must have done the math, seeing his men outnumber the invaders three to one. "NEVER! KILL THEM ALL!"

Olivia sighed. "Have it your way." She put a fist up and dropped it down.

The Brinkerhoff soldiers switched to offensive, all joking gone. Immediately, the battle turned as they knocked down guards left and right. Ander, Garret, and Blaze opened fire from the balcony with blunt tipped bolts. Within seconds, all dozen guards were down and unconcious.

The husband's face went ash white. His wife next to him buried her face in his chest.

Ander swallowed. This was more violent than he was hoping for. But they had given the owner the opportunity to end this with as little conflict as possible.

Olivia turned her hooded face to the plantation owner. "Where are your slaves kept?"

"You take my property?" Anger seeped through the plantation owner's words.

Olivia leaned close to the man, her hood touching his forehead. "They aren't *property*. You took their freedom away. So I'm enacting my own mirabetal. I'm giving them their freedom back."

The man closed his mouth and looked away.

"Garret, Blaze," Olivia called. "Tie them up."

Olivia stalked into the bedroom. Ander watched her pull a knife from her belt and carve a large DSS into the wood.

"What are you doing?" Ander asked.

"I leave this mark on all locations we hit. That way, all people know to fear the Desert Steam Soldiers. That way," she looked at the plantation owner, "they think twice before ever buying another slave. We will know."

Ander whistled. He had to admit he was impressed with Olivia as a commanding officer. She certainly was a stark contrast to Bragg, who was a coward and only thought of himself.

Garret and Blaze dragged the couple to the backyard next to the tied-up guards. Then Olivia pulled in Lieutenant Harper's team to make a full sweep of the house while the infiltration team and the Brinks kept watch. Lieutenant Harper's team returned after a few minutes with a string of servants and no slaves. That left only one location left—the outbuilding.

Freya led the way across the yard with one of the guard's clay oil lamps in hand. Ander and Olivia followed a few steps behind. The closer they got to the building, the more decrepit it became. When they reached the doors, Ander realized it was nothing more than a battered shack.

At Olivia's command, Freya removed the wooden crossbar and opened the doors. The scent of body odor and feces crashed against them like a wave. Although the night was dark, the moonlight shone through the opening enough to highlight the half dozen slaves inside. The slaves stared up at them with empty, wary eyes. Their thin bodies were huddled together on the dirt, probably for warmth from the cold night. Only a couple blankets stretched across them, which wasn't enough to cover all of them. Their clothes were threadbare and barely covered them, some with holes where their chains had rubbed through. The structure was even more dilapidated from the inside, with pieces of the roof missing.

The scene made Ander sick. How could any human being do

something like this to another? Any sense of compassion he had felt for the owners was now gone.

Olivia stepped in first, with Ander a step behind. As he entered, the frigid chill of power washed over him in an instant.

No! He thought with despair. *This can't be happening again!* He scanned around the room, looking for its source. Olivia lowered her crossbow and crouched down before a young girl with her arms wrapped around a little boy.

"Don't be afraid," Olivia said.

Where is it?! Ander's mind buzzed with alarm. The power was palpable and building, The only other people in the room were the slaves.

"We're here to free you," Olivia continued. She threw off her hood. In the same second, the building power released, plunging from rafters straight toward Olivia.

Ander tackled her to the ground as a dagger sliced through the air and buried itself into the earth next to them. He whipped around and fired at a dark, cloaked figure high above in the shadowy rafters. The figure dodged the bolt and slipped through a gap in the roof before Ander's crossbow could reload.

"Assassin!" he shouted, rushing out of the building and skirting around its perimeter until he faced the fields. The assassin was already halfway through the fields. Sergeant Allred's team chased after, but Ander knew it would be no use. The assassin would be long gone by the time the Brinks reached the end of the fields.

Ander cursed and returned to the outbuilding. Both Olivia and Freya were staring at the dark dagger embedded in the ground. Ander peered at the knife. Its black metal was... dissolving?

He moved in closer and watched the blade melt away into a curl of dark smoke. His jaw dropped.

"How did that just happen?" Olivia asked. "I've never seen magic like this." She circled the hole where the weapon once was.

"I don't know," said Ander, running a hand through his hair. This wasn't normal elementalist magic. "This much we do know. Someone wants you dead."

Olivia stared at the hole for a moment longer before squaring her shoulders. "We must be getting close to finding some answers then. This is a good sign."

Ander shook his head. "Since when is almost being killed a good sign?"

Olivia chuckled. "Welcome to our line of work. It's a good thing you were here. That was quick thinking."

"Almost like you knew what was happening a fraction before it did," Freya added quietly.

Ander's throat went dry, and he turned to cough in his arm. Olivia patted him on the shoulder.

"Thank you for the save. Now, let's get these slaves as far away from here as possible before that assassin brings in city guards."

"Yes ma'am." He helped the slaves up, avoiding Freya's eyes in the process. Worry grew inside his gut as Freya leaned against the post of the door gazing at the ground in contemplation. She was behind him when he saved Olivia. What did she suspect?

I need to find out why this is happening to me! he thought urgently as he led the slaves out of the outbuilding. *Why am I manifesting Gifted-like abilities?* Someone would discover his abilities soon, and if he didn't have an explanation, they'd label him as a Gifted. He'd be discharged from service or worse. He'd lose everything.

. . . .

Ander remained silent as he, Olivia, Garret, and Blaze hurried across the dark cracked plains with only two of the half dozen Brinkerhoff slaves in tow. The other slaves were split across the other teams, heading to different hideouts. As they traveled, Ander's mind spun around the predicament of his abilities. Who would understand what was happening to him? Where could he go for answers?

He wished Amelia were with him—even if only for someone to talk to. It was a selfish thought, of course. Her mission at the archives was far more important than him. Still, that didn't stop him from silently wishing the situation was different.

He sighed. *No.* He'd have to figure this out on his own. The problem was, he could only think of one option. Find a Gifted healer and take a memory restorative to see if he was Gifted or Commonborn.

He shook his head. If hiding his abilities was risky, visiting a Gifted healer was more so. When would he get an opportunity alone in the city? Not to mention his earliest memory was the day his parents died. Did he really want to relive that?

The answer was a clear *no.* Still, time was running out for him. Eventually, someone would catch on, and he needed to know what he was when that happened. If reliving his worst memory was what it took to make that happen, then he needed to face it head on.

Fine, he thought, steeling himself. If the opportunity presented itself to visit a Gifted clinic, he'd take it. Until then, he needed to keep a lower profile and stay focused on the mission before him: taking down the slave trade.

The sun peaked above the horizon when they finally arrived at a hidden cave at the base of a remote mesa. The inside was dark, cool, and filled with supplies.

"We'll lie low here," said Olivia. "Ander, could you get our guests something to eat?"

Ander nodded and found a basket full of brown dates in the back of the cave. He returned with them and knelt before the two children.

"Here you go," he said, offering the basket to a girl no older than eleven and a boy half her age. They ate quickly, wolfing handfuls like they'd never seen food before.

"What are your names?" Ander asked.

The girl cleared her throat. "Me name's Enga. This is Kinlock, my bruther."

"Thank yeu for savin' uz," Kinlock said in a high voice.

Ander gave them a sad smile. "I'm sorry you were taken in the first place."

Olivia crouched down next to them. "Could you tell us how you were taken?"

The girl's expression paled, and she stared at the wall unseeing. It was a moment before she spoke. "Me mum an' dah... they didn't... didn't 'ave money for the Shaoguan dageuon. So the Shaoguan... they took uz." Tears began to stream down her face, and her brother buried his face in her stomach.

Garret put a hand on the girl's shoulder. "You'll see your parents again. Don't worry about that."

"What happened next?" Olivia pushed.

"This is important, Enga," Ander added more gently. "If we can figure out how they transported you, we could rescue more children like you."

Enga wiped her eyes and nodded. "They put uz in a cart with others an' traveled to the coast. Then they put uz on a boat."

"What did the boat look like?" asked Olivia.

Enga shook her head. "Don't know."

"Surely you saw something?" pressed Olivia.

Enga shook her head again. "We were blindfolded until we were inside."

"What was the inside like?" asked Ander.

Kinlock answered this time. "Long and metal. And ship didn't bob like me dah's fishin' boat."

Didn't bob? That was strange.

"What happened when you landed?" asked Olivia.

"We were blindfolded again," said Enga. "But when they took em off, it was night and we were in Sadria."

"What about buyers?" pressed Olivia. "What happened before you were purchased?"

"We were sorted wit' blindfolds. By the time oor blindfolds were gone, maist everyone wiz gone."

"Thank you for telling us this," said Olivia. She turned to Ander. "We already know special slave transfers have been happening in the military quarter. I've never heard of a metal Sadrian ship that only docks at night. That's new. I need you to visit the slaver docks."

"The docks?" Ander repeated.

"Yes. This ship doesn't sound typical. Knowing slavers, they'd know a lot more about it. Head there now and come back with something useful."

Another undercover mission, Ander thought. He ran a hand through his hair. Undercover missions were *not* his specialty. But this would get him into the city alone. Perhaps he could stop by a Gifted healer's shop after all.

"Alright," he said. Stress seeped into his shoulders at the thought of both going undercover and visiting a clinic. Did he really want to do this?

"Find out about this buyer too," Olivia added. "This isn't the first time I've heard about a buyer with deep pockets."

"Yes ma'am," he gave her a salute.

"Do you want to kick Garret out too?" asked Blaze with a wink.

Olivia frowned. "Take Corporal Attwell with you."

Great! Ander felt knots form in his shoulders. The last person he needed tagging along was Blaze.

You might not get another opportunity to visit a clinic, echoed an annoying voice in his head. *Blaze at least knows you used the Everblade.*

Yeah, but Blaze is a loudmouth, he replied. *How am I going to pull this off?*

"Ready to go?" Blaze asked.

Ander sighed. "Yep, let's do this."

Chapter 14: Deep Pockets

Ander

Ander and Blaze kept their heads down as they pushed through
traffic toward the Sadrian harbor. Buildings rose on all sides,
but the view of the ocean was finally opening up as the city streets
sloped downward toward the bay. Dozens of ships were out in the
harbor and the scent of salt was strong in the air.

Ander's shoulders were tight from the tension he felt inside. He
hadn't seen a single Gifted clinic the whole way. The heavy crowds
did nothing to ease his anxiety, either.

Act like you belong, like you've been here a thousand times. He
repeated the mantra over and over, hoping it'd make him blend in
better. The words had become a drumbeat inside his brain, though
they had done nothing to ease the stress he felt now.

He glanced to the north, where the colossal palace walls and
domes scraped the sky. Amelia was somewhere around there, either

at the embassy just outside or in the archives within. If it was the latter, that meant those walls separated them now. The fact he also knew those walls had never been breached in all of Sadrian history only made the distance feel greater.

He sighed. Who knew how much danger she was in, and that was just to get information to *find* the Wayfinder. They'd still need to get it afterward.

"You thinking about the same girl I am?" Blaze asked, interjecting into his thoughts.

Ander jolted. "What?"

"Olivia?"

"Oh." He pinched the bridge of his nose. "No. Why?"

Blaze gave a sigh of relief. "Good. You gotta leave some women for the rest of us, man."

Ander frowned, not understanding what that meant. Then again, half of the things Blaze said made no sense.

The shorter soldier threw his hands behind his head. "Plus, I think she and I are hitting it off nicely."

Ander choked on a laugh. That wasn't even remotely the truth. On day one, Olivia had thrown Blaze off the side of a mesa after calling her a battle-ready babe.

Blaze continued talking, but Ander only half listened. The buildings were becoming more affluent the closer they got to the beaches. Odds were good they'd find a Gifted clinic soon.

They traveled a few minutes longer before a distant *stamp, stamp, stamp* reached their ears. The sound repeated itself in a steady tempo. Ander slowed to listen.

"I mean, it's not that I'm no longer interested in brunettes anymore, but—"

"Blaze?"

"–I've been realizing blondes really are more my type."

Ander ran a hand down his face. "Blaze, could you shut up for a second and listen?"

"I, uh, okay," he looked thoroughly annoyed until his eyes suddenly popped. "*Oh!* Is that what I think it is?"

Ander nodded. "Troops. Khaldun's back."

Horns blew as if in reply, along with the distant cheers of crowds.

Blaze stood up on his toes and looked toward the direction of the sound. "I wonder what's going on?"

Ander frowned. "Let's find out." They changed course, heading northwest until they reached the source of the commotion.

Columns of Sadrian guards and cavalry paraded down main street toward the military sector. Centered in their ranks was a line of six rugged and battle-scarred prisoners. Behind them rolled a flat cart with a final prisoner.

He was broad and well-muscled, with chains shackling him into a permanent kneeling position. An ugly scar stretched across his wide face, running from his right temple to the left side of his thick beard. The top of his head was shaved such that it proudly revealed a large Mirage tattoo. What caught Ander's eye the most, however, was the man's power.

Dormant power rolled off the man like sand blowing over dunes. Instead of being bright in Ander's mind, it was dark and clouded, similar to the assassin from the night before.

Blaze whistled. "Remind me to never get in a fight with that guy."

A familiar figure appeared into view, riding a warhorse behind the cart.

"Khaldun!" Ander whispered. They ducked behind the crowd and kept their heads down as the Sadhdron bellowed to the crowd.

"Chained before you is Abdulmalik, the Insurrector, leader of the Mirage, and Whisperer of the Sadriconda! Soon, he and the Mirage scourge will be sent back to the pit of Har where they crawled! Balance will be restored again to Sadria!"

The crowd cheered.

"We need to go," whispered Ander. They moved backwards to the alleyway they came from until Ander paused.

On the opposite side of the procession was a building with the words *The Healing Oasis* painted above it.

Ander sighed. Naturally, the clinic was less than fifty feet from where he stood, and yet still separated from him by hundreds of marching guards.

"What's wrong now?" asked Blaze.

Ander shook his head. "Nothing. Let's get to the docks." Perhaps afterward, he could make a trip back.

They headed toward the glittering bay, where sandy streets gave way to wooden boardwalks. Ships of all sizes groaned and creaked in the ocean breeze while sailors carried casks and roamed about. Taverns and mariner-themed shops lined the boardwalks.

Blaze took a deep breath and then turned to Ander. "Where do you want to start?"

Ander scanned the docks before landing on a bustling tavern. "There."

"The Screaming Maiden?" Blaze asked with a raised eyebrow.

Ander shrugged. "Sounds like the place a slaver would eat at."

They walked up to the tavern doors and pushed through. Circular tables covered a large dining hall and were filled to overflowing with the gruffest men and women he had ever seen. Laughter roared through the room and fists hammered on tables. Drinks sloshed as sailors swung them wildly as they talked. The room smelled like spicy food mixed with body odor and bad breath.

Ander felt like he was shrinking inside himself. How was he supposed to do this? This was the most raucous, disorganized, undisciplined environment he had ever stepped foot. This wasn't where he belonged. These men enslaved people and killed for money. He was *nothing* like these men. How was he supposed to *socialize* with them?

"Who should we talk to first?" asked Blaze.

Ander pinched the bridge of his nose. They should do *something* before they drew attention to themselves. "Umm," he scanned the room and spotted a table occupied by a single man. "Let's go there."

"You sure?" Blaze asked.

Of course he wasn't, but he was already committed. He led the way over and sat down. Blaze took a seat next to him.

The sailor was much larger up close than from the entrance of the tavern. Even sitting, he loomed at least a foot taller and twice as broad as Ander. He leaned back in his chair with his arms folded so his muscles bulged twice their size.

"You don't belong here," growled the sailor.

Well, this is starting out great, Ander thought. He held up his hands placatingly. "We're sailors, same as you."

The sailor glared at them. "Go find a tavern in the city."

"We're just here to get a bite to eat and some news. What's the word on the street for the slave trade?"

The sailor cracked his knuckles and stood. Ander rose as well, sensing a fight coming. Figures rose all around and turned on him and Blaze in an instant. In a blink, their faces were smashed flat into the table and their arms pinned.

"You want the word on the street?" asked the large sailor. "Two foreigners were thrown out for not minding their own business." The sailor jerked a thumb towards the door. A pair of burly men dragged Ander and Blaze to the door and threw them into the street. The men laughed as the tavern door swung closed.

Anger surged through Ander as he picked himself up from the dust. He glared at the tavern door and shook his head. Who was he kidding himself? He wouldn't ever get information from crooks like these. They were lucky to have come out whole.

Blaze shook himself off. "Well, that could have gone better."

"Not the time for jokes, Blaze." Ander closed his eyes and racked his thoughts for a new idea. They couldn't go back to Olivia without something to report.

Blaze put a hand on his back. "Here, let me try."

"And do what?" The question came out much angrier than Blaze deserved. Still, the last thing he needed was for the Blaze to make things worse.

"I'm going to talk to one of those sailors." He pointed to two men fishing off the pier.

"Okay, and do what?"

"Relax, I got it." He flashed his signature smile. "I'll just slide up all smooth like and pretend I'm one of them. Maybe I'll drop the name of someone I know, like... Asad, yeah. You noticed how everyone around here's named Asad? Kind of like how all the girls in the Republic are named Emmaline?"

Ander ran a hand over his face and let out a long breath of air. "Whatever. Go for it."

Blaze walked to the sailors with a bounce in his step. After a second, Ander followed. He'd need to be there when this went south.

"Oi, mates," he threw his arms around the shoulders of the two sailors. "Did you see this guy get thrown out of the tavern there? Oh goodness, you've got to hear this story."

"Who are you?" asked one of them.

"Oh, me?" he put his arms down. "Blaze. I'd ask who you are, but I'm sure there's identification in here somewhere." He handed the man his wallet.

Ander stopped a few paces away and ran another hand through his hair. Did Blaze really just pickpocket him?

The sailor took it with a frown. "That better have everything in it."

"Of course it does," Blaze winked. "What crew are you part of?"

The sailor grunted. "Name's Taz. This is Farid."

Farid nodded.

"We're part of the *Sea Scorpion*," Taz continued. "What crew are you part of?"

"That ship over there." Blaze pointed toward a mass of ships that were cluttered together.

Taz frowned and eyed him suspiciously. "Who's your captain?"

Blaze shrugged. "Asad."

Both sailors broke into grins. "We love Captain Asad! Here, come sit down."

"Does your friend talk?" Farid asked in a deep voice, pointing at Ander. "Or does he just stare at people?"

"Oh him, ha, he's harmless." Blaze waved for Ander to join them. Ander sat down on the other side of Taz.

"What got you kicked out of the Screaming Maiden?" Taz asked

Ander. Ander opened his mouth, but Blaze spoke first.

"He tried hitting on one of the girls. Totally didn't know she was already taken by a first mate."

Taz grimaced. "You gotta death wish?"

"Yeah, Ander here's terrible with the ladies," Blaze said with a grin.

"You got kicked out too," said Farid to Blaze.

"That's because I got her to wink at me."

Both sailors roared in laughter and slapped Blaze on the back. Ander watched the interchange with shock. Two minutes and Blaze had already become one of them.

Blaze's expression turned serious. "I'm excited to join Asad's crew, but I'm worried about those Republic airships."

Taz put his hands behind his head and leaned back. "Aye, I hear you there."

Blaze continued. "Word on the street is there's a new ship that's been raking in all the money while the rest of us are struggling with the Republic."

Farid spat to the side. "That's Kareem's operation, that vile bilge rat."

"Kareem?" Blaze asked.

"Ah, that's right, you're new." Taz sat back up. "Kareem's always been lookin' for a way to get a foot above the rest of us. Made a deal with the sultan and now he's got a plushy secluded port in the military harbor."

"From the talk, it sounds like he's pulling in a lot of slaves."

"Aye, he is. He's still takin' all the Brinkerhoff routes and somehow comin' out unscathed while we take the heat."

"How is he doing it?" Blaze asked.

Taz glanced in either direction before lowering his voice to a whisper. "Been tryin' to figure that out ourselves. Rumor has it that it's a sea serpent swallowing slaves up and spitting them out, if you take stock in that kind of thing. Kareem only ports at night and is gone by morning. Very mysterious. His crew are nearly all Gifted, powerful Gifted mind you, so anything could be possible."

Interesting, Ander thought. He didn't give much credit to the sea serpent theory, but the rumor was certainly an attempt to cover the real process.

"That's got to be expensive," Blaze leaned back as well.

"Aye, but Kareem's workin' with a buyer with deep pockets. I don't know his name, but he's been buyin' nearly all the slaves who can swing an axe or sledgehammer and porting them north."

Porting them north? What was north? "Do you know where?" Ander asked.

Both sailors looked at him as if they just remembered he was there. "Nope, but whatever they're doing, it's a massive operation."

A massive operation. So many questions swirled around Ander's head, and he didn't know which to focus on first. One thing was certain, however. This operation was a threat to the Republic.

He rose to his feet. Blaze looked at him and frowned. "Where are you going?"

"I need to stretch my legs," Ander replied vaguely. "I'll be back in a few minutes."

He retraced his steps back to where they watched the parade of guards. The guards were now gone, replaced by heavy foot traffic and carts. He caught sight of the clinic and felt butterflies flutter in his stomach in response.

I'm doing this, he thought. *I'm really doing this.*

His heart pounded as he crossed the street and pushed through the door. *Ding* came a bell from over his head. An attendant approached him from a desk and bowed.

"How might I serve you today?" the attendant asked in the desert tongue.

Ander surveyed the room, which seemed to serve as part waiting area and part shop. On the wall were rows of bottles filled with liquids and herbs. The environment felt far more organized and cleaner than the small village healer's.

Ander cleared his throat. "Do you have an elixir that can restore memories?"

"What kind of memories and how deep?" the attendant asked, switching to the common tongue.

"From when I was a child."

"Hmm." The attendant walked toward a wall and gestured to a row of bottles Ander couldn't read. "We carry many memory restoratives. They work if you can recall a fragment."

"I can do that." There were aspects of his parent's deaths that he'd never forget.

"Then these will do what you need," said the attendant.

Ander picked up a bottle and examined it. "How does it work?"

"A healer will administer the drink while you think about the memory. Then, when your mind and body are in a similar state as the memory, the memory will trigger." The attendant raised a cautionary finger. "Your physical and mental state must be real, however, and not imagined or hallucinated for it to trigger. Otherwise, it won't work."

Ander stared at the bottle as he processed the information. He'd have to be in a similar mental and physical state as the memory?

What kind of experience could do that for the day his parents died?

Images flashed in front of his eyes. He was on the *Legacy* again at night. A massive, horrible beast leapt onto Amelia and ripped her over the railing. Her screams rent the air—

Ander immediately set the restorative back on to the shelf and stumbled away from the attendant. "I'm sorry," he stammered. "I can't do that. I can't go through that again."

"What is this memory you are—"

Ander exited the clinic before the attendant finished his question. He briskly walked to the nearest alleyway, heedless of the people he bumped through to get there. As soon as he was alone in the shadows, he leaned over and ran his hands through his hair.

This isn't going to work, he thought. *I can't lose someone I care about again.*

Chapter 15: Interview

Amelia

A melia's fingers shook with nerves as she applied makeup in front of a long mirror with gilded edges. Her hair was already curled and piled neatly on top of her head, pinned in place with a jeweled comb. The comb matched her emerald green dress and was complemented by her dark overcoat.

The last formal event for which she had dressed like this was the masquerade ball at Castella Manor. She smiled at the memory. It felt like years ago, though she could vividly recall the terror she felt riding away on a stolen carriage while enraged Gifted soldiers chased after her and Ander. As frightening as that night was, it paled compared to this evening.

Within an hour, she, Amir, and Hammer would meet Khaldun for an interview. The high commander had returned yesterday from a conquest and accepted the Keeper's request to meet with Lady

Canterloch and her entourage. What the Keeper hadn't explained until a few hours ago was that the interview would happen over dinner.

Despite the fine furnishing of the embassy, her room reflected her inner state: chaotic. Her trunk was only half unpacked, her bed was a mess, and her lunch sat untouched on an end table.

Amir hadn't made the stress any easier. Ever since the interview was scheduled, he reminded Amelia every chance he got to not mess it up.

She was about to have dinner with the most dangerous man in all of Sadria. Messing up was the *last* thing she wanted to do.

There was one thing that she and Amir had agreed upon. She wasn't to attempt any more "magic." She got lucky last time. If the Keeper had been more observant, she'd be sitting in a prison rather than an excessively plush room.

She finished applying her makeup and gave a long exhale. She felt queasy, and the last thing she felt like doing was eating.

She looked into the mirror and thought again of the masquerade ball—where she met Ander for the first time. She smiled at the memory. He made a terrible dance partner, let alone an undercover agent. At the dance, he had even referred to her as ma'am.

Her smile fell. She wished he was here with her. She hadn't realized how comforting it was to have his steady presence around. He wouldn't be there to give her a stolen carriage ride if things went south.

A knock sounded at the door. She took another breath and said, "Come in."

The door opened and Amir and Hammer stepped in. Both were dressed in the finery of servants, though Hammer's outfit was much simpler given his status.

"Ready?" asked Hammer.

She nodded.

"You pretty."

She blushed. Hammer was always kind to her. Even after a couple weeks of him playing the slave role, it still pained her to treat him like a slave. She knew from experience that he would sacrifice his own life for hers in a heartbeat.

Amir folded his arms. "You're going to be late if you take any longer."

Amelia glared at him. "I don't see you wearing makeup and a gown." She stood up and slipped on a pair of silver laced gloves. "Now I'm done."

"Finally," Amir muttered. She ignored him, grabbed her satchel, and followed the men out of the room.

They passed through a sandstone hall that was covered with pastel paintings of the shining desert, the towering walls of the city, and the golden domes of the palace. Potted plants hung from ceiling planters and were filled with white flowered cacti, tentacled aloe plants, and many others she didn't recognize. No one was in the hall, but that seemed to be typical these last weeks. With the Sadrian-Republic Slave Conflict happening, very few diplomats were staying at the embassy, and she avoided any that were there. Every encounter she had with another person increased her chances of being found out and discovered. That strategy, however, wasn't going to work this evening. There was no way to avoid Khaldun if she wished to get into the archives.

They passed through the reception atrium and exited the building into the harsh sunlight. The late afternoon heat hit her like a suffocating wave, increasing the nausea she felt inside. She grimaced and used a hand to shield her eyes.

A covered carriage waited for them, with the Keeper standing by its door. The tall Keeper of the Embassy bowed deeply as they approached and offered Amelia a hand. She took it and allowed him to help her into the carriage. Amir followed, taking the spot next to her. Hammer disappeared to the back step of the carriage to take the only seat in the open sun.

When the carriage began moving, Amelia looked out the window at the gleaming golden domes of the palace. The domes disappeared from view as they approached the massive palace walls. They soared over eight stories high and cast long shadows across the bay. The height was so tall, she was sure it was impractical. The guards on top would barely see anything happening below.

Before they reached the palace walls, the carriage veered toward an adjacent segment of the city surrounded by a much shorter wall. When they arrived at a gate, guards stopped them and searched their carriage and bags. Then they were waved through.

Rows of utilitarian buildings rose along both sides of the street, with guards spilling in and out. The clanging of metal filled the air, along with the scent of molten steel. In the distance, an armada of red-sailed warships rose and fell next to the docks.

Amelia swallowed. No wild carriage ride would save her this time if things went wrong. She was walking into a lion's den.

The carriage slowed to a stop at a simple, two-story building. Khaldun emerged from its shadows, flanked by guards. Again, the Sadhdron wore a guard uniform similar to the others, but his eyes were dark with intelligence. He approached the carriage calmly and held out a hand to Amelia.

Amelia swallowed a sticky lump in her throat. Only days ago, this man tried to imprison her for no other reason than twisted tradition. Thankfully, she was in disguise at the time. He didn't even seem to recognize her eyes, which was good. She, on the other hand, would never forget his face nor the way he callously selected her for punishment.

She held her head high and took the high commander's hand, allowing him to lead her off the carriage. The others followed before guards closed in all around.

Amelia kept her expression aloof, while inside she felt like she was suffocating. Why did she accept this assignment? Getting into the archives was *far* more dangerous than what she had thought.

Khaldun let her hand drop before clasping his own behind his back. He greeted the Keeper and turned his attention to Amelia.

"Welcome to my city, Lady Canterloch." His voice sounded permanently parched.

"Thank you," she said in a haughty tone. "It certainly is a shining jewel, for at least this side of the great sea."

Khaldun's eyes narrowed slightly before responding in a cool, calculated tone. "Only the strong thrive in the harshest of environments."

A chill went down her spine, sending prickles up her arms. She was treading on dangerous ground. Khaldun was not one to be condescending toward.

He eyed her and her companions with a calculating expression before saying, "Come this way. Your servants too." He turned and began toward the building. Amelia hesitated only a breath before raising her chin and following.

Khaldun led them through a sparsely furnished reception area, down a hall, and into a room with a long table. The room looked suspiciously like a war room that was retrofitted to accept guests. Slaves were setting out wicker mats on the table with plain plates and utensils. They could have been the same place settings used in the guards' own mess halls.

Khaldun gestured around and said, "Take a seat." They each sat down around the edges while Khaldun took the head of the table. Some guards sat at the table with them while a couple took positions at the door. Hammer remained standing.

The guards are joining us too? That didn't bode well. As far as Amelia knew, they could be anyone from new recruits to generals.

More slaves arrived and ladled steaming bowls of soup to the group and set flatbread to the sides. The food was simple, just like the room's furnishings.

The Keeper grimaced and turned to Amelia. "Forgive the lack of adornment and finery. The Sadhdron makes a special effort to ensure he is offered the same degree of luxury as the soldiers he oversees, despite my attempts to convince him otherwise for occasions like these."

Huh. She always wondered why Khaldun never dressed differently from the other guards. Obviously, he didn't take stock in finery or in distinguishing himself above others. Instead, he endured the same things as the guards he led. There was something to respect in that.

Of course, what she saw at the Serenity Pools painted the Khaldun in a far different light. He was the Sadhdron, the high commander, the keeper of the peace, the balancer of the scales of justice. He was dangerous and cunning. Despite how he portrayed himself, he was no common man.

After a guard offered a brief prayer to Soleth in the Sadrian tongue, the group began to eat. Amelia eyed the soup and sipped a spoonful. The spicy warm liquid seared down her throat and it was all she could do to keep from coughing.

Khaldun didn't touch his food. Instead, he studied Amelia, Amir, and Hammer with calculating eyes. Finally, he addressed Amelia.

"Tell me. Why do you need access to the archives?"

Sweat beaded along Amelia's temples, and her mouth felt numb. She took a long sip of cold water before clearing her throat.

"My master, Lady Tornala, was tasked with a specific assignment from the Arcanum. My role was to assist. However, since we were attacked by a Republic airship, all I've been able to think about since was how the Republic will keep terrorizing from the skies until we Gifted find a way of flying too. I believe there could be a way to use magic to help our ships fly. I just need access to the archives so I can research my ideas."

Khaldun turned to Amir. "And you?"

Amir bowed respectfully. "I'm just a scholarly servant, here to help."

Khaldun clasped his fingers together and brought them to his lips. Then he turned to Amelia.

"Can you do magic?"

Uh-oh. Why would he ask that unless he thought she was a fraud?

She nodded. "Yes, of course I can do magic."

"Really?" His lips curved into a tilted smile.

"I can vouch for her," said the Keeper. "Lots of power and very little control. Lit herself on fire in the process."

Khaldun appeared unconvinced. "Your accent," he said, staring

CRAIG & JALEESA SNOW

at Amelia, "has traces of the Republic of Steam." It was a statement, not a question. "Your hands are also calloused, not soft like a typical noblewoman."

Cold sweat trickled down the back of Amelia's neck, having nothing to do with the spicy food.

Khaldun continued. "Your servant appears to be native and a scholar, like you've explained. Your slave, however, is more dangerous than the ordinary slave. Strong, coordinated. Not broken."

He leaned forward in his chair. "Tell me I'm wrong."

She swallowed. "No, you aren't wrong. I've spent time in the Republic of Steam as an undercover agent. I collected information about airships and their construction. I even worked as an apprentice carpenter."

The Keeper's eyes widened. "So you know how they're built?"

"In a manner of speaking, yes," Amelia replied. "But don't get too excited. The technology is complex and would be difficult to replicate outside of the Republic. But I do believe there could be a magical way to create an equivalent."

So far, all that she said was at least partially true. She had lived in the Republic, been an agent, and knew about airships. It was also hypothetically possible to use magic to power airships.

Khaldun didn't look convinced. "Prove it. Tell me how it could be done."

She let out a sigh of relief. This, at least, was an answer she had prepared for. Still—any information she gave about airship construction was dangerous. If enemy nations learned how to build airships, the Republic would no longer be safe. At the same time, if she didn't get into the archives and find the location of the Wayfinder, again the safety of the Republic would be at risk.

I'm in too deep now. She opened her satchel and pulled out a wire, napkin, and a small vial of oil.

"Airships," she explained, "rise because they are filled with hydrogen. Creating hydrogen requires electricity, which is a power we Gifted do not possess."

The Keeper cleared his throat. "There have been rumors in history about some having the ability."

Amelia shrugged. "Sure, let's assume the answer to that was a definite yes. You'd need one of those people to fuel each airship, but with such a small number of people, that's not a scalable option."

"Interesting," said the Keeper. Khaldun, on the other hand, remained silent.

Amelia swallowed. "What most people don't know is that hydrogen isn't the only way to make objects rise."

She bent the wire into a cylindrical frame. Then she wrapped the outside of it with a napkin. When she finished, it looked like a paper lantern. Then she applied a bit of oil on the wire on the inside and passed it to the Keeper.

"Would you ignite this? I would, but you know that would ruin the demonstration." She gave him a wry smile.

The Keeper ignited the wire, bringing a small, candlewick-sized flame to life.

"Heat also rises." She took the lantern from the Keeper and bumped the bottom of it into the air. The lantern rose and continued until it hit the ceiling. Several of the guards *oohed* at the sight.

"That is an impressive demonstration," said the Keeper. "But a ship is much heavier than a wire."

Amelia nodded. She was entering dangerous space now—some might even say traitorous. "You assume that an airship must actually be a ship. That's not a requirement. You could construct it to be anything lightweight and strong."

Khaldun now looked more interested. "You believe our archives hold answers?"

She nodded. "The Sadrians are known for their brilliance in ship designs and constructions. There's no better place to find inspiration, and our two nations have never had a more common enemy."

"What do you intend to do when you figure out how to create these ships?" asked Khaldun.

She smiled. "I will share it, of course. To all the Republic's enemies." As soon as the words left her mouth, she felt sick to her stomach, but based on Khaldun's smile, it had its intended effect.

"All right," Khaldun rose to his feet. "I'll grant you access to the archives. You will be escorted for each of your visits, and you will report directly to me at the end of the month. By then, I want to see schematics for how to make this a reality."

She swallowed. This was a much less ideal arrangement than she had in mind. But she didn't have much of a choice.

"Thank you."

"Good. Understand this, however." Khaldun leaned forward. "If any of you step out of line, you will be punished. Mirabetal. Understood?"

She understood clearly. Somehow, she was going to need to find out about the Wayfinder without getting caught or giving Khaldun more information about airships.

"Understood," she replied.

Chapter 16: Archives

Amelia

The carriage arrived with the rising sun. Amelia leaned back against the velvet pillows. Excitement filled her as she thought about the prospect of finally researching the Wayfinder. The feeling was surreal, especially after spending weeks working toward this moment. Not even bleary-eyed Amir's sour greeting was enough to bring her down. This was the day where she was going to prove that all the sacrifice was worth it. By the end of the day, she was going to come back with results, proving that everyone was wrong to judge and doubt her.

The driver whistled at the horses and set the carriage rattling forward. Adobe buildings passed on either side of them as they rode toward the rising golden domes and massive walls. Soon, the palace walls dominated the entire horizon and sky. As they neared its edge, dizziness took over her. The walls were so tall; they looked like they were perpetually about to fall over.

The carriage came to a stop before the palace wall gates. She stepped out and took in the size of the impressive doors, which were at least five times the height of a normal door and inlaid with a golden motif of a rising sun over desert dunes. Guards searched Amelia, Amir, and Hammer and their belongings before signaling the gates to open.

Stone grated upon stone as the gates opened into an entirely different world. The dusty road transformed into polished sandstone, with beautiful statues on either side that cascaded waterfalls of glittering sand. Bushes of exotic flowers filled the gaps between the statues and bloomed in reds, oranges, and yellows. More thick vegetation grew behind these, ranging from lush ferns to towering palms.

Beyond the vegetation rose magnificent buildings, each rising to new heights until they reached the palace itself, which soared above everything else and ended in its signature golden domes.

The sight was incredible, making the dusty streets behind them look colorless and barren in perspective. Even just the quantity of vegetation seemed at odds with the arid world all around.

"Miss Canterloch?" Two guards took positions on either side of the group. "We will be your escorts for your visit today."

Great, she thought sarcastically. *I almost forgot about the extra dead weight.* She put on a fake smile. "Thank you. Could you guide the way forward?"

They followed the guards down the path, passing more and more breathtaking scenery. After a minute, they deviated from the main path and angled to the left. Here, the gardens gave way to dusty construction and dozens of slaves. Task masters strode along the slaves, cracking whips as the slaves shaped sandstone blocks and mortared the blocks together with their magic.

The sight repainted the entire palace into a new light, replacing its beauty with gilded ugliness. *Was this how the palace was created? On the backs of enslaved people?*

So much for the sultan's stance on neutrality regarding slavery, she thought. Clearly it was all a lie, but she supposed she knew that before coming here.

Hammer's posture grew stiff as they passed the construction site, and she wished she could reach out and comfort him. Of course, for the sake of her persona she couldn't. But that didn't stop her from giving him a sympathetic look.

Soon they reached a three-story building with towers, arches, and varying levels of roofs. Hammer moved to open the doors.

They walked into an atrium with plush chairs and red carpet. An elderly woman wearing a shawl sat behind a polished reception desk before them. She stood as they entered.

"Welcome to the Sadrian Archives," said the elderly woman. "My name is Masovia." She walked around the desk and gave them a bow. "How might I help you today?"

Amelia opened her mouth and hesitated. She couldn't just ask for information about the Wayfinder with the two guards standing right there.

I need to get a feel for what's in the archives, she thought. *That'll help me plan how to disguise my actual research.*

Her lips parted into a smile. "I'm new here. Could we have someone give us a tour before we begin our work?"

"Absolutely," said Masovia to Amelia. "Let me get Fasiya, our guide." Masovia disappeared.

As soon as Masovia left the room, Amir groaned. "Do we really need a tour?" he muttered from the side of his mouth. "I could probably give one myself."

Amelia shook her head and subtly glanced at their guard escorts to emphasize why. He continued to stare at her uncomprehendingly.

She sighed. How could she silently explain to him that having her servant give a tour would draw attention and break their cover?

She didn't have an answer yet when Masovia reappeared with another Sadrian woman. The newcomer bowed to Amelia and said, "I am Fasiya. Are you ready?"

Amir gave Amelia a hard look.

"Yes," Amelia replied, keeping her eyes on Fasiya.

Amir ran a hand down his face.

"Great," said Fasiya, totally oblivious of Amir's silent complaints. "Right this way." She turned around and led the way through a set of double doors. Amelia followed closely, barely catching Amir muttering the words *infuriating* and *Steams*.

Fasiya stopped and, with a flourish of her hand, said, "Welcome to the central gallery." Behind her was a vast, three-story room, complete with a domed glass ceiling. Rows upon rows of books lined the edges; their cases stretched high into the air. Displays spread across the center of the room, filled with ancient armor, rusted weapons, conch shells, tarnished coins, sections of ships, and more. What pulled Amelia's attention the most, however, was the full sadriconda skeleton that wrapped around the ceiling twice. A few dozen people roved about the room and studied at tables.

She took a deep breath. If this was just the central gallery, she had a lot of work to do. There were thousands upon thousands of books in this room alone. Any one of them could hold the answers she was seeking. This was going to be a lot harder than she thought. Fortunately, she had Amir to help. Otherwise, the task would be impossible with the time they had.

"How familiar are you with Sadrian history?" asked Fasiya.

"Very," Amir muttered at the same time Amelia said, "Tell me everything."

Fasiya frowned at Amir and shifted her attention to Amelia. "When people come to Sadria, most only see desert dunes and barren landscapes. What only a few realize is that it was not always so. Long ago, the Sadrian Sands were once called the Sahadrian Seas. Those seas spanned across much of what is now barren landscape, and it teamed with life."

Amelia tilted her head. She never heard of Sadria once having seas. After flying over much of it, it seemed implausible. Still, she did her best to appear polite rather than skeptical.

"Come see this." Fasiya led them to a case that was filled with iridescent sea shells and fossilized coral. "These," she gestured, "were found in the deep heart of the desert, along with many other signs of sea life. Back then, the mainland and archipelagos were tropical and fertile. Our ancestors flourished under the watchful eye of Sarlketh, serpent goddess of the seas. It is said that gold coins were as plentiful then as the grains of sands are now."

Another exaggeration, Amelia thought. Still, she followed Fasiya to another case with tarnished gold coins, each embossed with a sea dragon on one side and a palace with a soaring, turnip shaped tower on the other side. Behind the coins was a faded papyrus illustration of the same palace.

"What changed?" Amelia asked.

Fasiya looked down. "Our ancestors allowed imbalance to

prevail over their way of life."

"Mirabetal?" Amelia clarified.

Fasiya nodded. "Wars broke out and grew so great, the gods intervened. Sarlketh ripped the seas from our lands, removing our source of prosperity and wealth. Soleth followed and scorched the earth until all that remained was desolate sands and broken mesas. Finally, Varis, hooded crow goddess of the underworld, rent the plains and opened pits straight to Har. From these slithered the dreaded scourge of our lands, the mighty sadricondas."

This is some intense history, Amelia thought. She glanced at Amir. The scholar had his arms folded and tapped his foot impatiently.

"The good news," Fasiya continued, "is that all of this happened nearly a thousand years ago. Since the founding of Sadria, our leaders have maintained the balance. Prosperity has returned, and we have again become a great people."

Based on what Amelia saw just outside these archives, she had a very different perspective on what balance meant, but she didn't argue the point.

"Come," said Fasiya, "let me show you more of the archives." They passed a group of scholars huddled around a table before exiting into an arched hallway. Fasiya led them past a series of study rooms and alcoves before taking them into a wide, rectangular room. A long table filled the center of the room and was covered with a single, massive map of Sadria. More maps were pinned to the walls, focusing on specific regions and cities.

"This is the map room," Fasiya announced. "On the table before you is the Great Sadrian Chart—the accumulation of a thousand expeditions into the sands. It represents our best understanding of

Sadria, acknowledging that many of these features are continuously changing."

Amelia walked around the table and examined the map with curiosity. Apparently, their flight out of the Southern Sadrian Range had taken them through Emberstorm Alley, which explained the storm they hit. She continued scanning through the names. Some were familiar, like the Sadrian Sands, but most were unfamiliar.

One feature in particular caught her eye. "What's this?"

Fasiya walked around the table to see what she was pointing at. "Oh, Shipwreck Sands." She paused a beat. "I'm not sure."

Amir cleared his throat. "During the days of the Sahadrian Seas, this region was a frequent target for raiders and pirates. As the seas departed, the bones of the sunken ships were left behind. They can still be seen today."

"Really?" Amelia asked.

"Don't even think about doing any treasure hunting," Amir clarified. "Many have tried. The place is infested with sadricondas."

Amelia gave him a raised eyebrow. "It was just a question." She made a mental note to revisit this room later. The details and scale of this map put her own to shame.

"Let's continue," said Fasiya. "Lots more to see." She took them next to a whole wing of the library dedicated to Elementalist magics. The wing alone boasted over several thousand books, ranging from magics relating to herbology, toxicology, desert survival, warfare, self-defense, alchemy, rituals, and many more. Amelia didn't see any sections on ancient magics or talismans, but they moved too quickly for her to be thorough.

They traveled next through the west atrium, passing a lone cherry oak door with archaic characters inscribed across the top.

Amelia paused in her footsteps. "Fasiya, what's that?" she asked, pointing to the door.

Fasiya turned around. "Oh, that's the door to the Arcanum section. Are you a member?"

"Not yet," she replied. "I hope to be soon."

"Then I'm afraid it's off limits to you and your companions."

"What's in there?" she pressed.

Fasiya shrugged. "I'm not a member of their order, either. However, I do know the Order of Arcanum's purpose is to bring back ancient usages of magic. I would assume the collection in there would help them with that purpose."

Ancient magic, she mentally repeated. Of all the sections, this seemed the most promising to her search. "Does the order ever allow guests?"

Fasiya shook her head no. "The Arcanum is very particular about who can access their research and collections. It's locked with a specific magical combination, so not even our Gifted staff have the ability to unlock the door for cleaning."

Amelia eyed the door again, noticing the subtle impression of a hand underneath the knob. If she took some time to study it further, she could probably figure out how it worked. She'd have to examine it unescorted, however.

"With your aspirations to join them, maybe one day you can tell me what's in there," Fasiya said with a wink. "Until then, it's off limits unless you wish to risk imprisonment under Sadrian law."

"Are there any other places we're not allowed to enter?" Amelia asked, curious if there were any other restricted collections like this one.

Fasiya looked up in thought. "There's no construction

happening this time of year. The only other place I can think of is in the records wing. Anything behind the service desk is restricted to staff only. Visitors aren't allowed to go through the census and tax records, of course. But you are always welcome to make requests at the service desk. Shall we proceed with our tour?"

Amelia nodded. They continued on through many more collections, making a full circle through the archives before finishing back in the central gallery. There, Fasiya stopped and clasped her hands together. "This concludes our tour. If you need help finding anything, just ask the aids here to help."

"Thank you," said Amelia. Fasiya bowed and left.

"Finally," said Amir, taking a seat at a table. "I thought that would never end."

"Amir! Maybe say that a little more quietly," said Amelia, watching Fasiya exit the gallery, passing their two guard escorts who had taken up position by the doors.

Amir followed her gaze and shrugged. "We're far enough away from our escorts. Besides, if they could hear us, I'm sure they'd agree."

Her jaw dropped open. "I was talking about Fasiya." She turned to Hammer. "Would you mind grabbing food for us? I believe that tinkling bell earlier was to signal lunchtime, and my stomach is growling."

Hammer nodded and left.

Amir folded his arms and lowered his voice. "You realize you just wasted half a day? That's another half day that my niece is out there somewhere, slaving in the hot sun."

"Don't you think it would be suspicious if we came in already knowing everything about the archives?" she shot back. "Besides, I thought the tour was very informative."

Amir shook his head disgustedly. "You're exactly like your grandfather. Stubborn and delusional."

She clenched her jaw and spoke in a heated whisper. "My grandfather was not delusional!"

Amir leaned forward and matched her intensity. "He came here paranoid that something dark from his nightmares was out to kill him. Something that could change shape into anything or anyone. He once thought it was me and nearly lit me on fire with his lamp! If that's not delusional, I don't know what is."

"That can't be right. He invented the you-know-what and founded the you-know-what. He was as sharp as a razor!"

"Well, get this. He came here looking for the fabled Wayfinder, just like you. Do you know why?"

She could sense Amir was setting her up with this question, but curiosity still propelled her to ask. "Why?"

"He was looking for *another* library, if you can believe it. As if there's not enough literature already here for a hundred lifetimes."

She screwed her face up. "What do you mean, *another* library?"

"He was trying to find the legendary Great Library of Illithador, which has been gone since the Great Collapse a thousand years ago. Point is, he thought the *mythical* Wayfinder would help him find it."

"How do you know if the Wayfinder's a myth?" she shot back.

"Did your wise old grandfather find it?"

Her back went rigid. "That's not a fair question! He left fourteen years ago on a voyage and never returned!"

Amir leaned back and folded his arms. "I rest my case then."

She stood and glared at him fiercely. "Maybe," she said in a heavy whisper, "he couldn't find it because *you* were his help."

Amir glared right back at her. "If that's how you feel, then you can research it yourself."

She balled her hands into trembling fists. "If that's how *you* feel, you can forget coming back here with me. I'll ask the guards to throw you out, and I'll work with the staff here instead."

Amir's eyes widened. "Finding the Wayfinder is delusional—"

"No, you are delusional!" She jabbed him with a finger so hard, he nearly tipped over in his chair. Her voice dropped to the barest of whispers. "This isn't some recreational pursuit. I have authorization from the highest levels of my government to find the talismans to the Source! There's a whole crew of us dedicated to this effort and dangerous powers trying to stop us. We've lost lives, and we've seen firsthand that the talismans are real. I know the Wayfinder is out there, and we will find it. The only question is if you will help me, or if I need to ask the guards to give you a swift kick to the rear on your way out of the palace. Good luck finding your niece then."

Hammer reappeared with three wicker bowls of food. He looked between Amir and Amelia. "Is there problem?"

Amelia turned away from the scholar and nodded to Hammer. "Yes, could you get the guards and have them escort—"

"Fine," said Amir with a stammer. "I'll do it, but on one condition. You have to help me get into the records wing."

She folded her arms. This wasn't their original arrangement. Her role was to get them through the gates, which she had done. Now it was his turn to help her with her research. Still, she knew there was no way to force Amir to help her, not when his only motivation was to find his niece.

"Fine!" she said while pinching the bridge of her nose. "I'll help you. Can we now move on?"

Amir gave a tired nod before grabbing a bowl of food from

Hammer. She and Hammer sat, and they all ate food in tense silence.

After a few minutes, Amir cleared his throat. "Where do you want to begin?"

She blinked. "Where do *I* want to begin? Didn't you help my grandfather? Couldn't you catch me up on what you found, and we start from there?"

Amir gave a long sigh. "This was over fourteen years ago. I can't remember much, and what I can remember I blocked out. We must have pulled over a hundred books, including some from the Arcanum section—which he had special access to."

She opened her mouth and closed it. *Great!* she thought. *We're starting from ground zero.* "Give me a moment to think."

In her mind, she ran through the words in the scroll she had stolen from the Library of the Chosen:

The Source of Great Power alone is not taken.
Four are required to make it awaken.

One finds the gate.
One leads the way.
One sparks the power.
One makes it stay.

The four were divided among the great nations.
Each was challenged to protect them from being taken.

A lens was given to the king of the sand.
An emerald of power for the general's command.
A sword of fire to the bearer of name.

And last, an amulet to those of fame.

Should this scroll in the wrong hands be taken,
A warning I give, the world will be shaken.'

The lens was what they were looking for, a talisman that could guide anyone to any location they wished. If the lens was originally given to the king of the sand, then a good place to start was to look through the history of the kings.

She shared this with Amir, and after finishing lunch, they began their search. They pulled volume after volume and looked into each. With each successive book, Amelia became more and more discouraged. The history of Sadria only went back about three hundred years when the first Sultan, General Sadria, took power. Everything beyond that was only vaguely referenced. None of it ever mentioned the Wayfinder.

When evening fell, they left the archives without any luck. Frustration burned through Amelia. Aesop's scroll was written a thousand years ago. Which meant, *if* the Wayfinder was originally given to Sadria, she had a gap of seven hundred years missing about its whereabouts. Unless, of course, that information was covered in the Arcanum section. But attempting that would put all of them at risk.

This is going to be much harder than I thought, she realized. Still, it was a large library with lots of possible routes to pursue. Maybe one of those routes would yield results.

Chapter 17: Discoveries

Ander

Waves rippled through the Sadrian harbor, slowly pushing Ander and Sergeant Allard toward the distant docks. The two soldiers floated silently in the dark with their spyglasses trained on the empty piers ahead.

A week had passed since Ander and Blaze reported to Olivia what they learned from the sailors at the harbor. Since then, Olivia ordered a nightly watch on the Sadrian military harbor. So far, all was quiet. No mysterious ships had been seen.

Ander lowered his spyglass and stretched his aching neck, making sure he didn't dunk his head in the process. Across his body were pig bladders filled with air. This allowed him to float without treading water. As convenient as that was, the occasional wave that crashed over his head was not. His eyes burned from the salt, and he couldn't wait for his shift to end.

Sergeant Allred, on the other hand, seemed like he was born for this type of stake out. He hadn't uttered a single complaint. In fact, it almost looked like he was enjoying it.

Ander let out a long, tired sigh. At least Freya wasn't on this mission. Ever since the plantation raid, she had kept annoyingly close to him. She volunteered for all the same assignments, and he felt her constant scrutinizing gaze. Fortunately, he hadn't needed to use his abilities again since the raid, but he knew it was only a matter of time before he did. What would happen then?

Hopefully Amelia finds the trail to the Wayfinder before that happens, he thought. That would allow him to close up his arrangement with Olivia. He could organize assignments after that and more easily deal with Freya.

Of course, he knew that wouldn't completely solve his problem. Whether it was Freya or someone else, he'd always have to hide his abilities. What he really needed to do was verify his blood status. He needed to prove that he wasn't a Gifted—just an ordinary Commonborn with an abnormal sensitivity to Gifted power.

Knowing that he needed to verify his blood status was easy. Figuring out *how* was proving to be difficult altogether. Short of taking a memory restorative, he still hadn't found another option. If he couldn't soon, he might have to concede and take one, but he hated the thought.

A sixth sense flared up in his mind, snapping his attention to full alert. Quickly, he scanned all around, trying to find its source. The waters and docks appeared just as they had been for the last few hours. Nothing was moving except for the rippling waves.

Sergeant Allard looked at him with a raised eyebrow. *What?* he mouthed.

Don't know, Ander mouthed back. Unease grew inside him, swelling like a thunderstorm. The feeling grew steadily until suddenly, the water all around them rose upward like a building tsunami.

The soldiers gaped in surprise as they were lifted and then dropped into rolling waves. A massive serpentine shape passed underneath them, shimmering with a murky glow of power. Ander stared with widening eyes. It looked like a mythical sea dragon, and it was heading straight for the docks!

His heart raced as his mind fought against what he was seeing. Sea dragons weren't real. They were myths, legends, folklore. As a child, he had heard fairytales about them.

His eyes told a very different story.

Goosebumps erupted across his whole body. He and Allred were exposed in the open water. If that thing turned around, they'd be sitting ducks!

"We need to go," Ander whispered urgently.

"Hang on."

The sea dragon angled toward an empty pier in the military dockyard. Then its whole body broke the water's surface with an explosion of frothy spray. Ander nearly dropped his spyglass in his haste to get a clearer look.

The serpentine shape wasn't a sea dragon at all; it was an iron-bound ship shaped like a sea dragon. Like a Sadrian warship, the strange ship was long and wide, and it even had a wrought iron dragon's head for a bow. The rest of the craft, however, was cylindrical, with rows of fins like oars, no sails, and a spiraled tail that looked designed to spin like a rotor. Magic radiated from the entire ship like molten steel.

He lowered the spyglass and ran a hand through his wet hair. *This* was how Sadria was importing slaves from South Brinkerhoff despite the Republic fleet. They were sailing underwater, completely undetected.

His blood turned cold with a new thought. The military implications of this were terrifying. If more ships like these were filled with soldiers and landed in the Republic, the Republic would have no warning of an attack until they beached. This—this was huge!

A hatch on top of the ship opened. Sadrian sailors spilled out and were followed by a line of blindfolded Brinkerhoff slaves.

Sergeant Allard cursed quietly. Fury burned in his eyes, and he looked ready to storm the beaches right then and there. The danger was too great, of course. Every sailor that exited from the vessel radiated power, and guards were assembling on the beach as well. There were far too many to fight, even if they had their entire network of Desert Steam Soldiers.

"We'll get them back," Ander said quietly.

The Brink gave a silent nod.

The sailors lined the slaves on the sand, allowing Ander to get a count. Forty slaves, thirty-four sailors, and two platoons of Sadrian guards in total. A large sailor, clearly the captain, walked out in front of the line and met a tall, thin Shaoguan.

Ander frowned. *What was a Shaoguan doing this far north?* The captain led the foreigner to the start of the line. Then the Shaoguan walked down the line and selected every slave that wasn't elderly, sick, or a child. Once the slaves were sorted, the selected portion was ushered back into the ship by the sailors. As that transpired, the Shaoguan waved a hand to a servant, who proffered a sizable chest to the captain.

Ander shook his head. None of it made sense. The Shaoguan Dynasty had conquered South Brinkerhoff and occupied it. If they wanted slaves, they could transport them by land into their own country. Why pay to have slaves shipped to Sadria, only to load them back onto a ship?

The hatch clanged shut, echoing across the waves. Then the vessel pulsed with power before sinking underneath the water. He watched the glow of the craft as it pulled away from the dock, passed beneath their feet, and turned north before disappearing.

North? That was the opposite direction from the Shaoguan lands. He drummed his fingers against his spyglass in thought.

Sergeant Allard leaned toward Ander and whispered. "We hae found our mysterious buyer too, mate."

Ander nodded. Hopefully, the Shaoguan was acting independently from his nation. Otherwise, there was now a third nation conspiring against the Republic. He swallowed. "We've got to report this back to Olivia."

"Yeu dae that. I'll keep watchin' a wee bit longer in case anythin' else happens."

"Sounds good." Ander turned and began swimming toward the shore of the main harbor. An oppressive foreboding closed in around his thoughts, threatening to sink him beneath the waves. How many nations were conspiring against the Republic? What were the Shaoguans doing in the north with so many slaves? Only one thing was certain in his mind. The Republic had to know what was happening.

He cut through the waves with urgent strokes. Soon, he arrived at an abandoned pier, where he removed his water gear and stored it in a hidden cubby underneath the boardwalk's planks. Then he was gliding through alleyways like a wraith. Guards patrolled through the empty streets with narrowed eyes, searching for anyone out past curfew. He carefully navigated around them and pushed deeper into the city.

After what felt like hours, he finally arrived at the side door of the Tipping Tavern. He knocked on it using the same unique pattern Amir did weeks before. Adeena, the burly tavern keeper, cracked the door open before letting Ander slog his way in.

"You look dreadful," she commented.

"Where's Olivia?"

"Burning the midnight oil." She pointed toward the hidden room.

Ander nodded his thanks and pushed straight through the stone fireplace into the tipping tower's secret room. Orange light glowed from the center of the room, highlighting Olivia behind a table full of papers and maps. Deep shadows shrouded the edges of the room.

She looked up at him as he entered and set down the report in her hands. "You're back early."

He rushed to the table and grabbed a quill, ink bottle, and parchment. "We've figured out how the Sadrians are getting slaves past the fleet!" Ander sketched the mysterious ship as he explained what they'd seen. When he finished, Olivia took the drawing and tapped a finger on her lips.

"An underwater ship?" she said thoughtfully.

He nodded. "It explains how they've been transporting so many slaves through the Republic's blockade, and perhaps far more slaves are being taken than we realized."

"And to the north," she added. She leaned back and exhaled. "This is big, Blackwell. I need to report this to high command. While we wait for a reply, we'll keep surveillance each night. I've got an agent planted inside the military sector. I'll task them with finding out more about this buyer and when this ship will appear next."

. . . .

The watch over the military dockyard continued for the next few weeks. Each time Ander made the trip for his shift, he passed the Gifted medical shop. Each time, his mind turned over whether or not he should purchase one.

As the days passed, the desire burned hotter and hotter. He wanted—no *needed*—to know if he was Gifted or not. One evening on the *Legacy*, the desire grew unbearable. He retrieved the key to the lockbox, which Amelia had left behind for safekeeping, and took out the Everblade. As soon as he held the sword again, a surge of rightness washed over him. The sword belonged to him. There was no doubt. He closed his eyes and willed it to life.

Nothing happened.

He put the sword back before anyone could see what he was doing. As soon as the sword was locked tight, a flood of questions and confusion came rushing back again. It took him a long time to fall asleep that night.

The next morning, he woke to the faint clicking of the *Legacy*'s telegraph. He rose and dressed quickly. When he opened his cabin door, Charles Rigg met him in the hallway.

"Ander, telegraph just came in."

"I heard. What's the message?"

"It's from Olivia. High command's come back with orders. They want us to take down the underwater ship."

Ander blinked. All sense of sleep left him.

Charles continued. "Olivia's calling all the officers, including airship officers, to a meeting at the Tipping Tavern at noon."

"Perfect, less bossy soldiers around," said Cid lazily from where he rested against the side of the ship. He took a noisy bite from an apple.

Ander ignored him. "Let's round up the officers then and be on our way." They gathered Garret, Veronica, and Freya up before making their trek over the cracked desert and through the bustling city.

When they entered the secret room of the Tipping Tavern, a full argument was in sway.

"How can yeu destroy the ship?" Sergeant's Allard and his two compatriots stood on the opposite side of the table from Olivia and her officers. "We don't know whaur it's takin' our people yet!" He leaned over the table with his palms flat on the table.

Olivia opened her mouth to reply and paused at the sight of Ander and his officers. "Good. We have everyone. Please take a seat." She looked to the angry Brink looming over the table. "That includes you too," she added firmly.

The group sat down, filling the table to the point of overflowing. Only Freya remained standing, taking a place against a wall.

Olivia clasped her hands together on the table. "We've gotten orders from high command to destroy the underwater ship. I know this news is controversial," she looked at the Brinks as she said this, "but orders are orders."

"I don't give a flyin' fish whit Major General Hawkes says," said Sergeant Allard. "That ship is our only lead!"

"Not to mention the impact on our operations," said Officer Brown, Olivia's second in command. "Khaldun's reaction will be swift and violent. We'll have to halt all rescue operations until his

CRAIG & JALEESA SNOW

vengeance settles!"

"I know many of you have reservations," said Olivia, "but I need you to understand the larger picture. General Hawke's strategy from the beginning has been to eliminate the oversea slave lanes. Doing so eliminates international slaving, which is his goal. That's within all our interests."

"What about recovery?" asked Ander. "There's lots of people enslaved that need to be brought back."

Olivia rubbed her temples. "Recovery is a long-term effort. Slaves are scattered everywhere. Nothing short of a full-scale war will force Sadria to give up *all* their slaves at once. Blackwell, you know as well as I do the Republic can't afford a war with Sadria. Not with the Enchantran conflict brewing."

She was right, he knew. If the Republic fought the Enchantrans by land and the Sadrians by sea, they'd be crushed. Still, that didn't stop him from adding his own uncertainty to the mix.

"Won't attacking a ship in the military dockyard be considered an act of war?" he asked.

Olivia shook her head. "No. Because we won't be attacking as Republic and Brinkerhoff special forces. We'll be attacking as the Desert Steam Soldiers."

"How does that make a difference?" asked Charles.

"Oh," Ander said. "Because both nations need plausible deniability."

"I still don't understand," said Charles.

"Oi," said Veronica, "it means the Republic will label you as renegades who acted accordin' to yer own agenda. It means if ya fail, there'll be no rescue or prisoner exchange. Yer on your own."

Charles' mouth dropped wide open. "How is that sanctioned by the soldier's regulations?"

"Regulations," Sergeant Allred shook his head darkly and chuckled like the word was a childish joke.

Olivia rose to her feet and looked out across the whole group. "Yes, this will be a hard mission. Yes, the price of failure means no return. It's the same price innocent Brinks are paying with each shipload. We have intel this is the *only* ship of its kind and privately commissioned. Destroying it will be a major victory against slavery. I know many of you feel unsettled about this. We will be on our own, but we're also the toughest band of fighters on this side of the seas. We'll succeed in this mission just like all the others. No matter the obstacle. No matter the sacrifice."

The words brought vigor back to most of the group. Sergeant Allred's group, however, still seemed unconvinced.

Olivia turned her attention to the Brinks. "If any of you would like to withdraw from this mission, please speak now."

Sergeant Allred shook his head. "We'll support ye. We Brinks don't shy awa' frae a fight."

Olivia nodded. "Good." She sat down and pointed at the map of the city on the table. "We have intel that the ship will make port tomorrow at midnight. Let's discuss our plan of attack.

The group discussed and debated for the next few hours until they settled on a plan. As soon as the slaves were escorted off the ship, Sergeant Allred and his royal marines would board the ship, load firestorm charges, light them, and escape. While that happened, Olivia and her soldiers would create a distraction to pull attention away while the Brinks did their work. Ander would lead a team of sharpshooters to overtake a nearby wall and provide cover fire in case the slavers spot the Brinks. The *Legacy* and *Thunderbreak* would hover out of sight in the clouds. When it was time for evacuation, Olivia's team would escape through the city, the *Legacy* would pick up Ander's team in the south harbor, and the *Thunderbreak* would pick up the Brinks in the north harbor.

When the meeting ended, Ander's nerves were uneasy. There was a lot riding on this mission, and everything was coming to a head quickly. How would Khaldun react after they destroyed the ship?

Garret put a hand on Ander's shoulder. "Do you mind if we talk about this for a moment?" He gestured to a corner of the room where Veronica, Charles, and Freya were huddled together. Ander nodded and followed him to the group.

The officers made room for Ander and quickly unloaded their thoughts.

"Ander, this is going to kick the bees' nest!" said Charles. "Khaldun's going to scour the whole city and desert for Steam soldiers!"

"Aye," Veronica agreed. "I'm worried about 'avin' the *Legacy* exposed in the desert."

"We think," said Garret to Ander, "that tomorrow needs to be our last night in Sadria."

Ander ran a hand through his hair. *Their last night in Sadria.*

"I agree," said Olivia loudly from behind. They all turned to face her. "Khaldun will not be forgiving and his searches will be more thorough than ever, especially since his forces are no longer hunting the Mirage leader, Abdulmalik. After tomorrow, we'll all need to disappear. But not all of you need to go."

She grabbed Ander's elbow and pulled him away from the others. "You're an invaluable asset here, Blackwell. We've had more successes in the last month than in the last three."

"Amelia," he said, barely hearing Olivia's words. "She doesn't know."

Olivia's expression fell into a deep frown. "Yes, I had forgotten about *Miss Steam*." She nearly spat as she said the name. "Naturally, she'll need to leave as well."

Maybe I could get to her at the embassy, he thought.

"Blackwell?"

Ander's attention snapped back. Olivia's eyes were locked on his.

Her voice lowered to an insistent whisper. "You're needed here in Sadria. The captured slaves of Brinkerhoff need you here. I need you here."

"You're asking me to abandon my mission," Ander realized out loud.

"No, I'm asking you to leave it in the care of *Miss Steam* and join my operations instead."

"I can't do that."

"Yes, you can," she pushed. "It's a reassignment, and I organize them all the time."

It would mean leaving the Wayfinder mission. Leaving Amelia.

He shook head. "No," he said firmly. "You have your orders and I have mine. We'll help with the mission tomorrow night, and that'll close our arrangement."

Anger burned in Olivia's eyes. "Fine. If that's how the wind blows, you are excused."

Ander saluted and left with his officers in tow. Once they were out of the secret room, Garret clapped him on the back.

"I don't think Olivia likes not getting what she wants," said Garret. "Thanks for sticking with us."

Ander nodded. They exited the building into a hot and humid alleyway. Once outside, a new thought struck him suddenly. He turned to the group. "You go back to the airship without me. I need to run an errand before getting Amelia from the embassy."

Charles folded his arms while Freya narrowed her eyes at him.

"Are you sure you want to do this alone?" Garret asked.

Ander nodded. "I can manage. It'll be easier alone. You all start preparations for the mission tomorrow."

They parted ways, traveling opposite directions down the Tipping Tavern's alleyway. Ander kept his trajectory north toward the embassy until the others were long out of sight. Then he pivoted and took off toward the harbor.

His heart pounded harder and harder as he passed each successive cross street. The palms of his hand grew sweaty with nervousness, and the feeling didn't diminish even when he finally stood before The Healing Oasis.

He stepped in and was immediately greeted by the same shop attendant from before.

"I see you came back," said the attendant with a bow.

"Yes, I'm ready to purchase that memory restorative." His voice had a nervous quiver.

The attendant raised an eyebrow. "You sure?"

The question was the one he had been warring against for weeks. But with this being his last opportunity, he finally knew the answer. "Yes."

He exchanged money with the attendant. Then he was led to a chair. The Gifted healer on duty appeared and clasped her hands. "Are you ready to begin?"

He swallowed and nodded to the healer.

"I need you to close your eyes and relax," said the healer, passing a hand over Ander's head. Static floated down from above and passed into him, sinking into his body. The scent of lavender filled the air and immediately he felt his tight shoulders relax. In his mind's eye, he saw the healer twiddling her fingers above him as power curled and swam through the air.

"Imagine the memory you wish to restore. Let it fill your consciousness completely."

Images appeared before his eyes. His father's blue eyes, his mother's curly brown hair. The Steam soldier toys he used to play with. Then running. Screams. Shouts. Enchantran soldiers. Fire. So entranced he was in the memory, he didn't realize the healer had put the restorative to his lips until the substance poured down his throat. The taste was sweet at first, but then turned bitter and spicy. Then power rippled through his body.

He gasped and sat up. His heart pounded in double time and his breaths came quickly.

"You're done," said the healer, placing a cork on the bottle.

"I'm done?" He blinked. The burning sensation faded.

"The memory you seek is now attached to the magic of mirabetal. When your mind and body are in a similar state as the memory, the events will flow back to you right there in the moment. It'll feel like stepping into a dream."

"In the moment?" Alarm peeled in his head. "You mean this restorative could take over any time?!"

"Yes. To others, it'll look like you pass out, so it's best if you stick with someone until the restorative completes its work. That way, your companion can ensure your safety."

Ander's pulse beat even harder, bringing perspiration with it. He was about to go into a major mission tomorrow, a mission in which people could die and where rescue would be impossible. He couldn't afford to pass out randomly.

The healer continued, unaware of the war waging in his head. "As the memory takes over, you will experience the scene as if you are actually there. Once it finishes, the scene will fade."

He ran a hand through his hair. This was the *worst* decision he could have made. With his own ability compromised, he couldn't lead the mission. He was a walking liability until the memory transpired.

He left the shop, completely consumed by the maelstrom he felt inside. So distracted he was that he didn't spot Freya, leaning against a nearby building, watching his every move.

Chapter 18: Visit

Amelia

"I just need you to—" said Amir.

"Create a distraction," Amelia finished flatly. She'd just spent another depressing day at the archives with no luck. They were now heading down the decorative halls of the embassy. "You don't need to repeat your plan a fifth time today. I've got it."

"No room for mess-ups," Amir pressed. "Got that?"

She rolled her eyes. Amir's insistence was giving her a headache. Her room was now in sight, and she was looking forward to the peace and quiet.

Over three weeks had passed since her first day at the archives. Each week had brought with it a string of dead ends. They'd searched through the histories of the sultans, volumes on magical relics, piles on magical lore, scads on magical techniques for finding, and that was only the tip of the iceberg. They had explored hundreds of other topics and had only found occasional references to a *lens of finding* with nothing concrete for where to find it. The weeks passed by with increasing frustration, all while Amir nagged and nagged about getting him into the records wing. Her deadline to Khaldun was now only three days away, and Amir had decided for them both that they were going to get him into the records wing tomorrow.

Her last lead was the locked Arcanum collection. It was the only place that made sense. The Wayfinder was a lost, ancient magic. Certainly, it was worth the attention of the Order of the Arcanum. Right?

She had brought the idea to Amir, and he had rejected it instantly. The risks were too high, he said. They'd have to break in, and that would certainly draw attention. He wouldn't have any of it.

The annoying scholar was still talking to her when she opened her door and bade him good night. As soon as she slammed the door on him, she took a deep breath.

Peace. Finally.

She dragged her feet to the mirror and began taking out her earrings. A faint knock sounded from her balcony door. She jumped and dropped her earrings.

What was that?!

"Millie," came a muffled voice.

"Ander?" She rushed to the door and opened it. There he was, crouching low behind her balcony railing.

"What are you doing there?" she asked. "You nearly gave me a heart attack!"

His expression was serious. "We need to talk, but not out here."

A chill ran down her spine. He found out, didn't he? Her hands began to tremble as she let him through the balcony door.

"I... I know what you must think," she started. "I can explain."

He gave a heavy sigh and ran a hand through his hair.

Yikes! This was not starting well.

"Millie," he said, "we need to get you out of here. Tonight."

She flinched at the unexpected words. "Tonight? Wait, huh?"

"We've got a major operation happening tomorrow that's going to send Khaldun in an uproar. It's not going to be safe for you to stay here at the embassy. Olivia's pulling in all resources, including the crew."

She narrowed her eyes suddenly and folded her arms. "She's not using my airship, is she?"

He swallowed hard, giving her all the answers she needed. She opened her mouth into a silent 'o.' Then words exploded out of her mouth.

"How dare that snobby, perfect-faced, domineering woman take charge of *my* airship?!"

Ander put his hands up. "She just wanted Veronica to pick up my—Garret's team after the mission."

"Using my airship?" She took off a shoe and threw it at him. He managed to dodge it before picking up a pillow for cover.

"It's not all bad news," he said.

"Oh, it's not, is it?" Her voice dripped with sarcasm. She held her other shoe now. "What else isn't wrong?"

"She got all the airship parts you ordered. Everard finished replacing them last week. He told me she's purring like a kitten now."

"You mean *he*? Why does everyone think my airship is a girl?"

He poked his head tentatively above the pillow. "I'm sorry. Have I caught you at a bad time?"

She ran her free hand down her face. Perhaps he had. She'd

spent weeks dealing with anxious, aggravating Amir. All that time she spent for nothing other than a pounding headache. A real Steam she was.

A wave of exhaustion passed over her. She dropped the shoe and sat on the edge of the bed, facing away from him.

"I can't leave yet."

"Why not?" He hesitantly edged into her view, the pillow still clutched in his hands.

She sighed. "I haven't found much about the Wayfinder. If I left now, we'd have nothing to go off of." She put her face into her hands.

Ander set the pillow down onto the bed. "You don't have any leads?"

She sighed. "I've got only one, but it'd be difficult to pull off." She told him about the Arcanum section with its Gifted lock. "Somehow, I'd need to lose my guards. And that would be on top of creating a distraction to help Amir get into the records wing."

"Why do you have to help him get to the records wing?"

She groaned. "Amir wasn't willing to help me translate texts unless I promised to help him find out where his niece was sent after being sold. We were going to do it tomorrow."

"Tomorrow night is the mission."

"I know. Which means I'd need to somehow do all of it tomorrow."

His eyebrows drew together. "Can you do it fast enough to get back in time?"

She raised an eyebrow at him. "If it means I'll be captaining *my* airship, you can bet I'll get back in time. Pulling it off will be the trick."

She looked at him and was caught off guard by his soft blue eyes and his concerned expression. Her breath caught in her throat, and she felt her pulse quicken. She glanced away, and the moment broke.

"I know you're capable," he said, "but... be safe."

She put a hand on her heart. "Me? Be safe? You're the one ticking off Khaldun."

"Well..." he looked away.

She frowned. "What?"

"I took your advice," he said slowly, taking a seat next to her. "I got a memory restorative and drank it."

"Yeah?"

He sighed. "What I didn't know was the cost." He took a deep breath. "The memory will only come when I'm in the same state as the memory. The problem is, I could be in combat and suddenly have a flashback take over. I'm a liability now."

He ran a hand through his hair.

Wow. That was a lot to take in. She put a hand on his arm. "Hey, you've got all of us to support you. Who knows, maybe the memory will trigger before tomorrow."

He met her eyes and gave her a tight smile. "I hope you're right." He stood up and crossed to the balcony door.

A thought crossed her mind, one that she kept pushing back. She needed to tell him about her past. Before anyone else did, if they hadn't already.

No one has told him, she corrected herself. This was too much of a normal conversation for that to be the case.

She reached out for his arm, but fear made her hesitate at the last instant. Fear of rejection. Fear of losing his friendship.

He swung a leg over the balcony rail, flashed her a smile, and said, "See you tomorrow."

"See you then, mophead."

He dropped to the grounds below and disappeared into the night. She stayed there, holding on to the open balcony door, wondering when she'd finally muster the courage to tell him.

Chapter 19: Distraction

Amelia

Two guards were posted on either side of the entrance to the records wing in the Sadrian Archives. Amelia eyed them out of the corner of her eye as she walked along the railing of the second level. Her own guards were knocked out and tied up in a closet; Hammer had seen to that. A stone stairway led from her level to the first level. The bottom was within direct line of sight to the guards, ending only ten yards away from them. Amir leaned against a wall to the right of the guards. In his hands was a book.

Amir looked up at Amelia and nodded.

Alright, she thought. *Time to fake an injury.* She headed down the stairs. A few steps from the bottom, she caught one foot behind the other and fell the rest of the way. Her body crashed against the floor.

She gasped and squealed in pain. The injury was *supposed* to be fake, not real. Sharp pain radiated from her ankle—the same one she had sprained while jumping out a window weeks ago. She cursed mentally.

"Someone, help please!" she said in her best damsel-in-distress voice. No one else was in the room except Amir and the guards. She looked directly at the guards and saw they were both hesitating. *Goodness? Was chivalry dead? Or were all men just dense?*

She tried lifting herself up and collapsed. Tears began to stream down her face.

That did it. Both of the guards bolted over. One took her hand and helped her to a sitting position. The other stood over hesitantly.

"Thank you! Oh, it hurts really bad." She twisted her face into an exaggerated grimace. She flinched with each movement, the act causing her ankle to twinge as well with real pain. From the corner of her eye, she could see Amir creeping to the entrance now. *That man better get a move on,* she thought. Otherwise, she'd give him a matching injury soon.

The hesitant guard started to turn back when Amelia grabbed his arm. "Could you both help me to one of those chairs?"

The guards glanced at each other before picking an arm, lifting her up, and walking her to the nearest chair. She whimpered and yelped along the way, hoping the noise would cover any sounds Amir made. They reached the chair and set her down.

"We have to go back to our post," said one guard. "But would you like for us to call a servant?"

She shook her head, checking for Amir in the movement. The man was gone.

"My slave should be around at any moment. Thank you."

The guards returned to their post. She sighed in relief. The plan worked... mostly. Pain still radiated from her ankle, but it was less now than before. Probably a minor re-sprain. She could see it was already bruising. *Great. Amir better get what he needs,* she thought in annoyance. Hopefully, this wouldn't slow her down for the next portion.

Hammer soon appeared and helped her up. Technically, she was supposed to stay and then "put on another distraction" at lunch so Amir could get out. As if the guards cared about who came out as much as who came in. Regardless, after Ander's visit last night, she had plans of her own. If it worked right, Amir would get his distraction and she would get what she wanted.

Hammer assisted her until they were out of sight from the guards. Once they were, Hammer pointed to her foot.

"You hurt?"

"Yes," she tested putting weight on it. Pain spiked up from her injury, but it was bearable. "I'll manage. Let's head to the west atrium."

She hobbled to the other side of the library where the door to the Arcanum section was located. Then they took a seat on a plush bench.

The west atrium had a glass skylight that glowed warm light into the room. Two hallways crossed through the room, along with a stairwell leading to the second floor. In the center of the main wall was the door to the Arcanum. Even a month later, she still had no idea what the archaic characters said across the top of the door. Maybe it was how to open the door?

She stretched out and yawned. This was the patient part. She needed to wait until lunch to give Amir time to find what he needed. Then she could begin. Still, that meant she had two hours to kill.

She had never been one for patience. The crew would be prepping the *Legacy* now. *Her* airship. It was tempting to make her move now, but she made a promise to Amir.

She passed the time reading a book about ancient ship designs. Apparently, some of the most innovative ship designs from the Sadrians were first created by pirates and raiders looking to get an advantage over their prey.

The hours passed slowly before a tinkling bell chimed, signaling lunch. *Finally,* she thought. She got up and proceeded down the hall into a women's lavatory and locked it.

She took a deep breath in front of a large vanity mirror. Then she began removing items from her person: A metal drill bit from inside the spine of her corset, two metal rods in her hair, a u-shaped rod from her shoe, and a wooden roller disguised as a button on her satchel. She set these down on the wooden counter in front of the vanity and began putting them together. When she finished, she had an auger.

She smiled at the clever tool. It was a shame she'd have to ditch it before this was all over. She placed it back into her satchel and removed four lipstick tubes. The gate guards must have thought she was overly vain when they searched her bag.

She took a deep breath and pushed out the door. Hammer stood in front of a wastebasket, blocking it from the view of passersby. She moved behind him, casually pulling the caps of her lipstick tubes and dropping the pieces into the basket. Then they walked back to their seats.

Seconds passed before the wastebasket ruptured with a loud crack and vomited thick smoke into the room.

Screams broke out all around, along with the Sadrian word for *fire.* Footsteps rushed away from the atrium where the whole area was quickly becoming consumed by a dense cloud.

Through the murky cover, Amelia rushed to the door with her auger in hand. The smoke was thick now, but it would dissipate in a few minutes. She jammed the auger into the wall by the doorknob and began drilling. Sweat beaded her brow as wood shavings spiraled out from the drill bit. She prayed her hypothesis would be correct. While the lock required magic to open, she hoped it operated on the same principle that all door locks operated. Typically, when engaged, a lock would slide a small metal bar into the wall next to it. But if she removed the wood that held the bar in place, maybe she could bypass the lock.

Half a minute passed and she could see the smoke was already beginning to thin. The commotion around the library was growing. People were evacuating—and probably bringing in Gifted elementalists to douse the "fire." Time was running out.

The auger reached the deadbolt and stopped spinning. She pulled on the door, but it wouldn't budge. The smoke was thinning out now. Footsteps pounded from a distance.

"They're coming," said Hammer next to her. He saw her struggling with the door. With one hand, he grabbed the handle and yanked. The deadbolt broke from the wall and the door opened.

"Go!" she whispered to Hammer before slipping inside the room and closing the door. Her heart pounded out of her chest. How long did she have before guards arrived?

No time to think about that. The room she was in was two stories high and rectangular. Shelves lined all four walls and stretched to the ceiling. Runic writing covered books' spines, completely illegible to her eyes.

Her stomach fell. How was she supposed to find what she needed here? She needed Amir to help her navigate through this. Of course, there wasn't any time for that. He was on the opposite side of the archives, and she had maybe a minute before she had to leave herself.

Without another thought, she rushed through the room, ripping books off walls at random and flipping through the pages.

"No, no, no!" She threw books left and right, searching for pictures, diagrams, or anything about the Wayfinder. Her heart pounded like a ticking clock. *Ba-thump. Ba-thump. Ba-thump.*

She only recognized a few useless symbols like water and fire. *Not helpful!* She needed a lens. Pounding boots echoed from the floor above her. She had to get out. NOW!

"Ughhh!" She backed toward the door, giving the room one last scan.

Her eyes landed on a leather-bound book on a high shelf. The spine held mathematical symbols that had caught her eye, but something about the runic writing looked familiar.

She took a step closer. Her mouth dropped open. "It can't be," she whispered. Her grandfather's handwriting shone to her as clear as day. Heavy footsteps pounded down the nearby stairs, propelling her to action.

She bolted for the book, climbing a ladder to the sixth rung and reaching out before yanking the book free. Then she was sliding down to the floor and barreling out of the room.

The smoke now layered the top of the atrium and blocked out the light from the skylight.

A rough voice came from the stairwell. "Secure the area and find where that smoke is coming from!"

She hugged the wall and bolted down the hallway that led to the main entrance. Pain shot from her ankle, making her wince with each step, but she didn't care. She had to get out.

She dropped the auger into the first wastebasket she saw and kept running. The pain in her ankle grew worse and worse. Before she rounded a bend, she heard a new set of footsteps pound toward her from the direction she was heading. Along with it came the jangle of armor.

Her heart raced. She looked back the way she came.

"The Arcanum section's been broken into!" someone shouted.

She was trapped between the guards she'd escaped and the new ones coming her way.

There had to be a way out. As she turned, her ankle popped. She crashed to the floor.

No! Tears sprang to her eyes. She pushed herself up and fell again. The incoming footsteps grew louder, like an incoming storm. Frantically, she looked all around for somewhere she could hide.

The lavatory! It was ten feet behind her. She crawled towards it, feeling her ankle throb with blinding pain. Tears ran down her cheeks and hit the stone floor beneath her.

She reached the door, turned the knob, and slipped in. As she did so, part of her dress caught underneath the door and prevented it from closing entirely. She reached for it and froze.

The footsteps rounded the corner.

Her breath caught in her throat. She could see a group of guards through the open sliver in the door. They stopped only feet away. Another guard approached from the west atrium and met them in the hallway.

"The fire started in a wastebasket and has since burned itself out," said the guard. "The lock into the Arcanum section is also broken."

"A book is missing!" shouted another voice from the other end of the hall.

"Show me," said a commanding voice nearby. "Reyhan, Kateb, Tamir, make sure no one enters this hall. Damjan, tell the guards at the atrium to look for a thief with a book." Two guards headed toward the atrium while three stayed.

Amelia's lungs burned. She hadn't taken a breath since the guards appeared. Slowly, she took a silent breath. Her mouth felt dry, and her ankle throbbed.

She was trapped here until the guards moved. *Or until they find me*, she mentally added. With her blue dress caught under the door, it was a matter of time before they saw it. Still, she didn't dare try to remove it and catch their attention. She clenched her teeth, feeling an overwhelming sense of helplessness.

One guard let out a sigh. "Wasn't expecting to be working during lunch. I'm supposed to be on shift tonight."

"We're all on shift tonight," said another.

"Everyone?" the first guard asked.

"Yes, all ten companies," said the second.

"Do you know what for?" asked the third.

"You know as well as I that Khaldun keeps that information reserved. All I know is my company is to hide in the northeast section of the military sector and wait for orders."

The military sector? Amelia thought. *That's strange.*

"We're southeast," said the first.

"Gatehouse," said the third.

Why would Khaldun hide his men inside his own military

complex? Unless....

A hand went over her mouth. The operation. Khaldun knew! It all was a trap!

"Hey, what's this?" The door to the lavatory opened to show all three guards peering down at her.

All the blood drained from her face.

Chapter 20: Falling Apart

Amelia

"**H**ave you been in here the whole time?" asked the first guard. "She's crying," said the second guard. He crouched down. "Hey, it's alright, miss. The fire is gone."

Wait... they didn't suspect her. Maybe she could get out of this mess. "Gone?" she repeated.

"Oh, I know you," said the third guard. "You're the misses who slipped down the stairs earlier."

She nodded. "I...," she quivered her lip, "I couldn't get away from the smoke. So I went in here, waiting for help, and you all arrived."

Maybe she was laying the damsel-in-distress thing too thick, but they seemed to be eating it up.

"Here, let us help you up," said the first guard.

They lifted her up, and she winced. More tears came to her eyes, and she didn't hold them back. "My ankle." She lifted the hem of her skirt to show the bruised and discolored joint.

"Two minutes at the healers will get that as good as new," said the first guard.

"Oh, good," she said, meaning it. They were kind. She had to give them that. Nothing like the guards at Enchantra. They would have left her on the floor. Then again, she *was* posing as a dignified guest.

"We need to keep this area closed for investigation, so we'll have to escort you out," said the third guard.

That was better than she could hope for. "Thank you."

"I'll do it," said the guard that helped her before. He wrapped his hand around her waist. They took two steps when the second guard put a hand on her shoulder.

"Hang on. What's that in your satchel?" He reached a hand in and withdrew a book.

"That's mine," she blurted. They all looked at her, and she realized her mistake.

"This looks archaic. You're coming with us." The guard holding her let go and grabbed her forearm and upper arm beneath her shoulder. Another guard did the same on her other side. They turned her around and dragged her back to the west atrium.

"Where are you taking me?" she pleaded. They ignored her. If anything, their grips tightened. She groaned inside. Why had she said the book was hers? They'll now all think she was the one that broke in, and if they dig deep enough, they'll discover they were right.

What about Ander and the others? She had to warn them.

They stopped before the broken door of the Arcanum. "Captain," said one of the guards beside her. "We found this woman fleeing the scene of the crime with a book."

"What have we here?" The captain stepped out and eyed Amelia with a wary expression. "Give me the book."

The guards handed it over. The captain looked at its cover and rifled through its pages.

Please help me get out of this. Please! She prayed silently over and over.

"She told us the book was hers." The guard to her right said.

"Did she?" He opened to the front page and frowned. "She may be right. This book doesn't belong to the library."

Amelia's breath caught in her throat. *What?*

"But—" said the guard.

The captain held the book out to show the seal-less first page. "There's no library seal."

"She was fleeing the scene," the guard stammered. "We found her hiding in the lavatory."

"Found her in the what?!" The captain rubbed his eyes and turned to Amelia. "I'm terribly sorry, miss. I'll have these buffoons escort you out of the building."

"Yes, sir," the guards replied stiffly. They turned around and helped Amelia hobble through the hall, past the front reception desk, and through the door. Sunlight gleamed down on her, warming her with relief. The guards handed her the book and gave a stiff bow before leaving with quick footsteps. She watched them go in stunned silence.

How in the world did that just happen? She shook herself. She needed to warn Ander and the others.

"Millie okay?" Hammer came over and supported her arm.

"Yes, I'm okay," she replied.

Amir appeared. His face was purple. "Good, because you're lucky we made it out."

She didn't have time for Amir's exhausting banter. She leaned in and whispered, "Khaldun's preparing a trap for Ander and the others. We have to go now."

"What do you mean—"

Amelia didn't wait for him to finish. She hobbled toward the gate, leaning on Hammer for support. The guards let them through without any trouble, but their carriage was gone.

She threw her hands up. "Great! We're going to have to walk?"

Using Hammer's help, she tore fabric from the hem of her dress and wrapped her ankle. The wrap was tight, but her joint felt slightly better.

Slightly was a good way to put it. She still gritted her teeth when they started up, this time at a faster pace. As they traveled, she briefed Amir on what she heard. When she finished, his eyes widened.

"I'll take us to the Tipping Tavern. That'll be the quickest way to get the message out. From here though..." he whistled. "It'll take us a few hours."

"A few hours!" Every step she took shot pain up her leg. Still, she wasn't going to be left behind.

They kept pace with Amir, switching between streets and alleys. Eyes followed them wherever they went—Amelia's blue gown didn't exactly blend in. Still, there wasn't any time to deviate to the embassy for a change in clothes. Not when every second counted.

True to his estimation, it was mid-afternoon by the time they reached the derelict part of the city. From up ahead, a plume of dust billowed up into the sky.

No, no, no! she thought as dread grew inside her chest. They rounded the corner and froze at the sight of the collapsed remains of the Tipping Tavern. Stone and warped beams jutted left and right out of the piles of rubble. Dust blew high into the air, drifting off the rubble in gusts.

"Mirabetal," Amelia breathed in horror.

"Adeena!" Amir broke free of the group and rushed to the ruins. They followed, Amelia limping to keep up. Dizziness grew inside her as she poured through the implications. This was her fault. She'd bombed the restaurant at the Serenity Square. She was the one that brought the wrath of Khaldun down on Amir's sister's tavern.

They reached the ruins and stopped before where the side door used to be. The door, the kitchen, the tower, all of it was destroyed. They couldn't see any bodies in the wreckage, but that didn't mean there weren't any underneath.

Amir turned on her and stabbed a pointing finger. "This is *your* fault!" he screamed. "If you hadn't come here to Sadria like your insufferable grandfather, this would have *never happened!*"

Bile rose up her throat and her knees grew weak. He was right. She slipped to the ground as nausea overtook her. It was like the factory fire, all over again. She had done this.

"Khaldun fault!" Hammer growled. "Khaldun flatten tavern. Not Millie!" He grew to his full height, towering protectively over Amelia. Amir shrank back, but his face was still a mask of fury.

Who was here when this happened? she wondered. *Was Ander?*

A creak came from behind them. They wheeled around to face a curved sword pointed at their faces. "No hasty movements," said the guard from an open doorway behind them. "You are surrounded." More armed figures moved out of the shadows on either side of the alleyway. They were trapped.

This can't be happening! she thought in panic. The figures on their sides closed in on them like a noose. Hammer raised his hands in submission to the guard in front of them. Then, in one movement, he knocked the guard's sword with one hand and slammed his fist into his face with the other. The guard crashed backward through the door with a loud thump.

The guards on their sides charged.

"In!" Hammer roared, grabbing both Amelia and Amir and throwing them toward the door. They scrambled inside, and Hammer slammed the door. Amelia dropped the lock bar down right as the whole door shuddered with impact.

They were in what looked like an abandoned residence. The empty room was covered with cobwebs and thick dust. Amelia and Hammer hurried forward while Amir stood frozen before the door, staring numbly.

"Adeena...." his voice was barely a whisper.

"Amir!" she shouted, turning around. "We need to get out of here!" He didn't react, so she grabbed his arm and yanked him out of the room.

CRASH! The sound thundered behind them, followed by pounding boots. They bolted down the hallway and out a back door.

They crossed a street and turned into another alleyway. Amir finally seemed to be out of his daze, though his eyes were wide and his face drained of blood. Still, he took charge again and led them down a winding set of twists and turns.

In the distance, a horn blew, sending chills down her spine despite the hot sun. After a few more turns, they paused behind a building to catch their breath.

Amir slunk down against a wall and put his palms over his eyes. "She's gone," he muttered.

Amelia's heart broke for him. As frustrating as the man was, she felt horrible for him. Adeena was his sister.

"There weren't any bodies," she said. "Maybe she got away?" He glared at her, and she fell silent.

"HOLD IT RIGHT THERE!" Two guards rushed toward them with their blades drawn. They slowed when they were ten feet away and adjusted their positions to block the exits. "TO THE GROUND! NOW!"

"No," said Hammer,. He rolled his shoulders and walked to the guards slowly. The guards adjusted their positions to either side of him and brandished their swords menacingly.

Emotion clawed up Amelia's throat. "Hammer, don't!"

"No hurt friends." He raised his fists.

Amelia turned her head away, unwilling to watch. Blades whistled, Hammer grunted, steel clanged, something hit the ground, and then silence.

She opened her eyes tentatively. Hammer held one guard against the wall while the other laid on the ground unmoving. Hammer's clothes were stained red, but his gaze was fixed on the guard.

"Tavern. What happened?" he growled.

"Don't... kill me," said the guard.

"What happened?" Hammer repeated. He lifted the guard higher.

"We ambushed the Tavern on Khaldun's order," the guard gasped. "Took everyone inside prisoner."

"How many?"

"A woman and three Republic spies."

"What else?" He raised the man higher up the wall.

The guard spoke even faster. "Khaldun learned about the

hideout and others. He's cutting off potential escape routes."

"What else?"

"I... that's all I know."

Hammer lowered the man and thumped him over the head. The man slumped over.

Amelia stared in stunned silence. Khaldun was routing the entire Desert Steam Soldier organization. She put a hand to the side of her head.

"How do we warn everyone now?" She turned to Amir. "Do you know of any other major hideouts where we might find Olivia?"

Amir didn't answer.

"Are there any other major hideouts?"

Amir shrugged dejectedly. "Many. All over the city. But you heard the guard. Khaldun is systematically taking them out. Who knows where Olivia's at or what hideouts have already been taken?"

That... was a good point. She leaned against the wall and processed the news.

The *Legacy*. They could go to her airship. She looked up at the sun. They'd have to hurry if they wanted to get there in time. She looked down at her throbbing ankle and gritted her teeth. "Let's get moving."

Chapter 21: Routed

Ander

Where are you? asked Ander from the stern of the *Legacy* as he looked out across the desert for the hundredth time. Darkness stretched across the desert, muting everything into shades of gray. Even the *Legacy* was bathed in shadow.

He tapped his fingers on the railing. *We should already be in the air,* he thought. If he didn't give the command to leave soon, they'd put the whole mission at risk. But he couldn't just leave Amelia and Hammer.

Has something happened to them? The three ground teams would already be in position now. He gripped the railing until his knuckles turned white. He should be out there with them, rather than staying back as support. Why had he taken that restorative? How long would he be a liability?

Veronica's footsteps approached. "Crews' finished readyin' for the mission, Lieutenant."

Ander took a deep breath. "Thank you." He let go of the railing and walked to the helm, where he could survey the main deck. Armed sailors looked up at him from their stations. Ballistae were locked into place along the railing, each loaded with long bolts that gleamed silver in the moonlight.

Ander nodded in satisfaction, though he felt the empty positions where his soldiers should have stood. He was the only Steam soldier in their midst. Granted, Axel and Bragg were both on the airship, but the former was still in recovery and the latter wouldn't have been of any help, anyway. Eugene was also onboard, readying the medical bay in case it would be needed.

"We've got incoming guards!" shouted a sailor from the rigging above.

Guards? The word sparked Ander into action. "Veronica, get us into the air!" He looked up at the sailor. "What direction?"

"South, toward the road!"

Ander sprinted to the stern and surveyed the south as the airship rose from its sheltered alcove. *There!* The movement was too vague to see details, so he pulled out his spyglass. Three familiar figures came into focus. He smiled.

"Veronica, take us south. We've found them." He kept his eyes on the figures as the airship lifted from the ground and began toward Amelia, Amir, and Hammer. His brows furrowed as the details became clearer. Was Amelia limping? Hammer was also bent over with a hand wrapped around his side. What had happened?

They dropped the ladder over the edge and soon the trio was climbing up. Amelia slipped over the edge first and collapsed onto the deck. Her blue Enchantran dress was soiled and torn at the hems, and her face was contorted in pain.

All of his worries about the restorative and the mission vanished in an instant as his attention riveted on Amelia. He rushed to her and helped her into a sitting position.

"What's wrong?" he asked quickly, taking her hand and putting two fingers on her wrist. "I see your ankle is wrapped. Where else are you injured?"

She shifted back against the railing and grimaced. "I'm fine. Hammer needs help."

Hammer climbed over the railing. His face was pale and his entire side was coated in blood.

Ander's eyes widened. He pointed to two sailors and shouted, "Get Hammer to the med bay, NOW!" The sailors rushed the large soldier to the hatch while Amir finally appeared last. The scholar's face was white, but other than that, he seemed uninjured. He muttered a string of curses along with the words *cursed flying machine* before following Hammer and the sailors.

"Ander?" Amelia's voice was dry.

"What happened?" he asked, refocusing on Amelia. Her auburn hair was matted with sweat and dust, and she definitely was in pain. He couldn't see any other injury, and her pulse was strong. Still, that did little to lessen the concern he felt building inside his chest. Something was very wrong. He could see it in her eyes.

"Ander, it's all a trap!" Her words came out in gasps.

"What is?"

"Khaldun. He knows about the operation!"

The words hit him like a hammer on steel. "Tell me everything." She explained her encounter with the guards at the archives and again after the Tipping Tavern. When she finished, the airship had reached elevation and was sailing high above the city toward the bay.

He ran a hand through his hair. "This is huge."

"I know." She let her head rest back against the railing. "Someone must have been on the inside. Someone who had access to all of Olivia's operations."

A traitor. The news was too much to process. He couldn't imagine anyone on their airship or in Olivia's corps betraying the whole group.

He shook his head to focus. The operation was already in motion. If he shot off a warning flare, the teams would retreat to their contingency hideouts—hideouts that Khaldun may have already captured.

He ran a hand down his face. How in the world could he fix this if Khaldun knew everything?

He took a deep breath. "We need a change of plans." He moved to the nearest lantern and lit it.

"Oi!" came Veronica's voice. "Whacha doin'? You'll give us away!"

"The enemy already knows we're here." The oil flared to life and cast an orange glow. He held it over the side of the airship and began to shutter and unshutter it in a blinking pattern. When he finished the brief message, he waited.

No response. Again, he repeated the pattern.

Amelia pulled herself up and groaned. "What are you sending?" she asked, settling next to him.

"Abort. Exfiltrate to south dock." He repeated the signal a third time.

Blink blink!

"There!" Amelia said. "That came from a sea tower near the

military bay."

"Garret's team." A wave of relief passed over him. Now he just needed to reach two more teams. He continued the message over and over until the *Legacy* reached their original destination: 8,000 feet above the military harbor. Neither Olivia's or Sergeant Allred's teams replied back.

Why aren't they responding? Can they see it?

"Here, take this." He handed the lantern to Amelia and took a few steps back from the railing.

Her eyebrows creased. "What are you doing?"

"Keep the message going." He slipped a pair of goggles over his eyes. "Tell Veronica to meet us at the south harbor." He put a foot on the railing and synched his magpack tighter.

Her eyebrows furrowed further. Then her eyes widened. "You aren't—"

The rest of her words were lost as he dove headfirst off the railing toward the sea far below. Cold, bitter wind ripped at him and increased to an overwhelming roar. His stomach clenched, but he kept his body in a pencil dive. Seconds passed before the clenching sensation passed. The bay grew closer and closer. As the details became clearer, he picked up a surge of water rising, heading toward the dock.

The slave ship. It was too early. That didn't leave him much time. He held his trajectory past his normal deploying point. The water approached fast, far too fast. When crashing felt imminent, he ripped down the lever to his glider wings.

Whoomp! He pulled up nearly ten feet away from the waves and accelerated at a parallel. The maneuver was risky by every standard, but he didn't have time to take this slow. The slave ship broke out of the water and slid to a stop at the beach.

Ander soared toward it. Details grew in size and clarity. He could even see the figures of Sergeant Allred's team stacking up at the rear of the vessel. A few hundred yards away, his glider began to lose speed. He took a deep breath, angled up to burn his remaining speed, and pulled his glider lever. The wings retracted back, and he dropped. He barely had time to tuck his arms in before he crashed feet first into the water.

The freezing water swallowed him whole and turned the world to black. He continued sinking for several seconds before his descent slowed to a stop. Then he swam to the surface. The way up was much harder than normal, and tense seconds passed before he broke through and took a deep breath.

The slaves and slavers were now exiting the ship to the beach in a long line. He had to get there before Sergeant Allred moved in. He dropped below the water and swam toward the ship. His gear slowed him down, but he didn't have time to slip any of it off.

He surfaced again, still a hundred yards away. Sergeant Allred's group climbed up the side of the ship, hoisting explosives with them. *No No NO!* "It's a trap!" he shouted, but his voice was lost with the crash of the waves. The Brinkerhoff soldiers climbed to the top and dropped into the ship. Ander swam harder, hoping against hope he could make some kind of difference. The static passed through the water, radiating from the ship. He could sense its use, but he was helpless to stop it. Every arm stroke felt more defeating than the last.

By the time he cleared half the distance, he was too late. Sergeant Allred and two other bloodied and bruised Brinks were roughly dragged from the ship by a mob of slavers, along with the explosive. The dead bodies from the rest of the team were carried out and thrown into the sea.

Ander slowed to a stop. Frustration poured over him, along with helplessness. Maybe if he had adjusted his trajectory, he could have saved them.

Maybe he still could save them? When he fought against the Mirage warrior near the Mesa Village, for a moment he had connected to the power of the Everblade again. It was brief, but it gave him exactly what he needed to win the fight. Maybe he could do it again and move in quick enough to get them out? He reached down for the sword at his hip and grasped its hilt.

He cursed. The Everblade wasn't on his hip. It was locked up on the *Legacy*. Besides, there were far too many Gifted slavers. The only chance they had now to save the rest of the group was if Amelia got to Olivia.

A new sight destroyed the thought. Just like slave exchanges before, guards came out from the military complex. This time, however, they had an additional line of slaves. Olivia and every operative Ander had met in the city were ushered onto the beach, bordered by two regiments of Sadrian Cavalry. Khaldun led the whole procession.

Ander closed his eyes. Khaldun had won. In one fell swoop, he had routed the entire Desert Steam Soldiers corps. Everyone was lined up on the beach except for Garret's team of sharpshooters and himself. His body felt like lead, threatening to sink him. He had failed all of them.

Khaldun waved an arm and a wall of sand rose and shoved Olivia sprawling from the line toward him. She rose back to her feet and guards surrounded her. Khaldun looked down at her with an upturned smile. "I finally caught the Desert Steam Soldier." His grating voice bounded off the waves and dripped with contempt. "Did you really think you could outwit me forever? There's a reason I'm the Sadhdron, and I've got quite the list of crimes for you."

"Greater than enslavement?" she shouted back. "Of ripping children and adults from their homes and *stealing* their future? You're no balancer of the scales of justice." She spat at his feet. "Do to me what you wish. I'd rather die a hero than live like you."

Silence fell across the beach. Khaldun clenched and unclenched his fists. Then he pointed to a guard. "Bring me the brand." The guard brought him a cruel metal object that looked like a fire poker with a symbol at the end. Khaldun took the handle in one hand and gesticulated his fingers with the other hand. Smoke spiraled off the end of the poker and the metal turned orange.

"You won't die a hero," Khaldun said harshly. "You'll *replace* the slaves you *liberated*. You'll die as property. Your fate is mirabetal!"

Guards yanked her forward and offered her wrist. Khaldun plunged the brand down on her wrist, and she screamed. Ander looked away. The guard dragged her back to the line and then took the next Steam soldier to be branded. They continued like such until they finished the entire line. Then they shoved Sergeant Allred and his two remaining marines toward Khaldun.

As they drew close, Sergeant Allred roared a *hurrah* and the three Brinks slammed into their captors as one. A fight broke out and immediately one marine fell. Power rippled outward and the second fell afterward. Sergeant Allred broke free from the guards and charged Khaldun with a boot knife in hand. Khaldun reached a hand toward the sea and ripped his hand toward the charging soldier. Sea spray surged toward the Brink and transformed into a solid glacial spike. The spike speared toward the soldier and—

A tingling sensation grew inside Ander, and immediately he looked away. He couldn't watch. Not only was it too horrible to see, but he could feel the memory restorative beginning to kick in right here. The tingling sensation hovered before fading away. He cursed and swam back out to sea.

His stomach felt like it was filled with lead. He couldn't understand how Khaldun could justify such horrible actions and call it justice. It was sickening. His insides ached from the loss of soldiers, of his friends. He hadn't known the marines for long, but he'd interacted with them enough to feel the blow deeply. Same with Olivia and her soldiers.

As he swam south, he looked back only long enough to see the remaining Desert Steam Soldiers enter the ship as fully branded slaves. Then, he felt the ripple of power radiate through the water and the mysterious ship disappeared under the water. They were gone.

. . . .

Hours passed before the *Legacy* arrived to pick up the band of soldiers treading water near the south docks. Ander grabbed onto the ladder last and climbed up as the airship rose. Shouts echoed across the bay, but the airship climbed into the night too quickly for even the sea catapults to take aim.

Ander climbed over the railing and joined the group of sopping wet soldiers, who were leaned over and gulping in breaths.

"What happened down there?" Amelia asked with concern. She tenderly climbed down from the helm and limped over.

"I didn't get to them in time," Ander said between breaths. He explained what he saw to the shock of everyone else.

"Why were we pulled out?" asked Lieutenant Harper, one of the few remaining soldiers from the Desert Steam Soldiers. "We could have provided cover."

"Because," Ander explained, "it was all a trap. Khaldun knew the operation was happening. We tried to pull everyone out. You would have been loaded onto that ship with everyone else."

"How could Khaldun know?" asked Charles.

Garret let out a long breath. "Because there was a mole in our midst."

"Who'd betray the Desert Steam Soldiers?" asked Lieutenant Harper.

Freya narrowed her eyes at Ander. "Maybe you should explain what you were doing at a Gifted clinic yesterday?"

Ander's mouth dropped open. She had tailed him? And she thought he was a traitor? "You think *I* did this?"

Garret stepped in between them. "Ander's not a traitor."

"I didn't say he was," she replied. "Only that it's suspicious that right after we made the plan, he left the group and traveled alone to a Gifted clinic."

"It does seem awfully convenient that he stayed behind on medical leave," added Charles.

Blaze stepped in. "The only crime Ander has committed is stealing all the girls. Come on, man! Save some women for the rest of us!"

Ander put a hand on his face. "Blaze—"

Lieutenant Harper turned on Ander. "If you were on medical leave, how was it that you just swam across the harbor just fine?"

Voices broke out, overlapping each other. The crowd of soldiers pressed in around Ander while Garret and Blaze tried to push them back. Soon, hands were reaching out for Ander and pulling at him.

BOOM! A starburst exploded off their port side, snapping

everyone's attention to Amelia. She stood wearily above everyone, leaning against the helm. In her hands the spent signal flare was still spewing out smoke.

"You idiots should be *ashamed* of yourselves!" she said. "*Ander* was the one that gave you the signal that saved your lives! *Ander* was the one that jumped off this airship without a second's hesitation to warn the other two groups."

She stared Freya hard in the eye. "As the captain of this airship, I know *why* Ander was on medical leave. I know *why* he went to that clinic, and I can assure you there was *no* nefarious intent. Use your brains, will you? If Ander was a traitor, he missed thousands of chances to turn."

The hands grabbing for Ander fell down and people's eyes turned downward. It was in this moment that Eugene arrived and pressed his way into the circle.

"I'm giving you all a medical order to disband right now," the medic shouted. "Go to your cabins immediately. None of you are in the right mind for this discussion."

"Lieutenant 'arper," said Veronica, "follow me. We'll make space for you 'n your comrades in the crew's quarters."

Ander watched the group dissipate around him. Amelia's words seemed to have sobered most of the crowd. There were a few, however, that eyed him with suspicion before they disappeared.

He let out a heavy breath and turned to Garret. "That was close to becoming ugly. Too close."

Chapter 22: Secret Journal

Amelia

Midmorning light gleamed through Amelia's cabin windows. The Sadrian coast was barely visible on the horizon. Everything else was blue seas as far as the eye could see. She laid in her bed with her injured ankle wrapped and propped up. The room was warm and the familiar rocking of the airship felt comforting.

It was the only comfort she had. Since the events of the evening prior, a solemn quietness prevailed across the airship. No one wanted to talk about what happened—how somehow the entire Desert Steam Soldiers corps were routed out in one night.

A layer of guilt churned inside Amelia. If only she had been faster, perhaps they could have prevented it all. Granted, she couldn't have predicted her injury, nor the Sadhdron striking at the Tipping Tavern. Still, maybe if she had sent Amir ahead to the *Legacy*, they could have gotten a warning out sooner.

It didn't matter now. The Desert Steam Soldiers were gone, and nothing could change that. Her only souvenir from their whole adventure was the book in her hands. The leather cover was old, and the pages yellowed, but the coded language was familiar.

The language was a mix of characters and mathematical symbols used to create a fake language. Her grandfather had taught her this code and had left her playful riddles when she was a little girl. The memories brought a smile to her lips. That was a long time ago, and she hadn't seen the language since.

She leaned over to her dresser and wrote notes on a piece of parchment. After spending an hour on the text, she had most of the cipher worked out. She needed the rest before she could begin reading.

A faint knock sounded on her door. She put a strand of hair behind her ear. "Come in."

Ander opened the door and closed it behind himself. He took a few strides before gently sitting on the edge of her bed.

"How are you feeling?"

She shrugged. "I've had worse falls."

Instead of smiling at her joke, he grimaced.

"Eugene said it should heal up just fine, so long as I don't walk on it for a few days."

That elicited a chuckle. "Good luck with that. I don't think I've ever seen you *not* busy. Even with you stuck in bed, you're still working." He gestured at the book. "Is that from the archives?"

She nodded. "It's the only thing I could come out with. I just need to finish the cipher."

He gave a heavy sigh. "If it doesn't have any useful information in it, I'm afraid this may be the end of our journey for the Wayfinder.

With no other leads and Khaldun—" He ran his fingers down his face. "We won't be able to return to Sadria."

"I'm sorry I didn't get back fast enough." Her voice was quiet.

"Sorry? You twisted your ankle, were attacked twice, and limped all the way to the *Legacy*. If it weren't for you, I'd have lost my whole team, not to mention the five others with them. If anyone's apologizing, it should be me. I should have calculated my drop more effectively. If I had, I could have at least saved Sergeant Allred and his team." He clenched his hands into fists and looked away.

She put a hand on his arm. "What you did was brave. I was worried you wouldn't come back." Her cheeks flushed at the admission, and she quickly pulled her hand away to brush some loose hairs that slipped back into her face.

"Thanks," he said simply. Then he sighed. "I wanted to thank you for standing up for me after the whole ordeal."

"Of course! I think they were all in a bit of a shock and were looking for a place to put it. I'm sorry that was you."

He shrugged. "I'm just glad that I can always count on you to have my back. There's no one on this airship that I trust more than you."

His words were kind, and she should have felt warm at the compliment instead of a sickening twist in her gut. He had *no* idea the secrets she was keeping from him.

They both fell into silence. After a long moment, he stood up. "Well, I've sent a telegraph to high command, briefing them on what happened. We're now waiting for a reply. In the meantime, let me know if you learn anything useful from that book. I could use a distraction."

"Will do," she said in a quiet voice. She watched him leave. Once he was gone, she put her head into her hands.

How am I supposed to tell him now? she wondered. With relations so strained on the airship, how was she supposed to confess to him she'd been keeping secrets from him all along? At this point, the information would crush him. He didn't deserve that.

She pulled at her hair and groaned. *Why was this so complicated?* Her empty room gave no reply, and it was a long time before she picked her journal back up to resume working on the cipher.

It helped to have something intellectual occupy her mind. The challenge helped push the impossible situation from the forefront of her mind to the back. After some time, she finally cracked the code.

She flipped the book to the cover and read *The 11th Secret Journal of Nicholas Steam.* Goosebumps erupted across her arms. She opened to the first page and read.

Day 1 at the Sadrian Palace
Sultan Aramah greeted me warmly, despite the late hour of my arrival. He accepted my request to study at the archives, though his guards were taken aback at the sight of the Revolution dropping into his palace gardens near midnight. I would have preferred not to have made such an entry, but, as you know, Cornelius, speed is the only advantage I have against our enemy, and I must get to Illithador before it's too late. From my research, the Wayfinder is our best chance at success.

Amelia brushed her fingers over the name *Cornelius* and felt tears come to her eyes. She hadn't read her father's name in years. The entry continued, but a line was scrawled across the margin in messy handwriting.

Begin reading the last entry.

Alright, she thought. She wiped the bottoms of her eyelashes with her palm before opening to the back. The second half of the book was blank pages, so she backtracked until she found the last entry.

Day 34 at the Sadrian Palace
He's here! Two of my colleagues are now dead, murdered in the night in their rooms at the embassy. I don't doubt he knows I'm sequestered here within the palace. Aramah believes I'm safe behind these walls. He is a fool. They are not impregnable to the one who hunts me. Nothing is.

There was a small paragraph gap before the next section. Here the characters here were sloppy and smeared.

Cornelius! The Sultan is dead, and the palace is in mayhem. I'm being hunted but I don't know whose face he's using. This library's no use. The Wayfinder disappeared long before Sadria was founded. I'm convinced the answers can only be found at the Lost Palace of Valera. Please see my notes within on how to find it. I'm leaving you this journal in case I don't make it. If I don't, you must complete the journey. The world needs to know who this dark entity is and how it can be stopped. Nothing else matters more.

The journal ended here, leaving her mind racing and her heart pounding. What had happened? What was pursuing her grandfather?

Was this the old age madness Amir had referenced? Or had there really been some dark power pursuing her grandfather?

A horrible thought struck her like lightning. Her grandfather had gone missing nearly fourteen years ago. What if he never made it out?

An icy chill swept over her, raising the hairs on her arms. She pulled her blankets closer and reread the words. The truth was, she didn't know what was true and what wasn't. Maybe her grandfather *had* become senile before he disappeared. She remembered the state of the Steam Invention Company before the fire. Her father, Cornelius, spent years doing everything he could to keep the business from going under. Apparently, her grandfather had mismanaged funds before he disappeared, taking out large sums of money before vanishing altogether. Why would he do that unless he had started to go mad? Unless he did it because of the dark entity, but if that was the case, wouldn't she have known about it? Wouldn't her father have mentioned something?

So many questions circled around her head. Still, the book in her hands and the handwriting—these were her *grandfather's* words. She closed the volume and held it close. Tears broke loose and dripped onto her blanket with soft plops.

Her family was gone. She was all alone.

The tears became a steady stream as loneliness consumed her. She held the book through it all as if it were a lifeline in a dark sea. The waves were familiar. She'd been battling them for years, but now she had something to cling to. This book contained her grandfather's voice. It was as if a piece of him were here in her arms.

She grabbed a handkerchief and wiped her eyes. It was a good thing she was working on this in her cabin. She could only imagine what it would have been like around the rest of the crew.

She opened the book again and ran her fingers over the letters. Her grandfather had penned these. His hands had touched these pages.

Another thought struck her. Her grandfather had gone to the archives to find the Wayfinder, and somehow fate had led her to do the same.

A strange warmth blossomed through her chest and filled her with purpose. The coincidence felt like destiny. Regardless of whether Nicholas was mad, she was now on the same path to the Wayfinder. The same desire he had to find it now burned through her veins.

The warmth transformed into passionate determination. She *had* to find the Wayfinder. Not only was this her mission, but it was her grandfather's wish. It might have been his dying wish. No other Steams were left to do this. No one else had the ability to read this book. This *was* her destiny. This was her part in her family's grand legacy.

With that thought filling her, she began reading through the entries, beginning again from the start. As she progressed, her excitement grew. Hours passed, but she couldn't stop until she read every single word. By the time she finished, she was grinning from ear to ear.

. . . .

Amelia couldn't contain her excitement as the officers filed into her office and took seats around the table. Not even Eugene's warning about injuring her ankle further could keep her down. Ander was the last person to enter, and he took the seat next to her.

"Are you ready to begin?" he asked.

She nodded.

"Alright." He stood and addressed the entire group. "I imagine many of you are wondering what Amelia found during her time at the archives. She is going to brief us on what she learned, and then we are going to discuss our next plan of attack. Amelia?"

"Thank you." She remained seated given her injury, but her voice carried nevertheless. "When I started my research, I came up with very little at first because the Wayfinder was lost long before the Sadrian kingdom was established three hundred years ago. In fact, my entire time at the archives would have been useless if I didn't stumble on a hidden journal from my grandfather."

She glanced at Amir to make sure he was listening. "My grandfather came to the archives nearly fourteen years ago, studying the whereabouts of the Wayfinder. He and I came to the same conclusion, but he connected several dots that I did not.

"Before Sadria was the great kingdom of Valera, which stood for nearly two thousand years until the Sahadrian Seas receded and dried into the deserts we see today. As the waters disappeared, the land grew inhospitable. The citizens left in masses to settle the eastern coast and Azure River.

"The final fall of Valera came when the aquifers collapsed underneath the great palace. In the course of one day, the entire structure sank into the earth and killed the inhabitants. As the years passed, the desert sands buried the remains, erasing any signs of its existence. No one knows where the city stands today, which is why it's now called the Lost Palace of Valera.

Amir put a hand across his eyes. "Please don't tell me you intend to search for it?"

"I'm not done yet," Amelia cut in. "We know that the Wayfinder was created nearly a thousand years ago and was given to the king of the sands. The greatest kingdom in this land during that time was Valera. Which means, if there's information about the Wayfinder anywhere, it would be there."

"So, we need to find this Lost Palace of Valera?" Charles surmised.

"Yes."

"Good luck," muttered Amir. All eyes turned to him. "What? Is that your brilliant plan? Let's go find the fabled artifact in the one place no one has found for hundreds of years? You're just as cracked up as your grandfather."

"Whoa," said Ander. "Speak like that in this room, and you'll be booted out."

"He has a point," said Charles. "How would we find Valera?"

"Exactly," said Amir with a smug grin. "How do you expect to succeed where others have failed?"

She clenched her teeth. "If you'd stop interrupting me, I'd tell you."

"Let's hold the questions until she's done," said Ander.

"Thank you." She took a deep breath before continuing. "The reason no one has found the palace is that the desert is thousands of miles long and thousands wide. You'd never find it by digging at random. That's where my grandfather's given us a missing piece.

"When Valera was at its height, traders came from all around the world to buy and sell. One of the major trade routes traveled through the Caves of Bailidan. A friend of my grandfather had once taken him on a tour. Inside the caves were ancient etchings. It wasn't until later that my grandfather realized the significance of the etchings—they were directions to get to Valera, preserved over the years. Now, if we could find these caves and translate the etchings, we could follow the directions and find where Valera was buried."

She leaned back with a satisfied smile. "Now I'm ready for questions and comments." The group stared at her in stunned silence. Everyone but Amir, but she was done with speaking to him.

"Brilliant work, Millie," said Ander next to her.

"I'm amazed you figured that out in only a few weeks," said Garret.

"I don't mean to rain on your parade," said Amir, "but do any of you know anything about the Caves of Bailidan?"

Amelia narrowed her eyes. "My grandfather said there was some political upheaval around the caves during the time of his visit to the archives. That was why he couldn't visit again."

"Political upheaval?" Amir chuckled darkly. "The Caves of Bailidan are the main headquarters of the Mirage. Khaldun's been waging war against those caves for fifteen years. He has troops stationed there as we speak. Good luck getting in."

"We've done the impossible before," said Ander. "We'll figure this one out too."

A knock sounded on the door. Freya pushed away from the wall and opened the door. A sailor entered.

"We got a telegraph from high command," said the sailor quickly. "They need this crew to stand testimonial against Bragg. They've ordered us to the Republic."

"What?" said Amelia in alarm. "But we just figured out our next step to the Wayfinder."

"We can't counteract a direct order from high command," said Charles. He withdrew an officer's handbook and began flipping to a page Amelia had no care to hear.

"Ander," she gasped, "you know we can't do that!"

Ander exhaled and closed his eyes. "Charles is right. We can't disobey a direct order."

"Ugh, soldiers!" She stood up quickly and immediately yelped in pain.

"Here, let me help," Ander offered, but she pushed him away.

"I'll do it myself." She limped past the group and out the door. When she entered her cabin, she slammed the door and fell to her bed. Her fingers found her grandfather's journal, and she clutched it to her chest.

This was supposed to be her destiny. This was how she'd join her family legacy.

She brooded until night fell, refusing to talk to anyone. When finally she began to drift off to sleep, a knock sounded from the door.

She let out an exhausted sigh. "I'm sleeping."

"Amelia, this is important!" the voice was Ander's.

She got up and unlocked the door. Ander and Garret stood there in full gear. Both of them had white faces.

"What's wrong?" she asked, feeling fear worm through her insides.

"It's Bragg," said Ander. "He's dead."

Chapter 23: Breaking Point

Amelia

Amelia stared at Ander and Garret in shock. "Bragg's dead? What? How?" She let the soldiers in.

"Slit throat," said Garret. "He was found on the floor with the knife still in his hands. We found his last will and testament on his bed. It looks like a suicide."

Amelia put a hand over her mouth. She never liked Bragg, but she never wished this upon him. "This is awful!"

"I know," said Ander. "It's sudden. I don't think any of us saw this coming."

"Why?" she asked. "Why would he do it?"

Garret shrugged. "Maybe he heard about his upcoming trial through the floorboards? Maybe that pushed him over the edge?"

Ander shook his head. "It's hard to believe. Bragg was many things, but at the heart of it he was always a coward. I can't picture him doing this."

Amelia frowned. "You don't think it was foul play?"

Ander rubbed a hand down his face. "I don't know. Maybe I'm jumping at shadows since the last mission."

Silence stretched out in the room.

"I don't think it was foul play," said Garret finally. "No one had been in his room except to deliver meals. I also don't see anyone on this airship wanting anything more than to see Bragg go to court."

"That makes sense," said Ander. "Well, we at least wanted to let you know. I'll need to report this."

"Alright," said Amelia. After they left, she stared at the door, her mind whirling with the news. The thought of Bragg dead opened a horrible pit in her stomach. It took a long time before she could get her mind to a place where she could sleep again.

Morning came bright and early. She and Ander organized the crew for a funeral service; and while no one liked Bragg, all were quiet and dressed in official uniform. Even Axel was there, though he wore an unkempt beard. The sight of him standing with the others was the only warmth in the otherwise somber service. This was the first time she had seen him outside the medical bay or his cabin.

Charles Rigg gave a few thoughts about his former commander. Then a sailor played a bugle while Bragg's remaining team wrapped his casket in a flag and tipped it over into the sea.

When the service closed, Amelia limped over to Axel. He noticed her coming and attempted to disappear, but she caught up with him before he could open the hatch.

"Axe, you're out and about," she said. She gave him a hug and immediately regretted it. The soldier smelt like he hadn't washed in weeks. She released him and looked into his face. His cheeks were hollow, and his eyes lacked their usual levity.

"How's your injury?" she asked.

He took a shallow breath and showed the stump of his right hand. It was healed over now with just a few scars.

"It looks great!" she said with a smile. The warmth didn't seem to reach him. He gave a tight smile and looked back at the hatch.

Something's wrong, she thought. She hadn't had time to talk to him about how he was doing with the loss of his hand, and now she was regretting that. There was clearly a lot that was pressing down on his normally loud and large personality. She opened her mouth to ask him how he *really* was doing when Charles stepped between them.

"Captain, we just got a telegraph from the Office of External Affairs. The *Firelancer*'s been spotted in the West Shaoguan Strait!"

"Oh..." That was only weeks away from Sadria, assuming that's where the Enchantrans were headed.

She closed her eyes and rubbed her forehead with her palm. If the Enchantrans were on their way, they were running out of time.

"That's not all, captain," said Charles. "We've been given new orders to maintain our objective for the Wayfinder."

She let out a breath of air. "Well, that's a relief. Make sure Ander knows about this, too."

"Will do." He left and headed toward Ander, who was talking to the remaining three members of Bragg's unit. Amelia turned back to where Axel was, but he'd disappeared.

She needed to set the *Legacy* on their new heading, but part of her wanted to hunt down Axel instead. The former need took precedence, though. With the Enchantrans so close, they needed every head start they could get. She'd have to snag Axel when the next opportunity came.

She limped to the helm and used her grandfather's journal to set course for the Caves of Bailidan. The caves were located on a lone peak just south of the western edge of the North Sadrian Range. The journey would take them all the way across the desert to the far north.

She gave sail configuration instructions to her crew while Ander reorganized the remaining soldiers from the Desert Steam Soldiers into Charles' team and created a new third team. Then they disbanded to below deck.

A few minutes later, Ander reappeared, with Garret, Eugene, and Blaze in tow. Hammer was still in recovery, and Axel was noticeably absent.

"Hey, Millie," said Ander. "We are starting up training. I know I've asked before, but if you're going to keep running into trouble—"

"Ander, she needs to recover," Eugene cut in. "She shouldn't be walking on that ankle, let alone piloting this airship."

"It's feeling better today," said Amelia defensively. It did hurt still, but not enough to force her to be cooped up all day again.

Eugene raised an eyebrow. "You're still limping."

"We could keep it easy, show you some basics?" Ander's eyebrows were scrunched close together. She opened her mouth to tell him *no*, but his concerned expression stopped the word from coming out.

After a pause, she gave in. "Fine, I'll join you."

"Great!" said Ander while Eugene folded his arms. "Garret, could you get the team started? I'll get Amelia outfitted."

"Outfitted?" she raised an eyebrow. "We're not playing dress-up, are we?"

"You'd have us all beat if we did," said Blaze. Heat came to her cheeks, and she was about to give a snappy reply when she caught his expression. His face was flat instead of grinning, and he kept glancing between her and Ander.

"Alright, let's get started," said Garret, pulling Blaze and Eugene with him.

"What's up with Blaze?" she asked.

Ander shrugged. "Ready to pick out some weapons?"

"Sure." They left the main deck and traveled down to the hold. As she stepped in, she stared all around. Crates and barrels filled every corner.

"Wow, when you told me that Olivia resupplied us, you weren't kidding."

He nodded. "Let's open these up here." They pried open a couple of crates that were filled with weapons of all types. Then he brushed his hands off and asked, "Any type of weapon you are interested in?"

That's such a boy question, she thought. She looked at the piles and scratched her head. "I'm not really a get-into-fights kind of girl."

Ander raised a mocking eyebrow.

"What?" She punched him in the shoulder. "Some of us aren't unruly ruffians."

He chuckled, pulled out a long sword, and handed it to her. She took it and held it with two hands. "Is it supposed to be heavy?"

"You're holding it wrong. Here, try this." He took her hands in his and adjusted several of her fingers to alter her grip. Warmth spread from the contact and sent her heart racing. She looked up at him and met his blue eyes. Her breath caught in her throat, and it felt as if the whole world slowed down. Then, all at once, awareness struck them both at the same time.

They both let go of the sword and took a step back from each other. The sword hit the floor with a loud clang. She turned away as he picked it up and put it away with the others.

She slipped a stray strand of hair behind her ear. "Sorry, I'm no good at this kind of thing."

"You're fine." His face was red and his posture was now stiff and soldier-like. "That blade is too long for your height. I'll find another one." He turned around quickly.

As he disappeared down the cramped aisle of crates and barrels, she looked down at her hands and wondered. What just happened? Had she really just lost herself in Ander's eyes? He was just her friend. She didn't think of him as more than that. Right?

She bit her lip. He was brave and honorable, and that was on top of being kind and thoughtful. Selfless—yes, he was that too. She couldn't count how many times he had risked his own life for hers. His appearance had grown more rugged over time, which she couldn't deny gave him a handsome appeal. And those eyes... Her attention drifted as she imagined his blue eyes, and how they always seemed to be softer when they were looking at her.

What about me? she wondered.

An icy chill settled over her with the question, blowing out the warmth from the moment before like it was a feeble candle.

I started the fire that killed so many people, she thought. *When I should have made amends, I ran away and lived outside the Republic. I'm loathed by the people of Steam, and for good reason. I'm selfish, stubborn, and end up hurting everyone I care about. I'm* nothing *like Ander.*

A wave of dizziness slammed into her as guilt filled her like a ballonet passed capacity. She leaned into a crate and put her face into her hands.

After a few steadying breaths, realization sank in. The truth was, it didn't matter whether or not she liked Ander. She could never be with someone like him, much less be friends. The only reason they were friends was because he didn't know the truth yet. She hid it from him, because she selfishly liked living this lie.

Ander's footsteps grew in volume, heading toward her. Fear rose inside her. He couldn't see her in this state. There wasn't time to escape either before he reached her. The airship wasn't *that* big. She took a few quick breaths and tried to compose herself.

He appeared with a shorter sword. "I found this," he said, offering it to her.

She looked at the sword and hesitated. If she took the blade from him, she'd have to learn how to use it. That would mean spending more time with him, thus perpetuating her predicament further.

She took a step back from him. "I'm sorry," she said without emotion. "I'm an inventor, not a soldier. Tools are more my thing."

His expression transformed into one of concern. "Millie, you need to learn to defend yourself. Otherwise, one of these days..." He swallowed and looked away.

A shiver went through her. He cared about her—it was clear in his expression. She'd let this go on for too long. If she couldn't tell him the truth, then she at least needed to stop living this lie. She couldn't keep pretending they could be friends.

She cleared her throat. "My ankle hurts, so I'm going to go."

She rushed from the room, ignoring his call after her. Tears threatened to spill out of her eyes, but she held them back. As she passed through the main deck, she spotted Axel hunched over the railing. Part of her wanted to stop and talk to him, but the pressure she felt inside was too consuming. She continued right past him and entered her cabin. Once inside, she threw herself on her bed and released her tears.

Chapter 24: Bailidan

Ander

Sweat dripped from Ander's face as he ran through drills with the team. Blaze stood opposite from him and matched his movements, blocking his strikes and striking in return. The sun was high overhead, blocked from view by the envelope of the *Legacy*. Despite the shade, the wind was hot and dry.

Regardless of the conditions, the drill was a welcome stress relief. There was only so much exercise you could get cooped up on an airship. The release in energy also helped ease the weight on his mind.

He had no idea what he said to Amelia that caused her to stop talking to him. One moment, she was his closest friend and confidant, and the next, it was like he never existed. It was driving him mad.

Blaze stumbled back a pace from the force of Ander's blows. Ander didn't let up. It was good practice, and they needed all the conditioning they could get.

There *was* one problem he was able to figure out in the storeroom after she left. In one of the new crates, he found an engineering magpack. The pack was outfitted with an assortment of dyed-black tools and was designed for high-risk missions that required repairs. It was a bit large and heavy, so he had taken it to the inventors to tailor it down to her size. It had taken several days, but they'd finally finished. There hadn't been an opportunity to give it to her yet. Now he wondered if the pack was a mistake entirely.

His train of thought halted as Amelia appeared and passed by them on her way to the crew's quarters. True to form, she didn't even spare him a glance. Instead, she bee-lined her way to the closed double doors and disappeared within.

Blaze's sword nearly took Ander's head off, snapping his attention back to right in front of him. *Right. Focus.* He shifted his position so that Amelia's return would be to his back and pushed her far out of his mind.

As they were wrapping up their drill, a sailor shouted, "Oi! City on the horizon!" They sheathed their swords and climbed up onto the forward quarterdeck to get a view.

Ahead, the blocky form of a city materialized on the dusty landscape. It rested between the end of a river and the edge of a rocky plateau. Where the plateau dropped off, desert sands stretched out on all sides. To the far right, the Northern Sadrian Range ran parallel with them and curved only slightly toward the desert. The last feature that caught their eye was a lone, jagged peak that rose separated from the rest of the range.

Ander glanced back to the helm where Amelia stood steering, tempted to ask her about the landscape. Then he thought better.

CRAIG & JALEESA SNOW

"Blaze," he said, "go get Amir."

Blaze returned with the potbellied scholar in tow. Amir's legs were shaky as he shuffled to them, and he stopped a good several feet before the railing.

"What do you want?" he asked irritably. "I don't like being exposed on top of this cursed flying machine."

"Could you tell us about the city ahead?" Ander held out his spyglass to the man.

Amir took it and raised it to his eye. "That's Vashi, the last settlement of the Sadrian kingdom." The man's face curved into a frown.

"You say that like it's a bad thing."

Amir huffed. "Being here is insane. Vashi is the front lines, the *front lines!* It's the place where Sadria and the Mirage war with each other."

"Really?" Ander looked through his spyglass again. Even from this distance, he could see the city was fortified and easily could have hosted an army of thousands. "Anything else?"

"That lone peak you see on the horizon. That's where the Caves of Bailidan are, the headquarters for the Mirage."

It was Ander's turn to frown. "That's not far away from the city. I'm surprised Khaldun's army hasn't conquered them."

Amir huffed. "Look at the sands between the city and the mountain."

Ander did and saw dunes moving of their own accord, kicking up dust. "Sadricondas?" he asked.

"Sadricondas," Amir confirmed. "A lot of them. No army has successfully crossed those sands."

"Why don't they just attack during the day then?" he asked.

"Don't sadricondas only hunt at night?"

Amir nodded. "That would normally be the case. Rumor has it, however, that Abdulmalik could stir the beasts up during the day. Some have even said he could influence them. Control them. That's how they've maintained the caves."

"There's a lot of smoke coming from the foot of the mountain," Garret observed.

"Maybe it's volcanic?" said Blaze.

Amir scrunched his eyebrows. "No, it's not."

Ander stretched his spyglass to its full length and felt his mouth fall open. Sure enough, on the northernmost side of the lone peak stretched an army with siege engines.

He turned to the scholar. "I thought you said no army has ever crossed these sands before."

"What? That's impossible," Amir stuttered. "The sadricondas, they've always repelled them. That's how the Mirage has kept their independence."

Ander raised an eyebrow and resumed studying the mount. The more he analyzed the mass of soldiers, the surer he felt they were Sadrian, not the Mirage.

"Well," he said, "it looks like the Sadrians have found a way."

"Judging by the marching lines in the sands," said Garret, "it looks like they took the shortest path from the edge of the northern range to the mount. It must be recent or they wind would've blown the lines out of the sand already."

Ander lowered his spyglass and ran a hand through his hair. "We need to get into those caves before they are overrun by soldiers. Otherwise, it'll be impossible to find those etchings to the Lost Palace of Valera."

"How are we going to do that?" asked Eugene. "If the Mirage is under siege, they probably have every entrance locked up tight."

"I have a way," said Amelia.

They all turned around to face her. Amelia focused on Eugene and didn't glance at Ander.

"We could go through the front entrance," she explained. "The original entrance."

Amir ran a hand down his face. "You realize the original entrances are collapsed, right?"

Amelia rolled her eyes. "Of course I do." She tapped a hand on her grandfather's journal. "I also know where time has worn them down so that cracks of sunlight are pouring in. I think we could break through."

"It's settled then," said Ander. "We'll prep the team to drop at nightfall."

"We?" she asked, addressing Ander for the first time. She folded her arms. "This mission doesn't have to be led by *you* and *your* team, does it? There are others who could accompany me."

"Yeah," said Charles, who was climbing up the ladder behind to join them. "Why does your team get all the action while the rest of us stay behind?"

Freya appeared next to him and echoed her agreement.

Ander took a step back, glancing between Amelia, Charles, Freya, and then back to Amelia. Why was she pushing him away?

"Millie, you're a part of our team," he explained.

She put her hands on her hips. "I'm the captain of this airship. I'm not a part of any team."

The words hit him like a slap. Pain and anger rose in him, but he kept his tone controlled. "If that's how you feel, then I don't see any reason, as the captain, *you* need to go on this mission at all."

"Who would read this, then?" she asked, holding up her grandfather's journal. "Besides, aren't you on medical leave?"

His back stiffened. Technically, he was, but he didn't appreciate being reminded of that fact. It wasn't like he was an invalid. He was fully capable, and he had half a mind to prove it.

He turned it back on her. "Aren't *you* still recovering from an ankle injury?" His voice was now rising.

"My ankle is FINE enough."

"So you think *you* are well enough to go, but *I'm* not?" They now stood face to face, glaring at each other.

"You're all raving mad!" said Amir. "Can't you see there is a *war* happening on those slopes?"

"Maybe this isn't such a bright idea," said Charles, who was now shrinking back. "Perhaps no one should do this mission."

"Since Ander is incapable and Charles is afraid," said Amelia, "then I'll just do it myself."

Something snapped inside of Ander. He wasn't incapable, and he wasn't going to let Amelia push him out of his job—even if the restorative hadn't done its work yet. His voice dropped to a steely calm as he addressed the group. "No. This isn't for debate. As mission commander, I am making an executive decision. My team *will* take this mission tonight, and I *will* be leading them."

"Then I'm going with you," said Amelia.

He glared at her. "Fine."

"FINE."

Awkward silence fell across the deck. Amelia turned with a huff and disappeared down the ladder. The rest of the group followed a beat afterward, leaving Garret and Ander alone.

Ander took his usual spot at the bow and gripped the railing. Garret joined him, and they stared out at the hazy city.

After a pause, Garret cleared his throat. "Is everything okay between you and Amelia?"

Ander let out a heavy sigh. "I don't know. I thought so, but now it seems like she wants nothing to do with me. I have no idea what I did."

"Hmm." Garret stroked his mustache in thought. "I could talk to her if you wanted."

Ander shook his head. "No. I can talk to her. I just need to find a time to do it when she's not so frustrating."

Garret put a hand on his shoulder. "Knowing you two, this'll blow over. You'll see."

He sighed again. "Thanks. I hope so."

The soldier pushed off the railing. "Well, let me know if there's anything I can do."

A thought struck Ander. "Actually, there is one thing. Could you have the inventors make a delivery? Tell them specifically not to mention that it's from me."

. . . .

The chilly night winds howled as the group prepared to drop from the airship. Smoke from the fires of a thousand torches drifted over, filling the air with the smell of war. A large black vulture swooped over their heads and continued onward, winging its way toward the commotion. Even from the opposite side of the mountain, they could hear the shouts and clang of steel, along with the pounding of war machines. The expenditure of magic drifted through the air like burnt ozone. Clearly, the Sadrian army was not holding back from taking the stronghold. The only question was, how long would the gates last before the caves were flooded with battle?

Amelia beamed from ear to ear as she showed off her new magpack to everyone but Ander. Black steel tools and pouches were strapped across the magpack, along with a steam-powered auger and a welding torch. Two canisters were clipped above a battery pack.

"I can't believe how thoughtful Emmett and Archibald are for finding and tailoring this to me," she said to Hammer. "It fits so well and is surprisingly lighter than I thought it'd be."

Ander watched the exchange, feeling distant and forlorn inside. He wondered if he should have told her the gift was his idea. It hurt seeing how happy she was but not being the recipient of that gratitude after days of her avoiding him. Still, he worried if he did tell her, she would reject the gift. He supposed it was better this way. At least she'd be safer.

The group finished strapping on their gear before putting on large hooded cloaks that covered everything underneath. Then they slipped on their mouth coverings and rappelled from the *Legacy* one by one.

They touched down in front of the rocky collapse of what used to be the entrance to the Caves of Bailidan. As soon as they were all down, Ander gestured a hand forward, and the group took up their positions around the collapse. The *Legacy* turned about and rose into the sky.

"Alright," Ander whispered to Amelia. "Guide us to where we need to break through."

She nodded without meeting his eyes. "My grandfather said he could see light from the top of the collapse. That's the weak point."

"Ander," said Garret. He knelt down and pointed. The cracks between the rocks were filled with what appeared to be melted sand.

Ander knelt down next to Garret and touched the rough surface—hard as rock with traces of magic.

A knot grew between his shoulders. "Let's see if the top has been sealed, too." They climbed over the debris and sure enough, all the collapse was sealed.

Amelia cursed. "There was supposed to be a weak point up here, one that we could get through." Her brow was furrowed as she bit her lip, thinking.

Ander studied the surrounding typography before turning to her. "Do you know of any other way in?"

Her expression fell further. "Not any reliable one. These caves were cut by water running through the limestone. We could look for a chute from above?"

That'll take too long, he thought. They needed to get into these tunnels immediately. "Do you think we could blast our way through this?"

Eugene shook his head and pointed a finger toward the north. "You realize there's an entire *army* over there? Not to mention another one *inside* this place?"

"We've got sound cover," said Garret. Ander hoped that was true, at least. Both armies' attention would be centered on the north side of the mountain, not here at the east. Eugene folded his arms in clear disagreement, but there wasn't time to argue.

"Millie, get us blast holes. Quick!"

She withdrew her drill and began boring holes into the rock. Blaze followed her, dropping charges in each. As they did their work, the conflict on the northern slopes seemed to grow in volume. War chants were shouted in tempo along with the rhythm of earth splitting pounding.

Second thoughts drifted through Ander's mind. *What if our break-in did alert the Mirage? What if we got into the caves too late? What if we became trapped between the two armies?* He shook the thoughts out of his head. *No, we have to succeed, no matter the obstacle, no matter the sacrifice.*

They lit the fuses and moved to cover. *BOOM!* Rock and fragments blasted everywhere. As the dust billowed out, the dark opening of a cave appeared.

He waved a hand, sending the whole group rushing to the dark opening. Amelia followed in the rear, holding up a lamp that glowed a dim phosphorescent blue.

The cave was wide, with a floor that was worn and mostly flat. Small ripples were carved into the stone, similar to the pattern of the dunes outside. The ceiling was coated with black ash, probably from the fires of travelers who passed through here for generations.

The rocks above them groaned. Ander's eyes widened. "Move!" The word barely left his mouth before the ceiling began to crumble. They tumbled forward as the cave collapsed behind.

More dust billowed past them. As the air cleared, they checked the passage behind. Blocked.

Eugene leaned over and took several shaky breaths. "There goes our exit," he muttered.

"Come on, Eugeney," said Blaze, slapping him on the back. "We've faced caves before."

"That's the problem," said Eugene. "I'm still working through the last cave."

Ander held up a fist, and the group fell silent. He strained his ears for any signs of the Mirage.

Nothing.

Still, they had made a lot of noise, far more than he had hoped. Someone was bound to investigate, and he wanted to be gone when they did.

He opened his hand and gestured forward. The soldiers readied their weapons and proceeded into the dark.

The passageway snaked back and forth as it rose in elevation. According to Nicholas Steam's journal, this had once been called the *Serpent's Corridor* during the time of Valera. After a few minutes, the tunnel opened into a walnut shaped cavern, with the path splitting to the left and right around a central pond. Within the pond, dark fish with white eyes darted around mossy stalagmites. Strange, bulbous bugs crawled above on the jagged stalactite ceiling. The whole bizarre scene would have been strangely serene if it wasn't for the impending sense of danger growing by the second.

Why haven't we run into anyone yet? Ander wondered. The blast and subsequent collapse would have been loud enough to echo a long way through the cave. Granted, he was grateful they hadn't run into a patrol yet. Still, the lack of resistance worried him more. Had the Mirage already lost the battle? Were Sadrian soldiers already flooding the caverns? Were they already trapped?

He picked up the pace, leading them around the pond and up a slope. By the time they reached the top, the path opened into another cavern filled with stalactites and stalagmites, except this time canvas tents were pitched throughout the space. Feeble orange light glowed somewhere ahead.

Ander motioned for Amelia to shutter the light. Then they proceeded forward in a low crouch. Once they reached the edge where the tents started, they paused and surveyed the environment.

Nothing moved.

They continued onward, passing tent after tent. Each was flung open and empty of life. Only scattered trash and the tents themselves revealed any signs that people had once been there.

They drew close to the only source of light in the cavern, which turned out to be the dim glow of coals from a campfire. It was positioned underneath a crack in the ceiling—a dried up water shoot, most likely.

Something moved ahead in the dark, freezing everyone to a stop. A figure materialized, hastily scurrying through the tents ahead of them and pawing through the trash on the ground. He was dressed in rags and had a mousy face. He pocketed a few items here and there before continuing on to another area in the room.

A scavenger, Ander realized. *Where had everyone else gone?*

BOOM! The sound echoed powerfully through the corridor and kicked dust from the ceiling. The scavenger leapt at the sound and disappeared deeper into the cavern.

The team followed the same direction, making their way carefully through the remaining tents and into a new cave. More *BOOMS* followed the first and continued in a regular cadence. Other sounds also grew into volume. Voices shouting.

Amelia slipped next to Ander and whispered. "We should be getting close to a fork in the path. The right will lead to the Coral Cavern while the left should lead to the overlook." She fell back before he could respond, melting into the back of the group. He sighed and continued leading forward.

When the fork arrived, they took the left path to the overlook. The sounds of commotion rose the farther they traveled. They were getting close now.

The path angled upward and ended at a drop off into a well-lit cavern. They lowered to the ground, crawled to the edge, and peered down.

This cavern was nothing like the previous two. The ceiling was covered with dried coral reefs. The reefs swirled around in flower-like arrangements, garnishing the ceiling with pearly wonder. Several sparkled in the torchlight, though most of their majesty was grayed and covered with soot and cooking grease.

The cavern floor was covered with wicker baskets and clay pots. People rushed to the supplies and carried them out through a cave to the left. On the right was a slightly open stone gate, which Ander guessed was the opening to the ancient guard outpost. The outpost was definitely not abandoned based on the light that poured through the opening and the shouts that echoed from within. More caves opened up throughout the cavern, including a large one that proceeded in the same direction that they had been traveling.

"They're evacuating," said Garret quietly. "Pretty frantically, I'll add."

"That's not a good sign," Eugene added.

Ander held a finger up to his lips. "This is the right place, right?" His barely audible question was pointed at Amelia.

She nodded, again without meeting his eyes. "It should be near the outpost."

Ander turned his gaze back to the walls by the outpost, studying every feature.

"There." She pointed to the left of the outpost opening.

Ander squinted. "I don't see it."

"It's a bit hard to see, but there's an impression there."

"I see it," said Garret.

It took a moment longer before Ander also spotted the

engraving. He withdrew his spyglass and could only make out a few indecipherable characters through the soot, ash, and grease covering the cave wall.

He pulled away from the edge and addressed the others. "It looks like it's obscured. There's no way we'll be able to make that out from here. We need to get closer."

"There's a lot of people down there," warned Eugene, "and our disguises aren't exactly foolproof."

"I'll go in alone," said Amelia immediately. "I'm confident I can blend in."

Ander's mind flashed back to the time Khaldun had singled her out in a crowd. She would have been taken if he hadn't been there.

He shook his head. "It's too dangerous to go in alone. Especially with the siege happening."

Her expression turned fierce. "I've done this kind of thing many times. Besides, you need someone to sketch the etching, and I'm the only one with a journal and charcoal pencil."

He closed his eyes. The continuous booming sound was now giving him a headache. "Fine. I'll go with Millie. Blaze, slip in and see if you can locate an exit while we get that inscription. Garret, Hammer, and Eugene will provide cover fire if things get heated. If we need to make a break for it, we'll move through that tunnel where they are taking supplies and pray we don't meet an army. Questions?"

The group shook their heads, though Amelia didn't look happy. He ignored her expression and said, "Alright, let's move." He clipped his crossbow underneath his cloak and led the way back, with Amelia and Blaze a step behind. They retraced their steps until they came to the fork in the tunnel. Then they took the sloping path down into the caverns.

As soon as they reached the entrance, Blaze split from them and hurried toward the supplies. He grabbed a basket and melted easily into the throng of people hurrying out.

Ander watched from the shadows, marveling how the soldier made blending in look effortless. There were so many people moving about, and so many chances of being spotted. He waited, watching for a gap in the crowd so he and Amelia could slip in toward the outpost.

After a few seconds, Amelia stepped in front of him in an attempt to block his view. Her hands were on her hips. "You don't need to accompany me. I can do this on my own."

"We're already underway," he whispered, trying to look past her. "Also, if you haven't noticed, we're in the middle of a siege." A gap opened between the hurrying people. He moved to join the crowd and was stopped by Amelia.

"Look." She pinched the bridge of her nose. "I know you are trying to help. But this isn't your strength—"

Whatever more she had to say was interrupted by a shout. A man, dressed in patchwork clothes, stomped toward them, shouting something in thick, unintelligible Sadrian. His hands gesticulated wildly, pointing to the baskets.

Ander instinctively reached for the hilt of his sword, but she grabbed his arm before he could draw it.

"He's telling you to grab a basket and take it down the tunnel," she said.

"Telling me?"

She nodded. "I'd do what he says."

Ander huffed. "Fine, but you stay here."

"Yeah right," she said. "I'm going to look at the carving."

"Amelia—"

"We don't have time for this. Go distract him, take the supplies, and circle back to me. Got it?"

Before he could respond, she was gone, weaving through the crowd like sand running through fingers. The angry Sadrian stared at Ander expectantly.

Fine! He walked stiffly toward the stack of supplies. It was all he could do to keep from bumping into others as they hurried by him. As soon as he grabbed a basket, the man roared in anger and pointed to a different one.

The blood in Ander's veins boiled, but he complied, picking up *that* basket instead. Then the man pointed to the cave everyone else was carting supplies through like Ander was slow-witted. He clenched his teeth as he headed toward the cave.

First, we're stuck, then Amelia's mad, and now this. He would have run a hand through his hair if he wasn't holding a stupid basket.

The angry man followed him and continued to shout. He didn't understand any of the words, but he got the intent. The man wanted him to move faster.

He picked up the pace, following the tunnel down twists and turns. All the while, the man continued to follow, making sure he was doing what he was told. The incessant noise and the knots in his shoulders grew. Same with the pounding headache. Every step he took pulled him away from the others, from Millie. He had to get back as soon as possible before it was too late.

An offshoot presented itself, and Ander turned into it quickly, hoping to lose the irate man. He set the basket down in the dark and turned right into him.

The man's face was purple, and he lurched over Ander menacingly as he vomited a scream of unintelligible words.

Restraint broke inside Ander, and without thinking, he grabbed the man's patched robe in one hand and yanked him so they were eye to eye. As Ander did so, his hood fell off his head, revealing his non-Sadrian complexion.

The man's eyes widened.

Great! Before the man could say anything more, Ander slammed his other fist into his temple. The man crashed to the ground, out cold.

Ander shook his head as an overwhelming sense of relief washed over him. He should have done that from the start. Quickly, he dragged the man deeper into the side passageway and retraced his steps back into the Coral Cavern.

He found Amelia hidden behind a stack of baskets. She must have stacked them herself, because they hadn't been there before. In her hand was a wad of ripped cloth, which she was using to scrub the wall. She handed him another wad, and he joined her in the scrubbing. The portion of the wall she was at was covered in ancient etchings and carvings. An ancient script surrounded a carving of a domed tower.

"What happened?" she asked. "How did you lose him?"

He grunted. "You have your strengths, and I have mine."

Her mouth fell wide open. "What did you do?"

Voices shouted from the outpost gate right next to them, silencing them both. Ander dropped the cloth and grabbed the pommel of his sword. Something was going on through those stone doors, and he got a feeling it wasn't good. He moved closer to the cracked opening, keeping low so he remained hidden behind the baskets Amelia had staged. As he neared the opening, the sounds within grew more distinct.

"What do you mean 'pledge the loyalty of the Mirage'?" said a strong voice in the common tongue. "Who do you think you are?"

"I'm your only chance of survival," came a calm reply—so calm it sent shivers down Ander's spine.

The first voice laughed haughtily. "You? An old man? You're our only chance of survival?"

A wave of coldness rippled from the room. Then the light underneath the door went out. A *crash* sounded and was followed by gasping.

"All right," groaned the first voice. "You've made your point clear."

"Send your warriors to Sadria. Storm the palace, and I will hand the kingdom over to the Mirage. All I ask of you is your complete loyalty."

There was something about the second voice. Ander was sure he had heard it before. He racked his mind but couldn't figure out where.

"Warriors to Sadria? Are you insane? Without the Insurrector's power over the beasts, we're being crushed by just a fraction of their army! Striking against Sadria now would be suicide."

Power rippled out again, and this time it was followed by a scream.

"Who do you think gave him that power?" said the second voice. "I made him into what he is!"

Ander crept closer to the opening, hoping he could catch sight of who the participants were. Right as he reached the crack, a hand grabbed his arm.

"I've got the inscription," said Amelia, holding up her grandfather's journal excitedly. "We can leave now."

Movement behind Amelia caught his attention: Garret, Eugene, Hammer, and Blaze heading toward them.

"Exit is just that way," Blaze said quickly, pointing a thumb to the entryway that the Mirage were carrying supplies through. "We'll just need to keep our heads down and—"

BOOOOOM! A deafening blast shook the cavern walls. Distant shouts followed, along with lots of footfalls and the clang of metal. Ander recognized it all with sickening dread. The gates were breached, and the Mirage were in retreat.

"That's our cue to go!" said Garret.

Ander led them around their hiding spot, but as soon as they emerged, he stopped. At the tunnel opening stood a familiar, now bruised, angry man. On either side of the man were cloaked warriors, each wearing mismatched armor made from animal hides and carrying spears tipped with sadriconda fangs.

The angry man's eyes found Ander and widened. "Steam soldier!"

Ander cursed as the warriors sprinted toward them. "New plan," he said, retreating backward. "We're taking an alternative exit."

The group scrambled into the maze of baskets and pots as the warriors pounded after them.

Amelia glared at Ander and said through gritted teeth, "Why does this *always* happen?"

"Not now," he replied, leading the way forward. Behind them, Hammer and Blaze knocked baskets and pots over to impede the path of their pursuers.

Static rippled past them, and a warrior leaped high above the barriers. Garret aimed and fired in one movement, catching the warrior in the chest as he flew. *Slam!* The warrior crashed into a pile of baskets nearby.

Two more warriors ran parallel to them along the side of the wall. In an instant, one of them kicked off toward the ceiling and slammed a fist into a coral stalactite. The rock exploded from the ceiling and launched toward them with blinding speed.

Slam! The rock missed Ander's head by inches and smashed into a bunch of pots, breaking them into jagged pieces. More warriors appeared behind the others, leaping across the piles of supplies.

"There!" said Amelia, pointing to a cave opening. They sprinted hard for the opening as the pursuit behind them grew more intense.

BOOOOOM! The sound blasted through the tunnel and shook the floor and ceiling. They threw their hands over their heads as rocks showered all around.

The tunnel turned in a wide u-shape and exited right back into the coral cavern again.

Ander cursed and sprinted hard toward an opening on the opposite side of the cavern. The others followed close after. The Mirage warriors screamed after them, which pushed them to run faster. They entered the new cave and heard their pursuit abruptly stop.

"Ander," gasped Eugene. "They're retreating."

"Retreating?" said Ander, without slowing. "Why would they be—"

A new sound echoed toward them from the direction they were running. Growing shouts and the clanging of steel. The passage opened into a cavern filled with ranks of banded armored soldiers.

Sadrians!

Ander's eyes widened, and he immediately pivoted. "Back! BACK!" He shoved the others as the Sadrians charged after them with curved blades drawn.

Static energy flooded through the cave like an electric tsunami, sending piercing shivers all up his spine. Boots pounded after them at an inhuman tempo.

"BLOW THE CAVE!" shouted Ander.

"UHAHHH!" screamed Blaze, two octaves higher than normal. The soldier threw a canister over his shoulder, which bounced off the top of Ander's head. Ander dodged two more before the explosives ripped through the air.

Three deep BOOMs went off behind them. Searing heat and rock exploded behind them, followed by screams and collapsing rock. The group burst out of the tunnel into the coral cavern, barely escaping being swallowed by the collapse entirely.

The Coral Cavern was now empty of people. All that was left was a stream of Mirage warriors, sprinting from the outpost to the exit cave beyond.

The group caught their breath.

"That's our exit," said Blaze, pointing to where the warriors were leaving.

"Our cover's blown, you idiot!" hiss Eugene.

"If we keep our heads low, and don't draw attention to ourselves," Amelia looked meaningfully at Ander, "we could probably make it out."

BOOM! The cavern shook violently again. "Fine!" said Ander. "Let's move!"

The group ran into the maze of supplies when the flow of Mirage soldiers suddenly changed to screaming Sadrian warriors.

"Down!" called Ander, and the group complied, ducking behind stacks of baskets. He watched through a sliver of space between baskets as the last of the Mirage warriors disappeared into the exit cave. Then the cave collapsed behind them with a horrible, grating sound.

"BREAK THE OPENING!" screamed a Sadrian general, pointing a weapon at the collapse. Magic rippled outward as soldiers charged forward and threw their fists out in complex patterns. The rock pile cracked and groaned.

"We're trapped," said Eugene. He put his head down and took in shallow breaths.

Trapped. The words seemed to hit the group like a punch to the gut. Expressions fell.

"There's got to be another way out," said Garret, looking at Ander.

"Millie?" Ander asked.

Amelia took a stressed breath, looking around. "Well, I suppose we could try the original exit?" She pointed behind them to a large opening that angled downward.

"You realize it's probably sealed and unstable like the front entrance, right?" asked Eugene in a critical tone.

Blaze shivered.

Amelia glared at him. "Unless you'd like to dig a grave right here, that's our only option at this point."

"Fine," said Ander. "Those Sadrians haven't seen us yet, so let's pull out slowly and quietly."

In a low crouch, the group crept through the supplies toward the back of the cavern. They made it all the way to the opening before the Sadrian soldiers spotted them and began pursuit.

The team broke into a hard sprint, running headlong into the tunnel. The path gently sloped downward, increasing their pace.

"How many soldiers are after us?" asked Ander from the front.

"Too many," said Eugene from the rear.

"I know what you're thinking," said Blaze between breaths. "We're being chased because I'm just too darn noticeable to all the lady soldiers—"

"Shut up, Blaze!" said Amelia.

The passageway twisted and turned before it stopped abruptly at a collapsed dead end. Behind them, the pounding of boots grew like an incoming avalanche.

"How in the *world* are we supposed to get through that?" said Eugene in exasperation.

"Blow it," said Ander. "The rest of us will lay down cover fire."

"What?!" Eugene said. "You'll bring the whole cave—"

"Shut it," Amelia said, shoving him aside. "We don't have time for this." She began boring holes into the ceiling while Blaze followed with charges.

"Let's back up the tunnel a ways," said Garret. "That way, we have some space from the explosion."

Ander nodded and led the way back around a bend before setting up position. The pounding of boots grew louder and louder until suddenly the cave flooded with soldiers.

The team opened fire on the incoming Sadrians, shooting bolt after bolt. The front line of soldiers fell, but more replaced them. One soldier threw a fist toward Ander and his team, and a howling torrent of wind blasted toward them. Their shots became inaccurate and weak in the unrelenting torrent. The Sadrians closed their ranks and moved toward the team in unison.

"WE NEED THAT OPENING—" Ander's words were cut off by a horrible, deafening blast. The cave shook like never before, and nearly every person crashed to the floor. Dust rushed through the tunnel and snuffed the torchlight.

Ander's ears rang horribly, but that didn't stop him from grabbing the magpacks of the Steam soldiers around him and pulling them back toward where the blast came. As they rushed back around the corner, moonlight showed high above. Amelia and Blaze stood there in the dim light, bathed in dust.

"Quick!" Amelia shouted.

The group spilled out of the cave and tore down the mountainside.

Boom! Amelia fired a flare into the sky as they ran, signaling for the *Legacy*. Behind them, Sadrians scrambled out of the cave shouting war cries.

The mountainside gave way to a sea of sand, and the group kicked up a cloud of dust in their haste. In the distance, the hum of airship rotors grew.

Ander glanced over his shoulder and saw the Sadrians stop at the edge of the desert. *That was good, right?*

They slowed down in the sandy dunes to catch their breaths.

"That... was... too... close," said Eugene. "No more caves."

"Agreed," said Garret.

"It's a good thing they stopped following us," said Blaze. "I told you, my looks definitely have their effect. Next, they'll be fainting left and right."

"Blaze, I don't think that's why they stopped," said Ander suddenly. All across the horizon were dozens of dunes, moving like enormous waves across the landscape.

Sadricondas.

One dune changed course and headed straight for them.

He swallowed hard.

"The airship is almost here," said Amelia, pointing up. She took a step away from the group and waved to the airship. Then suddenly, the sand collapsed underneath her and sucked her into its depths.

Chapter 25: Depths of Har

Amelia

The ground beneath Amelia's feet broke like ice over a lake, and she fell straight into darkness. *SLAM!* She hit the ground on her back so hard, her lungs seized. Seconds passed before she could gasp in a breath. She was in a circular tunnel of compacted sand. The ceiling above her was almost three times her height.

Ander's face appeared in the hole above, blocking the only light. "MILLIE!" Desperation flooded his face, contrasting with his usual composure under stress.

"I'm all right," she gasped. She pushed herself to her feet and felt a familiar ache in her ankle.

The ground rumbled underneath her feet and seemed to echo down the tunnel.

"We're getting you a rope!" Ander shouted. "Just hang on!" His face disappeared.

She glanced down the tunnel as the sound grew. *What was a tunnel doing all the way out here?* The arch of the tunnel was so uniform it seemed almost unnatural. Unless... it *was* unnatural.

Her eyes widened. "GET ME THAT ROPE! NOW!"

"It's almost here!" shouted Garret.

Pure terror flooded her body with ice. The rumbling grew louder and louder. Her heart pounded out of her chest.

A knotted rope fell down, and she scrambled onto it.

"MRAHHHHH!" The sound bellowed at her from down the tunnel. It *was* close. Ander stood above her, pulling the rope up as she climbed. His eyes held a terror she'd never seen in them before.

Air rushed toward Amelia from the cave as the sound intensified. She rose foot-by-foot from the ground, but she was only halfway up when the sadriconda appeared with its amber eyes, curved spikes, and rows of long, jagged teeth. All of her muscles froze as it hurtled itself at her.

She closed her eyes and bunched her body up for the impact. Suddenly, she was yanked upward right before the world exploded.

She hit the ground as the sand erupted feet from her. The massive sadriconda blasted from the ground in a long, soaring arc. It was so close that a couple of its spiked black scales knocked against the toes of her boots.

Ander yanked her backward onto an airship ladder and held onto her waist as it rose. Sense slammed into her, and she scrambled for purchase on the ladder and then scaled up like a madwoman. By the time she reached the top, she slumped against the railing and stared at her feet. Her arms were shaking violently.

Ander put an arm around her. "Millie. It's okay. It's okay." He repeated the words as she clung to his Sadrian cloak and sucked in ragged breaths. Gaping jaws played across her eyes, over and over.

The shaking slowed as Ander's warmth comforted her. The sadriconda was gone. She was safe now.

She looked up at Ander, realizing he had risked his life for her. He could have easily run. In fact, he *should* have run. If the sadriconda had surfaced only a few feet sooner, they would have all been swallowed.

"Thank you." Her voice felt small.

"Of course."

She realized with a jolt where she was. Quickly, she pulled away. She was supposed to be distancing herself from him, not clinging to his cloak like a lifeline.

She gave him a grateful nod and said, "I need to go." Without another glance, she stood and made her way toward her cabin.

"Wait!" He caught up to her at the door. "Millie, what's going on?"

She swallowed. This wasn't a question she had expected. She had hoped that she could just distance herself from him and that things would just work out. Apparently, it wasn't that simple to stop being friends with Ander Blackwell, especially when you were both stuck on the same airship.

She hesitated.

"I've been trying to figure out what I did that upset you so much. You've barely even talk to me anymore."

She grabbed a loose strand of hair and pulled at it. "I'm... I'm working through a few things and need some space. It's not about you. But yes, I do need space."

With that, she opened her cabin door and disappeared within.

. . . .

Morning came quickly, waking her with gleaming rays through her cabin's windows. It felt too early, especially after the exhausting adventure the night before. The only motivation that got her out of bed was a growing anticipation to learn more about what she discovered.

Within an hour, she was at the helm. She steered with one hand and held the journal with the other. Her fingers drummed against the wheel with excitement.

Amir took his time before appearing above decks to frown at her. She had sent for his help with the transcription, but she hadn't expected him to be *this* sluggish. It wasn't like *he'd* done anything special the evening before.

He cautiously climbed up the helm and stopped by her. "All right," he said with a sour tone. "What do you want?"

She opened the journal to her transcription of the etchings from the Caves of Bailidan. Centered was a depiction of a palace with a soaring, turnip-shaped tower. Underneath was ancient writing she couldn't decipher. She showed him the page.

"Could you translate this?"

"Hmm," he took it from her hands and squinted. "It's a late Valeran script, though your penmanship could use some work and these lines aren't exactly straight."

She looked at him sidelong. "Sorry, I guess next time I'm trapped in a cavern between two armies, I'll make sure to draw straighter lines. Now, could you tell me what it says?"

He raised an eyebrow. "In my profession, the details are very important—"

"Just tell me what it says."

He frowned and returned to the transcription. For a long

moment, all that came out of his mouth was a series of *hmms* and *uh huhs*. She waited as patiently as she could, continuing to drum her fingers on the airship wheel.

Finally, he cleared his throat. "This first word is *the*."

"Are you kidding me?" She nearly took the book from him so she could smack him over the head with it. "I thought you said you were *fluent* in ancient Sadrian languages?"

"Ancient *Sahadrian* languages, and I'm jesting. Goodness, you Steams are always so impatient. I've translated the words, but interpreting is another matter. It describes the way to Valera, but it uses landmark names that are antiquated. As best as I can interpret this, we are to follow an old highway north along a mountain range, until it curves into the northwestern part of the peninsula. That's as much detail as it gives. I'm guessing back then that would have been plenty of directions to get there."

"Oh, this is perfect!" she flipped through the journal excitedly until she found the map drawn by her grandfather. She found the region and pointed to a labeled landmark called the *Depth of Har*. "That would put Valera right here then!"

Amir's eyes widened and his face grew pale.

"What?" she asked with annoyance. "You look... shouldn't you be excited or something? This is *huge!*"

"If this etching is correct," said Amir slowly, "then there's a reason why Valera has been lost to the ages."

She frowned. "Care to explain?"

He shuddered and spoke in an urgent tone. "That region is cursed. No one who enters ever comes back."

She put a hand on her hip. "Cursed? Do you mind offering specifics?" Amir was really testing her patience.

"You aren't planning on going there, are you?" he asked, grabbing her shoulders with a fearful passion.

She flinched at his sudden intensity. "Of course we are. According to my grandfather, we need to find the Lost Palace of Valera to pick up the trail to the Wayfinder. It's the only way."

He pulled away. "This pursuit of the Wayfinder has gone *too* far! My job was *only* to help you at the archives, not galivant with you straight into the jaws of death! I insist you turn this flying abomination around straightway."

She shook her head. "I can't do that, Amir."

He scowled and pointed a finger angrily at her. "You and your family's delirious obsession with this fable is going to be the death of us all!" He pivoted and disappeared down the ladder. She would have stared daggers into his back if he hadn't tripped on the last rung and crashed to the deck. He quickly recovered and disappeared below deck.

Amelia patted her airship and smiled. If there was one thing she could always count on, it was her airship.

She worked with the crew to set a course due north. As the hours passed, the landscape changed from dunes to flat, cracked plains. These plains stretched far into the distance before dropping off into sheer cliffs. As she watched this transition, she envisioned a great sea gently lapping against the cliffs. If her imagination was correct, the sea would be expansive, stretching west as far as the eye could see.

As the sun reached noon, Ander appeared above deck and traveled to his usual place at the bow to scan the horizon with his spyglass. She kept her gaze away from him, but her mind rebelled. After working so hard to distance herself from him, all it took was one adventure to make things so complicated. How was she supposed to do this? She couldn't be his friend, but she also hated how much it pained them both when she tried not to be.

Ugh. Who knew that one mistake years ago would make her life so messed up? Her life was broken, doomed to be forever haunted by the consequences of one thoughtless act. Nothing seemed to make it go away. Building her airship didn't. Working outside the Republic didn't. Getting the Everblade didn't. Even this mission, thousands of miles from the Republic wasn't far enough to separate her from her past. If only she could turn back the clock. Then maybe her life wouldn't feel broken.

Broken. That seemed an adequate word for it. She felt broken and unrepairable.

"Hey, Millie?"

Ander's voice made her jump out of her skin. She hadn't realized he had come over to her and was now climbing up the helm. What was she supposed to do? Had their moment yesterday somehow shifted their relationship back to friends? Should she push him away farther? Tell him to go away?

Both those options felt exhausting at the moment. It took so much mental focus, and it hurt each time to see how it affected him. Maybe today she'd take a break from it all.

He stopped next to her and held out his spyglass. She looked at it and then back at him. The wind seemed to tousle his hair in a messy sort of way. *His hair had gotten a lot longer over the weeks in Sadria.* She tried not to focus on that too much. Instead, she took the spyglass and asked hesitantly, "What's this for?"

He gave her a grin that somehow seemed to overlook the fact she had ignored him for over a week.

"You should look over the side," he explained.

She raised an eyebrow. "Okay?" She took the spyglass and handed him the wheel before proceeding to the side of the airship. At first, all she saw was cracked earth, but as she zoomed in, her breath caught in her throat.

Faint lines and boxes covered the landscape in a distinct pattern. There was once civilization here!

"I bet we wouldn't be able to see that on the ground," he said. "It'd just look like flat tablelands with random bumps."

"We must be getting close then?" She looked out across the horizon and noticed a new feature. Ahead, the land looked pockmarked with many depressions.

"Miss Steam?" Amir's voice came from the main deck, sounding frantic.

"Great," she muttered. Amir was back for round two. She moved to the front railing. "Yes Amir?"

He stood with his arms scrunched to his sides, while his eyes darted from side to side. "You have to turn this balloon dinghy around!"

She closed her eyes and grimaced. "This is not a dinghy, and we've already had this conversation, Amir."

"Please! The land ahead is cursed."

"Uh huh. Tell me. How is it cursed?"

He gritted his teeth. "Long ago, there was a civilization that lived here. I only know them as the *ruptured ones*. They angered the gods and so were cursed. The ground shook and fell away. Great holes formed, so deep that the people felt straight to Har, the dark underworld. Everything was destroyed, and the place was abandoned."

She tilted her head. "You realize that story matches very well with the story of Valera?"

"But the curse is real!" His expression was deadly serious. "I've read many accounts of people entering these lands. Archeologists, adventurers, bandits—most don't return. The few that do were covered with *thousands* of sores and completely mad! They called it a curse from Varis herself!"

She pinched the bridge of her nose. "Have you considered that those stories were invented to keep people away?"

"I strongly disagree," he said. "If you intend to continue, I insist you let me off this airship immediately!"

Ander interjected. "You realize we'd be stranding you in the middle of the desert? Not to mention, the closest civilization is at the caves of Bailidan, which are now scores of miles away?"

"We aren't dropping anyone off," said Amelia firmly.

"You can't make me go!" said Amir.

Amelia sighed. "Ander, could you escort Amir back to his cabin?"

"You can't just—"

Ander dropped to the main deck, turned the man around, and pushed him toward the hatch. "You heard the captain. Down you go."

Amir grumbled all the way. When he and Ander disappeared, she felt an immediate sense of relief. Ander reappeared a moment later, and returned by her side. He was silent, which suited her just fine. It was also confusing and comforting to have him there. Amir's antics had planted a seed of worry in her mind.

The pockmarked landscape grew into focus. Soon, crumbling walls and broken buildings littered the plains. Wide pits broke the landscape as well.

Ander whistled, breaking the silence. "Well, do you think this is Valera?"

"I hope so," Amelia replied. They passed over a pit, which yawned with impenetrable darkness. She shivered. *No wonder the natives think this place is cursed.* Hopefully, it was just a story. She had no desire to repeat an Insula Tranquilitas experience again.

Ander took out his spyglass and scanned the horizon. "Any idea where we start searching?"

She looked out with him. Clearly, there weren't any standing palaces—only the stone ruins of a once great city, ravaged by the winds of time.

"Since the palace collapsed into the ground, I think we're looking for a hole or depression large enough to collapse something that large?"

"Okay, like that?" He pointed toward the center of the ruined city, where a hole three times the size of any other rested. Around the hole was a crumbled wall with broken towers.

She blinked. "Yeah, that would fit the description."

He chuckled. "I was afraid you'd say that."

"Let's take a closer look." She guided the airship until they hovered over the pit. Like the others, it was impenetrably black. The size was impressive, large enough to easily swallow the airship. Word spread that they had arrived, so crew members and soldiers crowded above deck to look over the edge.

"How deep is it?" asked Charles, looking at Ander.

"No idea," he replied. "Could you have Axe bring out his flares?"

Charles saluted. A moment later, he returned with a disheveled Axel. The large man still didn't look like he had bathed. His face and eyes looked hollow. Across his shoulder was a belt full of flares and explosives.

"Axe?" said Ander. "Could you drop a flare below?"

Axe nodded with little enthusiasm, ripped one off the belt, and dropped it down into the abyss. Amelia watched the light grow smaller and smaller until it faded.

"I didn't see it hit the bottom," said Charles.

"Oi, it kept on goin' and goin'," added Veronica. "Almost like there's no endin'."

The Depths of Har, Amelia thought with a shudder. Was it possible to have pits extend to the underworld? This seemed abnormally deep for just sinkholes. Perhaps there was something unnatural here.

Ander turned to Amelia. "I think we can count out using the winch to get a team down there."

Amelia swallowed. "I can navigate us in. Veronica, light the lanterns and prep the crew for descent."

"Aye Cap." Veronica turned to the crew and began shouting. "Oi! You 'eard 'er! Light the lamps! Loose the sheets! On the double."

Amelia called down the horn to reduce the hydrogen, and the airship dropped slowly into the pit. As the sides rose all around, the sun and desert heat disappeared. A chill crept in and the light dimmed until the only light came from the lanterns. The darkness was so thick, the surrounding walls disappeared into nothing. Only the echoing rumble of the engines reminded her that there were walls at all.

Amelia shivered and wrapped an arm around herself. "Veronica, have the crew keep an eye out for any protrusions from the walls and the floor. We don't want any accidents. I'd hate to find out how deep this goes that way."

"Aye, cap."

"Axe," said Ander, "drop another flare."

Axel complied, and the spectators watched in silence.

"Do you think this goes to the center of the earth?" asked Blaze.

"Or to the land of the dead," added Charles quietly. "Heard Amir say this place was cursed."

"It's not cursed," said Amelia with a firmness she didn't feel.

Hssssss! The sound echoed through the space, seeming to come from everywhere and nowhere at the same time. The crew felt quiet.

"Wha—what was that?" whimpered Axel. It was the most personality he had expressed since losing his hand.

"Quiet everyone," whispered Garret.

Hssssss! Amelia wheeled her head to the right, only to catch a blur of movement fly by the airship. "Um, was that just the cave?" She could feel the unsteadiness in her voice.

"Ready your weapons," whispered Ander, grabbing a crossbow from over his shoulder and cocking it. Other soldiers followed suit with their own various weapons.

HssssSSS! Something flew right over Amelia's head and latched its fangs straight onto James Cole. He screamed and ripped off a snake like no other Amelia had ever seen.

The snake was all black with thin red stripes. Along its head was a wide, flat hood that doubled also as wings. Long white fangs gleamed as it hissed in the soldier's hands. James' eyes went wide before he hurled the snake over the railing. Then he stumbled and fell face first to the deck.

Eugene rushed to the fallen medic and checked his pulse. After a second, Eugene paled and began chest compressions.

HsssSSSS! In an instant, the darkness swirled like a tornado. Snakes flew in from every direction. Amelia let out a blood-curdling scream and threw her hands over her head. Hundreds of snakes flew in, their hisses like nails on a chalkboard to her ears. She ducked underneath the wheel and took a fetal position. Their wings beat the air with a frenzy, and as they passed, their scaly bodies slid over her exposed arms.

One landed in her hair, and she completely lost it. She screamed so hard, her lungs emptied of air and her stomach clenched like she was in free fall. Frantically, she shook her head and batted at the creature with her hands, but that only seemed to make the situation worse. The snake's wings wrapped around her half-falling-out bun, tangling it more. Its white teeth flashed in her vision as its head whipped into her view.

In an instant, the snake was ripped from her hair, and arms wrapped protectively around her. She closed her eyes and felt Ander's warm embrace shield her from the terror all around.

Nearby, Axel's voice roared and was followed by the whooshing of fire and the banging of explosions.

The beat of wings became frenetic before scattering away from the airship. Soon, silence fell across the airship. Ander slowly pulled away from Amelia.

She lifted her head cautiously and looked about. Flares were scattered across the deck, burning bright against the dark. The snakes were gone, but they left devastation in their wake. Sailors and soldiers lay on the deck unmoving, while others groaned and muttered with mounting volume. Eugene fell to his knees and rocked nearby, whimpering about swirling water and caves. Veronica sobbed by the door of the captain's cabin, repeating Otto's name over and over. Charles rolled along the floor, moaning about failing a regulations test. The hysteria grew in volume and intensity.

What in the world was going on?! Had half the crew gone mad?

Ander rose to his feet and ran a hand through his hair. As he raised his arm, her eyes bulged. Latched onto the back of his arm was a green and black striped snake.

"Ander!"

He noticed it and immediately ripped it off with a wince. It hissed and zipped off the airship. Amelia rushed to examine his arm. A red and purple bruise was already forming.

"Ander!" She looked up to see his eyes turn bloodshot. He stumbled, and she grabbed him before he could fall to the deck. His eyes grew unfocused. Terror seized her heart.

"Ander? Ander!"

He looked over her shoulder, and the blood drained from his face. "No! No! NO!"

He pushed her aside with surprising strength and ran to the railing. "MILLIE! IT'S GOT MILLIE."

Amelia rushed to his side. "Ander! What are you doing?"

He acted like he was attaching something around his waist. Then he put a foot on the railing and leaned over.

"ANDER!" She threw her arms around his waist right as he tried to jump.

"Ander! DON'T!"

Garret and Hammer rushed in and together, they helped her pull Ander away from the edge.

"Ander!" Garret slapped him in the face. "Get a hold of yourself!"

"It's taken Millie!" Tears grew in Ander's eyes. "The beast. It's taken her!"

Amelia crouched next to him as the soldiers pinned his struggling form to the ground. "Ander," she took his hand. "I'm right here."

"It's taken her!" Tears streamed down his face. The light in his eyes faded.

Tears were coming to her own eyes now, too. She kept hold of his hand and brushed her other hand through his hair. "Ander. I'm right here. I'm right here."

"Not Millie," his voice grew weaker.

She squeezed his hand tighter. "Ander? Ander! Don't leave me!"

A hand gripped her shoulder, and a deep voice spoke. "What color were the stripes?" She looked up at Lieutenant Harper, the leader of the new team created from Olivia's remaining corps.

She blinked. "What?"

"The snake that bit him?"

"Oh... uh, green, I think."

The soldier let out a sigh. "He'll be alright. Green is mean, but red means you'll be dead. The hallucinogens should wear off soon."

"Hallucinogens? Oh." She turned back to Ander. Was this what it was like for him when the beast had taken her over the edge? She never realized how horrible that would have been for him. Her own memory was spotty. All she could remember were vague pieces here and there. Her body had been in so much pain, and she had been delirious at the time. It wasn't until the Enchantrans woke her that her memory became somewhat lucid again.

Ander's eyes closed, and he drifted into a sleep.

Garret rose and began barking orders, directing people to carry the injured below deck and clearing the upper deck of all nonessential crew. She stayed with Ander until soldiers carried him away.

He'll be okay, she told herself as his limp form disappeared below decks. *He'll be okay.*

She wished she could go with him. But she was still captain, and with her first mate indisposed, everyone needed her at the helm right now.

She leaned against the wheel, exhausted. Axel remained on the deck lighting a continuous stream of flares. Hopefully, it was enough to keep those horrible snakes away. Just the thought of them coming back sent creeping shivers up her spine.

"I see something, port side," shouted one of the few remaining sailors.

Amelia looked left, out across the darkness, and sucked in a breath. A crooked tower rose from the depths. On top was a golden dome that was shaped like a fat, upside-down turnip. The sides of the tower were rounded and made of polished sandstone that glittered majestically in the lamplight. Grooves and designs were cut into the stone, featuring a repeating motif of palm leaves and ocean waves. The shape of the dome and tower matched perfectly with the drawing from the caves of Bailidan.

This was it! This was the tallest tower. They'd found the Lost Palace of Valera!

She looked over the railing and was surprised to see the bottom of the pit rapidly approaching. The points of several other towers broke through dirt and sand, but nothing else of Valera was visible.

The palace... it's buried. Still. This was Gifted engineering from the Era of Wonder. Somehow, the iconic tower survived the fall. Perhaps the rest of the palace had survived as well.

There was only one way to find out.

Chapter 26: Lost Palace

Amelia

Dirt and sand crunched underneath Amelia's boots as she walked toward the solitary tower. Soldiers fanned out from either side of her, Blaze and Freya to her right and Lieutenant Harper and a soldier named Bracks to her left. Amir plodded behind them.

Amelia paused and exhaled a cloud of fog. Holding up her lantern, she studied the area. Aside from the barely visible points of the other towers, the terrain was mostly flat. Water gurgled somewhere nearby—which was odd considering the climate outside the pit. Ferns grew in spotty patches and black scarabs scurried through the sand. Somehow this deep in the earth, life survived.

"All right," said Lieutenant Harper. "We're going to make our entry point up there at that break in the dome of the central tower."

"I can get us a line," said Freya. "We just need to get a little closer." The group moved ten paces when suddenly the sand began to shift.

Lieutenant Harper held a hand up. "No one makes a move. Who knows what critters burrow in these sands?"

Amelia stopped and scrutinized the sand intently. The last thing she wanted was another winged snake.

"I can't believe you're forcing me to come," said Amir grumpily.

"You were just barely gabbing about how huge this discovery was and the books you were going to write," said Amelia.

"Quiet!" said Lieutenant Harper. The two fell silent. When the shifting sand stopped, Harper waved a hand forward, and they continued.

Crkkkkkkkk! The sound seemed to come from underneath their feet. Amelia froze to the spot. "Everyone stop! Right now."

"Fine by me," said Freya. "I think I could shoot a line from here."

Blaze smirked. "I know what this is, Amelia. This is the part where you confess to everyone that you always loved me, and you can't go another step without admitting that I'm more dashingly handsome than And—"

Something crunched behind her, and in a blink, the ground broke underneath her feet. She screamed as she dropped into complete darkness. Three seconds of sheer terror passed before she slammed onto a pile of sand and felt the wind rush out of her. Soundlessly, she struggled for breath, but her lungs refused to expand. Sand and dirt continued to cascade over her like she was in an hourglass, slowly suffocating her. Then the pressure released in her chest, and she gasped frantically for breath while throwing her arms out of the sand.

Slap! Her hand contacted someone's face in the dark.

"Ouch!" said Blaze. "First, you're falling for me and now you're abusing me? No wonder why Ander took a snake bite instead of coming here."

"Shut up, Blaze!" She ripped a flare off her belt and lit it. They were in a domed circular room, large enough to fit the *Legacy*. Sand fell around them in a circle, cascading from a hole in the ceiling high above. The rest of the ceiling was covered by a large fresco of a gleaming bay full of ships pulled by gigantic sea serpents—serpents that looked almost exactly like sadricondas except with blue scales and ridged fins instead of spikes. The walls were polished sandstone with gold bands depicting the repeating palm leaf motif. Piles of sand sloped from the walls in regular piles—likely where windows once stood. Rubble and skeletons littered the floor, all the way up steps to where a sultan-like figure remained on a broken throne.

She used the flare to light a bent lantern from her pack and caught sight of another figure.

"Cid!?" She took a step back. "Why are you here?"

He frowned and gestured rudely to the room all around, as if somehow that was enough explanation.

"You're supposed to be on the airship!" she said. "It's too dangerous for everyone to come."

"It's not my fault you broke the ceiling," said Cid.

"*I* broke the ceiling? I bet we were fine until *you* secretly joined us on the already precarious roof!"

"Agree to disagree."

She flexed her fists.

"This hole is the royal ceremony room," said a fourth voice. She whipped around to Amir, who was now also picking himself out of the sand.

"Great!" she threw her hands up. "I'm in this hole with *all* my favorite people."

Lieutenant Harper's voice echoed from high above. "Are any of you injured?"

"No," Amelia replied.

"Hang tight!" said Lieutenant Harper. "We'll bring the airship around and lower the winch to get you out."

"Look at the architecture," said Amir, drifting away from the group. The other two also stepped out of the sand pile to explore.

She growled at the others and pointed back at the sand pile. "He said we need to hang tight. That means stick around in case your thick heads didn't catch that!"

Blaze held up a fancily dressed skeleton and said in a falsetto voice, "Come on Millie, join the party. We're dying to meet you."

"Don't do that!" said Amir quickly.

"Do what?" said Blaze.

"Disrespect the dead! They'll come back to haunt you."

Amelia rubbed her temples and muttered, "You're all here to haunt me."

"So many valuables... all abandoned?" Cid's voice was less gruff than normal.

"Don't touch those!" said Amir, changing direction to stop Cid. Amelia watched them and folded her arms. Was she the *only* adult here?

Cid raced away, running up the stone steps toward the throne. Amir and Blaze followed only steps behind.

Crrrkkkkk! Amelia looked up. Cracks grew across the dome's ceiling and stretched outward.

Her eyes widened. "Guys?"

Cid was now rummaging through the skeletal remains of the

Sultan while Blaze was chasing Amir with a skeleton.

"GUYS!" She rushed over the debris and up the stone steps. She yanked Cid's arm with one hand and grabbed Blaze's collar with the other. Amir stopped in his tracks.

She glared at them all. "The ceiling is getting worse!"

All three men looked up at the same time. The cracks were growing right before their eyes, creating jagged lines that branched out like lightning.

"Uh," said Blaze. "Back to the center?"

The four of them scrambled back to the sand pile, bumping into each other in the process. More sand cascaded around, growing the pile farther and farther out. From somewhere above, the airship engine roared with life.

A jagged piece of sandstone crashed down to the ground.

"Uh, Miss Steam," said Amir. "I'm afraid the ceiling won't last much longer."

She hated it when annoying people were right. It created an illusion that they weren't *always* stupid.

The airship would take a few minutes to get settled over this hole, and that was precious time they didn't have. When this structure collapsed, it'd bury them with it.

She gritted her teeth and looked around. On the opposite side of the room from the throne was a large opening into a foyer beyond.

Crash! A large block slammed the sandpile near her. She jumped. "We aren't going to survive here. Follow me!"

She bolted toward the opening with the other three in tow. More blocks crashed around them and shattered into broken shrapnel. Rock pelted them as they weaved left and right through the debris. The ceiling groaned overhead, threatening imminent destruction.

Come on! Come on! Her legs burned as she dodged white skeletons and broken debris.

Amelia zipped through the opening, the others on her tail. An ear-splitting *CRACK* shuddered through the room behind them as they rounded a corner and ducked down.

BOOOOOM! The world rocked. Dust blasted past them and filled the room with a suffocating cloud. Violent aftershocks followed before the world stilled.

All four of them coughed in the dust, and it was a long moment before it settled. Then they slowly peeked around the corner. The path they took was now completely filled with large blocks of rubble.

Cid growled. "Now you've blocked our way out, too."

Amelia glared at him. "You know, just shut it, Cid."

"Oooo," said Blaze.

Cid rolled his eyes and turned away.

"I knew coming here was a bad idea," said Amir. "I warned you all. Now we're going to die down here."

Amelia threw her hands up. "Oh, so everybody's a critic now? You think *I* want to be stuck with you all?"

Blaze looked down as if slapped. Then he snapped his head back up, his face serious. "What are your orders, Millie? Need me to scout?"

She exhaled loudly. "Give me a second to think." She paced the room, which was a grand atrium of some sort that was shaped like a fat plus symbol. At each end of the plus was an opening. On the inside corners were ascending staircases. Above them were balconies, lined with railings. A crystal chandelier miraculously still hung, swinging, from the center of the ceiling.

As her head cleared, a plan formed. "Blaze, I want you to take the second floor and look for a way to the central tower. From there,

I need you to contact Lieutenant Harper and let him know we're okay."

"Yes, ma'am." He withdrew a lantern from his pack, lit it, and disappeared.

Amelia continued. "Cid, I need you to...." She trailed off. Cid was gone. She hadn't even seen him light a lantern or torch. *Idiot*, she thought. They'd find him later, assuming she didn't decide to leave him here altogether.

"I guess that leaves you," she said finally to Amir.

"I'm staying right here," he said firmly.

"You are?" She gave him a hard look. "Do you even have a lantern?"

His expression fell, but he gritted his teeth. "I'm staying here. You've pushed me far enough."

"Fine, suit yourself. I'm going to search for the library." She turned and began walking toward the entrance directly opposite from the royal ceremony hall. She'd barely exited the atrium when Amir quickly stumbled after her.

"Wait!"

She rolled her eyes and examined the new room ahead of her. She was at the top of a stairwell that branched left to right. The railing was polished gold and still gleamed in the torchlight, despite a coating of dust all around. She leaned over the railing and took in the sight below.

Ahead of them looked to be a grand entryway into the palace. Rock and sand spilled through the opening of a gate. Warped golden doors barely hung on long rusted hinges. On either side of the gate were gold statues holding poles with tattered, faded banners. On each banner was the emblem of the palace structure, with palm leaves underneath and sea serpents lining the edge as a border.

Amir gasped. "The seal of Valera." He glided down the stairs to inspect the banners closer.

She shook her head. *Leave it up to a scholar to only have eyes for the seal and not the gold.* There was so much of it all around. It was inlaid into the cracks of the walls, and even the railings were made of gold. The sheer quantity of it made her wonder if the stories were true. Had gold coins once been as plentiful here as the desert sands are now?

The notion was fanciful and impractical, she knew. But that didn't stop her from feeling a rush of excitement from the vision it conjured.

Temptation pulled at her to take out her tools and cut out a gold bar from the railing. She resisted the impulse, though the thought didn't leave her mind entirely.

She waited until Amir finished taking notes in a journal before proceeding back to the atrium. Here, they turned right down a passageway. They passed a series of guards' quarters, which were strewn with skeletons, rusted armor, and decaying bed frames. Mattresses had shriveled and become overgrown with moss. Everywhere stank of foul mildew.

The hallway ended in a square room with broken columns and a single iron door. The iron door still stood intact and looked thick enough to survive a siege even now. It was locked, probably forever if it wasn't for a column that had crashed into the wall next to it, opening a hole into the room beyond.

Curious, Amelia climbed up the angled pillar and crawled through the cracked opening. As she reached the top, she slipped and fell through onto her back.

"Oof." Underneath her back was a bed of hard, cold, clinking metal. She slowly sat up and raised the lantern.

Her mouth dropped open in a silent gasp. The room was *filled* with gold coins. They obscured the floor and rose halfway up the walls. There must have been hundreds of thousands of them. Despite the dust coating, they glittered magically at her in the lantern light.

She rubbed her eyes to make sure she wasn't dreaming. The sheer magnitude of what she was seeing was impossible to comprehend. It was like falling into a fairytale.

Amir was shouting something from the room on the other side, but she scarcely heard his words. She scooped a handful of the coins and inspected them in the light. Each was embossed with a palace on one side and a sea dragon on the other.

There was enough wealth in her hands alone to purchase an entire estate. Add the amount in this entire room—there was no limit as to what it could buy!

She sank back as realization flooded into her. If she took home even a fraction, she could rebuild her family's company to greater heights than ever before. More than that, she could rebuild her reputation. She could change the way people viewed her and treated her. This could buy her life back.

Desperate longing filled her as she thought about the years she had spent trying to redeem her past. Now the answer was right in front of her. With this gold, she could have everything she ever wanted.

She stared at the gold, feeling the desire for a better life build inside her with an unbearable crescendo. Soon its pull became irresistible, and she found herself slinging off her magpack and stuffing coins into its pouches.

Euphoria grew inside her as her magpack began to fill. Her heart raced with each added handful. Every bit promised of a better life—a life of freedom, esteem, and belonging.

"What are you DOING?"

Amelia jumped. Amir's face stuck out of the hole above, and it was clear the rest of him didn't fit through. His expression was one of disgust.

She shook herself. What *was* she doing? She probably looked like a madwoman. Her cheeks flushed, and she shrank away from Amir. She suddenly felt exposed and vulnerable.

Amir wasn't finished. "I knew insanity ran in your blood, but I didn't think you'd stoop so far as theft!"

"Theft?" Anger rose inside her. "How is this theft if it's been abandoned for centuries?"

"Would you rather I use a different word? Like looting? Plundering? Are those any better? I thought you were better than this."

Hot tears sprang to her eyes, and she turned away. Shame and embarrassment filled her to the brim. She *was* a fool. How did she expect money to change anything for her? It didn't matter how much money she had. People would still only see her as the girl who started the fire.

The tears continued, dripping onto the coins with metallic *plinks* as horrible despair washed over her. There really was no escape from her past. Not as long as there were people who knew who she was. There was no redemption for her. This was her fate.

She gripped her fingers into fists. *No.* She'd finish what her grandfather had started. She'd find the Wayfinder, and when she got back to the Republic, she'd use this money to take a one-way voyage as far as she could go. Maybe she'd travel to Brinkerhoff or somewhere farther south. With enough gold, she could buy herself a comfortable life and escape all the pain. Maybe she could forget her family name and past altogether.

She rose and threw her magpack back on. The gold weighed her down, but it was nothing compared to the weight she'd been carrying for years. Sure, maybe it was selfish to take the gold, even if it was abandoned. Still, it was far better than continuing with a false hope that maybe things would get better. At least with this, she could start a new life, far away from everyone who knew her.

Without looking at Amir, she said, "There's no library on this side of the palace, so I'm going to keep searching."

They returned to the main atrium, where Blaze waited. He rushed to them as they approached.

"I found the central tower," he explained, "but the bottom is filled with rubble. So, I found another way in the tower and got a message back to Lieutenant Harper. They'll have to clear the path to get to us, but we have a way out."

She cleared her throat. "Oh, good." She gave him a smile she didn't feel.

He frowned. "Are you alright?"

She nodded. "I'm fine."

"Good," said Cid, materializing from the dark. "Because I've found your abandoned library."

Chapter 27: Tomes of Secrets

Amelia

A melia, Blaze, and Amir followed Cid from the foyer down a hallway strewn with debris. They ducked under fallen timbers and squeezed through small gaps where the ceiling had given away entirely. Some gaps were so small, she had to wriggle her body just to get through. It would have been significantly easier if she wasn't carrying a pack full of gold.

Amir whined at each obstacle. Many of the gaps required him to suck in his gut and squish himself through. She got the sense he wasn't one to get much exercise outside walking or using a quill and parchment. This was far outside his typical trip to the library.

His whining, though, was incessant. Maybe even torturous. He'd stop at each point and question again why they were exploring the ruins in the first place. Then he'd see something and become as giddy as a schoolgirl. It took massive willpower not to leave him behind.

Still, they needed him. He was the only one who could translate ancient writings.

They passed several rooms, including a dining hall and a kitchen. After that, they wound their way through a hallway that must have once been filled with suits of armor on each side—only now the pieces were scattered across the floor like a battlefield. Finally, the passageway ended at a set of closed gold doors. Hinges groaned as they pushed through into a wide and open dark space.

"Here's your library," said Cid with little enthusiasm.

"Can't see much," said Amelia, raising her lantern up in the dark.

"Oh, I got it!" said Blaze. He pulled out a signal flare and set it off. *Boom!* The light shot up, revealing a large oval chamber filled with row upon row of tipped and broken shelves. Books covered the ground in haphazard piles. The flare continued upward, revealing a second, third, and fourth floor ringing around the chamber. Sandstone pillars supported each level and were carved to look like sea serpents. Cracked and broken bridges spanned from each level to the next, cutting diagonally across the open center space in a crisscross pattern. Tattered banners hung off each level in alternating patterns.

"Ohhhh," said Amir, as if in a daze. "All the books."

The flare bounced off the ceiling and dropped back to the main floor, where it stopped in a pile of books.

The pile burst into flames.

"The books!" Amir nearly tripped over himself as he ran to the fire and began stamping it. Amelia and Blaze followed and helped while Cid hung back and laughed darkly.

Amelia stamped out the last ember and glared at Blaze.

"What?" said Blaze, holding his hands up. "How was I supposed to know that would happen?"

"You realize we're in a *library?* An ancient library? With *books?*"

"Oh... right."

She rolled her eyes. "You're lucky it's contained. The last thing we want is this whole place in flames."

They all fell silent as a deep rumble echoed through the forlorn library. The sound was low and resonant like distant thunder; yet it vibrated their insides with an unsettling intensity.

"What was that?" Blaze whispered.

"I don't know," Amelia replied. "Maybe it's the collapsed part of the palace settling?"

The room groaned again, and with it came the creaking and groaning of stones. The sound continued, shifting its source as if moving through the palace. Goosebumps prickled across her arms, and the air in the room suddenly felt thick and heavy.

She swallowed. "We need to find what we need and quick!"

They rushed through the main floor, stepping over rubble and debris to pick up disintegrating books from piles on the floor. Clearly, the collapse of the palace had put the entire library into a chaotic mess. Rats scurried from place to place, and twice, Amelia spotted winged serpents darting after their furry forms. Despite the mess, it looked like time and critters had created natural paths through the debris. It was as if someone had taken a rake and had pulled debris to the side to create aisles that snaked back and forth through the chamber. The floor along these aisles was rubbed and scarred, as if the rake used to clear it was as sharp as knives and pulled across a thousand times.

Amir seemed oblivious to all of this. He ran excitedly from one pile to the next, picking up a book, reading the title, and setting it down for another. "This is incredible!" he said breathlessly. "We have records of their culture, agriculture, architecture—look here." He held up one particularly large volume with a torn spine. "Here's one about taming the sea serpents. *Sea serpents!* They actually had them and used them to pull their ships!"

His words echoed hollowly around the grand chamber, stretching and extending the sound before diminishing. The effect was unnerving in the oppressive dark. Amelia suddenly wished Ander was here with them. Or even Garret or Hammer. She felt exposed and vulnerable in such a dark and open space. That effect was further enhanced by the bumbling fools she was stuck with. They were making so much noise in a place that had so long been undisturbed.

As if to make her point, Blaze asked Amir, "Do they have any books on ancient practical jokes? Asking for a friend, of course."

She stepped between them. "Guys, focus! We're here to find books about the Wayfinder. Amir, where do you think that'll be?"

The scholar glared at her. "Miss Steam, we're in one of the most incredible archeological finds in all the lands and all you can think about is still just the Wayfinder?"

She put her free hand on her hip and opened her mouth, but Cid spoke first.

"Stop bickering like children and shut up!" he hissed. He pointed to an ear. The creaking and groaning of stones was back, and this time it was much closer. They froze and listened as a new sound joined it—a continuous grating noise like the scraping of metal against rock.

"I don't think that's the palace settling," whispered Blaze.

Shivers went down Amelia's body. She turned in the direction of noise. The scraping, scratching sound was now entering the room, and she recognized it for what it was.

"Get off the path!" she hissed in the barest of whispers. They scrambled away as a massive, scaly form slithered just barely into view.

A sadriconda! Her breathing froze and her heart increased in tempo. Its head rose and was nudging the pile of books Blaze had accidentally lit on fire. She swallowed hard and stilled her breathing.

Their lamps still glowed with light, but the predator didn't seem to notice. It probably couldn't, she realized. Sadricondas lived underneath the ground after all and rarely came out in daylight.

The detail gave her a small measure of comfort. She locked eyes with Amir and mouthed two words. *Wayfinder. Where?*

His face was drained of blood as he pointed a shaky, trembling finger upward.

She nodded. That made sense. This bottom floor appeared to be general access. Even back in the time of Valera, the sultans wouldn't have wanted everyone to know about the Wayfinder.

She put a finger to her lips and led them carefully across the rubble-strewn floor toward an arched bridge. Their pace was painstakingly slow. Debris was littered everywhere, and even the smallest *crunch* echoed. She took them in a wide arc around the sadriconda, since its long body stretched across half of the cavern.

Finally, they reached the bridge. It rose diagonally across the oval room, traveling directly over the sadriconda. With careful steps, they climbed up the smooth arch, which was covered with thick dust and rat droppings. The gold railing was likewise covered with cobwebs.

Midway across, part of the floor gave way underneath Amir. He stumbled forward and hurried away as chunks of stone crashed to the main floor below. Quick as a flash, the sadriconda struck at where the rocks hit the floor, sending up a spray of dust and rock into the air.

The group scrambled the rest of the way and ducked behind a collapsed bookcase. Seconds passed before the grating, slithering sound resumed, roving through the chamber below.

Amelia breathed through her mouth in an effort to be even more quiet. Still, her heart pounded, and it was all she could do to keep from gasping in great gulps of air.

Cautiously, they moved from behind cover and scanned the second floor. Similar to the main floor, this level was filled with tipped bookshelves. Mounds of sand sloped out from the wall where windows once stood, their glass shards twinkling in the lamplight. They began a tour around the ring, passing tipped reading tables and mice-ridden, plush chairs. Cid followed a ways behind, pausing here and there to inspect a skeleton for valuables. When they completed a circuit, nothing stood out to them, so they proceeded to the next level.

As they rose, the light illuminated glimpses of the sadriconda below. It was rising up the arched bridge to the first level, sliding to where Amir had nearly fallen through.

It's following us, she realized. The thought quickened her already grueling pace. There was only so much tiptoeing you could do with a pack of gold before your calves burned. Still, she told herself it would be worth it in the end.

They continued their search on the third and fourth levels. Both were much like the second, except the damage worsened the higher they went. Cracks ran through the floor and up the pillars of each level. A portion of the fourth floor had also given way entirely into the third. They still hadn't found anything when they reached the last bridge. It rose from the fourth floor to an alcove in the ceiling.

"Look!" Amelia pointed at the alcove. When she raised her lantern, she could just make out a golden door gleaming with runic symbols on the far side of the bridge.

Amir raised an eyebrow and gestured to the bridge. The center was broken, leaving a gap over twenty feet wide. Only the warped railings remained to connect both sides.

Blaze waved a dismissive hand. "Amiry," he whispered, "we do this kind of thing in our sleep. Watch and learn." He walked to the edge and stretched his arms.

Amelia cautiously approached him. "Blaze, I've got a rappelling line and a harness."

He shook his head. "I got this." He winked at her before climbing onto the railing and scooting up it with his hands and legs. She held her breath and felt her heart skip a beat when the railing emitted a low groan as he passed through the bent middle. Then he was on the other side.

She ran a hand down her face. There were a thousand ways that could have gone wrong. She looked over the edge and tried to catch a glimpse of the sadriconda. All was silent. Perhaps it had finally left?

Cid bumped past her to the railing. The smell of his unwashed body rivaled that of the mildew all around. He shimmied over the gap and got across in no time.

Blaze waved for her to come next. She approached the railing, took a deep breath, and then thought better. A minute later, she had a harness strapped on and was attaching a rope to a nearby pillar. Then she climbed onto the railing, sitting on top of it rather than dangling underneath like Blaze and Cid had done.

The railing felt much more precarious than it looked. A knot grew in her stomach, but she had to get across. She began to scoot over it and felt it wobble underneath her. Quickly, she clamped her legs tighter until the wobbling ceased. Cold sweat formed across her forehead and her palms, making her grip more slippery.

Come on, Amelia, she urged, forcing herself onward. The gold coins in her pack weighed her down considerably and threatened to pull her off the edge each time she moved. Second thoughts were going through her mind about the money. Maybe she should have left her pack behind at the atrium? It was too late for that now. She was already halfway across.

Finally, she reached the other side and took a gulping breath. Blaze gave her a big thumbs up and waved Amir on next.

Amir shook his head.

"Come on," Blaze whispered. "All the cool kids are doing it."

Amelia frowned at Blaze.

He rolled his eyes. "Alright, all the cool kids and Cid are doing it."

"More like the dumb kids," mumbled Cid.

She ran a hand down her face and focused her attention on Amir. "Hey," she hissed, "I left you a harness. Slip that on and then attach this rope." She threw a rope over to him. "If anything happens, we've got you."

Amir continued shaking his head. "I'm not doing it. I'm not good with heights."

"You can do this," she urged. "We need you. You're the only one who can translate these texts."

Amir's expression became pleading. "Miss Steam, I can't do it. I really can't."

"*We* can't do this without you," she insisted. "Look, I know you aren't invested in finding the Wayfinder. You're more concerned about finding your niece, but what if finding the Wayfinder is the *only* way to find your niece? You could spend your whole life looking for her and never find her. By looking into the Wayfinder, you could find her in a heartbeat."

That got his attention. She continued. "Amir, you might be the only person in all of Sadria who can do this. Who else knows ancient Sahadrian like you? We need you. Your niece needs you."

Amir's hands clenched and unclenched. Then he sucked in a deep breath. "Fine. I'll do it for my niece."

She let out her breath as Amir cinched on his harness. Then he climbed on top of the railing, closed his eyes, and began to scoot.

"You're doing great," she said. "Almost halfway there."

The railing groaned again, and he froze. "I can't do this. I can't do this!" He wrapped his arms tighter around the railing. As he did, his weight shifted to the side and pulled him underneath.

"AHHHHH!" His scream echoed through the room. Then his feet slipped out, and he hung from the railing with just his hands.

"He's going to fall," muttered Cid.

"Swing your legs back on," said Amelia.

Amir kicked his legs wildly.

"I'm telling you, he's going to fall," repeated Cid.

"NOT HELPING!" snapped Amelia.

"Brace yourself," said Blaze quietly. She tightened her grip on the rope. Then Amir's fingers slipped. He plummeted downward, rending the air with a horrific scream. Then he reached the end of the rope line with a jolt.

The rope nearly ripped straight out of Amelia's hands. Both she and Blaze stumbled forward under the immediate weight. They

WAYFINDER

groaned and pulled with all their might. Amir continued to jar the
rope as he flailed and screamed. Somewhere far below, the
sadriconda stirred. It grated its scaly body and began up a level and
then the next.

Amelia's and Blaze's feet slipped a few inches toward the gaping
edge. Fear rose up in Amelia's throat like bile. They were losing the
fight. Why hadn't they tied off the line on *this* side? Amir was going
to fall, and if the drop didn't kill him, the sadriconda would.

Sweat dripped down her temples as her feet continued to slip
forward until they reached the edge. She could feel Blaze's arms
shaking behind her. Her toes began to creep over the edge. If she kept
holding on any longer, she was going to get pulled over after him.

Someone huffed behind them. Then suddenly the rope yanked
backward.

Cid? She'd forgotten he was there. He never helped with
anything. He didn't even clean up his own plate after meals on the
airship.

Slowly, they pulled Amir up and over the ledge. Once he was
over, they each dropped to the ground and sucked in deep breaths.

"When this is over," whispered Amir, "I'm never associating with
any Steams again."

"No 'thank you'?" asked Blaze. "We could have let you fall!"

"We would've had to if it weren't for Cid." She turned to eye Cid
with a newfound gratitude.

Cid folded his arms and huffed. "I told you he would fall."

Of course he'd say that, she thought. Still, he had helped when it
mattered most. They continued their breather a moment longer,
listening to the grating sounds of the sadriconda as it continued to
roam about below. It hadn't passed above the third level, which she

347

was grateful for. The last thing they needed was it launching out at them while they were suspended so far from the ground level.

Once her heart had settled down, she dusted her hands off and rose. Speaking again in a whisper, she said, "Well, should we see what's behind this door?"

Together, they approached the golden door. As they neared it, the runic symbols glowed brighter in the lamplight, along with ancient words along the top.

"Royal Athenaeum," Amir read. He turned to Amelia. "Looks like we've found the Sultan's personal collection." He tried the handle. Locked.

"Alright," she said, sizing up the door. "We can crack this."

"Or you could ask Cid to give you the key," said Blaze. He put his hand out. "I saw you swipe it from me."

"That was after you swiped it from me," Cid replied defensively. "I've stolen it twice, fair and square."

"That last one doesn't count. I was trying to keep Amir from becoming a pancake."

"Not my fault you were occupied."

Amelia ran a hand down her face. "For goodness' sake, just give it to me."

Cid and Blaze stared at each other for a long second. Then Cid finally handed over a golden key, the length of which was carved into a sea serpent and the handle into palm leaves.

"It was on the sultan," said Blaze.

Amir's jaw fell open. "You desecrated the last sultan of Valera? Haven't you heard about royal curses?"

"I didn't do it," said Blaze quickly. "Cid did. So if there's a curse, he has it."

"But you stole it from me," said Cid angrily, "so you'd just as likely be cursed."

Amelia's head pounded. In a harsh whisper she said, "If you all don't SHUT IT right now, I will personally leave you all behind when we take the *Legacy* out of this pit."

The group fell silent. *Finally*, she thought. She plunged the key into the lock and turned.

Stale air rushed out of a small, oval room. In the center of the room was a reading table with two plush chairs. On the left and right sides of the room were two sets of standing book shelves that rose to the ceiling. The surrounding walls were covered with faded frescos.

Cobwebs stretched across the bookshelves and up to the ceiling. Books still lined the shelves, though their rune-covered bindings were layered with dust. A strange odor filled the space, not musty or moldy like everywhere else. It tasted like sea salt and palm leaves—the scent of an era long forgotten.

Amelia set the lantern down on the reading table and surveyed the books. "Alright, Amir, how can we help?"

"Wipe down the spines, will you? I need to be able to read them. Same with this table."

Amelia began wiping down the bookshelves while Blaze wiped the table. Cid only hung at the doorway, opting to lean against it rather than help.

Most of the texts were distinctly older than the rest of the library. Several would have been ancient even in the time of Valera. Though some spines had decayed, most of them were well preserved considering the rest of the palace.

As she dusted, Amelia noticed a few empty places in the shelves that were missing books. She paused. In the empty slots, the dust layer was much thinner. As if—they weren't the first to visit this library since the collapse. Someone else had too, and based on the lack of dust, it was relatively recent.

Was it my grandfather? she wondered. The thought gave her goosebumps. It had to have been. Who else would have known where to find this palace? Who else would have needed the knowledge it contained?

Amir began perusing the collection, pulling out books and then piling them on the table. There was nothing she and Blaze could do at this point. Neither of them had any hope of translating this literature. So, as Amir began to flip through the books, they toured the mural around the room.

The mural depicted a series of scenes, showing Valera over time. The first showed a battlefield between warriors and sea serpents on orange sands. In the center was a brawny warrior with a circlet who was raising both hands in the air. On either side of the warrior, waves rose, the tops crusted with sharp ice. Sea serpents cowered and bowed to the warrior. In the distance lay a city with a half-built palace. Underneath it all was a caption in gold calligraphy.

She turned to the scholar. "Amir, what does this say?"

He paused in his study to squint at the words. "It says *Liberation of the Sahadrian Seas.*"

"Do you think there really were sea serpents?" Blaze asked Amelia quietly.

She shrugged and continued walking to the left, where the scene changed. Blue waters lapped against orange sands, while the mighty palace of Valera rose in the distance. An armada of warships filled the bay, and each were pulled by a great sea serpent. Borrowing Amir's help again, the caption for this painting was *Rulers of the Sahadrian*

Seas.

"Maybe there were sea serpents?" she hypothesized. "But they only existed in these seas and during the time of Valera. I've never heard of sea serpents like this anywhere else in the world."

"Whoa, look at this," said Blaze, pointing at the next scene. Valera stood, shrouded in deep shadow. Most of the plaster above the city had fallen, but whatever had been depicted was primarily black, purple, and gray. Dark purple lightning appeared from the edges of the broken section and struck at the city. Sadricondas attacked the city, rising from the earth and crashing into buildings. Near the beach was a sea serpent in the act of getting struck by the purple lightning. Half of it had the blue sheen and fins of a sea serpent while the other half was black-scaled with jagged spikes just like the sadricondas. The sight sent cold shivers down her spine.

Had sadricondas once been sea serpents? She staggered backwards and put a hand to her head. Sea serpents hadn't just gone extinct nor had sadricondas suddenly risen from Har like the Sadrians believed. They were the same, just transformed.

What would be so powerful to cause that? The top portion of the mural would have held the answer, but it was gone, broken into dust on the floor. All that was left was a suggestion of dark power, power similar to what had stirred within the Nardoowe beast.

She let out a breath and searched for any other context clues. The scene stretched to the left, where the sea lapped against the mountain range. Warriors appeared to be using magic to carve a channel for the waters through the mountain range. She stared at it for a full minute, trying to glean its meaning in context. She came up with nothing.

"What does the caption for this dark one say?" asked Blaze.

"*Fall of the Sahadrian Seas,*" Amir grunted.

Blaze chuckled. "Fall? Ha. They should have called it *Fall of the Sahadrian Sky*. Get it? Because part of the sky fell off the wall?"

Amelia rolled her eyes and walked to the final scene, which depicted Valera like before, but now the lapping sea was gone. Great ships laid on their sides and wild sadricondas roved the sands. The caption underneath read *Age of the Sadrian Sands*.

She brushed her fingertips over the long paint strokes and felt the loss of the once great kingdom. There was no final painting to show how this grand palace would one day sink into the sands to be completely forgotten by the rest of the world.

"I found something," said Amir.

Amelia jumped and hurried to stand over Amir's shoulder. Before him was a dusty tome with yellowed pages. He pointed at an illustration of a glass lens mounted on a gold, sea serpent frame. The serpent's tails braided together to create a handle.

Amelia's mouth fell open. "Is that—?"

"The Wayfinder," Amir finished. He began reading. "*It's said to hold the magic of Saldranon the Shrewd, and is one of the four most powerful talismans in the world. All the user has to do is look into its depths and visualize what it is they wish to find. The lens will show them the path to get there.*"

"Wow," said Blaze, who had now joined Amir's other side.

"What else is there?" Amelia asked.

"It begins to talk about the Wayfinder's true purpose, but whatever else was here is gone." Amir flipped the page. Sticking up at them was the remnant of a torn page.

"I can go look for a free-floating page," said Blaze.

Amir shook his head. "This page didn't fall out. I've seen what that looks like more times than I care to count. No, this was ripped out."

"It probably talks about the Source," said Amelia. "It makes sense that the page would be ripped out or stolen at some point. It's incredibly dangerous and should've been forgotten entirely. What else is there?"

"We've got a bit of history. The Valeran sultans used the Wayfinder to discover treasures of the earth. Many called it the *Lens of Hope* because it brought in carts of gold during a time when the seas were drying up and the trade routes became more treacherous."

He flipped a couple more pages. "We have accounts of two wars fought over the Wayfinder. It's been stolen multiple times and reclaimed the same."

"Could you skip to the end, where we learn about its last whereabouts?" asked Amelia.

Amir raised an eyebrow before flipping several pages forward. Then he pointed again. "Here, it says that the Wayfinder was stolen by Rasharr Voh, the Dread Pirate Lord. He used the lens to rob the world of its greatest treasures and then used the Wayfinder to hide them in a trove no one else but he would be able to find."

Interesting. The book had a drawing of his ship, the *Dread Reaper.* It was a long warship with a sharp steel ram on the front and three rows of slave oars. Unlike warships of its time period, however, this particular ship was gaff-rigged rather than square-rigged.

"What else?" she asked.

"If you could give me a second, I'll tell you," said Amir grumpily. "As I was saying, Rasharr Voh was tracked down by the Valeran Navy and sunk to the sea. The Wayfinder was never recovered."

Amelia put her hands to her head and sank down in the chair

opposite from Amir. "So... the Wayfinder really is lost."

"Many have tried to reclaim it over the years," said Amir. "There is no shame in accepting that this is a lost cause."

"There's got to be something. Where was it sunk? Do we have a landmark or general location?"

Amir sighed and turned back to the page. After a moment, he began reading, *"The Valeran Navy tracked Rasharr Voh and laid a trap near the Red Crossing. The narrows to the Sahadrian West Sea were a favored raiding ground for the dread pirate lord, and when he saw a heavily laden trader ship—a decoy—he immediately struck.*

"While the dread pirate lord was occupied, the Valeran Navy closed in with three royal warships. The Dread Reaper *was speared through below the waterline while elite officers leaped onto its deck and engaged the malignant pirate swine. The death toll was heavy on each side, both refusing to yield. Eventually, the pirates fell. Rasharr Voh was pressed back and took his last stand in his cabin. His last words were 'You'll never find the Wayfinder on my dead body!' He then used magic to rip a hole straight through all three decks to the sea below.*

"Water flooded into the cabin in a torrent. Rasharr Voh attempted to escape through the hole he created, but an officer speared him through the gut and pinned him to his own desk. After that, it was all the officers could do to get off the ship before it sank beneath the sea.

Amir cleared his throat. "The rest talks about attempts they made to recover the Wayfinder. All were unsuccessful. The Red Crossing was the feeding grounds of the remaining wild sea serpents, and the sea floor was filled with thousands of sunken ships to search. So, that's how the tale of the Wayfinder ends." He shut the book with a loud thunk.

"That's something," she exclaimed, coming to a stand. "We know the region the ship was sunk in."

"The Sahadrian West Sea is an extensive region," said Amir, "and who knows where this Red Crossing is?"

"Yes, but it's a good starting point. Hang on." She paced while she tapped a finger on her lips. "It'd be a place filled with the wreckage of over a thousand ships, but in our day and age, it's no longer covered with water. It'd be dried up."

"And probably buried under a mile of sand," he concluded.

"What if it wasn't?" She snapped her fingers and broke into a large grin. "Do you remember the map room? The one we toured at the Sadrian Archives?"

Amir raised a sarcastic eyebrow. "How could I forget?"

"Do you remember the name of that location that was common for raider and pirate attacks? Where the bones of sunken ships can be still found today?"

"Shipwreck Sands?" He inhaled sharply and then nodded excitedly. "Yes! That would fit both historically and geographically. Shipwreck Sands is in the western region of the Sadrian desert, by the burning flats. Back then, it would've been a bottleneck channel for traders, making it the perfect ambush point for ships. If Drywind Bowl was once the Sahadrian West Sea, then that would mean Rasharr Voh went down at Shipwreck Sands. That fits!"

They stared at each other in pure excitement. After so much research, they finally had a solid lead—the last whereabouts of the Wayfinder.

Blaze cleared his throat. "So, based on the light gleaming in your eyes, I'm assuming you know where we need to go next?"

Amelia nodded and then hesitated. "Amir, do you know where Shipwreck Sands is on a map?"

His bushy eyebrows pressed together. "I know the general region, but I couldn't point to a map and say where it is exactly."

"Me neither." She slunk back down. "Without an accurate map, we could spend years combing the western desert."

"There's only one place you're going to find that kind of map," said Amir. "The Sadrian Archives."

"Maybe there's something here?" She paused as a smell hit her senses. *Smoke.*

Cid rushed into the room. "Hate to break up your book party, but Blaze's pile of books reignited and has gotten a little crazy."

Amelia took the book from Amir's hands and crammed it into her already stuffed magpack before rushing out the door. They reached the edge of the bridge and looked down.

The chamber now glowed bright from the flames of several piles of books on the floor. Their flames licked out and jumped to other piles in seconds. Her eyes widened as she processed what was happening in double time. The fire was growing, and she understood too well how quickly it would spread.

"We need to go!" she said urgently.

Amir's face was stricken; his gaze flicked back to the room they were just in. "But the collection? What about all the history?"

"There's no time," she explained. "This is going to spread fast, and if the heat doesn't kill us, the lack of oxygen will. We need to get out. NOW!"

Blaze jolted into action, jumping onto the railing. She grabbed his arm before he could begin scooting.

"There's no time! We're rappelling straight down. Quick, help me get set up." They wrapped a line around multiple points at the base of the railing. As they did, the smoke quickly filled the ceiling above and began to descend upon them. Within a minute, the air became hot and dry, and the four of them coughed.

Once the line was secure, they strapped on harnesses and looked out below. The bottom floor was an inferno, and the flames now licked at the second level.

"It's growing!" said Amir with fear.

"We can't drop to the first floor," said Blaze, "but I could probably swing us to the bridge to the second." He latched himself onto the line and dropped without delay. She watched him fall and then swing successfully to the bridge leading to the second floor.

Cid didn't wait before dropping right after Blaze.

"Amir," Amelia coughed, "you're next."

Amir hesitated, and she could see the fear in his eyes. She took him by both shoulders and said, "You have to do this for your niece. We are the only ones who know where the Wayfinder is."

Amir swallowed before stepping off the edge. He zipped down and nearly crashed at the bottom.

The smoke was so thick now, and it was all she could do to latch her harness to the line and drop over the edge. She fell quickly, gaining speed. As the landing neared, she squeezed the rope against the rappel device. She wasn't slowing like normal, but her weight was much greater than normal with the gold. Panic surged through her and she squeezed the rope harder. The rappel device squealed at her before she hit the bridge with a thud. Coins jangled loose and rolled away down the bridge.

"This way," Blaze shouted. They sprinted the rest of the way to the second floor while ancient tapestries burned on either side of them. Cid was way ahead, tying and dropping rope down to the main entrance. In a flash, he was over the edge and gone.

Wow, he's fast. That was as much thought as she could give because suddenly, a pillar crashed feet from her with a deafening blast. This spurred her to run even faster.

They reached the line Cid had tied and wasted no time throwing themselves over the railing and sliding down. Even Amir offered no complaint, somehow finding his courage in the face of imminent danger.

They hit the floor right as a loud *CRACK* reverberated through the room. Behind, the top bridge finally broke loose of its shabby mooring and fell straight into the next bridge in line. That bridge broke as well and continued to the next in the series.

No one paused to watch the pattern continue. They hurtled toward the main entrance in a frenzy, heedless of the debris and flames around them. As soon as they passed through the main doors, the bridges hit the ground with a deafening *BOOM!* The blast sent a shockwave wave so powerful, it threw them forward while shaking the entire world all around them.

"This place isn't going to hold!" Amelia screamed as she tore to her feet.

"I can get us out!" yelled Blaze. "Just follow my lead."

They crashed through the hall filled with fallen suits of armor, sending pieces flying. They dove under fallen timbers and wrenched their way through the small gaps in the passageway. A pouch on her pack tore free and spilled clicking coins all behind her. She gritted her teeth and pressed forward, not looking back.

Dust and debris rained down on their heads. Cracks grew in the ceiling over their heads, racing them toward the atrium. They barely won the race and emerged into the plus-shaped room.

"Up here," Blaze shouted, rushing up a stairwell. She dashed after him and then skidded to a halt.

"AMIR! WHAT ARE YOU DOING?"

He was still at the base of the atrium, leaning over and panting. "Hang on!" He wheezed back. "I need to catch my breath!"

Without warning, the wall next to him exploded like a thunderclap. From it launched a dark maw with rows of long, jagged teeth. In an instant, they closed around Amir and he was gone.

Amelia stared at where Amir had just stood in frozen shock. She had spent weeks with him, first at the embassy, then the archives, and now here. The weeks were filled with incessant jibes against her and her family, and his complaints were endless. He had been a prick in her side since day one, but now he was gone.

The loss hit her so suddenly and painfully, she wanted to double over and curl into a ball.

The sadriconda rose its head and turned to her. Pure terror poured through her in an instant. She bolted toward the doorway Blaze had gone through.

The sadriconda launched at her, crashing where she'd stood a fraction before. Its jaws slammed shut with a sickening clap. Then she was in a tower stairwell that was tilted at a 45-degree angle.

She scrambled up the wall and climbed over each circular row of railed steps. The massive predator followed, struggling at first to squeeze through the door until it forced the walls to crumble around its snout. Amelia screamed. The sadriconda inched through the small space, forcing itself closer and closer to her.

She became more manic, throwing herself over each subsequent row of stairs. Blaze appeared at the end of the tower ahead of her, eyes wide and shouting. His words were lost over the pounding of her heart and the sounds of the beast behind her.

The sadriconda lurched after her, its scales grating against the stone like nails on a chalkboard. She pushed herself harder, feeling each additional crash against stone and metal add more bruises to her already fatigued body. The pack on her back felt like an anvil now, pressing down on her, slowing her ability to escape. But there was no time to pull off the magpack.

A long-forked tongue slapped against her back like a wet bristle brush. It cast a smell so horrific, it sent bile choking up her throat.

Blam! A bolt flew inches past her face and impaled itself into the beast. It howled and filled the whole tower with the smell of death. The bolt bought her just enough time to reach the top.

Blaze helped her squeeze through a hole into another, wider tower. This one also had a stairwell, but it was much wider and only partially tilted.

"Where's Amir!" he shouted.

Tears threatened to break, and she couldn't trust her voice. She only shook her head.

His expression fell. "Oh...."

They tore up the stairs while the walls and floor trembled, threatening to crumble apart. Below, the entryway blasted apart. The sadriconda tilted upward and roared a mighty *MRAHHHHH!* Then it pushed itself upward, crushing the stairs below them as it wriggled toward them.

She screamed and pounded up the stairs. Her pack felt terribly heavy, and her legs burned like they were being seared by a hot iron.

Just above, Lieutenant Harper's voice shouted down at them. "That's them! Drop the ladder." His face came into view at the top of the stairs, just one flight away. And yet, the sadriconda still snapped not far behind them.

As Blaze and Amelia reached the top level, a violent shudder ripped through the tower, pitching the floor. In an instant, Amelia lost her footing and flipped over the railing.

She barely caught herself with a single hand, grasping a golden rung. Beneath her, the sadriconda roared and wriggled toward her in predatory delight. Sweat slicked her hand, and she could feel her grip slipping.

Blaze appeared in a flash and grabbed at her hand and pulled. Veins bulged along his arms and face, but the combined weight of her and her pack was too much.

Cold waves of horror washed over her as she began to slip. She was going to die. Not just that, it was about to end horribly and painfully. As soon as she fell, the sadriconda would close its jaws and rend her to pieces like it had Amir. There was no redemption for her, no redeeming of her family name. Her story would end here, falling to a horrible and violent end.

Regret ripped at her heart as she thought about all the stupid things she had ever done. All of it she'd done out of stubborn selfishness. Even the good things were motivated by the same thing. Perhaps, this was what she deserved.

Their hands slipped to just their fingers.

"Millie! NO!" screamed Blaze.

Tears filled her eyes, wishing and praying for a second chance. Then her fingers slipped entirely.

Her arms and legs flailed outward as she fell straight toward the gaping maw of the sadriconda. Her heart beat once.

This was it, she thought. Then tendrils of thick darkness flooded the entire tower and something smashed into her body, throwing her to the side. She crashed into a wall, and her entire world went dark.

. . . .

Something was dragging her, carrying her away. She moaned, debating whether she wanted to open her eyes. Her limbs felt like lead, and the bliss of sleep was so much more attractive than the growing throb across her whole body. Sounds grew sharper with a tinny ring: crashing stones and the ear-splitting shriek of a monster. Was she in its stomach? Was she already dead?

Her mind grew more lucid, and her eyes blinked open. Blaze and Lieutenant Harper were at her sides, supporting her beneath the arms. Their expressions were focused and intense as they were rushing her up the last tower steps.

"Wha...what happened?" she moaned, trying to get the words heard above the shrieking below. Goodness, her head and body hurt. She scrunched her eyes shut again.

"Millie, you're back!" Relief flooded Blaze's voice. "You're okay!"

Okay was a stretch. Pain radiated down her neck, spine, and arms. She tried opening her eyes again. The world swam, but she couldn't tell if that was just her head or if the world was actually spinning. "What hit me?"

"No idea," said Blaze between ragged breaths. "It was too dark to see. Whatever it was, you're lucky to be alive."

Lucky... Her vision fuzzed around the edges. Below, the large beast writhed and squirmed downward, away from them.

"Millie, stay with us..." The sound faded away as she drifted out of consciousness again. Then she was staring up at the inside of a turnip-shaped dome. A winch line hung down through a hole in the ceiling. Figures were scrambling around her, strapping her into a harness. Things were falling from the ceiling. Her eyes closed again.

She woke up again on the deck of the *Legacy*, this time feeling more lucid than ever. Hammer and Garret were there this time, moving her onto a stretcher. Sailors and soldiers scrambled left and right. She tried to sit up and then immediately regretted it. Pain shot through her whole body, making her head swim again.

"Whoa there, Millie," said Garret, easing her back down. "You're not ready for that yet."

"What's happening?" she coughed.

"Palace crumbling," said Hammer. They hoisted her up. The crashing grew louder, along with the blood curdling shrieking of the sadriconda. Then it all cut off suddenly.

Great plumes of dust blew up past the airship. She didn't need to look out to know the palace was gone, finally buried after standing so long.

The soldiers set her down on the bed of her cabin and laid her magpack against a wall. Its pouches were torn and shredded. Most of its contents were gone, with exception to her main pouch. The edges of golden coins peaked out of the rips and tears, gleaming at her in the low light. She turned her head away, sick with disgust. Her greed had nearly killed her.

She closed her eyes and was immediately woken by a soft knock. "Come in," she croaked.

Garret entered with an apologetic expression. "Sorry to bother you. Veronica's still out so we're running with only a skeleton crew. They're raising the airship out of the pit and need a heading afterward."

"Sadria," she said tiredly. "We need to go to Sadria,"

Garret nodded and exited. She stared up at the ceiling. Her whole body seemed to throb just from existing.

I should have died. A tear leaked from her eye, running down her face into her pillow. *How did I survive?*

Something had pushed her, intervening in what she had thought was her certain fate. *Something dark.*

She drifted off into emptiness.

Chapter 28: Return

Ander

"What happened to her?" Ander asked with alarm. He sat straight up despite how woozy and queasy he felt. In his lap was a wooden bucket, ready in case he needed to hurl like the others in the room. It was the body's way of getting rid of the venom, or so he was told.

Garret sat on the edge of his cot and held up a placating hand. "She's okay. I'm no medic, but I can tell there's nothing broken. A concussion? Probably, but she'll pull through."

Ander ran a hand through his hair. "How long ago was this?"

"About a day. We've been managing with just a portion of the crew since."

Ander leaned back into the wall. Apparently, he had missed a lot in just one day. A third of the crew recovering from bites, James Cole passed away from poisoning, and Amir killed by a sadriconda. On top of this, Amelia had nearly died as well during her expedition into the palace. It was a lot to process.

He cursed, wishing he hadn't gotten bit. Maybe he could have saved Amir. Maybe he could have kept Millie safe.

Technically, he *had* kept her safe—that was how he got bit by a venomous snake. Still, that didn't stop him from wishing things had been different, or that the launch party had waited at least.

He rubbed his head. "Thanks for the report."

Garret nodded. "I'll keep things running until the rest of command are in better condition to resume their posts. In the meantime, I recommend you get some sleep."

Ander did so. Days passed before he felt like normal. He visited Amelia in that time, checking to see how she was doing. She was very quiet during his visit, sharing only briefly what had happened and what they discovered. He could tell she was holding a lot back, but he didn't want to press her. The fact she actually talked to him without hostility was progress. Still, she seemed distant and withdrawn—a far cry from the close confidant from before.

They held a brief funeral service for Amir and James Cole. There was no body to bury for Amir and no ocean to tip James into, so they settled for a memorial out in the desert, complete with a carved headstone.

By the time they reached the city of Sadria, Amelia was back to her regular duties as airship captain. She was kind to him, but still distant. Something was going on with her, he just wished he knew what it was.

Darkness covered the city when they arrived. Only scattered pinpricks of orange light revealed there was a city at all. That and the soaring palace with its walls. They continued flying until they stopped

10,000 feet above the palace.

Amelia stood next to Ander, dressed head to toe in black. Her pilot goggles hugged her forehead. There was a subtle tension in her posture as she pulled at her sleeves. She was nervous, and he couldn't blame her. This was her first sky jump at a significant height. They were even higher than normal for today's jump, too. Khaldun would watch the skies, and they needed every advantage they could get to avoid detection.

He gave her a tight smile. "You sure you want to do this? Once we step off the *Legacy*, there's no turning back."

"We have to get to that map," she said, rubbing her hands together and then breathing in them to warm them up. "Without it, we could end up spending years canvasing the desert."

"I get that. But I could easily do this on my own. We don't need to risk your life too, especially since you just started feeling normal."

She gave him a sidelong look. "Then make sure you don't botch the landing." A nervous smile played at the edges of her lips.

"Millie," he said, shaking his head, "I'm more worried about once we get *inside* the palace. It's going to be teeming with guards."

She put a hand on her hip. "We've talked about this already, Ander. You're going to need someone who knows the archives."

He ran a hand through his hair, tempted to keep pushing. But her jaw was already set, and he knew that stubborn look in her eyes all too well. She was going whether or not he liked it.

Garret appeared before them. "You ready?"

They nodded.

"Alright. Millie, since this is your first sky jump at high altitude, we are going to strap you into a tandem." Garret lifted an especially large magpack with twice as many straps on the front. "Ander knows how to use this and will control it every step of the way. All you need to do is mirror what he does with his hands and legs and keep on your feet for the landing. Questions?"

For an instant, her eyes glanced to the drop below. Then she shook her head no.

"Okay," said Garret. "Let's get you set up."

Ander strapped in first, and then Amelia stepped in front of him. Then Garret cinched her in too. It wasn't until this moment he realized how incredibly close she was to him. Her back was pressed up against him, and strands of her pinned back hair blew teasingly into his face. He gritted his teeth and forced his mind to focus on anything but her. *Think about the mission. Think about the mission.*

Her arm brushed against his, breaking his concentration and sending his pulse racing. He pulled his hands away, flapping them awkwardly as he tried to figure out where to put them. No where was safe, so he finally opted with putting them behind his back like a drill sergeant.

Garret noticed the movement and, rather unsuccessfully, held back a smile. "You're good to go." He patted them each on the shoulder and stepped away.

They awkwardly shuffled to the edge of the railing and leaned over. The palace lights flickered far below; its imposing structure was only a small circle from this high up.

Amelia sucked in a breath, and a tremor ran through her body. Her hands bobbed up and down, as if searching for something to hold on to.

"Hey," he said quietly, "you can do this."

She tilted her head up and looked at him through her goggles. Her eyes were wide with worry, and he could almost see the second thoughts whirling in them.

"It's not too late to opt out," he added with a grin.

Her eyes narrowed and grew defiant. "Just shut up and give me your hands." She grabbed his hands and wrapped them tightly around her stomach. Then she closed her eyes. "Okay. I'm ready."

He cleared his now suddenly dry throat. "On my mark. Three. Two. One." They leapt over the railing and dropped into the darkness.

His stomach lurched at the sudden fall. Amelia screamed before the wind ripped away the noise. Then the world spun.

Her grip on his arms was like a vice. It took all his strength to unwrap them from her waist so they could stretch their limbs out to an X shape. Then the spinning slowed and weightlessness overtook them.

He felt Amelia relax. He even may have heard a giggle. Her hands clutched his tightly, no longer with tense terror. She even looked up at him through tear-streaked goggles and gave him the most breathtaking grin in the world.

Warmth filled him from his head to his toes, and despite their intense speed, it was like everything had slowed down. She was the most beautiful girl he'd ever met, his best friend and most trusted confidant. In this moment, everything felt right. Being here with her, holding her hands like this.

The moment broke as details of the palace grew clearer. He pulled their hands into a dive, angling their heads downward. Then he ripped down on the glider lever.

Large wings shot out and gripped the air with a *whoomp*. He angled them up and then glided down in a slow spiral. His mind was now focused on what he was doing as they dropped below the palace walls like a large black bird.

Their landing area approached quickly—a wide lawn with chopped green grass. He pulled a cord and both their feet dropped from the wings like stretched out talons. Then they hit the ground in a run.

Their feet pounded together the first ten paces in unison before they tripped into a roll. They tumbled wildly before crashing into a manicured hedge.

Ander groaned.

"Yep, that hurt," she winced.

"You okay?"

"I think so."

"Good." They listened out for any signs of alarm.

Nothing.

She met his eyes and broke into a big smile. Then, all at once, her expression changed and became distant again. It almost seemed... pained.

There it is again, he thought. *That wall she's been putting up.*

They detached themselves from the tandem and picked up the broken pieces of the wings. An ugly scar scored the lawn from where they crashed. It'd be visible by morning, but hopefully they'd be gone by then.

They shoved the broken pieces into a nearby rubbish wagon. Then they removed what gear they could salvage from their tandem magpack and shoved the rest underneath the pile of garbage.

With less energy than he had before, he turned to Amelia. "Where to next?" he whispered.

She pointed to a large building with towers, arches, and multiple levels of roofs.

"Got it." He took point, gliding from cover to cover. She followed a few steps behind in a lowered crouch. They passed through a garden and then paused at the edge of a road. Two guards passed by them, lazily scanning the environment while they talked to each other. When the guards had gone around a corner, they hurried across the road, pushed through bushes, and reached the northern edge of the archives.

"Boost me up," she said. "I can unlock the shutters."

He crouched down with his hands cupped. Amelia stepped into his hands and he lifted her to the window. Then she went to work, grabbing one tool and then the next from her belt.

Snick. In a flash, it opened and she was climbing through. A beat later, Ander jumped up and pulled himself after. Once in, he closed the shutters and locked them.

They were in a dark reading room. In the center was a round table with a pile of books in the middle. Around the edges of the rooms were plush chairs.

Amelia led the way now, creeping to the door and slowly opening it. A lonely hallway stretched out before them, bathed in moonlight and shadows. Slowly, they slipped through the archives until they pushed through into a wide rectangular room filled with a long table covered by a single, massive map of Sadria.

"Here we are," she said. "Give me a second to plot out what we need."

He nodded and propped open the door to keep watch of the hallway. All was quiet.

"This is it!" she whispered. "Shipwreck Sands."

He glanced back to see what she was pointing to when a sharp pain pricked his neck. Instinctively, he snatched at the spot and pulled away a dart.

Alarm bells went off in his head. He tried to shout at Amelia, tried to warn her, but her back was turned and his tongue felt fat and his body numb. He took a step toward her and fell over. Two guards caught him on either side before he could hit the floor. He hung uselessly and watched as more guards silently flooded into the room around Amelia.

She spoke faster with growing excitement. "Now all we need to do is make our way toward these coordinates—"

Turn around! he screamed, but his mouth wouldn't respond.

"—and find a gaffed rigged warship with three rows of oars and a steel ram."

Get out of here!

"The sadricondas shouldn't be a problem since we'll fly over the worst of the desert."

Stop talking! A tear leaked out of his left eye from the effort to speak.

"The book indicated that Rasharr Voh kept the Wayfinder close, so I'm guessing if we find his remains, we'll find the Wayfinder."

She turned right as the guards snatched her and slammed her against the wall. He screamed inside, willing his body to move. If it could, he'd take down every one of those guards in a heartbeat.

Khaldun entered, clapping slowly. "Well done! I congratulate you on your discovery."

"How *dare* you treat me this way!" shouted Amelia. "I am an Enchantran ambassador!"

The guards dragged Ander next to Amelia. He wanted to apologize to her, but the best he could do was drool out of the left side of his mouth.

One side of Khaldun's lips turned up into a sneer. "Miss Steam, I was never convinced you were an ambassador. What I didn't know was *why* you were here. Now I do, and I must commend you for unraveling the whereabouts of the Wayfinder."

His eyes narrowed on Ander with gleeful recognition. "I wondered how long it'd be before we finally caught you. There is much to balance out for *your* actions."

An icy chill ran down Ander's spine.

Khaldun turned back to Amelia. "I'm sure your information will be very useful to my colleague here."

An elderly man in Enchantran robes stepped into the doorway, wearing an expression of pure victory.

Master Honorhorn! Great. They'd just given the Enchantrans everything they had about the Wayfinder.

The master's face was one of pure victory. "Looks like the tables have turned, only this time, it's us barging in on *your* meeting. And I can assure you, Miss Steam, your airship won't rain fire to save you this time."

Anger burned through Ander. He hated hanging there, limp from head to toe. How had they snuck up on him, and what did they put in that dart? Some sort of paralysis drug from Nardoowe?

Master Honorhorn turned. "Darvin, did you catch all of what she said?"

A young man in his twenties stepped forward. His appearance matched the Enchantrans. "We need to find Rasharr Voh's sunken ship at the Shipwreck Sands, master. I didn't catch the type of ship, however."

"A gaffed rigged warship," answered a cold feminine voice from behind Ander. A black-hooded woman stepped around him and leaned uncomfortably close to his face.

"Miss me?" the Huntress whispered from beneath her cowl. She ran her black fingernails down his face. The sensation felt like nails grating against a chalkboard.

"Don't you dare touch him," said Amelia. Her hands were gripped into fists.

"Oh? You don't like that?" The Huntress said in a mockingly sweet tone. Then her tone flipped from sweet to venomous. "Then you *really* won't like what Khaldun will do to him!"

Amelia struggled against her captors, but they kept her pressed back against the wall. The Huntress walked past her and then moved to Honorhorn.

Master Honorhorn and Darvin were in a conversation, pointing to Shipwreck Sands on the map. Honorhorn nodded at his apprentice. "You're right. That does align nicely with the information we have from the Library of the Chosen." He clapped his hands together. "Tell Captain Marshall to ready the *Firelancer* to depart immediately."

"Yes, master." Darvin exited from the room.

Honorhorn turned back to Ander and Amelia. "I'm afraid the race ends here." He gave them a deep bow. "Enjoy your time in prison."

Pure frustration poured through Ander as the guards dragged him and Amelia out of the room and down the hall. He wanted to shout back, to fight back. Nothing he tried made his body respond. He was completely helpless, and it burned him to the core. Worst of all, no one on the *Legacy* would know what happened here. They wouldn't know they were captured. They wouldn't know the Enchantrans had *everything* they needed to get the Wayfinder.

Chapter 29: Lowest Moment

Amelia

Defeat tore through Amelia as she was roughly escorted through the palace gates. She could barely see Ander's limp form as they dragged him along. Her stomach roiled with apprehension. Would they kill them? Torture them? Sell them to slavery?

She looked up to the sky and desperately searched for the *Legacy*. If she could spot it, just maybe she could send a message. Maybe she could signal for help.

No luck. The dark sky was as obscure as ever.

Stupid! she thought. They shouldn't have come. She should have known the archives were too dangerous to return to. They should have tried something else, anything else.

It was too late now. They were captured and, worst of all, Honorhorn now had *everything* they had fought for. What would happen to the Republic, now that she had failed?

More guards joined their procession, increasing their ranks as they headed directly toward the lower walls of the military sector. Each addition widened the gulf of hopelessness consuming her. By the time they reached the gate, the number of soldiers was twice that of the full crew of the *Legacy*. Even if help came, rescue was impossible.

They traveled down the utilitarian streets until they reached a circular monolith of a building. The outside walls were smooth stone straight to the top. No windows broke its surface. Attached to the base of the building was a shorter, crenelated structure with guards roving the top. Heavy iron doors marked this as the only entrance to the entire building.

When they reached the building, the guards shoved her and Ander through the doors into a dimly lit atrium. There they were separated into different rooms where they changed, or were changed in Ander's case, into dull linen prison clothes. Then they were escorted out and taken through a final set of iron doors into a prison unlike any she'd ever seen before.

The room was a cylinder with five levels ascending upward. On each level were barred cells packed closely together. Stone walkways with metal railings and ladders extended out from these. Hanging from the ceiling were more cells, which were individually suspended so high, if their occupants fell, they'd most certainly die. The inside of the room was clear except for the very center where a watchtower stood.

Guards roved the top of the watchtower, commanding a clear view of every cell in the prison. The only light in the room glowed from a dim brazier at the very center of the watchtower. This created a reverse lighthouse effect, where the light feebly stretched to the entire room except for where the guards walked. Where the guards walked, gigantic shadows rose up the walls, dark and imposing.

Amelia and Ander were yanked into the room and shoved up to the second level. Prisoners watched them as they passed, staring at them with empty eyes and sunken faces. Soon they reached two empty cells next to each other. The guards threw Ander in the first and then Amelia into the second. Then they slammed the doors and locked them with a *snick*.

Amelia rose to her feet and glared at the slowly approaching figure of Khaldun. He finally stopped in front of her cell and gave her a cold, self-satisfied smile. She clenched her fists and withheld the urge to reach through the bars and smack his smug face.

The Sadhdron cleared his throat. "Miss Steam, by stepping onto Sadrian soil as an illegal, foreign trespasser, mirabetal. You will receive thirty Gifted lashes and a life sentence in prison."

She flinched. "Just for being from the Republic?"

Khaldun's expression darkened. "Thirty Gifted lashes are enough to require healers to keep you alive long enough to finish it. Don't interrupt me again or I'll increase it."

She took a step back and fell silent.

"For your crimes of false impersonation and espionage, mirabetal. You will continue what you promised me. You will design an airship powered by magic. If you attempt to resist, you will be tortured until you do. That is all."

That's all? She sank backwards into the back wall. *That's a whole list!*

"As for you," Khaldun's tone turned dark as he stepped toward Ander's cell. "As an illegal foreigner, thirty Gifted lashes. For your crimes against the slave trade, mirabetal. You will rebuild the complex you destroyed, brick-by-brick. Finally, for killing several of my warriors, mirabetal. You will meet your end under execution from my hand. I will separate your head from your proud shoulders and mount your skull for all to see at the gates."

He turned to address both of them. "You'll take your lashing within the hour." He turned and left.

Amelia slumped down and put her hands over her face. "We shouldn't have come back, Ander. This is all my fault."

The paralysis must have worn off because Ander slowly rose to his hands and dragged himself to the bars separating them. "Hey," he groaned, "it'll be alright."

Tears built in her eyes. "They're going to torture us! And then... they're going to kill you!" Guilt sparked in her and took flame.

He gave her a tired smile. "We'll think of something before then. Maybe we'll—" he began listing off a series of ideas, none of which she heard. Pressure grew in her chest, closing off her breath and filling her heart with unquenchable regret.

Everyone that grew close to her always got hurt. Everyone. Her parents, the workers at the factory, and now Ander.

Hot tears streamed down her face unbidden. *She* had brought this upon Ander. *She* had brought him to the palace—the most dangerous place in all Sadria. *She* was the one to blame.

"Hey," Ander's voice was soft. "It'll be alright. Even if we don't escape, I'm okay with this."

"You don't deserve to be here," she said behind her hands.

"You don't either," he replied.

"You're wrong. This is *exactly* where I belong."

"What? That makes zero sense!"

She turned her back to him. "You don't understand."

"Understand what?"

Fear rose in her throat and froze her tongue. She knew he needed to know the truth. He deserved to know the truth. Yet, she hesitated again. She didn't want to lose another friend, but of course, that bridge was already about to be burned.

Burned.

She took a shaky breath and in a small voice she said, "I caused the Steam Invention Company fire."

A beat passed. "What are you talking about?"

"I caused the Steam Invention Company fire."

"You mean the fire that killed over a hundred people?" Disbelief filled his voice.

"One hundred and twenty-seven." She could list all their names, too. Every single one. Tears streamed down her face.

"I don't believe that."

She glanced at him and saw his soft eyes were full of confusion.

She didn't deserve those soft eyes. She looked away and took a shallow breath. "It was late evening on New Year's Eve. My mother and I went to pick up my father at his office. He... he was working late, and we were scheduled to go to a stuffy banquet party. My mother made me wear this stupid white dress I hated, and... and I didn't want to go."

The image of her mother pulling her along the sidewalk to her father's factory came to mind. She was struggling, trying to pull away the whole time, but her mother dragged her along. She ran her thumbs along her fingers, wishing she had never let go.

The tears grew thicker, but she couldn't stop now. "We got to the waiting room by my father's office. There was yelling coming from his office. My mother set the lantern down on an end table and told me to wait out in the lobby. She left me and entered my father's office."

"I... I was so mad. I didn't want to go. So... so I kicked the lantern and left." She took a shaky breath and her voice hitched. "I was so mad I didn't look back. Minutes later, I smelled the smoke and *knew* what had happened. I felt horrible, so horrible. I tried to go back, but the hall was on fire and spreading."

Her pulse quickened as her eyes replayed the scene. Fire spread down the hall like liquid. "I ran to the construction bay to warn the workers, but something... something was wrong with the bay doors. The lobby was engulfed and I couldn't go back either. We were trapped." She remembered the fear in the worker's eyes.

Her body shivered as she continued. "The only way out was a duct used to push scrap to the dumpster. I was the only one that could fit, so the workers set me in it and pushed me out."

She remembered hitting the base of the dumpster onto saw dust. Screams rose behind her, screams of pain that would haunt her dreams for the rest of her life. She was choking on sobs now.

"I ran for help while it snowed ash. By the time an airship appeared with water, it was too late. They were dead. All of them."

She wiped her face with a soaked sleeve. "When authorities arrived, I told them what happened." She remembered the horrible sick feeling in her stomach when she told them about the lantern.

"I was too young to sentence, and the authorities said the details were too inconclusive to convict me—even though they found the fire started around my father's office. But *I* know I'm to blame. How else could that fire have started? I never looked back... so I'll never know."

She fisted her hands and put them to her forehead. "There. Now you know my secret. Now you can hate me like everyone else." Her voice broke on the word *hate*.

Silence stretched out between them.

After a long moment, he spoke, "I—"

Guards approached and stopped in front of Amelia's cell. They opened the barred door and yanked her from the floor.

Khaldun appeared behind the guards and gave her a cruel smile. "I see you've settled into prison life quickly." His tone was mocking.

Shame shivered through her. She should be strong. She was a Steam. She represented the Republic. Instead, she probably looked like she'd broken down already.

She *had* broken down, but this prison wasn't the reason for it. Khaldun wasn't the reason for it.

An overly muscled guard appeared in front of her. In his hands was a leather whip with multiple tails. He gave her a vicious smile.

Her shoulders sank, and she lowered her head. Resignation filled her as she slowly followed the guards out of her cell.

"Khaldun!" said Ander. "I invoke ulesibli mirabetal!"

Khaldun stopped and turned. "Ulesibli mirabetal?" He narrowed his eyes and looked between Ander and Amelia. "Why should I honor your ulesibli mirabetal?"

"I killed your men," said Ander. "I tarnished your honor."

Amelia blinked slowly. *What was he talking about?*

Khaldun's eyes narrowed further. "Sixty? This would wear even the healers out."

"Please," Ander begged.

Something new flashed in Khaldun's eyes. Anger? Respect? "Guards," he said, "put Miss Steam back in her cell."

The guards grabbed her arms and threw her tumbling to the cell floor and slammed the door after.

"What?" She rushed back to the barred door. "What is happening?" She looked at Ander. "What are you doing?"

He gave her a sad smile. Realization dawned on her. "No! Nooo!" She reached out for him through the bars as the guards pulled him away.

"Ander!" Tears fell down her face again, unbidden and uncontrolled. Why was he taking her whippings? How was he supposed to survive sixty Gifted lashings?

The darkness in her cell grew as the guards walked away with their oil lanterns, taking Ander down a ladder to the main level. "Ander," her voice was weak as she slid down the bars and put her face into her hands. He didn't deserve her punishment. He didn't deserve this.

Clink clink. She looked up from her hands and watched Ander get chained to the watchtower. The guards then ripped his shirt down his back and stepped backward as the muscled guard with the whip approached.

She couldn't watch this, couldn't bear this. Through tear-streaked vision, she crawled to the darkest, farthest portion of her cell as the whip fell.

Crack!

Crack!

Crack!

She curled into a ball and tried to tune out the horrible noise. The whipping sounds stopped briefly, and she knew it was to let healers take over so Ander could continue his torture. Tears continued to stream and soon soaked her hair. Ander was quiet at first, but as the beating continued, his painful groans raked across her heart.

"Ander," she whispered. "I'm so sorry! I'm so sorry!"

The darkness of the cell pressed in around her and filled her mind with visions of her worst memories. Factory flames roared before her eyes. Crowds spat and screamed hate at her as the enforcers took her away. Cold wind blew at her as she stood before her parents' graves.

"I'm so sorry!" she repeated the words again with desperation. "I didn't mean for any of it to happen."

Hammer's burned, unmoving body rested on the deck of the *Legacy*. A sadriconda burst from the walls and sank its teeth into Amir. And now Ander—every crack of the whip, every heartbreaking yelp he made—all of it was her fault.

"Why do I always make things so much worse?" Asking the question did nothing to comfort her. It only highlighted what she already knew. Everyone, *everyone* she ever cared about or got close to—they always received the same fate. Death and torture.

Guilt, shame, and hopelessness wrapped around her chest like a large, squeezing snake. She could barely breathe, barely think. Her whole being felt like shattered glass, helplessly broken beyond repair. The darkness pressed down on her, threatening to consume her entirely. Only a single thread tethered her from giving way entirely.

She looked up at the ceiling and asked, "Is there no hope for me?"

"We all make dumb mistakes," said a gruff voice.

She jumped at the sound and turned to its source. In the cell next to hers was a large, old man leaned up against the wall. The sight of him surprised her. She'd been so consumed by her own emotions, she had forgotten she wasn't alone in this prison.

"It's one thing to make them on purpose," coughed the old man, "it's another to do it by accident."

She continued to stare at the man, unsure of what to say.

"You're never too far from redemption," the man's voice filled with emotion. "Even here, you can change."

Something about the way he said the words struck her chest and filled her with a warm feeling. She rose to her knees, brushed her wet hair from her face, and asked, "Who are you?"

"A sorry old man, one who's done a lot worse than you."

"I doubt that." She wiped her sore, puffy eyes with the palms of her hands.

The man coughed multiple times into his sleeve before wheezing for breath. "If you want my advice, do what you can to make things right. Find your redemption. Learn to forgive yourself. Do that, and these bars will disappear."

She raised an eyebrow in the dark. "Make the bar disappear?" She didn't mean to make her tone sarcastic, but it came out that way anyway.

The man broke into another series of fitful coughs before replying. "We all make mistakes. Even your friend out there has made his share of mistakes."

She opened her mouth to give a sarcastic reply, but the words stopped in her throat. The man was right. Ander wasn't perfect. She didn't know anyone who was.

"The real question in life," continued the man, "is what you *do* after you make those mistakes. Have you ever tried to run from them?"

She shifted uncomfortably.

"How about hiding what you did? Or explaining them away?

Rationalizing that you had no choice?"

Her discomfort grew. "What's your point?"

"Those things don't help. They only create distance between you and the truth. If I've learned anything, it's that guilt is a hunter that won't give up until you face it head on. So if you want my advice, learn to face the music. Take responsibility. Apologize, seek forgiveness, and restore what you can. It takes real strength and a higher power to take the broken pieces of your life and turn them into a masterpiece."

The man slowly stood and bowed to her. "I've said enough. Good luck, kid." He padded away from her and laid down on the opposite side of his cell to rest.

She sat there in the dark for a long time, pondering over the old man's words. *Do what you can to make things right. You're never too far from redemption. Take the broken pieces of your life and turn them into a masterpiece.*

How long had she lived outside the Republic? How long had she tried to run away from the pain or bury it? Maybe it *was* time for her to face the music.

She looked up and felt an overwhelming sense of peace come over her. Maybe she could make it right. Maybe she could rebuild her life. It'd be hard, but she was a Steam. Doing hard things ran in her blood. She could do this.

Of course, she wasn't going anywhere, not while she sat in this cell. She had to escape. She owed it to the people she hurt. She owed it to the Republic.

Slowly, she rose to her feet and squared her shoulders. Gone was the oppressive guilt from before. Gone was the feeling of hopelessness and worthlessness. All of that was now replaced by a determination that burned through her and filled her with hope. She *could* do this. She *would* do this. And she could be a force for good.

Footsteps approached, along with a moving light. She shielded her eyes as guards appeared, opening Ander's cell and dropping a limp figure to the ground.

Ander! She rushed to the bars that separated them and put a hand to her mouth. His hair and ripped shirt were drenched in blood.

"Ander? Are you okay?"

He didn't respond.

Fear rose inside her chest. "Ander? Ander?!"

Chapter 30: Lost Memories

Ander

*L*ightning flashed, briefly illuminating the windows of the small home. Raindrops pattered against the thin glass panes, running down their lengths in long tears. A young Ander sat on the floor and played with wooden toy Steam soldiers.

The dream felt strangely lucid and yet detached at the same time. He felt the smooth wooden texture of the toys, saw the smallness of his hands, and heard the storm raging outside. Yet, he experienced all of this as if he was only an observer with no control within his own body.

Thunder boomed again and shook the floor. He jumped and looked around for his mother. She smiled at him from where she leaned against the wall. Her blue eyes were soft and her brown curls lazily bounced around her shoulders.

His father stepped into the room and tousled Ander's hair with a hand. *"How's my little Steam soldier?"* he asked. *He stopped and leaned up against the wall by Ander's mother. Like his mother, his father had brown hair, but his eyes were brown and a thick mustache grew across his upper lip. His arms were strong and his hands callused.*

Tears would have come to Ander's eyes if he could control them. He'd forgotten what his parents looked like. They couldn't have been older than their late twenties. Looking at his father was almost like looking into a mirror. His eyes and smile, however, came from his mother.

Ander resumed playing while his parents talked to each other in soft whispers.

"You know... you really shouldn't have made the toys," his father said. *"People will wonder how you got them, and if they put two and two together—"*

"I'm not worried," said his mother. *"Every child needs toys, and it's the least I could do given my situation. I'm more concerned about that knife you gave him."*

His father chuckled and ran a hand through his hair. "Every boy needs a knife, Claire."

"He's five. You really think that's a good idea? He thinks he's a Steam soldier, and he's been using it to chop my flowers. And the cat... he nearly scared it off for good."

His father chuckled again. "I wouldn't complain if the cat disappeared—"

"William!" she gently punched him in the arm. He only smiled and put his arm around her in turn. The room grew quiet with the gentleness of their affection.

Ander's heart ached with a loss he had long forgotten. Here he was, back in the warmth of his home in the presence of his parents!

That all was about to end.

CLANG-CLANG CLANG-CLANG!

"That's the city bell!" said his mother. The worry in her tone sent shivers through Ander.

"The bell?" said young Ander.

His father threw open the front door and stepped outside. A sharp wind blew in and put out the fire in the hearth.

"What's wrong?" asked Ander. A deep chill settled in the room.

His mother gave him a tight smile. "I'm sure it's nothing, dear. Keep playing with your toys."

His father reappeared and gripped the door. "Claire! We need to leave, NOW!"

The room burst into motion. His mother swept him up in her arms. The toys fell out of his hands and hit the ground with dull thuds. Ander reached for the toys and gave a small cry when she hurried him toward the door. His father followed, grabbing a pack and an old sword that hadn't been oiled in years.

Ander held on to his mother as his parents ran from their home. Screams echoed from the street behind them and filled him with cold shivers.

"Mom? What's happening?"

"Nothing, honey," she said between breaths. He wiggled in her arms until he could peer over her shoulder. Fire jumped from home to home in quick succession. Metal clashed in the distance and rang with discordant harmony against the ever-pounding bell.

"Legionnaires!" gasped his father.

They turned so quickly into a side street, Ander barely caught the sight of gilded armored soldiers with winged helmets. They looked much scarier than the toy versions he had.

He tucked his face into his mother's neck. "Daddy, I'm scared. Where are the Steam soldiers? Where are the airships?"

"Airships can't fly in this weather," his father said in a worried tone. "We're just going to have to run."

"William," gasped his mother, "we're heading north. You know they won't let me take refuge there."

"We aren't leaving you," said his father with determination. "I'm sure they'll understand in a crisis."

The screams and commotion were rapidly gaining on them. They turned a corner and merged into a throng of fleeing people. Shoulders bumped into them left and right. Claire's arms tightened around Ander. Then something rammed into them and sent them crashing to the ground.

His mother swooped over him and covered him with her body as people kicked, stomped, and rammed into her in their frenzy to get past. Each hit sent a shudder through her body, but she held fast to Ander, protecting him from it all. Twice she tried to rise and was shoved back down. It wasn't until the crowd thinned she could finally stand.

"Claire!" shouted his father, somewhere nearby. "CLAIRE!"

"Here!" she replied. Ander clung to her as she ran to the voice. When they caught up to his father, his eyes were full of fear.

"Claire, run!" He drew his sword. His mother and father locked eyes with each other.

Ander knew what horrible understanding was passing between them. He wanted to close his eyes, but he couldn't. His mind was trapped in the memory—the memory he forgot for a reason.

His mother sprinted away, never looking back. Ander screamed and climbed up onto her shoulder. "Dad!" Gilded legionnaires ran toward him with bloody swords. Their feet moved impossibly fast.

He buried his face into his mother's neck, but that did nothing to mute the brief clang of steel. Tears streamed down his mother's face and dropped into Ander's hair. They turned a corner as crunching footsteps followed. The soldiers were pursuing them!

They sprinted through an open doorway into an empty tavern. Chairs and tables were turned over and a serving bar was covered with unfinished meals. Legionnaires stormed through the door after them.

Pure desperation flashed across his mother's face. As they passed a vertical support beam, she slapped her hand across it. Static energy poured from his mother with a torrent like nothing Ander had ever felt. The beam exploded from the raw power and blasted wood shrapnel into the assailants behind.

The realization of what had just happened crashed into Ander all at once. His mother was Gifted! Too much was flashing before his eyes, however, to fully process the implications.

Energy continued to flow as his mother's movement quickened like lightning. Legionnaires engaged, swinging their blades at her only to catch air. She dodged them all, continuing to blast building support structures left and right. Soon, there was only one left. She touched this and dove into a cellar stairway as the entire ceiling above gave way.

They tumbled down the stairs in a wild fall. Behind, deep screams ripped the air and then silenced abruptly as the world crashed down upon itself.

They hit the cellar floor right as splinters of wood slapped into them and dust poured into the room. The noise was deafening, and the ground shook like an earthquake. The ceiling above them groaned but held. Long heartbeats passed before the tumult silenced and the dust settled.

Claire crawled toward Ander and picked him up. "You okay?" she asked, cupping his face with both her hands.

"I hurt my elbow," he replied, showing a scratch. Tears filled her eyes, and she hugged him tightly.

After a long moment, she cleared her throat. "We need to get out of here." The stairwell was clogged with debris, and the ceiling above them bulged menacingly. The only exit was a thick glass window that let in a sliver of light.

"TRAITOR!" shouted a muffled voice somewhere above. "We know you're in there!"

The blood drained from Claire's face.

"Thought you could get away with it? Didn't you! Living with the enemy," continued the voice.

Energy rippled through the floor from above. Then the crackling began. Immediately, the cold cellar warmed.

Claire's eyes widened. She rushed up the stairs and began to clear the rubble.

"Mom," said Ander. "I'm thirsty."

"Hang on, honey," she replied, stress seeping through her voice.

CRASH! A portion of the ceiling gave way and fell into the room, bringing with it burning timbers and smoke. She picked up Ander and frantically looked around.

Smoke burned Ander's throat, and he coughed. "Mom, I'm scared."

She zeroed in on the small, thick glass window. She rushed to it and put her hand on the pane. BOOM! Shards exploded outward, creating a hole wide enough for just one of them.

Tears ran down her face as she picked him up, ran a hand through his hair, and looked into his eyes. "I need you to run north, Ander!" Her voice hitched. "I need you to be a brave little Steam soldier!" Then she *pushed him through the window. A second later, the building collapsed.*

"Mom!" Ander rushed to where the window once stood, but roaring flames repulsed him farther and farther back. "MOM!"

"Ander?" said his father. His voice was weak, but it sounded close by.

He ran to the sound and found his father lying on the ground.

"Dad!"

His father put a hand to cover the spreading red stain across his chest. "Ander... where's... where's...?" His eyes clouded over.

He grabbed onto his father's arm and with tear-filled eyes screamed. "Help!"

A crunch echoed down the street, followed by a deep voice. "Run away, boy." He spun around and saw a hulking legionnaire step into the street. The legionnaire had a wild look in his eyes and a javelin in his grip.

Be brave, my little Steam soldier, *echoed the words of his mother's voice. Ander stepped in front of his father and drew his knife.*

"You're a bad man!" Ander shouted, pointing the knife at the Enchantran. "Go away!"

"Suit yourself." The legionnaire lifted his javelin up and threw.

Quick as a flash, a figure jumped in front of Ander and intercepted the weapon with a barrel lid. Ander gawked at the figure's dark metallic armor and magpack covered with gadgets and gear. A Steam soldier!

The Enchantran and Steam soldier stared each other down. "You need to run, kid," said the Steam soldier before tossing the barrel lid to the side and drawing a hose-fed war hammer.

Ander scooted closer to his father, but his eyes stayed transfixed to the scene. The Enchantran drew a broadsword and moved in a slow arc. The Steam soldier pivoted, so he was always in front of Ander.

In an instant, the legionnaire closed the gap and swung his broadsword at the Steam soldier's head. The Steam soldier ducked, pivoted, and slammed his war hammer into the Enchantran's back with a powerful, hissing CLANG. The Enchantran's momentum sent him crashing into a building.

"Run, kid!" the Steam soldier yelled again.

The legionnaire didn't stay down for long. In a blink, he was leaping back at the Steam soldier, swinging his broadsword in a blinding series of strikes. In seconds, he had the Steam soldier pinned to the ground with his blade locked with the soldier's war hammer.

The broadsword inched closer and closer to the Steam soldier's neck. The soldier groaned with physical exertion. "Kid! Run! He... coming... for... you... next!"

Ander couldn't. His mother told him to be a brave little Steam soldier. So that was exactly what he was going to do.

He took his knife and shakily threw it at the legionnaire. The knife swished through the air without any strength and missed the legionnaire entirely, slicing instead into the hose of the Steam soldier's war hammer.

Compress steam hissed out of the hose in a torrent, firing straight into the legionnaire's eyes. He began screaming, and in seconds the soldier pushed him off. Then the soldier rose his war hammer up and—

Ander looked away, not wanting to watch the rest. When he looked back, the battle was over.

The Steam soldier gave a heavy exhale and wiped his brow. Then he approached Ander and knelt down. "You didn't run."

Ander shook his head. "I was trying to be brave, like a Steam soldier."

The soldier gave him a grateful smile. "You made one great Steam *soldier today. I owe you one." He handed Ander back his knife. "Now, let's get you out of here."*

"What about my parents?" Ander asked, pointing to his unmoving *father and the burning inn.* "Will they be okay?"

Ander watched Julius Blackwell choke up with emotion.

"Don't worry, kid. I'll make sure you are taken care of."

Chapter 31: Mixedborn

Amelia

S he watched Ander's vague form moan and convulse for over an hour. Her fingers ached from gripping the bars, and her voice was hoarse from calling out to him. He seemed to be trapped in some sort of nightmare. Her eyelids grew heavy watching him, but she knew she owed it to keep watch over him. She only relaxed when, finally, he stilled and his chest rose slowly up and down in a steady rhythm.

What felt like seconds passed before she woke to the clanking of metal. Blearily, she blinked from the dim morning light that glowed from an open skylight at the top of the prison. At the front of her cell was a metal cup and a ripped scrap of bread.

Her stomach growled at the sight. She rose and winced as she stretched her body out. The stone floor had been the furthest thing from comfortable, but apparently, she'd been exhausted enough to sleep anyway. She grabbed the bread and was about to take a bite when Ander moaned.

She could see him clearly now in the increased light. His face and hair were caked in dried blood, and his linen shirt was shredded and stained. At the moment, he seemed to be trying to reach for his cup and bread with a hand, but they were both a few feet out of reach. He moaned as he tried to shift himself forward, but his face grimaced each time he attempted.

"Hey, take mine," she tossed her bread to him.

"Thank you," he groaned. He held the bread in his hands for a moment before slowly putting it into his mouth. His face was pale and his body was shivering.

She wrinkled her eyebrows. "You look awful. Let me pull you closer so I can help." She reached her hand out to him. He took it and she pulled him to the bars. He moaned painfully as she did so, but within seconds, he was next to the bars.

She put a hand to his forehead and grimaced. "You're burning up." She ripped a strip of cloth from the bottom of her pants, dipped it into her cup, and placed it over his forehead.

"You shouldn't have taken the whipping for me," she said while she ripped another strip of cloth.

"I had to," he replied weakly.

"Why?" She dipped the new strip into her cup.

"Some people are worth getting whipped for."

Amelia froze her movements and looked at him. Her heart swelled with warmth. She reached through the bars and tenderly dabbed at the blood on his face. Stubble had grown in from the evening before, giving him a handsome, rugged look despite his disheveled appearance. At the corner of his lips was also a small, white scar she'd never noticed before.

She cleared the emotion from her throat. "Even if that person has a horrible past?"

"You're not a horrible person. Not to me," he breathed, his eyes closed.

A tear fell down her cheek. Her stomach rumbled, and her throat was parched, but she didn't care. For the first time in years, she felt incredible inside. Gone was the oppressive weight of guilt. In its place was an unexplainable calm. That, and an overwhelming incredulity. Somehow, Ander hadn't rejected her despite him having every reason in the whole world to do so. Instead, he had sacrificed himself for her.

A soft, tender feeling wrapped around her like a warm blanket, filling her with a depth of care and concern she'd never felt before.

She surveyed his condition again. "How much do you hurt?"

He chuckled and then winced.

"That good?" she raised an eyebrow. "I need to see your back."

"I'm okay if you don't."

"Ander?" Her tone was stern.

He exhaled before slowly rolling over. It took him a full minute to shift his way onto his other side. She lifted the torn flaps of the shirt out of the way and let out a gasp. Hundreds of long purple stripes covered his back, remnants from the many strands of the whip. From the scars over each, it was evident they were once open wounds before the healers sealed them over. Given the number of scars, he would have bled to death fifty times over. Still, it looked like the healers only sealed the wounds. They hadn't addressed the bruising or the trauma.

Her stomach felt sick. She tore another strip of cloth from her pants, which were starting to look like shorts. She soaked the strip and dabbed his back.

He groaned and flinched at the soft touch. "Gently, please?"

"I am being gentle. Ander, this... this is horrible." She continued to wash the blood from his back, but she was running out of clean water.

He cleared his throat. "The restorative worked. I saw the day my parents died."

"Oh..." It had been weeks since he had told her about it at the embassy. She'd forgotten about it entirely.

"I know my heritage. My father was a Commonborn from the Republic. My mother... she was a Gifted from Enchantra."

"Oh." She paused her work. "That means—"

"I'm Mixedborn." He let out a heavy breath. "It's one step below Gifted."

"Mixedborns aren't illegal in the Republic."

He tilted his head back so she could see his raised eyebrows.

"Okay," she hedged, "so they aren't popular, either."

He laid his head back down. "Mixedborns are rejects."

She tucked a wild strand of hair behind an ear. "You wouldn't be the only one."

Both of them fell quiet, though instead of awkward, the silence felt comfortable.

After a moment, he spoke again. "I think I understand why I can't make the Everblade work. The Warden said I was like an oil lantern, full of potential but without any fuel for the spark. It makes sense now."

She frowned. "How so? I thought Mixedborns don't have any magic?"

"I think that's true in a sense, but I don't think it's complete. I didn't inherit my mother's power, but I think I inherited her ability."

Her mind processed the information, putting pieces together. "So that's why you can sense power but not use it?"

He nodded and winced. "That's why I could use the Everblade when Kadesh pushed power into me."

"Oh." This *did* make sense. It made a *lot* of sense. She had wondered why he had special abilities but didn't register any power on an electrodetectualizer. This explained why.

"I see," she said. "So, Kadesh giving you power was like a starter motor to an engine...."

"A what?"

She rolled her eyes. "The analogy works. Go on."

He paused a beat before saying, "I think I can get the blade to work again."

"Huh?" She tilted her head. "I thought you just said you don't have any power."

"I don't have my mother's power," he corrected.

"But you said your father was a Commonborn?"

"He was."

She shook her head. "Are you feeling alright?" She put a hand to his forehead.

He grabbed her hand from his head. "I'm not crazy."

Her lips curved into a mocking smile. "You sure?" He still held her hand, which sent tingles up her arm.

He rolled his eyes before turning serious. "When Kadesh pushed power into me, it ignited power inside me." He let go of her hand and pointed at his chest. "I felt power inside that wasn't his. What I felt was my own."

"But Commonborns—Mixedborns don't have power?" His words were hurting her brain.

"Okay, call me crazy then." He turned his face away from her.

She opened her mouth, then closed it, then opened it again. "I don't think you're crazy, but what you're saying doesn't add up. If what you are saying is true, Mixedborns and Commonborns have power—which we both know isn't the case, otherwise we'd see evidence of that."

"I've got one. Do you remember when the Everblade was stolen? I was able to get it to work again that time, though it was just briefly. How else could that have happened if I didn't have a small degree of power?"

"I don't know," she said hesitantly. "I feel like we're missing something. If you had power inside, that would have registered on the electrodetectualizer. I also think you would have been able to power the sword again other times."

He gave a long, wheezy sigh. "I suppose you're right. It just feels like the answer is so frustratingly close."

She set the rag down on the ground and leaned into the bars. "Why is it important, anyway?"

He sighed. "I've been thinking about the Nardoowe beast. Same with what you told me about sadricondas once being sea serpents twisted by dark power. I get the feeling the Everblade was created to fight those kinds of evils."

She frowned. "I thought the Everblade was created to cut the path to the Source? That's why it was hidden."

He shrugged and gasped from the movement. "Maybe it has more than one purpose. Regardless, I have this feeling I'm meant to have it and use it. If that's true, there's got to be a way for it to work.

I have to find a way."

"Well, neither one of us are doing anything until we get out."

He frowned at her. "Why are you grinning then?"

"I'm not grinning," she said with a smirk.

He raised an eyebrow. "And you think I'm the crazy one?"

"Hey!" She looked around to see if the guards or prisoners were paying attention. Then she lowered her voice conspiratorially. "It's a good thing none of these guards are women. Otherwise, they would have thought to pull all of these out." She reached into her hair and removed a hidden hair pin. "All we need is a plan and the opportune moment."

Chapter 32: Prison Break

Ander

Ander shuffled through his cell, walking for the first time in five days. The pain was excruciating, but he knew he had to push through it if they had any hope of escape. He hated the feeling of helplessness that accompanied the pain. People were depending on the information they had. Every moment that passed was a moment closer to disaster—a moment lost to stop the Enchantrans from getting the Wayfinder.

The first two days after the whipping were horrible. He could barely breathe, barely speak. If it weren't for Amelia, he wasn't sure how he would have made it through. Her constant presence and encouragement were like a ray of sunlight in the oppressive darkness of his cell. She helped him pass the time by discussing improbable escape plans and sharing stories from her childhood. He shared many of his own, including the "operations" that he pulled to escape the annual Steam Military Academy dances six years in a row. By the end, they were both laughing so hard, tears came to his eyes from the pain. It took both the prisoners and the guards telling them to be quiet for them to stop.

On the third day, two healers visited his cell and argued with each other on how to heal him just enough so he could cut sandstone soon while still leaving him in pain. Apparently the Sadhdron was eager to have him join the slaves reconstructing the bombed slave complex. The conversation was cruel, but it worked out on Ander's behalf. After the healing, he could move again without the same intensity of pain.

Five days had now passed since they were interned, and finally he was feeling partially able-bodied. He could at least walk, albeit painfully slow and only with one hand on something for support.

"You there!" *Clang clang!* "Steam soldier."

Ander's attention snapped to where a guard stood rapping on his cell.

The guard opened a rolled parchment and said, "We've got orders to take you and thirty others to the sandstone mines tomorrow, and your girlfriend's not on the list." The guard's face broke into a sneer.

Ander glared at the guard and didn't say a word. Amelia wasn't his *girlfriend*. She was a close friend, but he could see the angle that the guard was going for. The guard was trying to rile him up, and it was working. His knuckles were turning white from how tightly he was clutching his bars.

"She, on the other hand," the guard continued, "is scheduled to get chained to a desk at the archives tomorrow until she starts talking. Sounds like loads of fun all around. Enjoy your last night together." The guard chuckled darkly as he walked away.

Ander growled and slammed the meaty side of his fist into the bar. Pain exploded through his back from the movement, and he winced until it subsided.

Amelia leaned in close from the other side of the bars. "Ander, we need to do it tonight," she whispered. "There isn't any more time."

He let out a long sigh. They already had this conversation multiple times, and it had always ended the same way. Their likelihood of success was next to zero. He had calculated the guard rotations himself. Shift changes happened only three times a day. Then the guards would slowly pace around the top of the watchtower in a circle, scanning the whole room as they went. There was a ten to thirteen second window for every two minutes in the loop where the guards didn't have eyes on them. It was enough time for Amelia to unlock her cell door, but that was it. In the next loop, she'd need to unlock his own cell and make it back to her own. Then, in the next loop, they'd have to slip out and keep in the guards' blind spot as they made their way to the closed entrance on the main floor. *If* they were to make it that far without being noticed by prisoners or guards, they still had to unlock that door as well and make it past the guards stationed there. In his condition, there wasn't any way he'd be able to keep up.

He growled again in frustration. The Sadrians had done well in making the prison impossible to escape from.

"Ander, we have to try." Her expression was pleading.

He closed his eyes and shook his head. "You'd have more success leaving me behind."

She moved closer to him and waited until he met her eyes. "I'm not going to leave you," she said firmly. Her jaw was tight and her expression was stubborn. He ran a hand through his hair and then winced.

"You know how impossible this is, right? And I don't mean Amelia Steam level of impossible. I mean *actually* impossible."

"What if we had help?" She subtly gestured up at the isolated cages that hung high above the open space of the prison. It didn't take a genius to know these held the largest, gruffest, and most dangerous Gifted prisoners: the most striking example being Abdulmalik, the Insurrector and former leader of the Mirage. Their cages were hoisted up by a winch system attached to the side of the tower. Each could be dropped in an instant. Ander had seen it happen once. A prisoner screamed obscenities at the guards. They dropped his cage the full five stories until it hit the ground. The prisoner did not survive.

"You mean from them?" he clarified.

"Yep," she said.

His eyebrows shot up in incredulity. "You want to start a fight... in the prison... in the middle of the military sector?"

BOOM! The door to the panopticon slammed open and several guards ran into the watchtower.

He frowned. "Something's going on."

"They're distracted," she said excitedly. She fished out her hairpin and began unlocking her door.

"We're doing this now?"

She nodded as the door clicked open. "Take this," she handed him the hairpin. "Open the clip with your thumb and forefinger until the lock snicks. Then twist counter clockwise. "

She slipped out of her cell before he could say another word. He watched her in stunned silence as she ran in a low crouch toward the stairs to the main level.

MOVE! screamed his mind. He shuffled to the lock of his door and began working it while he kept an eye on the guard situation. The new guards appeared on the top of the watchtower and spoke with the others in hushed, urgent tones. Then, as one, they all drew their swords.

Something definitely wasn't right. He felt the lock snick and began to twist, but he couldn't remember what direction.

"Hey! What's she doing?!" The voice came from one of the cells on the main level—a prisoner. Amelia froze in her footsteps, halfway to the watchtower. The guards hadn't spotted her yet.

GO! Ander wanted to scream. The door to his cell clicked open, and he fell through. He slammed into the walkway railing as the door to his cell crashed open. The noise was so loud, he could practically feel the entire room's eyes on him.

He cursed under his breath and decided on a new strategy: distraction. "Hey!" He pushed himself up onto the railing and waved to the guards. "You forgot to lock my cage."

"GET BACK IN THERE, FOREIGNER!"

Yep, that got their attention. One guard disappeared down the watchtower, likely to come and get him. The rest continued to shout at him while he shuffled along the railing.

Amelia was now at the base of the watchtower, just beneath their gaze. She just needed to make it a little farther around to the winch system.

Hoping to keep their attention, he shouted back, "What's happening? You all seem frazzled? Did you make Khaldun mad or something?"

"BACK TO YOUR CELL!" The guard who disappeared down the watchtower had now emerged and was charging toward him.

Ander knew he couldn't run, nor did he really care to. All he cared about was keeping Amelia safe. He already survived one beating. What was one more?

Boom! The ground shook with the sound of distant thunder. He stumbled and caught himself on the railing.

The door into the panopticon flew open again, and a guard sprinted into the room shouting, "They're after the Insurrector! Drop the cage! DO IT NOW!"

Clack-clack-clack-clack! Every single cage began to lower from the ceiling. Amelia had successfully gotten to the winches and was now skirting around the opposite side.

All the guards dispersed from the watchtower in a mad rush, pounding down the stairs within. Even the guard heading toward Ander changed direction toward the winches.

The guard who had given the initial warning turned around and sprinted toward the entrance. "Lock it down!" he screamed. "Seal them in!"

Ander groaned. They needed that entrance open if they were to escape. Without another thought, he gritted his teeth and leapt over the railing. He hit the ground and crumbled entirely. His body exploded with pain and his vision clouded over. Then, with gritty determination, he forced himself to stand and began moving unsteadily to the entrance.

Amelia joined him in a flash, throwing an arm around his waist and helping him rush forward. Behind, the guards' attention was completely focused on the winch system. "The system's jammed!" one of them screamed.

Of course it was. Ander would have smiled if he didn't hurt so badly. That and if the entrance hadn't shut in front of them, closing with the finality of a coffin lid.

"No, no!" breathed Amelia. They reached the iron doors and pushed against it. No luck. The doors would be locked now and, based on their thickness, not even Gifted power would be able to rip them from their moorings.

They turned around and frantically scanned for another exit they knew wouldn't be there. There was nothing, nowhere else they could go. They were trapped.

The guards were in a panic now. They had foregone trying to unjam the winch and were now hacking at the chains in a fearful frenzy. Something about their manic focus gave Ander pause.

"Uh, Millie?"

"Yeah?" she said, still looking for another exit.

"Do you think there's a good reason why they want to cut the chains so badly rather than come get us?"

CRACK! The cages, which were now about halfway down the chamber, suddenly all dropped. They crashed to the floor and threw a cloud of sand into the air.

Silence followed.

"Is he dead?" spoke one guard.

A deep, malevolent chuckle echoed from within the cloud. The temperature dropped, raising the hairs on Ander's neck. Cold energy rippled outward, carrying with it more dust. It coiled up and outward like tentacles.

Then, in the half light of the haze, a dark figure rose, easily four times the size of a regular man.

Ander swallowed as pure dread poured into him. What had they just unleashed?

"HE'S NOT DEAD—" The shout cut off abruptly and was

followed by the screams of guards as their forms were sent hurtling through the air. The dark figure moved swiftly, and where it went, chaos followed.

Ander stood frozen there with Amelia. There wasn't anywhere safe they could go. All he could do was step protectively in front of her as she hugged into his arm.

"I think you were right," she said in a shaky voice. "This really wasn't a good idea."

He opened his mouth to reply and then stopped. The hulking figure was now stopped, and the guards were now dead or silent.

"Your oppressors are gone!" roared the figure. "You are now free!"

Tendrils of dark sand shot up and slammed into the lock of each level with precision. Barred doors opened in a discordant chorus. Gasps followed and then were overtaken by cheers.

Well, Ander thought. *Our prison break just grew in size.* He was about to voice the sentiment to Amelia when the hulking figure turned and stalked toward them. As it emerged from the dust, the figure faded and shrunk. In its place was Abdulmalik, the Insurrector.

The Insurrector was still an imposing figure, despite him losing some weight while in prison. He walked toward them with his broken chains dragging from his wrists. The captured sword in his right hand dripped with blood. The scar that stretched from his right temple to the left side of his beard looked much more intimidating now than when Ander had seen it weeks ago, when Khaldun had paraded the Insurrector's capture. The large Mirage tattoo on the side of his bald, wide head also stood out in the light.

Six other muscled men emerged on his sides, each clutching

weapons of their own. Ander recognized them as the same six warriors that had been captured with Abdulmalik.

Ander pulled Amelia away from the doors, anxious to get out of their way. Even in good shape, this was not someone he wanted to get into a fight with.

The Insurrector didn't spare them a second glance before he and his companions sprinted and rammed into the doors with startling power. The entire frame and wall shuddered.

Shreeeeek! High overhead, a hole opened up in the skylight. Sadrian archers appeared above it and drew back recurve bows.

"Millie!" said Ander. "We need cover!" He grabbed her hand and pulled. They scrambled to the nearest open cell on the main floor right before a volley of arrows flew in the room. People screamed as the arrows struck their mark. Chaos erupted as people scrambled everywhere.

The Sadrians had created a death trap, likely prepared if the prisoners ever rose up against them. Abdulmalik threw up his arms and sand erupted again from the ground, obscuring the archers from accurate shots. Then just as quickly, dozens of fake Mirage figures appeared in the haze, each charging up levels and climbing chains to reach the top. All of them were a clever diversion as the Insurrector threw a fist into the ground and poured power into it.

The ground rumbled underneath their feet and then was followed by the horrifyingly familiar *MRAHHHHH!* A sadriconda burst into the prison from a nearby wall. It screeched again before rising up the levels toward the archers' opening.

"Quick! To the hole!" said Amelia. She pulled Ander through the hazy dust, keeping her head down as stray arrows whizzed by. Ander struggled to keep up. His adrenaline was fading, and no amount of grit and determination was helping him push past that now. Other prisoners joined them, pressing into them as they all exited the building and into a full-fledged war.

Sadrian troops fought in scattered units against raging Mirage warriors, who struck at them from all directions and melted into clouds of sand. Molten sand blasted left and right, searing through armor and flesh. Gales gushed back, ripping arrows from the air and sending them spiraling back. Walls of sand rose up and were shoved toward adversaries. The sheer quantity of spent power drifting through the air was like smoke from wildfires. Above it all was the terror-gripping calls of sadricondas as they crashed through buildings and sent warriors on both sides in retreat.

Amelia froze in her footsteps, bringing Ander to a stop as well. "It's like with Valera," she breathed.

"We need to move," he said wearily.

They hurried out onto the street and took cover in an alley right as chunks of rock blasted through the street. As they stood in the cover, overwhelming exhaustion pulled at Ander, and soon he was slumping down the wall.

She grabbed his arms and pulled him up. "Come on. We can't stay here."

"I'm not going to make it," he breathed. "I'm too weak. You need to leave me behind."

"I'm not doing that. We just need to make it out the gates and then lie low." She looked up at the angle of the sun to get a direction and then burst into excitement. "I see the *Legacy*!"

The airship was dropping from the sky, heading toward the entrance of the prison. She pulled his arm around her shoulders and looped hers around his waist, making sure to keep clear of his injuries. They stumbled toward the lowering airship.

The crew spotted them, and soon Steam soldiers were dropping from rappelling lines and surrounding them. Quickly, the soldiers helped Ander and Amelia into the airship and then the *Legacy* was under way, pulling away from the prison.

As they rose, he and Amelia looked out at the city. It wasn't just the military sector that was in chaos. Other portions of the city burned with fire while dozens of sadricondas crashed through buildings and leveled streets. The entire city was under attack.

How in the world had sadricondas gotten to the city? This was *very* far away from the deep Sadrian Sands and it was broad daylight, too.

Garret put a hand on his and Amelia's shoulders, interrupting his thoughts. "I'm glad we got to you in time."

"Me, too," said Ander.

"How did you know where to find us?" asked Amelia.

"Well," said Garret, "we actually have Cid to thank for that. After you didn't return, he helped us contact the Mirage. We made a deal with them to discover your whereabouts."

Ander frowned. "What were the conditions?"

Garret now rubbed his neck, his voice lowered. "Between you and me, they wanted a high-powered explosive. An Axel-grade explosive, but I wouldn't let that slip to Charles."

Amelia scrunched her eyebrows. "Why would they need a high-powered explosive?"

BOOOOOM! Rock, dust, and fire exploded from the palace gates and rained down into the city. As the dust settled, an army of Mirage warriors surged into the palace.

Ander's jaw dropped open. The Mirage had just broken through the impregnable palace walls. And they'd inadvertently helped the Mirage do it.

He ran a hand through his hair. "We just helped start a revolution," he said breathlessly. *What would the Republic think*, he wondered.

He shook his head. What was happening before them wasn't their fault. This conflict had started long ago and was fueled by the Sultan's slaving policies and Khaldun's oppressive measures. As dire as the situation was for Sadria, it was out of their control. They needed to get the *Legacy* to Shipwreck Sands before the Enchantrans found the Wayfinder and started another war on Republic soil.

Chapter 33: Transformation

Amelia

After giving Veronica a heading, helping Ander to the medical bay, and surviving a lung-popping hug from Everard, Amelia returned to her quarters and washed all the prison grime off herself in a basin. Then she changed into fresh clothing, pulled her hair back, and proceeded below decks to the serving area.

Garvin's cooking had never tasted better. His spice soup tasted divine compared to the stale bread and tinny water of the prison. She took a second helping and then, sheepishly, took a third and fourth.

When she finished, she rested her head and arms on the serving counter in satisfied bliss. "Garvin," she said lazily, "next time we get thrown into prison, we need to bring you with us."

The cook chuckled and took her bowl and spoon for her.

Eugene poked his head out of the medical bay. "Oh, good. I need to check on you. Come on in."

She followed him into the medical bay and sat down on a cot. Ander rested nearby, sleeping on his stomach with his back exposed. On his back was a sludgy poultice of some sort.

"How's Ander?" she asked, while the medic retrieved a stethoscope and magnifying glass.

Eugene gave a heavy sigh. "I'm not sure. It's fortunate prison healers administered aid during and after the whipping. If they hadn't, I'm confident that at best he'd be permanently disfigured, have little to no mobility in his back, and would live with chronic pain for the rest of his life. At worst, it would've killed him.

"As it is, I'm confident the bruising will clear up. The scars will be permanent, of course. What I don't know about is his internals—how it'll impact his muscles, ligaments, bones, and organs. Only time will tell. No doubt, he will be slower for the next while until he recovers."

She looked over her shoulder at Ander. His back slowly rose and fell as he slept soundly. Soft tenderness warmed inside her chest as she thought about how much pain he had taken for her. It was pain he'd continue to take for her for the next while.

Why had he done it?

Eugene began her own checkup. After what felt like a thousand questions, he concluded that she was malnourished and in need of extra bedrest. Her bruises from the Lost Palace were now faded; she barely noticed them at all. Her concussion was long gone as well, though her memory was still hazy from the time she escaped the Lost Palace to when she woke up in recovery later. All in all, she was doing well enough, considering the circumstances.

That was her physical health and the extent of Eugene's survey. Deep inside, she felt whole. Instead of oppressive guilt continually weighing down on her shoulders, she felt light and... strangely free. It wasn't that she couldn't remember the fire anymore; that hadn't changed. She still felt remorse at what had happened. The difference was the memory of it didn't burden her anymore. In its place was an overwhelming desire to do good and to make reconciliation. In short, she felt like a new person.

She rose to leave and found her gaze drifting to Ander. He had sacrificed so much for her, and in that moment of sacrifice, she had been changed. What he did meant far more to her than he'd ever know. On a whim, she bent down and kissed him lightly on the temple before leaving the room.

A quiet peace rested on her as she returned to her cabin. She didn't have any problems obeying Eugene's order to rest. Her bed was infinitely soft compared to the stone floor of her cell.

She fell onto her bed and closed her eyes. Hours passed, waiting for sleep to come. As the afternoon wore on, a growing anxiety crawled into her mind. The *Firelancer* had a five-day head start on them. By her calculation, it'd take the warship a total of eight days to reach Shipwreck Sands from start to finish. It'd take the *Legacy* about seven days to make the same trip. Doing the math, that meant the Enchantrans would have a full four days to search the region for Rasharr Voh's ship before they arrived. That was a lot of time. Too much time.

The anxiety grew until she became restless. She needed to do something to increase their speed. With that, she rose and exited her cabin.

The sun was low on the horizon, and the crew was taking their evening meal in rotation. She found Veronica at the table in the mess hall and sat down on the opposite side.

CRAIG & JALEESA SNOW

"Veronica, I need your help figuring out how we could shorten the time it'll take to get to Shipwreck Sands."

Veronica swallowed a mouth full of food. "Yer askin' me, cap?"

Amelia nodded. "Collectively, you and I have flown across much of this desert. I bet we could map the wind patterns and plot our course accordingly."

A smile grew across Veronica's face. "Course, cap."

They spent the next half hour combining their knowledge into a map. Then they plotted out what they saw was the most efficient route. It'd shave *some* time off their trip, but it wasn't nearly enough.

She traveled next to the engine deck and found Emmett and Archibald. The two inventors were huddled over a stack of schematics, pouring over them. They paused and turned to her as she approached.

"Amelia," said Archibald, the younger of the two inventors. He leaned onto the table, obscuring the drawings. "Fancy seeing you here."

"I need your help increasing our speed," she said, cutting right to the chase.

The two men looked at each other. Something unreadable passed between the two. "Increasing our speed, you say?" said Archibald.

"I'm not an idiot." She stepped around him and began flipping through the schematics. "I know you both have been *dying* to modify my airship." There were drawings for three-bladed and five-bladed propellers, high-efficiency boilers, gyroscopic deck designs, spinning three-barreled steam cannons, and even a recipe for magnesium-based fuel pellets.

"Hey!" said Archibald, throwing his hands on top of the pile.

"Those are proprietary!"

"So is my airship you've been studying," she replied, still flipping through the corner. She stopped at a schematic of the *Legacy*'s engine deck.

"Like this!" She pulled out the schematic and placed it on top of the stack. Notes were scribbled around its sides. There were measurements showing metrics and formulas for fuel consumption, boiler temperatures, steam volume and force, and rotor speeds.

"Your airship is fast because it's small, not because it is efficient," said Emmett flatly.

She swallowed the urge to argue. "Alright, tell me how it's less efficient."

A big smile grew across Archibald's face. "Well, it all starts with the thermodynamics of your airship—"

"The short version," she said, turning her gaze to Emmett.

"You could raise the temperature in your boiler," said Emmett.

Archibald jumped in. "Higher temperature means greater steam pressure which'll generate more spin force for your rotors—"

Amelia put up a hand. "I got that. We usually burn at standard temps. Going higher is risky. I don't want the boiler to explode."

Emmett nodded. "You're burning at the recommended Steam Engineering Corps Standard. That standard was designed with regular airships in mind. Your boiler is smaller, more compact, and most importantly, thicker than regular boilers. It can handle the increase of heat."

Excitement grew inside Amelia. "Perfect. Let's do it."

Archibald blinked. "Really?"

She nodded. "What else?"

Archibald flipped to the schematic of the three-bladed and five-bladed propellers and then dove into how either option would be more effective than their current two blade set up. They went back and forth on options and finally settled on a plan to fabricate new five bladed propellers using spare parts and to install them late the next day. By the end of their meeting, both inventors were animated and eager to get started.

Amelia left with a smile on her face. It was fun seeing both inventors light up. It made her realize they had a lot more to contribute than what she had been asking from them up to this point. To be honest, she hadn't really thought about them since they left the Nardoowe jungle. She'd been so consumed by her own problems she hadn't reached out to them for help. As she fell asleep that night, she resolved to work with them more.

First thing the next morning, she rose and checked on Ander. He was awake and sitting up while Eugene wipped paste across his back. Already, his bruised skin was looking much better.

"... want you up and moving," said the medic. "It will need to be slow, but I can't have you stiffening up."

Amelia quietly sat on the edge of a cot and watched as Eugene instructed Ander through a series of movements. Ander stiffly completed each, groaning any time he lifted his arms above shoulder height. Twisting motions were also painful for his back, but he had full mobility. It was significant progress from a few days ago when he couldn't even stand. Still, he had more recovery to go before he was back to normal.

Eugene finally finished his exam and stood in front of Ander, looking him dead in the eyes.

"I'm going to clear you for training because I need you to stay mobile, but it needs to be *very* light. No swinging swords or moving your back a lot. Those muscles are going to be in recovery for a long time." Still looking at Ander, he said, "Can you make sure he sticks to that, Amelia?"

Ander gave a start of surprise and turned around, groaning at the sudden movement.

Amelia held back a smile. "Sure can! Get your shirt on and I'll meet you up there." She walked out of the med bay and went to her cabin. She grabbed her newly repaired magpack and strode out onto the deck. Garret had already started the team on warm-ups. Everyone was there except for Axel, who was absent once again from the group.

She cleared her throat, causing everyone to stop their calisthenics. She held up her magpack.

"Can I join you?" she asked a little sheepishly. She had been asked by Ander and Garret for months to join them, but she had always given excuses. She was a little afraid they wouldn't want her there, but she shouldn't have worried. Her question brought nothing but grins from the soldiers around her.

"Come on in," Garret said. "I see you brought your magpack with you." He nodded to it hanging from her shoulder.

"I did," she agreed. "I know you all train with your gear, so I thought I'd bring mine."

Garret directed her to a spot on the deck where she could do the warm-up exercises without hitting anyone else. Then they moved into small groups after that, each group working on drilling their weapons. She didn't have any weapons, so she disappeared into the hold and came back with a steam-powered wrist crossbow that seemed to suit her nicely.

Garret helped her strap the crossbow to her arm and hook in a hose to the steam canister on her magpack. The crossbow was surprisingly light, much more so than the large alternatives the soldiers used. The only downside was she had to manually cock it before each shot. Still, the draw weight wasn't bad, and it used compressed air with each shot to help propel the small bolts with more power than would have been possible with just the string alone.

Garret instructed her on all the basics, from loading a bolt magazine to firing at a target. As she began practicing, she became so focused she hadn't realized Ander had appeared on the deck until she retrieved her bolts from the target tacked to the deck railing. She caught him watching her and grinned. He smiled warmly in return.

Over the next few minutes, she kept finding herself unintentionally glancing his way and meeting his eyes in return. Each time, she felt a small thrill of warmth dance through her. The awkward tension from days before was gone, removed by their time together at the prison. Now, everything in the world finally felt right.

On her fifth round, she lifted up her now-tired arm, fired, and hit the bulls-eye. She squealed in delight and swiveled around to see if Ander had noticed too. Instead of catching him, she turned right into Garret.

He clapped her on the shoulder. "Nice shot! Now you just have to keep practicing until you hit the center *every* time."

She slumped a little.

"Don't worry," Garret said. "You'll get there."

She nodded and sighed as she left to retrieve her bolts. As she returned, she detoured from the shooting position and made for Ander.

Ander was partnered with Hammer, moving slowly and stiffly through the sparring forms. The large man was thankfully taking it easy on Ander, but she could tell that the movements still hurt. His face grimaced in pain with each movement that required turning his abdomen. They paused when Amelia made her way over.

"Did you see that?" Amelia asked excitedly. "I hit the center of the target!"

"I did," he said proudly. "Great job!"

"Millie did well," Hammer said.

"Thank you." She glanced at the rest of the group, who were sparring, aiming at targets of their own, or doing strength training.

She frowned. "Where's Axe?"

Ander and Hammer shared a glance. "He's... umm... he hasn't joined us yet," said Ander.

Amelia was confused. "Why not? His arm is completely healed. He could start training again. *You're* here, Ander."

"He sad," said Hammer.

"Oh...." She didn't know how to respond to that. To be honest, she hadn't taken much time to check in on the large pyrotechnician since returning from the archives. Now that they mentioned it, Axel had seemed sad. At each meal, he kept himself withdrawn. His eyes usually were empty, yet full with some kind of emotion she couldn't name. In some ways, it reminded her of herself, especially after the fire.

Her thoughts suddenly broke, and she turned to the two men beside her.

"I need to go. I'll see you later." She strode away without another word, disappearing down the hatch.

Within a half-minute, she knocked on Axel's cabin door.

Silence.

She waited before knocking again, this time more insistently.

"Axe, this is Amelia. Do you have a second?"

She took the huff from inside as a yes and opened the door. A wave of stench slammed into her as she entered the room. Axel laid on his bed, staring at the ceiling. All around were dirty plates, bowls, and clothes, along with burnt matchsticks and piles of explosive powder and canisters.

Her eyes widened. If she had known about all of these combustibles, she would have been here much sooner. She walked across the room and opened the porthole for fresh air.

Axel shielded his eyes and spoke with a loud, husky voice. "I suppose Ander sent you?"

"No, *I* wanted to check on you. I'm worried about you." She bent down and began sweeping up the explosive powder into her hand and dumping it back into its original can.

Axel gave a long and heavy sigh.

She raised an eyebrow. "Would you like to grace me with words?"

He frowned. "I can't join the others for training. No matter how much they want me to."

"Why not?"

Axel waved his stump vigorously at her. "I don't have a hand anymore—my *dominant* hand. I can't even—" He looked up at the ceiling and heaved out a great breath. "I can't make explosives anymore."

She frowned. "Just because you don't have a right hand anymore doesn't mean you are incapable. My father used to employ injured Steam soldiers." She finished cleaning the powder and began setting the dishes in a pile.

Axel sighed again. "Your father must have been a rare man. People like me—" he put his left hand over his eyes. "People like me aren't fit for service or anything else. Most cripples—most people like me end up on the streets."

She paused her cleaning and sat on the edge of his cot. "That's not true. I thought parliament gave a stipend for injured heroes."

Axel chuckled darkly and shook his head. "Not much. Besides, I don't want government support. I joined the military so I could fight. Now..." his voice cracked, "I don't have a purpose anymore. I'm broken." His voice sounded dead as he turned away from Amelia, facing the wall.

Amelia's heart was wrenched. Axel was normally loud and jovial, but this... this was a shell of the man. Was this how Bragg felt after he lost everything? Was this what led him to do what he did?

"You aren't broken," she said in a stubborn tone.

"Whatever. Just leave me alone."

No. Determination flooded through her. This wasn't going to continue. She wasn't going to let Axel think he was broken or that his future was to live on the streets. He was capable and strong. He was going to make it through this.

"You're not broken," she repeated, "and I'm going to prove it."

She stood up, picked up the pile of dishes, and left. After she dropped off the dishes, she headed straight for her cabin. As she walked, the beginnings of an idea formed in her head.

Ander stiffly caught up to her as she entered her cabin. Leaning against the frame he said, "Is everything ok?"

"Sorry, I have something I need to do for Axe." She dropped her magpack on her bed and went to her desk, already reaching for a charcoal pencil and parchment.

"Oh." His expression fell slightly. "Well, is there something I can do to help?"

"Umm, yes, actually! Could you bring extra drafting paper from Emmett and Archibald? In fact, let them know I'll need their help with a project within the next day or so."

"Sure?" He raised a curious eyebrow. "What are you planning?"

She grinned. "I'm not ready to share yet, but it will be worth it."

"Alright."

After Ander fetched the parchment, she spent the rest of the day in her cabin, sketching and re-sketching. The only times she exited were to grab food and once to take detailed measurements of Axel's arm and shoulder, especially around the stump of his arm. He eyed her quizzically when she did this, but she just smiled and didn't offer any explanation.

She continued her work all morning. By the time lunch came around, she brought the two inventors into her cabin and had them review her designs. When they discovered what she was doing, they became excited and innovated on the ideas further. By the end of the evening, the three of them had begun prototyping at the inventors' table.

News about the project traveled to the rest of the crew the next day. As the word spread, people came to pitch in various parts they needed, whether it was gears from old pocket watches, parts from broken weapons, and more. Soon the entire airship was involved in one way or another. It wasn't until afternoon of the fourth day they finally finished the project. When they did, Amelia assembled the whole crew onto the main deck. Then she went down to Axel's cabin and knocked. He answered, looking even more glum than before.

"I need to show you something," she said, grabbing his left wrist and pulling him out of the room.

He resisted the tug. "What is it?"

"Just follow me to the main deck."

He sighed before letting her lead him up the stairs and out into the sun. When he stepped out, he put left hand up and blinked in the harsh light.

"Surprise!" shouted the crew.

He stared with an open mouth at the whole crew assembled around him. "Is this an intervention? Or my birthday? What is this?" Then his eyes landed on the large, shiny mechanical prosthetic on a table in front of him with hoses that ran into a magpack.

"Come here." Amelia pulled him toward the contraption and helped him slip on the magpack. Then she slid on a soft, padded sleeve over his right arm and strapped on the mechanical prosthetic. He complied, all with an incredulous stare.

"The end here," said Emmett, pointing to the hand portion of the arm, "is designed to swivel different types of attachments when you do this." He manipulated a part, and a hook appeared, then a pincer, then a knife, then an open socket.

"Here's where you can lock in a steam crossbow," Archibald added, pointing to a rail on the side of his arm. "And the open socket attachment is so you can screw in a war hammer, hypothetically."

"Millie, do you want to tell him about the last item?" asked Emmett.

Amelia grinned. "Sure. This pipe that runs down your arm is a flamethrower."

Blaze giggled. "I got to test it. It's beautiful if I say so myself. Also, it's named Franchesca."

Amelia smiled broadly at the hesitant light that had come into Axel's eyes. The large man pointed back at the canister on his magpack. "Is this the same canister you told me not to touch when we first toured this airship?"

She nodded. "As long as you are part of this airship, you'll always have a purpose."

Tears formed in his eyes. He looked down and fiddled with the arm. Then he stumbled to Amelia and wrapped her in an enormous hug.

"Thank you," he whispered.

Tears came to her own eyes as she hugged him back. She knew what this felt like—to be broken and then made whole again. Yes, she still had a past and Axel was still missing an arm. Those hadn't changed. But now, there was a peace inside her, a peace that unexplainably filled in the holes she felt inside. That same peace was now filling him as well.

A thought struck her suddenly. If it wasn't for her experience in the prison, would she have noticed how badly Axel was struggling? Or would she have overlooked him because her own challenges were more than she could bear? How many others had she been overlooking?

She pulled away and watched the large soldier stare at his new arm in delight. So consumed she was that she barely heard Veronica calling to her from the helm.

She turned around and climbed up to stand next to her first mate. Veronica pointed delightedly at the horizon. "Do ya see what that is, cap? Cliffs and stretchin' tableland!"

Amelia squinted and then blinked. "It can't be! We're only four days into our journey."

Veronica nodded excitedly. "It worked! The plottin', prop replacement, all of it. I expect we'll be arrivin' to Shipwreck Sands by tomorrow mornin'!"

Chapter 34: Shipwreck Sands

Ander

Ander woke early the next morning to the thrumming vibrations of the airship and the sound of activity. Something was going on and it was confirmed a moment later when a knock rapped on his door, followed by a sailor's voice.

"Oi, Commander. We spotted the canyon!"

Ander blinked his eyes several times before stiffly sitting up on his cot. His muscles were still tight, but he was grateful to be back in his own cabin. Last night was his first night back in his own space instead of in the med bay.

He rose and splashed his face from a basin of water, trying to shake off the last dregs of sleepiness that clung to his mind. He had dreamed of his parents again—just like every other night since the memory restorative had kicked in. Despite it being several days since reliving the memory, it was still fresh and raw in his mind.

The revelations he had gained were also fresh, and he was still trying to come to grips with how this changed things for him.

His whole life, he had believed he was Commonborn. *Just* Commonborn. Just like every other person in the Republic of Steam. He'd trained for years at the academy to fight Gifted. He'd made being a Steam soldier his life's purpose. And yet, he was half Gifted. Enchantran blood ran through his veins.

You are more like your enemies than you realize, echoed the voice of the Warden through his head.

The news shouldn't have surprised him. Ever since the vault to the Everblade, he began to suspect something was different about himself. Now he knew the truth, and it was far worse than he was suspecting.

Hurried footsteps pounded in the hallway outside, bringing his attention back to the present. If they were nearing Shipwreck Sands, then the *Firelancer* would likely be near too. His team and the others would need him on deck. They'd need him acting as their mission commander, regardless of his physical and mental state.

He sighed and changed. As he did, he put on his armor, magpack, and sword just so he would feel more like himself. It worked, though the process hurt like crazy. The pieces on his back were especially difficult to cinch into place, requiring him to take it all in slow, painful breaths. After a few minutes, he finally got everything settled.

He emerged above deck and blinked in the bright morning sunlight, which glowed orange and pink above the rusty-orange horizon.

"Ander!" Garret waved for him to come over. "Just in time. Take a look."

He followed Garret to the bowsprit and looked out across the horizon through his spyglass. Ahead of them, the vast tableland they were flying over ended abruptly and dropped thousands of feet into a sandy basin miles wide and a hundred miles long. Within the basin were dunes with hundreds of broken, wooden ships of every kind.

He let out a whistle. "That's a lot of ships."

Amelia appeared next to him. "My grandfather thought there may have even been thousands of shipwrecks here. His journal mentioned it." She looked up at him, her eyes taking in his full gear. She raised an eyebrow and flicked the front of his armor with a finger. "You better not be planning on using that today."

"Don't worry. Eugene only cleared me for mild exercise. I'm just... re-acclimating."

"Mm-hmm," she said, not seeming to believe him. "Sure you are."

He frowned. "A guy can't wear what he wants anymore?"

Amelia turned to face him. "Not if that guy is particularly good at getting into trouble!" She put her hands on her hips.

He shrugged, unable to argue against that, and let his gaze drift back out at the basin. The *Firelancer* was out there somewhere. At least, hopefully it was, still searching. Otherwise, if the enemy had already found the Wayfinder, their trip here would be all for nothing. Everything they sacrificed for the Wayfinder would have been for nothing.

After a moment, he caught her studying him. He frowned. "What?"

"You seem to be doing better."

"I feel better."

"Good." She gave him a tender smile that felt like warm

sunshine, melting away all the aches and pains of the last days.

Garret cleared his throat, causing them to both jump and look away from each other. He grinned and shook his head before saying, "What I don't understand is how these ships haven't been plundered in the years they've been sitting here."

Amelia shrugged. "Maybe they have, though I doubt it. This part of the desert is very far from any town or village, even the remote ones. The heat is even worse out here since we're so far from the ocean and any water source. Going out on foot or even on a sand sailor would be a death sentence."

They took in her words and continued to stare out at the approaching basin. Much of it was shrouded in shadow from the plummeting cliffs. Those shadows likely wouldn't change until the sun reached higher in the sky.

"Umm," Garret said suddenly, "the sadricondas may also have something to do with it."

"The... what?" She lifted her spyglass to her eye, and Ander followed suit, stretching his to its fullest extent. His jaw dropped open.

Dozens of dunes moved of their own accord, weaving their way through the shipwrecks. Every so often, black scales rose out of the sand before diving back under. As he watched longer, he noticed similar movements throughout the entire basin, increasing his initial estimate.

There were also the miniscule forms of desert sprinters, trying to keep away from the moving dunes. He watched as the sand underneath one flock gave way and was swallowed whole by an exploding trio of sadricondas.

"There's got to be hundreds of them," he said finally.

"Maybe they're just as trapped here as these ships are," she said. "You weren't on deck yet when we passed near the opening into the basin. It was *really* narrow."

"Good thing we have an airship," said Garret.

"Assuming we didn't get here too late," added Amelia.

"Oi!" shouted a sailor. "*Firelancer!* Northeast 30 degrees in the basin!"

"They're still here?" gasped Amelia. She turned to Ander. Her eyes were filled with excitement. "We still have a chance!"

Ander quickly scanned the position of the enemy craft. Sure enough, the large warship flew low to the ground. "They're flying from the east. That'd mean anything behind them they've already scanned. So if we got ahead of them—"

"We could find the ship before them!" she finished with a wide grin.

Excitement surged through Ander with a rush. "Garret, rally the soldiers. We need to be ready in case of a fight. Millie, we'll need to stay out of sight until we're ready to dive in."

"Already on it," she said.

The deck exploded into activity. Steam soldiers and sailors rushed back and forth, arming themselves and mounting ballistae into position. Amelia took over the helm while Ander took position next to her so he could supervise preparations from an elevated position. Soon, all three Steam soldier teams were assembled on deck before him.

He cleared his throat. "My team will take the bow and prepare the steam cannon, with exception to Axe. Axe, I want you on the stern keeping us apprised of the *Firelancer*'s movements. Harper, your team will pull out the barricades and prepare for ranged combat.

Charles, get your team ready to drop once we've sighted our target."

Everyone broke into action except Charles. He stared at Ander and blinked. Ander could see the flicker of doubt in his eyes before he finally called his team to start attaching harnesses around their waists.

Once everyone was at their positions, including the crew, Amelia addressed the airship as a whole. "Once we drop into the valley, we're going to keep our eyes peeled for a ship that looks like this."

She opened the book from the Lost Palace and showed off the picture of Rasharr Voh's ship, the *Dread Reaper*.

"It's long, pirate class, and gaff-rigged," she explained, "designed to move fast and hit hard. Once you've spotted it, call out. Questions?"

Everyone shook their heads.

"Once we drop into the desert," said Ander, "there won't be any cover. We'll be in plain sight of the *Firelancer*. The goal will be to keep ahead of the Enchantrans and avoid engagement. If that's not possible, we'll sink them here to join the rest of the ships."

The crew cheered. Ander turned to Amelia. "We're ready to enter."

The airship dropped lower and lower to the ground. It was only morning, yet they could already feel the suffocating heat radiating from the sand below.

The cliff edge approached quickly. Sand blew over it in swirls before plummeting thousands of feet down. *Here we go!* he thought.

They flew over the edge and rapidly dropped into the basin. As soon as they did, he felt the sheer magnitude of how many shipwrecks there were before them. Amelia's estimate of thousands was very accurate. Their hulls were of all shapes and sizes. Most were tipped over with wooden frames so dried out the cracks were visible even from the sky. Masts were tipped over and, in most places, gone all together.

"Oi, Cap!" said a sailor. "Nothin's rigged out here. Only bones of ships are left."

"Use your imagination," said Amelia.

"*Firelancer*'s changed course," said Axel from behind them. "They're heading our way."

How in the world are we going to sift through all of these in time? Ander wondered. "Millie," he called, "we could really use your help! No one knows ship construction like you do."

"Veronica," said Amelia, "take the helm." Veronica took the wheel, allowing Amelia to take a spot next to Ander at the railing. She stood close enough that her arm brushed his own, sending tingles from the contact.

Ander, focus, he told himself. *The Republic is depending on you.* Amelia, on the other hand, seemed to have no problem focusing.

"Nope, nope, nope. These are square-rigged merchant ships. You can tell by the size of the hull and the placements of the masts." Then she grabbed his arm and pointed excitedly. "Oh! There's something! Definitely pirate class! Still square rigged, but Ander! Look at how it's sheared in half!"

"*Firelancer* is picking up speed!" said Axel with a growing note of panic in his voice.

She waved a hand. "We'll outrun them. Nothing can match the *Legacy*."

Whomp! Wind blasted past them from the rear, whipping across the deck. Traces of static followed its wake, passing through Ander just as quickly. He turned his head toward the source—the *Firelancer.*

What were the Enchantrans doing? He left Amelia's side and proceeded to the stern and raised his spyglass.

The *Firelancer* was flying directly toward them, moving so quickly that sand blew up and curled in its wake. Amelia appeared beside him and cursed. "They re-rigged it, Enchantran style."

She was right. The airship looked different from before. When they last saw it, the bow had been ripped apart by an explosion—and that was before they riddled the deck with ballista bolts. Now the airship was repaired and had twice as many sails, all of which were full of air.

"It's gaining on us," said Axel.

Amelia cursed. "Veronica, increase our speed."

BOOSH! A sadriconda exploded from the ground behind them, arcing toward the *Legacy* before crashing back to the earth. Then another burst up toward them. Its jaws snapped hungrily in the air after them.

Everyone took a step back from the railing. Axel gulped audibly. "Anyone else feel like a grasshopper surrounded by fish?"

"We're high enough they can't reach us," said Amelia. Tentatively, the group resumed looking for the pirate ship as the *Legacy* increased in speed. Soon, the details seemed to blur around them.

"Oi," called Veronica, "we're reachin' the end soon. The narrows are comin' up." In the distance, the basin's towering cliffs closed in on either side to create a canyon only a couple hundred feet wide.

Ander took in the landscape and a thought struck him. "Millie, if I were ambushing a marauding pirate, that canyon would be right where I'd want to do it."

She gasped and slapped herself in the forehead. "Of course. The narrows to the Sahadrian West Sea. I assumed it was this whole basin, but I bet you're right." She called out to all sailors to scan the canyon entrance ahead for any signs of the ship. As they drew closer, it became apparent that there were more shipwrecks here than anywhere else.

The *Firelancer* continued to gain on them, growing larger and larger by the second. Sadricondas chased after both of them, making the sand look like it was boiling.

"I'm seeing trading ships and warships," said Amelia excitedly. "They're all surrounding a—" She gasped suddenly. "That's it! Suspended between the walls of the canyon! That's the *Dread Reaper!*"

Ander squinted until he caught sight of the ship. It hung in a narrow spot, caught on both sides of the canyon. He smiled and approached the railing overlooking the main deck. "Charles, is your team ready to drop?"

"Ander," cut in Veronica next to him. "I'm not going to be able to slow or stop without risking collision with the *Firelancer.*"

Charles' face went white. "Are you crazy? You want us to rappel down at high speeds with all *that* on our tail?" More sadricondas had joined in the chase, coming in at them from more directions than just their rear.

Ander ran a hand through his hair. "Make it a sky jump then and glide to the *Dread Reaper!*"

"Half of us aren't trained to sky jump," said one of Charles' soldiers.

"Same with my team," said Lieutenant Harper.

Stress seeped into Ander's shoulders, filling them with aching tension.

"*Firelancer*'s closing on us!" said Axel. The large airship loomed behind them, growing more imposing by the second. Legionnaires hung off the sides and screamed at them while the smoke of pitch blew off their deck like a war machine of the apocalypse.

"I'm increasing to full speed!" Veronica pulled a lever and the props behind them hummed harder.

Ander stared at Charles and Freya. They could do it, but inside he knew they wouldn't. They were the product of Bragg's leadership. They'd hesitate until it was too late to jump. Even now, the entrance was seconds away.

"Coming in hot!" said Veronica.

The tension grew inside Ander until it reached a breaking point. There was no one who could make the jump except for Garret and the rest of the team, but they were at the opposite side of the airship, loading the steam cannon. Besides, there wasn't any time to ask. They were entering the canyon.

He gritted his teeth. "Millie, make a loop back for me."

Her eyes widened. "What? Wait, you can't–"

He leapt off the stern and deployed his glider.

Swirling dust swallowed him whole. The *Legacy* disappeared completely from his view as violent turbulence hit. The gales ripped and pulled at him, yanking him this way and that. His body screamed at him, and it was all he could do to keep aloft. The *Dread Reaper* was completely obscured from his view; there was no chance of landing on its deck through the haze. Even the hurtling forms of the sadricondas crashing below him were cloaked. It was just him, the turbulent gales, and the dust.

Agonizing seconds passed before the ground suddenly appeared before him. There was no time to pull his release cord and stretch out his feet. He crashed into the sand and rolled head over heels before careening to an abrupt stop against a cliff wall.

Excruciating pain exploded through his body in a raging torrent. His vision grew dark, and suddenly he was back in the prison again, feeling the whip's tails strike him over and over. His back was in flames, searing with unbearable heat. At each strike, he bit his tongue to keep from crying out, from letting Amelia hear him. Even still, horrible groans escaped from his lips of their own accord.

The pain subsided, and his vision cleared. He was back in the narrow canyon. Dust clouded everything, leaving only a hazy light. He rose and groaned.

Why had he dropped from the airship? He realized now how dumb that was. His whole back felt like someone had cut it open and poured Sadrian spices all over it. He was not in condition for this kind of activity.

His thoughts were interrupted as the *Firelancer* streaked overhead, whipping gale force winds in its wake. He stumbled onto his knees and coughed hard in the dust as it flooded into his lungs. Then the sand beneath him vibrated with a pounding rhythm.

The sadricondas! He stumbled to his feet and then was yanked back into the cliff wall by a steel hook. Black scaled serpents careened past. The force of their passage shook the canyon walls and rained rocks and sand all around. Then the rumbling moved on, fading down the canyon.

Ander turned toward the owner of the hook. "Axe?"

Axel's bearded face stretched into a wild grin. "I thought *I* was supposed to be the insane one." His grin made him look more normal than he had in months. If Ander had any doubt the soldier was feeling more like himself, the bandoliers covered with explosive canisters removed all suspicion. The man carried enough payload to level half a city.

"Thanks for the save," said Ander.

Axel nodded.

"Could one of you help me up?" said a third voice.

They whipped their heads toward Amelia, who was twisted up in a broken glider and half buried in the sand.

Ander gasped. "Millie?" They stumbled toward her and helped her up. "What are you doing here? You could have gotten killed!"

"What am *I* doing?" she repeated, while disconnecting her mangled wings from her magpack with a vengeance. "What are *you* doing here? You're supposed to be taking it easy! You're in recovery, for goodness' sake! What if your jump set you back? What if you injured something permanently? You aren't invincible, Ander!"

She opened her mouth to say more when a loud shriek cut her off. The sound echoed toward them from up the canyon.

"Uh, maybe we should hurry to the ship," said Axel in a high, panicked tone.

They glanced at the *Dread Reaper.* The sun-bleached warship was suspended nearly twenty feet above them. Even centuries later, the steel ram on the bow looked sharp and solid despite the grit and rust. Between the bow and stern was a row of square, open portholes that ran along the upper third of the ship, each with hooks for oars.

Aside from the obvious age and weathering, the ship's hull was surprisingly intact. Only two large holes were visible, one on the side just below the waterline and another straight through the bottom of the ship near the stern.

They hurried to the ship, feeling the sand beneath their feet vibrate with increasing intensity. As soon as they got there, Ander turned to the others.

"Any ideas on how we get up?" he asked, trying to keep his voice calm against the hammering of his heart. They didn't have Garret here to shoot a line, and he and Axel weren't in condition to scale the cliff wall, either.

"I've got a grapnel," said Amelia, "or we could throw a lasso up?"

"I don't care how we do it," said Axel. "Just do it fast!"

She quickly fished out a rope and grapnel and handed it to Ander. He grabbed it as a mound of sand rolled around a bend in the canyon.

He fumbled the grapnel, dropping it to the ground as panic filled him. Then, in a flash, he had it back in his hands and was moving backward to give himself room to throw it.

"Ander..." Axel squeaked.

"Working on it," he growled back. He threw the grapnel and hit the side of the ship. It fell back toward them and landed in the sand with a dull thud. Quickly, he reeled it back in for a second throw.

Axel gave a terrified squawk as the incoming mound grew larger, heading straight toward them. The tremors in the sand grew.

"I don't want to push you, Ander...." said Amelia.

"I do!" Axel interrupted. "Throw the stupid thing!"

Ander squared up and threw. The hook flew up through the hole in the hull's side. He pulled back and felt it lock into place.

"It's good!"

Without saying anything more, the three of them scrambled up the rope—Amelia first, followed by Axel, and then Ander.

As soon as Ander's feet were free of the shaking ground, he worked on pulling himself up as quickly as he could. His back and arms throbbed painfully, but the approaching sadriconda was all the motivation he needed to move. He hadn't gone too far when his head slammed against Axel's boots.

"A little faster there, Axe." The mound was now reaching where they'd just been.

"You try climbing a rope with a hook and one hand!" he called back, irritation coloring his voice.

Ander swallowed. *Right.* The sadriconda hadn't broken the surface yet, but it was only a matter of time.

Amelia reached the top and pulled herself over. Then she peered back over and cried, "Come on!"

Axel muttered something to himself.

"I don't think you want to hear a response from him right now," Ander called up.

It was another minute before the two soldiers finally pulled themselves through the opening and collapsed on the floor.

Ander's back was on fire and he tried, unsuccessfully, to keep the moans of pain from escaping past his lips. He felt a tender touch on his arm and looked up. Amelia stood over him, eyebrows furrowed.

"You okay?" she asked softly.

He nodded, rolling to his side before getting up. He took some deep breaths and looked down through the hole they had just come up through. The sadriconda slowly circled beneath their ship like a shark in waves.

"We're safe for now," he said.

"Yeah," said Axel. "Perfectly safe. We're not dangling in a wooden cage above a sand shark at all!"

Ander rolled his eyes before looking around. They were in a large cargo hold. Broken chests and crates were scattered all around. Sand was everywhere too, rising up the walls and covering the floor in mounds. Mingled with the sand were gold coins, their luster muted by grit but still recognizable in the morning light.

It was clear the ship had been in the sea for some time because the walls were stained dark and old dehydrated barnacles still clung all around. Sunlight also glowed through cracks in the worn, ancient wood slats.

The timber floor creaked underneath their feet as they moved deeper into the ship. As they walked, more signs of cargo appeared: piles of tarnished pots and pans, rusty tools, and barrel hoop rings.

As they traveled, Axel's foot suddenly went straight through the floor. He gasped as he caught himself and pulled away. Sunlight peeked up through the hole his foot had just created, and farther below were black scales circling around where the broken pieces had fallen.

Ander swallowed. "We need to go nice and slow."

"Walk over to the keel," Amelia added, moving to the center of the room. "That'll be where we'll get the best support."

Axel was frozen for another moment before cautiously following. His face was white.

"Where are we headed?" Ander asked Amelia.

"Rasharr Voh met his end in his cabin. My guess is that's near the main deck."

"I'll be a lot happier once we have more than one level between us and the canyon floor," said Axel.

They followed along the ship's length, keeping to the center. Soon, they reached a door that sagged on broken leather hinges. It creaked as they passed through it into another room. This room was empty except for some decayed chests.

"This must have been where the crew kept their belongings," Amelia said. She pointed to rusted rings in the ceiling. "Hammocks would've hung from these."

As they continued carefully through the debris, they spotted some personal effects—an old bone comb, a rusted knife, and a dried leather shoe. Another door hung limply across the room, revealing an ascending staircase on the other side.

"I'll go first," Ander said. He carefully tested each step before trusting his weight on it. The wooden planks creaked mournfully as he climbed up, but they all held firm. Amelia and Axel followed behind.

He reached the next level and paused, letting his eyes adjust to the harsh light coming through rows of open portholes. In front of him was a long room that stretched almost the whole length of the ship. On each side were three rows of crumbling benches, with an aisle spanning down the center. Spaced periodically along the aisle were rising support beams. These all continued until the room ended at a wall with another door.

He took in all of these details in a heartbeat and found his eyes riveting on the forms still sitting on the benches.

Amelia let out a sharp gasp and grabbed his arm.

Mummified remains of slaves were chained to their seats. Their skin still clung to their bodies, stretched thin and dried like leather. Teeth and limbs were missing from some while others still had hair rising from their skulls. Many still clutched parts of oars in their hands.

Ander swallowed. "I'm glad Hammer's not here to see this."

Amelia shuttered. "It's horrible. They couldn't get away." Some bodies were stretched toward the aisle, as if they had died in the act of trying to escape.

Ander and Amelia walked down the aisle with a quiet reverence while Axel followed, making periodic sounds of disgust. He had his arms pulled in tight to his body and made an extra effort to navigate far around the corpses when their limbs stretched out toward the aisle.

They reached a door and pushed through into another stairway. Carefully, they rose up the steps, passing more dried out corpses. These had been better protected from the winds and sun. Underneath rusty armor, they could see swaths of dull-colored clothes on some, while others wore bright colors with the Valeran seal. The trio wove their way through the remains, rising until they arrived at the main deck.

The main deck was a mess. All the masts were broken off, with pieces lying across bleached, warped planks. Dried pieces of rope, broken spars, and other debris littered the deck, poking up through mounds of sand. Fallen bodies were also present, though the elements had worn these away to just white bones. A few wore breastplates so rusted they were crumbling away.

Axel eyed the unstable-looking deck. "Umm, maybe I'll just wait," he said, shifting nervously from foot to foot.

"I'm sure it'll be fine," said Ander. "We've got three levels between us and the ground."

In the distance came the faint *booming* of a steam cannon and the *twang* of ballistae.

"They better be taking care of my airship," Amelia muttered.

"The sooner we find the Wayfinder, the sooner we can get off this ship," said Ander. He pointed to a set of double doors on the opposite side of the deck. "I'll bet you that's the captain's cabin."

She nodded. "Seems about right. Well, here we go." They climbed carefully over the wreckage, testing each step before committing their weight. Twice, their feet broke through the planks. Each time, they circumnavigated around the area until finally, they reached the double doors.

Ander pushed them open and halted. Before him was a gaping hole, cutting off access to the rest of the room. One look across the other side confirmed that this was indeed the captain's cabin.

Faded wallpaper and dusty golden sconces adorned the walls. A large wooden bed frame was tucked against the far wall, just underneath large windows. Trunks laden with treasure lined the rest of the walls, their contents spilling out through cracks in the wood. In the center of the room, a corpse leaned against a desk—pinned through the gut with a rusted metal spear.

"That's him!" said Amelia. "That's Rasharr Voh!"

The corpse was well preserved, with leathery skin that still showed faded ink tattoos up his neck and down his arms. He wore fine clothing and an abundance of jeweled rings and necklaces. His mummified hand still clasped a golden saber.

"Sooo," said Axel slowly, "Beef Jerky's got the Wayfinder then?"

"Beef Jerky?" Amelia giggled. "I suppose the name fits. Yes, his last words were, 'You'll never find the Wayfinder on my dead body!' That was right before he ripped this hole and sank the ship."

"We need to get across," said Ander.

All three of them looked down the hole. It plummeted all the way through the ship to the swirling sand below.

Amelia stepped back and put her hands up. "I'll be honest. I have no desire to search through a corpse."

"Not it!" blurted Axel.

Ander looked at both of them before letting out a sigh. "Fine. I got it."

He wrapped a hand around the doorway and shuffled along the thin, broken edge of the floor. The boards creaked ominously underneath his feet. Halfway across, he looked down. The drop looked much longer from where he stood. Black scales rose from the sand below, reminding him of what waited there if he did fall.

"Umm," said Amelia in a higher tone. "Maybe we should have tied you off first."

"Too late now," Ander said. He continued, feeling his heart beating in his ears until finally he reached the other side.

Amelia let out a sigh.

Ander approached the dread pirate lord, who was even more gruesome up close. The pirate's eyes were gone, his hair was thin and mangy, and Ander could have sworn the pirate still smelled like decay even hundreds of years after dying.

He scrunched his nose and tried not to breathe too deeply. "Millie," he called, "what am I looking for, exactly?"

"A lens, like a magnifying glass or a looking glass, except mounted in a gold frame that looks like a sea serpent."

Ander grimaced as he looked over the leathery body. He tentatively patted the pockets, pulling out coins, jewels, and knives. Nothing he found was remotely similar to a lens.

He continued to Rasharr's hands, inspecting the jeweled rings. Then Ander pulled up the necklaces on tarnished gold chains, but again, found nothing.

"Are you sure it's on him?" he asked.

Amelia nodded. "He told the officers that they'd never find it on his dead body."

Ander paused. "Wouldn't that mean it's not on his dead body?"

She put her hands on her hips. "It's an expression. Plus, he sank his own ship right after saying it. To me, that sounds like it would be on his person. Are you sure it's not hanging from one of the chains?"

Ander removed each necklace, one at time, and dropped them on the desk.

"It's not here," he said, feeling agitated.

Amelia grimaced. "Maybe take off his coat and vest?"

"Ew," said Axel with a shiver of disgust.

"Not helping!" said Ander. He pulled the coat off and shook it, searching for any additional internal pockets he had missed. He did the same with the vest.

Amelia rubbed her forehead. "I don't understand. It's supposed to be on him. If not, where else could it be?"

She stared at Ander, her gaze distant and unfocused. Her shoulders sank. "If it's not here, then I don't know where it would be."

Ander swallowed. "Maybe it's in one of the chests back here?"

Axel pointed at Rasharr. "Is that what the Wayfinder looks like?"

Ander looked back at the body, but saw nothing different. "Where?"

"The tattoo over his heart. Is that what it looks like?"

Ander peered down and caught where Axel was pointing. Now that the corpse's coat and vest were gone, a large tear was visible across his shirt, revealing a faded tattoo of a golden, mirror-shaped lens.

"Millie?" Ander asked.

Amelia leaned forward and scrunched her nose with distaste. After a moment, she nodded. "Yes, that's what it looks like."

Ander eyed the tattoo. The inked Wayfinder was surrounded by treasure. All of it was bordered by lines. Curious, he ripped the shirt further to expose more of the tattoo.

The lines continued, forming a maze—no, a path.

"Millie," he said excitedly. "This isn't just a tattoo. It's a map!"

He ripped the shirt off and exposed Rasharr's entire torso. The tattoo on the front was a cave system, with dotted lines and inked instructions leading the way toward the Wayfinder. Ander traced the lines as they curved over Rasharr's side to his back, but the desk stopped him short. "It goes to his back," Ander called. "I'm going to have to detach him."

Ander grabbed the spear protruding from Rasharr's gut and pulled. The spear yanked free, throwing his balance back. He teetered at the edge of hole, wildly wheeling his arms forward.

Amelia yelped.

He caught himself and his body balanced out. Then he exhaled and wiped a bead of sweat off his brow. "That was close."

The other two were quiet, breathing in deep, steadying breaths. Then the floor beneath Ander groaned and sagged.

Ander threw himself forward as the ground sank several inches, tilting toward the hole. The desk slid toward him, grinding its way toward the gap in the floor. He wrenched the dread pirate lord off the desk and dove out of the way.

The desk slid to a stop just at the edge, teetering at the brink. Below, the ship groaned, sending deep vibrations through the floor.

Ander swallowed. He needed to get out of there. "Axe, catch!" He threw the body across the hole.

Axel caught it before dumping it next to him. "Gross, gross, gross!"

The groaning of the ship grew louder, followed by a jolting crack.

Amelia's face went white. "Ander! The room is shifting again!"

"I worked out as much." He backed up against the wall. Then he sprinted toward the hole and leapt. He flew over the gap and crashed onto the other side. Axel and Amelia yanked him up, and they all staggered away from the room.

The cabin floor continued to sink behind them. They turned and watched the captain's chests and massive bed frame slide down and crash into the desk. Everything slipped down the hole, crashing and banging through all the levels. They leaned over and watched the furniture fall until it smashed to the sand far below.

The sadriconda roared and ripped through the fallen wreckage, flinging shredded debris.

Ander swallowed. That had been close. Too close.

They took a break to calm their pounding hearts. Rasharr Voh rested at their feet, lying face first on the warped deck. Ander marveled at the tattoo etched there.

"So," he said, "when Rasharr Voh said on his dead body, he literally meant on his actual body."

Amelia nodded and then knelt to look closer at the tattoo on the pirate's back. "It's a regional map of a cove just north of Sadria." She pointed a finger to an X marked on the side of a mountain. "This must be where he hid his treasure, including the Wayfinder."

She looked up excitedly at Ander. "It all makes sense now. No one could take the treasure from him because no one else would be able to find it without him."

She pulled off her magpack and withdrew supplies to copy the map. As she drew, the ship groaned again.

"Uh," said Axel. "Do you think the ship is done settling?"

Amelia paused in her sketching and looked up. "I imagine we should be fine. This ship has sat here for hundreds of years."

The ship groaned again, this time for much longer, resonating through its entire length. All three of them fell silent. Then came a loud snap.

All at once, the ship started tearing apart, hinging from the hole that had once been the captain's quarters.

"Run!" Ander shouted. He grabbed Rasharr and sprinted. The ship tilted as they scrambled past the wreckage of the main deck, trying desperately to escape the epicenter. Then the entire rear of the ship broke free from the rest.

All three of them lost their footing and fell as the deck plummeted into an angled dive. The ship hit the bottom of the canyon with a bone jarring blast.

Ander was launched up. The body flew from his hands and he windmilled his arms before slamming back onto the deck. He gasped for air. But before he'd fully caught his breath, a black scaled shape crashed through the helm before him, ripping it to shreds. He pushed himself away and scrambled toward the raised bow.

"Ander! Axe!" Amelia shouted. She was pinned under a pile of debris, sliding toward the sadriconda.

Ander rushed to her. He grabbed her arm and pulled, but there was too much on top of her. Frantically, he hurled off wood fragments left and right. Axel sprang beside him. "On three."

They each grabbed Amelia's hands. "One, two, three!"

Amelia let out a squeal as they yanked her free.

Without any more delay, they scrambled up the bow. There they took in deep, gasping breaths.

Amelia locked eyes with Ander, her gaze urgent. "Where's the body?"

"The body?" he repeated. Then he opened his eyes wide. "It fell out of my hands in the fall!"

All three searched feverishly for the mummified captain.

"There!" said Axel. He pointed to Rasharr's body. It lay in the open sand, which was rippling from the sadriconda's movements.

They watched in horror as the body began to sink.

"No!" Amelia cried.

Ander took a deep breath and stumbled to the edge of the ship, but Amelia beat him to it.

"Not this time, mophead!" She leapt over the edge and hit the sand, sprinting toward the dehydrated body. Sand sprayed up behind her as she pounded toward the mummified captain. The sadriconda paused in its destruction and turned toward her.

"MILLIE!" Ander yelled.

She reached the Rasharr, grabbed him, and sprinted back toward the ship. The beast launched toward her. She leaped away, and the sadriconda snapped straight through the pirate's leg.

When she reached the ship, Ander pulled her up onto the stern. The sadriconda pivoted and charged toward all three of them.

Axel screamed and threw canisters from his belt like mad. The explosives went off, blasting up plumes of sand all around the beast.

The sadriconda flinched back and roared before diving beneath the sand.

Ander held his breath as silence followed. After a moment, he turned to the others.

"Do you think that scared it off?"

Clack-clack-clack-clack! The anchor winch spun wildly nearby as the attached chain rapidly disappeared into the sand. His eyes widened, and he opened his mouth to warn the others when the chain reached the end of its line.

Crash! The bow ripped away from the rest of the ship so quickly that all they could do was grab onto the railing before their entire section was dragged out of the canyon and into the basin.

"It's the sadriconda!" yelled Amelia.

Axel wrapped his arm around the railing. "What?"

"The anchor must've caught on it somehow," Ander called. "It's dragging us!"

The bow raced across the sand at breakneck speed. Sand sprayed up at them while pieces of the ship crumbled off behind them.

"Axe!" Ander shouted above the noise. "Break the winch! We need to—"

MRHAAAAH! The roar came from right behind them.

"What in the world?!" said Amelia.

More roars joined the chorus. Ander whipped his head around and saw dozens of mounds heading toward them.

"AXE! DON'T BREAK THE WINCH!"

Amelia grabbed a signal flare and blasted it into the sky. It burst into a gigantic starburst above them, barely audible over the rumbling pursuit behind them.

They climbed their way higher on the bow so they were overlooking the sharp ram in front of them. Pieces of the deck were still breaking off the rear, leaving a trail of debris. The remaining ship looked closer to a sled now. Fortunately, the steel ram on the front held strong—at least for now.

"They're getting closer!" yelled Amelia.

The mounds raced toward them. Then, as if sensing they were close to their prey, the sadricondas started bursting out of the sand.

The beasts arced toward them through the air and crashed just barely behind them in deafening blasts.

Axel cried out in panic and began throwing explosives behind them without regard. The sand between them and the sadricondas exploded. Then one rogue canister slipped from his hands and rolled down the angled deck.

"Oops!"

"Duck!" shouted Ander. The canister exploded, blasting boards off of the end of the *Dread Reaper*'s remaining timbers.

The blast must have impacted the sadriconda pulling them, because its speed increased again as it turned. As it whirled, their ship-sled skidded across the sand, whipping fast toward a shipwreck.

They all yelled and ducked behind the railing. The *Dread Reaper*'s ram crashed through the shipwreck, slicing the wreckage in two. Boards flew up around them, pummeling them with debris. Then they were through, still skidding at reckless speed.

The pursuing sadricondas tore through the rest of the wreck, leaving nothing intact.

"I see the *Legacy*!" Amelia yelled, pointing up.

The *Legacy* swung into view. The deck was smoking, and the sails were riddled with holes, but sweet relief passed over Ander as he stared at their worse-for-wear rescuer. Then without warning, their momentum slowed until they came to a stop.

Behind, the pounding grew as the sadricondas hurtled through the sand.

"Uh!" said Axel.

"Get ready to bail!" shouted Ander.

The crowd of sadricondas were almost upon them when, with a whiplashing jerk, the ship was yanked so hard the chain broke. The remains of the *Dread Reaper* were thrown forward, straight into another ship.

All three of them were launched into the air, sailing over the bow before tumbling through the sand. Ander grunted in pain as he pushed himself to his feet.

"Quick!" said Amelia. "They're still coming." Ander snatched the pirate's body out of the sand and scurried after the other two. The wreckage behind them blew apart as the beasts plowed through in their madness to get them.

They sprinted away, heading towards where the *Legacy* was now swooping down. The rope ladder rolled down and slapped the ground. Amelia reached it first and scrambled up. Axel went next. Hauling the mummy under his arm, Ander grasped the ladder before the *Legacy* lifted into the sky.

He let out a breath of relief as they rose away from the swarm of blood-crazed serpents, feeling the tension drain from his body. As the airship turned towards the east, his view opened to a smoking *Firelancer*, soaring out from the canyon, hot on their tail.

Chapter 35: Northbound

Amelia

The *Firelancer* chased the *Legacy* relentlessly across the Sadrian deserts and past the northeastern Sadrian coast. Amelia tried everything to lose the Enchantrans. They flew at top speeds, barreled through dust storms, and even weaved through the treacherous crumbling canyons in the Abyssal Rift. Nothing seemed to work. They would lose the *Firelancer* for a time, only to find it the next day, edging closer.

The map they had recovered on Beef Jerky, as the rest of the crew had now come to call the dread pirate lord, pointed to a cave located in a cove on the north side of the Northern Sadrian Range. It was a tucked away region, remote from all civilization—the perfect place to hide away treasure.

They were now flying over the ocean, having passed the northern Sadrian shores only hours ago. Night was falling, shrouding the glimmering rusty deserts behind them and making the seas underneath them look purple. Amelia held the helm's wheel in one hand while she tapped her fingers against her leg with the other.

She leaned toward the horn. "Everard, how's our coal supply?"

"Hang on," came the reply. "We've got roughly a day and a half's supply left at the rate we're going through it."

A day and a half. She swallowed hard and looked back. The *Firelancer* was only a mile behind them.

"They can't sustain what they're doing," said Ander, climbing up the ladder.

She jumped at the sound of his voice. "I didn't see you there." She brushed a loose strand of hair out of her face.

He pointed at the airship behind them. "We've proved the *Legacy* is much faster than the *Firelancer*. The only reason they've held on is because of their elementalists manipulating the winds. They'll eventually burn out."

Amelia wasn't convinced. Marshall Grease captained the *Firelancer,* and she had no doubt the vile brawler would stop at nothing to reach the *Legacy* and send it down in flames. If that meant pushing their elementalists to the brink of death, he'd do it.

"We're almost out of coal," she said, worry coloring her voice. "We've got a day and a half before we're left to use only the wind. What then?"

She met his eyes, sensing the thoughts passing through them. Neither of them needed to voice what would happen. The answer was quite clear. Without their engines, the Enchantrans would catch them and a battle would ensue. However, unlike times before, there would be no escape and no sleep-inducing melons to save them. They would be boarded, taken down by magic and superior numbers.

She rubbed her forehead with her palm. "You realize if they catch us, we'll lose both the Everblade *and* the map to the Wayfinder? And with the Wayfinder, they'll find the other two talismans in no time."

Ander took a heavy breath. "I know. That's not an option." He stared out across the horizon. After a moment, he said, "We could try sending a message to high command? Maybe we can get a military warship to support us?"

She shook her head. "We're too far north. The nearest warships will be down patrolling the overseas slaving routes. That's assuming, of course, we aren't out of telegraph range already."

Lightning flashed in the north, briefly illuminating thick storm clouds in the distance.

He folded his arms. "We could always turn around and take a stand?"

She narrowed her eyes at him. "And give you another excuse to reinjure yourself?"

"I'm feeling better," he hedged.

"Uh-huh?" Amelia said, with a mocking tone. "No, thank you."

Truthfully, he *was* getting better. She'd seen him training and he was getting closer to his previous intensity. But she didn't want to tell him that. Ander wasn't invincible. He'd been rash at Shipwreck Sands, and he might not be so lucky next time.

She scanned the sky, pausing on the distant storm front to the north. The billowy clouds rose out of a dark, wide base before spreading out like an anvil. Jagged lightning flashed from within.

Ander followed her gaze and raised an eyebrow. "You're not thinking what I think you're thinking?"

She hesitated. Navigators like her avoided storms like this one for good reasons. All it took was a stray bolt of lightning, and their entire ship would explode into flames.

"Do we have any other choice?" she asked. "We're not going to lose them over the open sea. At least with the storm, we have a chance of escaping."

He grimaced. "The crew won't like this."

"I'm sure they'll like not being dead even more," she said with a wry smile. "Besides, we need to veer northwest anyway, and I don't want the Enchantrans to follow."

"Alright, I'll warn everyone below decks that it's going to be a bumpy ride." He turned to leave, then paused, looking back at her. "I'll be back soon."

She could have sworn he glanced at the light scar across her temple—her token from the last dangerous storm—before disappearing off the helm. Somehow that show of concern warmed her from the inside out. With that feeling invigorating her, she squared her shoulders.

"Veronica, I'm turning us due north. Have the sailors swap the working sails out for storm sails."

"Oi, ya sure cap?" Veronica asked. "That storm is lookin' mighty dangerous."

Amelia nodded. "I wouldn't attempt this if we weren't desperate. Quick now. I don't want the Enchantrans catching up."

Veronica relayed the order to the sailors on duty. They stared up at Amelia like she was mad before Veronica's shouts sent them scrambling. The *Legacy* slowed as they transitioned to the heavier duty canvas sails. Behind them, the *Firelancer* closed the gap from a mile to a half mile before they were fully underway, coursing through the air toward the oppressive clouds.

The storm grew larger as they flew toward it, as if it was stretching its arms in a deadly embrace. The anvil top soared higher into the sky as well. Lightning flashed, highlighting roiling darkness.

Ander rejoined her. "Everyone below decks is assembling at their stations. I've also got the soldiers on standby, just in case."

"Hopefully it doesn't come to that," she said with a shiver. She glanced over her shoulder at the warship, which now loomed close. She cursed. "Looks like Marshall Grease knows what we're doing and is trying to stop us."

Instinctively, she reached for the lever to increase their speed, but it was already maxed out. Their transition to the storm sails had cost them both time and speed, and the Enchantrans were capitalizing on both.

She clenched the wheel as the *Firelancer* edged closer. The storm did the same, growing darker in the dying sunlight. A cold chill came with the dimming light, sending prickles up her arms. She pulled her pilot overcoat tighter around her neck and slipped on her goggles.

The airship rattled as the wind grew rougher. "Lifelines!" she shouted, quickly clipping hers on.

BLAM!

"Incoming!" Ander shoved her down as a grapnel crashed on deck and yanked tight against the back railing. Then he was at the grapnel in a flash, slicing the rope so the metal hook clattered to the deck. The limp rope fell back to the *Firelancer*.

Amelia scrambled back to her feet and righted the wheel as the world disappeared in a deep mist. Visibility dropped to a murky blur, shrouding everything around them. She could barely see the bow.

The damp soaked into her overcoat. Mist collected on the airship, gathering until it dripped off the envelope and ran down the masts in rivulets. The sheer quantity of moisture in the air felt suffocating. But they were hidden now from the *Firelancer.*

She yanked hard to port and began a complicated series of turns, shouting at the crew to follow suit with rigging configurations. They were flying blind, with only the instruments to guide them. Despite this, she plotted their route mentally, trying to keep the *Legacy* within the outer layers of the storm where lightning would be less likely.

Powerful updrafts yanked them upward and were quickly followed by heavy downdrafts. Amelia gripped the wheel with white knuckles, feeling each shudder through the airship jolt through her own body and make her teeth rattle. This continued while the sound of thunder boomed from the depths of the dark storm beyond.

She was beyond soaked by the time the turmoil settled again into billowing mists. By that point, it had been some time since they had lost sight of the *Firelancer.* Through their harrowing journey, they only saw the warship once, trailing far behind them before the mists swallowed it back up.

She slowed the airship and cut the engines, hoping to eliminate any sound of their presence. As the rumble of the engines died down, the world suddenly felt eerie. The mist blew across their airship, moaning like a specter in the night. Swirls of clouds formed dark, looming shapes all around them. Amelia watched warily, waiting for the *Firelancer* to charge out at them.

Nothing.

"Did we lose them?" she breathed, looking at Ander hopefully.

Lightning flashed in the distance behind him, backlighting the silhouette of a large warship for a split second. It was higher than them and slowly moving in their general direction. Then it was gone, vanishing into swirling mists.

Waves of icy dread washed over her, sending her heart racing. The *Firelancer* was so close! Dangerously close! Worst of all, it was at a higher elevation, so the Enchantrans could easily fire down on their exposed envelope.

Panic raced through her, freezing her to the spot as her eyes remained glued to where the silhouette just was. Everything inside her screamed to move, to get them far away, but she knew it would be futile. They wouldn't escape in time. By the time the rotors reached speed, they would be boarded or worse.

She could feel the crew's eyes staring at her, waiting for her orders. Perhaps they expected her to hatch some daring plan to save the day. That was, after all, what a Steam would do in a moment like this. But her mind was blank. She stared at where the *Firelancer* had been.

A bowsprit speared through the mists above them, followed by a dark, creaking hull. It cut through the mist like a shark's fin in turbulent waters. Everything above the lower decks was obscured by swirling clouds, cloaking the legionaries and elementalists that were, no doubt, readying to fire.

She waited for grapnels or ballista bolts to fly, but strangely, nothing did.

Amelia tilted her head. the *Firelancer* was flying perpendicular toward them rather than turning to their broadside to fire. If she didn't know better, it was almost like the Enchantrans didn't see them at all.

The thought broke her mental paralysis. Maybe there was a chance they could escape unseen. Hurriedly, she leaned into the horn and, in a whisper, said, "Everard, lower our altitude. Quick!"

Her stomach knotted as the *Legacy* dropped. As they sank, the warship drifted above their heads, disappearing from their view as it passed over their envelope. She held her breath and clung tightly to the wheel.

A second passed. Then another.

The *Firelancer* reappeared on their other side and continued onward until it faded entirely.

She let out her breath and felt her shoulders sag.

"That was close," said Ander quietly.

She nodded. They waited there longer before turning northwest and sailing onward. A full hour passed before they exited the storm. As they did, she checked the dark horizon for any signs of the *Firelancer*.

The warship was gone.

They kept their lamps extinguished for the entire night as they continued on their heading.

As the morning broke, they could see the eastern edge of the Northern Sadrian Range and a long coast to the north. As the day progressed, that coast became clearer, stretching out into a rugged, bleak landscape of sparse grasses and hardy trees. The air was much brisker here than Sadria, but not so brisk as to feel like winter. Even so, Amelia put on a scarf and a thick hat to ward off the cold.

By noon, they found the broad river tattooed on Beef Jerky's back. Even centuries later, the slow-moving channel was still present, following along the northern edge of the mountain range. They followed it for two days while cold fog from the storm front blew its way into the region.

When Amelia was starting her evening meal on the second day, Ander appeared from the main deck and hurried toward her.

"Millie," he said, "You need to come see this." Something about his expression seemed worried and yet excited at the same time.

Puzzled, she left her food and followed him up to the bow. He pointed down below.

The river ended at a large lake that overflowed with fog. The fog drifted beyond the lake, stretching out to the sides of a valley. Something glowed beneath the fog.

She squinted at the terrain, then turned to Ander. "What is it?"

"Look."

A wind blew through the valley, picking up the fog in curling rolls. Steadily growing into focus underneath were dozens of wooden forts, with lines of chained figures being ushered into each by horsemen. There must have been hundreds of the chained figures. Beyond the forts were massive quarries, timber yards, and rows of buildings. In the center of these was a large-scale construction project, though what was being worked on was indecipherable beyond the dozens of canvas-covered mounds. All of this was in the valley at the base of the mountains. The mountain itself was riddled with caves and mines.

Amelia's jaw fell open.

"There's more." Ander pointed toward the bay. She followed his finger to where a strange, iron-bound ship was moored next to a dock.

He cleared his throat. "I think we just found where all the Brinkerhoff slaves have been taken, and it's right in front of where Rasharr Voh hid his treasure."

Chapter 36: Shackled Secrets

Ander

"**O**ur comrades are down there!" said Lieutenant Harper. The man was half standing and half sitting in the captain's office, his palms pressed into the table. All around the edges of the table were the *Legacy*'s officers. Ander sat at the head of the table. Amelia, oddly enough, had sat next to him rather than at her usual seat at the opposite head.

Lieutenant Harper stabbed a passionate finger into the table. "We need to mount a rescue!"

"With what army?" asked Charles, gesturing his arms all around. "Did you see how many Shaoguan slavers are down there?"

"A covert rescue won't need an army," Harper pushed.

Garret stroked his mustache. "Let's say we managed to rescue the Desert Steam Soldiers. What would we do about the remaining slaves?"

"Oi," Veronica rubbed her forehead. "We 'aven't room for boardin' more than a dozen, slaves or soldiers."

"Fine," said Harper, "then we backtrack until we're in telegraph range and bring in the fleet."

"Backtrack?" said Amelia. "The Wayfinder is right in front of us! It's in one of those caves; we just need to find which one. We can't abandon everything now, not after everything we've gone through."

"We can't mount a rescue," Ander said. Harper opened his mouth, but Ander put up a hand to forestall him. "Not because we couldn't pull it off, but because saving a few people would lose us the element of surprise for saving the majority. It's not a strategic move. The best chance these people have is a united, coordinated strike from the fleet."

"What about the Wayfinder?" asked Amelia.

He nodded. "The Wayfinder *is* our primary objective, and we can't abandon it now. So, here's what I propose. We send in two ground teams, one to recon the mountainside for our cave and another to contact Olivia's team to get intel. At the same time, we could send the *Legacy* to backtrack to get a message to the fleet. This way, we could work on both objectives simultaneously without jeopardizing one for the other. Thoughts?"

The room was quiet.

Emmett cleared his throat. "With the supplies we got from Olivia, I think we could boost our telegraph signal with Charles' help. That would save us from having to fly back into range."

"Even better," Ander said. "Alright, it's decided. We'll drop the ground teams within the hour. This meeting is adjourned."

. . . .

The two teams moved silently through the trees with their

crossbows trained out for threats. Downhill from them they could just see the tops of buildings through the branches. Acrid smoke drifted up from the roofs. Its sulfuric tang blew through the trees.

Ander inhaled. *I know that smell,* he thought. *They're smelting iron.*

The question, however, was *why.*

The teams paused as they neared the camp. The camp was close to the mountainside, where dozens of caves were visible. Here, armed Shaoguan horsemen roamed, cracking whips as slaves wheeled out carts of ore.

Ander made eye contact with Freya and pointed up the mountain. She broke off, leading all the other soldiers except Garret and Harper. She had instructions to search for a triangle shaped cave opening that matched the one on Beef Jerky's back.

When the recon team was gone, Ander, Garret, and Harper crept through the vegetation toward the camp, careful not to make a sound. Ander was relieved to feel more himself out in the field. His back was still stiff, but it only ached periodically when he twisted too far.

They slowed to a stop near the work camp's edge. The buildings were scattered haphazardly across a wide clearing. There were stamp mills, smelting furnaces in the open sun, lumber yards, and many other buildings with chimneys that spouted dark smoke. The construction of the work camp was crude. Time hadn't been taken to shape the logs that supported buildings. Apparently, the Shaoguans had prioritized function over form. Perhaps the entire operation was intended to be temporary.

They watched the slaves rove back and forth, looking for anyone they might recognize.

Ander eyed the Shaoguan warriors who supervised on horseback. They looked otherworldly in their armor of scaled, red-iron plates. Their sleek helmets were pointed at the top, with metal masks that latched over their faces. The effect made them appear inhuman. Only their height differences gave them any sense of individuality. As for weapons, each wore a set of curved, thin short swords strapped in an X on their back.

"There," whispered Harper, pointing to a slave working at a tall stone furnace. "That's Corporal Walker. I did two tours with him."

Ander faintly recognized him, despite his sweaty face and threadbare clothing. He was surrounded by pallets of raw iron ore and stacks of wood. The furnace he was working by glowed red with heat.

"Alright," said Ander. "Let's make contact."

They followed along the edge of the trees in a crouch, keeping plenty of foliage between them and the Shaoguan riders. Then, when they were directly behind the furnace, they hurried toward the back of the furnace.

Harper cupped his hands over his mouth and made a low clicking sound.

"Harper?" Corporal Walker stepped around the furnace and dropped his mouth open. "With Blackwell and Mills. My goodness." He looked over his shoulder and turned suddenly, as if he was inspecting one of the pallets. "I can't believe you tracked us!"

Ander was grateful the corporal's back was turned, otherwise, the man would have seen Ander swallow a sticky lump in his throat. It was by sheer accident they had found them.

"Walker," said Harper, "we need intel. What's happening here?"

Walker shook his head and picked up a stack of wood. "I wish I knew. These Shaoguans don't say much. All I know is our camp's processing ore from the mountain. They cart down iron, copper, and coal to here. We process it and then send it down to the other camps."

"Have you seen what they are using it for?" Harper asked.

Walker threw the wood in front of the furnace and shook his head. "I don't make the trip, but it doesn't matter if I did. They're keeping the camps isolated from each other. Whatever it is they are doing, they've compartmentalized it. I suspect they're keeping us separated so we can't coordinate an uprising."

That makes sense, Ander thought. Though, something inside him wondered if there was more to it. Everything about this slaving operation seemed so strange. It didn't make sense for Shaoguans to buy enslaved Brinkerhoffs when they already occupied half of their country. Stranger still was that these Shaoguans were then transporting slaves to a remote region far away from their lands to mine, mill, and work in such a way that even the slaves weren't privy to what was going on. What were the Shaoguans really doing that required so much subterfuge?

"Anything else you know?" asked Garret.

Walker paused, then added. "Most of our materials go to one central camp. There are whispers that it's heavily guarded. No one goes in or out of it, aside from Shaoguans. If you want answers, that's where you'd find them."

"Hmm," said Ander. Infiltrating the central camp was risky, and it wasn't their priority. They had to get the Wayfinder, assuming it wasn't found already. "Walker, how much do you know about these mines? Have you heard anything special about them?"

The enslaved soldier shook his head. "I'm not part of the teams that go up there, but I see Niels. He's been working the mines longer than most. I'll get him."

Walker disappeared and then returned with a hunched over older Brink. "Niels," he said. "Pretend you're talking to me and don't turn around."

"Huh?" Niels began to turn his head, but Walker pulled him back.

"Don't."

"Whit's this all about?" asked Niels. "Yeu are going to get us intae trouble!"

"Calm down," said Walker. "It'll be worth your time. Blackwell?"

"Neils," said Ander, "what can you tell us about the mines on the mountain? Is there anything special about them?"

"Special?" Niels shuddered. "Many o' them are cursed. Rich in ore, aye, but cursed."

"What are you looking for, exactly?" ask Walker.

Ander hesitated, trying to figure out how to respond. He settled on another question. "Niels, has there been treasure found in any of them?

"Treasure? Yer serious? I thocht yeu said this wis important?"

"It is," said Ander quickly. "Have the Shaoguans been pushing you to find treasure?"

"Oi no. Only a daft loon wi' a dead wish would hide treasure in those mines. Nay, they hae us minin' for iron mainly."

"Would you know if they had found treasure?"

Niels nodded his head. "Certainly."

Okay, Ander thought. Perhaps this whole mining operation around the Wayfinder was coincidence.

"You said the mines were cursed?" Garret asked.

Niels shuddered. "We're nae the first tae mine here. The

passages are pure ancient, wi' crumblin' bones. But that's nae all there is."

Ander felt a chill go down his spine. "What else is there?"

Niels swallowed hard and lowered his voice. "Many o' the shafts feel like somethin's awatchin' yeu frae the deeps. Some've even seen dark, twisted things lurkin' in 'em."

"Dark twisted things?" asked Garret.

Niels nodded. "Those o' us who are wise stay away frae the deeper caverns an' always carry a light. Those who don't go missin'."

"Carry a light?" Ander said to himself. He shared a knowing look with Garret. Too much of this sounded like the Nardoowe beast. It too lived in the dark and avoided light. That adventure had nearly killed them all. Were there more beasts like that inside this mountain?

A thought struck him suddenly. Amelia had told him that the dread pirate lord used the Wayfinder to hide his treasure in a trove no one else could find. Was the danger why no one could find it?

"Niels, are there any caves that are more prominent than the others? Any you haven't explored?"

Niels was silent for several heartbeats. Then he spoke in the barest whisper. "There is one cave at the base o' the mount. We call it the Silent Shaft. It's the wurst o' the lot an' oldest. Built long before uz. The Shaoguans use it tae get rid o' the troublesome slaves. No one who goes down returns."

"Why do they call it the Silent Shaft?" asked Harper.

Niels swallowed. "It's the place where a slave's scream echoes afore stoppin' suddenly."

"Where is it?" asked Ander.

Niels pointed across the camp to a path that looked far less used that the others. "Follow that till yeu get tae a tunnel wi a wooden barricade in front o' it. Yeu cannae miss it."

Someone barked a command in their direction. Walker shrugged apologetically. "We need to go. Hope you got what you needed." The two slaves disappeared.

Ander, Garret, and Harper waited there a moment longer before slipping back into the trees. Thoughts poured through Ander's mind as they moved away from the camp and angled their trajectory toward the path Niels had gestured to.

They followed the trail from the cover of the woods, following its windy path until they encountered Freya's group.

Freya looked excited and whispered, "We think we found our cave." She turned around and led everyone up the same path until they reached a yawning, triangular opening with a large boarded barricade stretched across.

Ander started into the deep darkness beyond the barricade. Something about its unfathomable depths sent a chill through him.

This was definitely the cave they were looking for.

He let out a long breath before saying, "I think it's time we report back to the *Legacy*.

The sun was dropping below the western peaks by the time they were picked up by the lake's edge. Ander climbed onto the main deck as long shadows grew across the foggy lake. Amelia poked her head from the hatch to below decks and quickly emerged to greet him.

"Oh, good," she said. "Did you find anything?"

He nodded and shared everything they discovered. As they spoke, Emmett, Archibald, and Charles worked nearby, trying to connect a long metal pole to a telegraph. As Ander was wrapping up, the telegraph began clacking.

"It's working!" said Archibald.

"Quick!" said Charles, grabbing a charcoal pencil and parchment to write the message.

Ander and Amelia rushed over. Charles dashed down the pattern, but the tapping fluctuated from strong to indistinct. As such, the words were fragmented and broken.

They read over his shoulder.

EX--RNAL AFF--RS OF--E TO LEG--Y.

"That must be Secretary Drake's office," said Amelia quickly.

"Sending confirmation of receipt," said Charles, tapping a message back.

A moment passed before the message continued.

WAR--NG. TRA--TOR IDE-T-FI-D. SU--ECT G--S BY NA-- OF --. RESP---- F-- STO-EN SCHM--TICS. APP--END ON SIGHT. REPEAT. APPREHEND ON --.

Ander read the words over and over, trying to grasp the full meaning.

"The traitor's been identified?" Amelia said. "But it doesn't say who."

"They're sending this information to *us*," Ander added slowly. "Which means... that traitor is here. With us."

They shared a look with each other.

"Charles, ask them to repeat!" said Ander. "We need to know who's the traitor!"

"Oi!" shouted Veronica. "*Firelancer*'s sighted! *Firelancer*'s sighted!"

"What?" Amelia's face grew pale. "How is that possible? This is so far away from where we lost them. Not unless—"

She paused, and Ander's mind filled in the rest. Unless the

traitor on board gave them away.

He ran a hand through his hair. "If the Enchantrans know we're here, what else do they know?"

They locked eyes with each other. Then Amelia said, "We need to find that Wayfinder as soon as possible."

Chapter 37: Silent Shaft

Amelia

Ander shouted for the soldiers while Amelia rushed to her cabin. She tugged open the door and quickly entered before stopping in her tracks. Something seemed... off. Nothing was wrong with her bed or her clothing. Nothing was wrong with her desk; it was just as messy as ever. She stepped in front of it, opened a drawer, and pulled a latch for the secret compartment within. The map that had been sitting in there was gone.

The *traitor!* They had been in *her* quarters!

Who in the world had been watching her so closely that they found *this?*

With a huff, she threw her magpack over her shoulder and shoved her way out of the cabin. She made a beeline for where Ander and Garret stood. Soldiers were assembling all around them, clumping together in their teams.

When she reached Ander, she skipped all preamble and said, "The map is gone."

"What?!" said Ander. Garret closed his eyes and exhaled.

"I think it's the traitor that took it," she continued. "And I wasn't just leaving it around for anyone to find. I had hidden it too. Which means they've been watching us—me—very closely."

Ander ran a hand through his hair. "We need a new map."

Garret turned to the quickly massing soldiers and shouted, "BLAZE!"

The door to the hatch crashed open, and Blaze scrambled over to them in a rush. He stopped short of Garret and stood up straight. "Yes sir! Here sir." He gave Amelia a wink.

"Blaze," said Garret. "Bring Beef Jerky here."

Blaze's smile faded. "How did you know—I just barely set him up?"

"Now!" Garret pointed an urgent finger at the hatch.

Amelia watched Blaze hurry away, nearly slipping as he climbed down into the hatch. She shook her head. Only Blaze would plan a practical jump scare at a time like this. How he ever got into the Steam Special Forces was beyond her.

"Charles," said Ander, "I need that message repeated!"

"I sent a reply," said Charles frantically, "but the signal went dead. It's not even drawing power anymore."

Ander clenched his jaw. "Emmett, Archibald, I need you to figure this out. Charles, gear up. The rest of you listen up."

Amelia watched Ander brief the assembling sailors and soldiers on their situation. In moments, Blaze returned with Beef Jerky. Amelia pulled out her grandfather's journal and quickly began transposing the map, focusing on the caves that housed the

Wayfinder. The path was a maze of tunnels and branches, with instructive text and symbols she hoped would make sense when they got underground.

She half listened to Ander as he spoke to the assembly.

"... we're going to send two teams down into the caves—mine and Charles'. Harper, your team will stay on deck in case of an attack. Keep an eye out for the traitor. At this point, it could be anyone. Amelia, you and the crew—"

"I'm coming with you," she interrupted. "Don't even try to argue that, mophead."

The crew chuckled.

Ander sighed before nodding. "Veronica, we'll need you to take the *Legacy* north and keep it out of sight. We'll come to you for a pickup. The last thing we need is an air battle over this slaving operation."

As Ander coordinated instructions for the pickup, Amelia's eyes dropped to the sword mounted on his hip.

Why does he have the Everblade? Given the circumstances, it was oddly suspicious.

She shook the thought out of her head. There was no one she trusted more than Ander, and it was probably for the best. With how much the traitor knew, nowhere on the airship was safe for the blade.

"Again," said Ander, "we have confirmation from the Republic that there is a traitor in our midst. It's someone on this airship, and we need to keep our eyes open because now is when they'll make their move. We don't know who it is yet, but we suspect it's just one person. If we're vigilant, we'll spot them."

"Fat chance," Eugene mumbled. Garret elbowed him. "What? We've all been together on this airship for weeks. Months. We've all

477

talked with each other and done things together for so long." He looked at each of them. "If we couldn't spot a traitor then, how will we now?"

The group was silent.

"We also didn't know there was a traitor on the airship," Amelia said. "Maybe now that we know, we will see their tells." She focused her gaze on each one of them. "Look, I don't want it to be anyone either. But the only thing we can do is our best."

"Nicely said, Millie," said Ander, giving her a quick smile. He faced the rest of the team. "Check your gear. We drop in five."

. . . .

Night fell across the woods as the team moved silently through the trees. Cold fog turned the world into muted shades of grey. Goosebumps grew on Amelia's arms as her mind conjured up potential horrors that lurked in the mines ahead. Who knew what the slaves had meant when they said dark, twisted things lurked in them?

The team was deathly silent. Not even Blaze spoke a word as they stole up the path to the abandoned mine. The only consolation they had was that the whole team was here: Ander, Garret, Blaze, Eugene, Axel, and Hammer. It was the first time they had all been on a mission together since the vault to the Everblade.

Hopefully this time will go better, she thought. The notion didn't dispel the creeping worry growing in the back of her mind. At least with the Everblade, they knew what danger they faced. Here, they didn't have that luxury. They were going in blind, relying on a faded tattoo for a map.

The mine appeared before them, opening up like a triangle portal to the underworld. Charles, Freya, and three others were already there, having come another way. Amelia only vaguely knew the three soldiers that were added to Charles' team: Edgar, Frederick, and Percival—all former Desert Steam Soldiers.

The two groups joined together and looked into the mine. Amelia's heart began to beat faster with nervous anticipation. After so many months, they were finally here at the precipice. Somewhere in this cave was the Wayfinder—the same talisman her grandfather sought years ago.

Axel shivered in front of her. "Well... I'm not going in first."

Everyone looked at each other in a silent debate. After several long seconds, Charles cleared his throat.

"Do we even need to go in there?" he asked with a slight tremble in his voice. "Clearly, the Wayfinder's been protected for this long."

Ander muttered something under his breath before saying, "I'll take point. Charles, your team can cover the rear."

Amelia stepped up next to Ander. "I'll join you. You don't have to be alone."

He gave her a grateful smile before turning a serious gaze into the dark. "Here we go."

They slipped past the barricade and proceeded into the musty dark. Once they were all in, Amelia lit a lamp and raised its orange glow.

The tunnel was relatively straight, traveling deeper into the mountain. The air was musty and the hard ground was grooved from the ancient passage of wheelbarrows and carts.

Their soft footsteps echoed loudly in the quiet, traveling both forward and backward. After a few minutes, they reached a hollowed rectangular room with a hole in the center. Around the hole were the remains of rotten framing and broken railings. Amelia lifted her lantern to inspect the lift swinging silently over the pit. The pulley gleamed in the lamplight.

"At least the lift's been replaced," she said, scanning the cables and lead counterweights. All of it was new compared to the wooden framing around the pit.

"Is this the Silent Shaft?" asked Axel in a whisper.

Amelia looked down the shaft, but her lamp light didn't travel very far below the platform.

Blaze slapped Axel on the back. "What's wrong, Axey? Afraid something's hiding down in the dark?"

Axel glared at him. "Want me to throw you over to see?"

Eugene ran a hand down his face.

"Alright," said Garret, putting an arm around Axel and Blaze so he was in the middle, separating them. "Let's see how this thing works."

"I can help with that." Amelia pointed to a crank on the lift platform. "We turn that to wind the platform up or to unwind it down. These were designed to take heavy loads of raw material, so we shouldn't have to worry about overloading the platform."

Ander stepped onto the platform first. It swayed slightly before settling. He nodded. "My team will go down first. Then Charles's will come next."

"Why can't it be their turn?" Axel muttered to Amelia before gingerly stepping onto the platform. She followed, taking a spot next to Ander again. Once everyone was on, Hammer turned the crank.

The lift dropped slowly into the shaft, squeaking with each rotation of the crank. Walls rose around them, framed by rotting wooden timbers. The room above them rose higher and higher until it was just a small glow above them.

Amelia shivered. The temperature was dropping steadily now,

seeping through her pilot's overcoat. She tucked her fingers into her side pockets and breathed out a puff of steam into the frigid air.

Axel's mechanical arm rattled slightly as the husky soldier aimed his flamethrower below at the darkness between the platform's edge and the shaft's framed walls.

Garret put a hand on the husky soldier's shoulder. "Relax. There's no reason to get wound up yet."

Axel's eyes widened. "What about that?" His voice was a whisper as he pointed a trembling finger at the framework lining the walls.

The timber was scored with deep cuts, as if something large and powerful had attempted to climb up the shaft. A whole other type of shiver shook through Amelia, running down her spine and raising the hairs on her arms.

What did this? she wondered.

The marks continued, marring more and more of the timber framework until the supports had become twisted and warped. Then the supports ended abruptly in broken splinters, leaving the rock behind exposed.

Everyone but Hammer raised their weapons now, pointing them to the sides all around. Amelia's wrist crossbow felt feeble compared to whatever ripped out the thick timbers.

The squeaking of the crank suddenly seemed loud in a shaft that should have remained like its name. Silent. Was whatever made these marks still down here? Would it hear them? Would it come for them?

Her heartbeat measured the seconds that passed with a loud thump-thump in her ears. As the minutes grew, her wrist crossbow arm bobbed unsteadily. Then, without warning, the shaft opened up.

They lowered down to the ground with a *thump* in a circular chamber with a wide tunnel. Piles of broken timbers lined the sides of the chamber, as if the Shaoguans had scooted them to the side to make way for the lift. White human bones littered the floor.

She swallowed. Maybe she should have stayed on the *Legacy*.

The soldiers scanned the room with their weapons before training them toward the open tunnel before them. They waited, and when nothing happened, Ander flicked a hand forward. They silently took position on either side of the tunnel opening.

Amelia yanked the cable several times before stepping off. Then the lift rose back up. She watched it go, suddenly feeling trapped with their only source of escape disappearing into the darkness above.

She let out a breath and wrapped her arms around herself. Ander caught her eye and gave her a quick smile. It might've comforted her if it wasn't for the tight lines around his eyes.

She took a moment to steady herself before joining the others. Then, at a silent signal from Ander, they moved in deeper.

They passed a half empty rack of tools hanging on the wall. Pickaxes, shovels, chisels, and sledgehammers were all just starting to rust. She didn't want to think about why the Shaoguans had abandoned them. The creeping feeling she felt up her spine was more than answer enough.

There were remains of ancient tools on the floor as well—rusted bits of metal, the head of a pick, and broken drill bits. These were pushed to the side, away from the center of the path.

Ander leaned in close to Amelia. "There's power here in this mine," he whispered. "Subtle, but distinct."

Power. Was that the Wayfinder? Or something else?

They passed a wheelbarrow full of red rock, some of which gleamed with a metallic sheen. It now stood strangely abandoned by the slaves that had once used it. Another one laid on its side just up ahead, its contents spilled out.

"Looks like they were in a hurry to shut this place down," said Eugene.

Hammer pointed to the ground. "Blood."

Amelia studied the ground, which was splotched with brown spots. In one place a set of handprints were smeared across the floor—as if the hands had been dragged backward.

Axel swallowed audibly. "Maybe I should cover our rear. Just in case."

Ander shook his head. "We'll post behind these wheelbarrows and wait until Charles' team arrives.

Long minutes passed as they listened to the squeaking of the lift platform grow louder and louder before the lift itself settled on the ground. Then, just like Ander's team had done, Charles' team scanned the room and proceeded into the tunnel with their weapons out.

"It looks like the Shaoguans tried to reclaim this place before abandoning it," whispered Charles as he approached.

Amelia nodded. It certainly appeared that way.

"We need to be careful," added Freya. Her eyes were unnaturally wide and her expression was tense. "I measured the claw marks. Whatever made them is big."

"Big?" asked Axel.

Freya nodded.

Ander put a fist up for silence. "Same order. My team in the front, Charles' team covering the rear. No speaking unless you need to. Millie, you've got the map. What are our directions?"

She opened her journal. "We follow this tunnel until we reach a chasm."

Ander nodded and led the way forward. Amelia stayed next to

him, taking care to tread quietly with each step.

The tunnel continued forward, with an occasional offshoot. They passed these warily, conscious that anything could be down them.

The tunnel opened into a large cavern, with a floor that sloped downward until it dropped off into a wide chasm that cut across the center of the room. A single bridge spanned across the chasm, built with old rotting timbers on top of a twisted metal frame. Part of the bridge's railing was gone, broken such that its remaining fragments angled downward into the chasm. In the gap between the two sides of the railing were long claw marks cut into the floor of the bridge, as if something from the chasm had reached up from the depths and ripped it apart. On the other side of the bridge, the cavern floor sloped upward until it converged into another tunnel.

Garret elbowed Amelia's side and pointed to a metal cable anchored to the wall. It ran downward to the opposite side of the room. What it was used for was a mystery to Amelia.

"That's not up to code," Charles whispered, pointing to the bridge.

"Really?" asked Eugene with a mocking eyebrow.

Ander put a hand up for silence. "We go over the bridge one at a time. That way, we can cover each other. I'll go first." He took a step forward before Amelia grabbed his arm.

"The map says not to." She showed him the map, which had an X crossed through the bridge. "It says to go around on that side."

She pointed to the left side of the chasm, where two rows of rusted spikes stuck out of the wall. They were probably nailed in back when the workers were first making the bridge and needed someone to cross over to the other side.

"You want us to go over on *that*?" said Charles. "The bridge would be much safer."

Amelia silenced him with a single glare. "You forget, Rasharr Voh used the Wayfinder to hide a treasure trove no one else but he could find. If that wall is the path he used, then there's a reason why he used it and not the bridge."

The group fell silent. Then Ander proceeded to the wall where the spikes began. He tested the first on the lower row with his boot, before stepping on and grabbing onto the higher row. Then he slowly moved from spike to spike over the chasm. Garret followed next before Amelia's turn came.

As she rose over the chasm, she peered down into its fathomless depths. Something about the yawning darkness felt... unsettling. It wasn't the height—she was well used to that. No, it felt like the darkness below was *thicker* somehow. But how could darkness be thicker? Maybe it was the feeling that something—or some *things*—were down there in the darkness. The thought invaded every corner of her mind and set her heart beating faster.

Keep yourself together! she chided herself. They still had a ways to go, and she was already freaking herself out.

She kept her head up after that, focusing only on climbing from one spike to the next. That didn't stop the knot of dread tightening in her stomach, making it harder and harder to breathe.

She finally reached the other side and scrambled up the slope to another tunnel opening. Only then did the sensation subside.

What just happened? she wondered. Now that she stood here on the other side, everything that had gone through her head seemed irrational. It was just a chasm, and the darkness was just that. Normal darkness.

She looked back the way she came and spied the cable anchored to the wall. *Rasharr couldn't have carried treasure across the spikes,* she realized. *He must've used the cable to send it over somehow.*

The others crossed over the chasm now until only Axel remained, creeping along the spikes. Amelia could see the perspiration growing on his face. She gave him a thumbs up to encourage him.

SNAP! A spike broke underneath him. He clung to the one by his head and scrambled to the next step as the broken one dropped into the chasm.

Ping... ping... ping....

Amelia held her breath and stared into the hole.

Seconds passed.

She let her breath out and waved for Axel to keep coming. When he reached the other side, he balled his hand into a fist with his arms tight at his sides. "Never again."

Scritch! The sound echoed from the chasm like metal scraping against stone. Icy fear poured into Amelia. "Run!"

Everyone hurried through the tunnel as more scraping followed. Instead of hanging in the rear, Axel ran just behind Ander and Amelia.

After a few moments, the noise faded. The group slowed to take a breath.

Amelia leaned over, feeling her heart pounding.

"What was that?" asked Edgar. "It sounded like it was climbing toward us."

Amelia closed her eyes. She imagined the Nardoowe beast, with its long claws, climbing to her. She immediately opened her eyes and shook the image from her mind.

"We need to keep moving," said Ander. "We have to assume the Enchantrans know the Wayfinder's here. We can't afford to lose any time."

The soldiers reshouldered their crossbows and continued forward. The tunnel here was windy, snaking back and forth. Other passageways cut from the main path, flowing out like tributaries in all directions. Rotten ladders leaned against walls and boards were stretched over gaping holes. But the main path was clear.

Amelia's heart rate was finally calming down when the tunnel opened into a cavern so black the path disappeared in the gloom. They halted. Their light seemed feeble against the expansive darkness.

They walked a few steps forward before stopping abruptly. The path before them fell away into deep darkness. Amelia pulled out the map.

"This cavern is wide and has lots of levels and offshoots," she explained. "Where we are needing to go next is on the other side."

They looked out at the darkness.

"We need a visual," said Ander. "Axe, would you shoot a flare? One without a burst?"

Axel pulled one off the array on his chest and angled it up before lighting it. It shot up, giving them a wide view of the cavern.

They were near the top of what appeared to be a cylinder-shaped pit, which dropped below them into darkness. The diameter of the chamber was as wide as the *Legacy* was long. Along the curved sides were dozens of tunnels, all at various locations and levels around the cavern. Rusted, warped bridges and broken scaffolding connected some of these together, while others had become isolated from the ravages of time. Several hoists also came down from the ceiling, their lines broken and gently swinging.

Back in the day, this would have clearly been the heart of the mine, with arteries of activity all around. Now, however, it was still and lifeless.

The flare bounced off the ceiling, fell away into the wide depths, and vanished immediately.

"Beef Jerky must have been tough to have hidden his treasure in a place like this," said Blaze. "Perhaps he was a *seasoned* adventurer? *Tough* maybe? *Lean—*"

"Shut up, Blaze," said Amelia, looking over the edge. "That flare went out too quickly. Is there water down there?" All she could see was darkness now.

"I didn't hear a splash," said Ander next to her.

Axel cocked his head. "My flares burn underwater. It's possible it burned out prematurely?"

"Let me try," said Charles, taking a flare out and dropping it over the edge. It fell about fifteen feet before passing into what appeared to be a cloud of darkness. As soon as it passed into the darkness, the flare snuffed out.

A chill ran through Amelia, cutting straight through her overcoat to her skin. She swallowed a thick lump in her throat. "I think we should stop doing that."

Ander's voice dropped to a whisper. "Which tunnel are we supposed to go to next?"

She ripped off a flare again and set it down at her feet. It created enough light that they could see the other side. She referenced the map and matched it with her view ahead.

"There." She pointed to a ledge sticking out on the opposite side.

"Hmm," said Charles thoughtfully. "If we tied off a rope, we could drop to that bridge there," he pointed to a bridge that ran below them to the other side. "Once we get across, we could climb that scaffolding to the platform."

"But that takes us dangerously close to... whatever snuffed out those flares," Amelia said. "And it's not the path Beef Jerky laid out."

"Where are we supposed to go?" asked Garret.

She glanced at the map and pointed to the left, where a thick chain hung down from the ceiling. "It wants us to climb that."

"And then what?" asked Garret.

She studied the map further before raising her eyes high to the ceiling. "There are rungs up there, see that?" She pointed a finger and traced a path across the ceiling to where a ventilation shaft had been cut. The rungs continued past the shaft, leading all the way to the other side.

"That's the way?" said Charles with a raised eyebrow. "Half of those rungs look rusted through.

Amelia put a hand on her hip. "You're all forgetting that Rasharr Voh—"

"Beef Jerky," Blaze corrected.

"—used the Wayfinder," she continued, "so he could hide his treasure somewhere no one but he could get to. Clearly, he chose somewhere dangerous, where the wrong misstep adds our bones to the collection at the entrance."

"Maybe I'll make my blood smear into a smiley face," said Blaze.

"Will you please SHUT UP!" Her last words echoed through the chamber like an outburst in a solemn church ceremony. She immediately clamped her mouth shut.

A wave of cold blew up from the pit.

The group fell deathly still and trained their weapons into the dark.

Nothing happened, but she was sure they were all thinking the same thing. Something was wrong with this mine. Everything about this place felt unnatural.

"I'm with Charles on this one," said Eugene in the barest of whispers. "How many of us could actually make that climb?" He pointed to Ander. "Your back is still recovering." He pointed to Axel. "You would have to do it with a hook." He pointed to Hammer. "You'd probably break each rung."

Now that she thought about it, she wouldn't be able to make it either. They'd have to climb thirty feet, swing from rung to rung going up and then back down the sloped ceiling to the other side. It'd take someone seriously athletic or Gifted to make the climb. In fact, perhaps that's how Rasharr Voh did this part. He used Gifted power.

Ander sighed. "Eugene and Charles are right. We aren't going to get everyone over the top. Can anyone think of any other ways across?"

The group was silent.

"We could go back?" said Axel with a sheepish voice.

Ander shook his head. "With a traitor in our midst, I suspect we'll have Enchantrans in these mines by morning. No, we have to keep moving forward."

He looked down at the void before sighing. "We'll go with Charles' plan and use the bridge. I'll test it first. The rest of you can then follow. Watch your step because there's probably a reason why Rasharr didn't take this path."

They anchored a rope and dropped it to the bridge below. Then Ander clipped his crossbow to his magpack and climbed.

Amelia watched nervously as Ander slowly lowered himself down the rope. He winced a couple of times on the way—which reminded her that he was still recovering. She could only imagine how his back felt. Frankly, it was foolish of him to even be here. What if the bridge broke underneath him and he was forced to climb back? How would his injuries respond to that?

She fidgeted nervously with her overcoat as Ander lowered himself onto the warped bridge. The structure groaned under his feet but held firm. He gave a thumbs up and waved the group to come down.

Garret slipped over the line next and then Blaze. Amelia watched the trio traverse slowly across the bridge, spreading their feet out wide to distribute their weight.

Her turn came next. She hugged the rope tightly as she swung over the side. The bridge looked farther down from this vantage than from the safety of the platform above. She clenched her teeth and slid down. When she reached the bottom, she carefully stepped onto the bridge.

The walkway was made of thick, eroded planks anchored into a metal frame. The frame itself was rusted and warped so the walkway was far from level. It almost looked like someone had put the structure under a press, forcing the metal to bend until it had a permanent twist in its shape. Looking over the metal railing, her light stretched down and then stopped abruptly at a layer of darkness.

The darkness was smoke-like in texture, yet as black as burnt grease. It slowly moved like simmering water, except it seemed to radiate a bone chilling cold. The cold numbed her thoughts to the point of lethargy. She took several slow, shivering breaths in an attempt to clear her head before she walked forward.

The railing was like ice to her fingers, burning with each touch. A creeping dread grew inside her chest as she walked away from the rope and toward the center of the cavern. The pressure built inside her until she felt like she was suffocating. Every part of her wanted to run back or to curl up in a fetal position.

Her mind played tricks on her, making it seem like the lamp she carried was growing dimmer—even though it had plenty of oil to burn. At the same time, she felt a growing sense of certainty that there *was* something below, watching her as she passed. The thought sent chills raking down her back like nails grating across a chalkboard.

She hurried faster to the other side and reached the end, where a tunnel opened up. Here, there was scaffolding that was bolted into the wall next to the cave, with a ladder rising to where Ander, Garret, and Blaze stood, waving her up.

Her muscles felt like lead as she grabbed and lifted herself up each rung. As she reached the top, Ander took her hand and helped her rise over the edge.

His hand was warm and comforting compared to the frigid cold below. He looked down at her and furrowed his brows. "You're freezing!"

"Yeah," she said quickly, giving him her other hand. He took it and held it as well.

Garret cleared his throat. "That's the last person down." He pointed out Edgar, who was now reaching the bridge.

More of the group were now climbing up to the top. Blaze stood up on his tiptoes and then said, "Freya, are your hands cold, too?"

Freya didn't respond. Her face was ash white as she hurried away from the scaffolding.

Edgar reached the halfway point when the flare on the other side of the room fizzled out. The bridge fell into total darkness.

Just as quickly, the room echoed with the sound of claws on stone.

Scritch click scratch! CLANG! That last sound was the bridge.

Pure fear flooded through Amelia. Whatever had been in the darkness below had now come above.

She let go of Ander's hands and ripped out a flare. Its light extended only half of the distance that the prior flare did, because the opposite side of the bridge was now shrouded in darkness. Then the darkness moved along the bridge toward Edgar, who stood frozen with a third of the bridge left to cross.

"MOVE!" Ander shouted. Edgar jolted up and ran.

The darkness followed like a flood, swallowing the bridge as it went. The soldiers ripped out their weapons and fired blindly into the darkness. From the plinking sound of their bolts hitting stone, all of them missed.

Ander holstered his weapon. "I don't think we're hitting anything! GET EVERYONE UP."

They yanked Charles onto the ledge and then Frederick. Edgar reached the base now and scrambled up as quickly as he could. The darkness surged up after him. As he neared the top, long white claws reached up from the darkness and sank into his back.

Edgar screamed. Charles and Ander grabbed his arms and pulled while the others fired at the darkness to no avail.

RIP! Edgar slipped from their grasp and disappeared into the darkness below. His screams rent the air.

Ander grabbed his sword, readying to dive. Amelia pulled him back.

"NO!" she screamed, fear washing over her in waves. "DON'T!"

Edgar's screams ended abruptly, throwing the entire room into unearthly silence.

Edgar... Edgar is gone.

The thought washed through her, making her legs feel unsteady and her head numb. Then the darkness moved again, rising up the scaffolding toward them.

They stumbled away from the edge as it rose. Amelia's mind screamed for her to run, but her muscles felt frozen to the spot. Chills raced through her veins, and her stomach felt like it was sinking at an alarming rate. The sensations grew, building inside her until all she wanted to do was curl into a ball and scream. Instead, her eyes remained unblinkingly locked on the rising darkness.

Long claws, now dripping with blood, curled over the top of the landing.

"Run," Ander breathed.

Chapter 38: Darkness

Amelia

Pure hysteria broke out across the usually disciplined group. As one, they scrambled headlong into the cave behind them, shouting, screaming, and bumping into each other in their haste to get away. Amelia's heart hammered against her chest as sheer terror poured through her veins. Her breaths came in quick, shallow gasps as she sprinted faster than she ever had in her life.

They rounded a corner and halted. Before them, the tunnel had caved in from the ceiling, leaving only a tight gap near the top.

"COME ON!" shouted Axel, pushing the group forward.

People scrambled up the mound of rock, pushing themselves through the gap. When Amelia reached the top, she scooted herself through like a madwoman.

"It's coming!" screamed Charles from the rear.

She crashed down on the other side, bumping her head, arms,

and legs against rocks.

"I'M STUCK!" shouted Axel.

In a rush, soldiers were at the large soldier, pulling him out through the wreckage. Then Eugene and Charles came last just as claws reached through the gap.

It's going to reach us! Without another thought, Amelia ripped a canister from her belt and threw it. Too late, she realized it wasn't the explosive she intended but a flashbang. It blew up in a flash of searing light. The dark presence reeled back violently and collided with the ceiling, sending a torrent of rock crashing down onto itself.

The group scrambled away, coughing, as rock and dust showered into them. Seconds passed before the dust settled. When it did, there was nothing behind them except for a sealed wall of rocks.

"Is it gone?" Axel breathed.

Everyone stared at the wall of rock, expecting darkness to seep through. Nothing did.

Charles rounded on Amelia. "You just blew up our way out!"

"Really, Charles?" she said between breaths. "Would you rather I'd let it get us?"

"I think it was quick thinking," said Ander, cutting off Charles' response. "And we just learned this thing doesn't like light, like the Nardoowe beast." He put his hands on his knees. "We need to recollect ourselves. We aren't through this yet."

They sat down while Eugene checked for injuries and passed out rations. Garret stood guard on one side of them while Freya monitored the collapse behind.

Ander sat next to Amelia. Then he let out a deep breath. "I guess we know why Rasharr Voh took the higher path."

She nodded shakily. "I hope that was the worst of our adventure here."

"Me too."

They both fell silent.

After a moment, he opened his mouth and then hesitated. He lowered his voice. "That thing radiated some kind of power. And there are more of them. I can feel the power everywhere."

"Power?" she asked.

He nodded. "Not normal power. Dark power like the Nardoowe beast and the sadricondas."

She pursed her lips. "If Sadricondas were once sea serpents, and the Nardoowe beast was some kind of dire wolf, what do you think these are?"

"No idea."

She pictured the way the darkness moved and how *claws* had extended out of it. A shiver went through her, and she shook the image out of her head. "On second thought, I don't want to know."

They waited there until the group had composed themselves. Then they rose, dusted themselves off, and proceeded onward.

The tunnel turned in a wide downward arc.

Amelia checked her map and then swallowed. "Ander? You know the room with the darkness? The Heart of the mine?"

"Yeah?"

"Um... we're going to have to go back in again. Except this time, we'll be *lower*."

"Lower?" clarified Eugene next to her. "Like where the darkness was hiding?"

She nodded.

"We should turn around," said Charles. "Like I said before, this mine is clearly secure enough for this artifact."

"There *is* no way back, dummy," said Freya.

"That's enough," said Ander. "Everyone light your lanterns and keep a flare and flashbang handy. If we can create enough light around ourselves, perhaps we can keep these things back."

"What if we can't keep them back?" said Charles.

Ander put a palm on the pommel of the Everblade. "Then we'll improvise. Quickly now." Each member of the group withdrew their lanterns and lit them.

Some of the chill Amelia felt inside dissipated with the abundance of light. With it came a rush of confidence. Maybe they could do this.

She followed one step behind Ander down the sloping tunnel. As they descended, the passage grew darker and murkier. The glow of their lanterns dimmed strangely, shrinking the light around them until they could only see five feet in front of them.

An anxious knot grew inside Amelia's stomach. Going down here didn't feel safe. It felt like they were walking into their graves.

The cave ended in a metal caged structure with zigzagging wooden stairs going straight down. *Scaffolding*, she corrected, with a metal mesh wrapping to prevent loose rock from hitting the workers that once worked here. Outside the scaffolding yawned the thick darkness of the Heart.

Amelia caught Ander's eye and pointed while mouthing the word *down*. He nodded and carefully stepped onto the scaffolding. She hesitantly followed, keeping her distance as far away from the mesh wall as possible.

They climbed down a level in complete silence. Only the wooden planks gave any sign they were there, periodically squeaking as they softly applied their weight. Amelia barely breathed. The darkness around them was thick and suffocating, yet she didn't dare gasp for breath for fear of being heard. A sixth sense inside told her there were more of those dark apparitions in this cavern.

They reached another level and turned. As she stepped onto the first step, the plank broke. She gasped and froze.

She didn't need to see into the dark to feel the dark apparitions suddenly turn their attention toward her. Sickening dread washed through her, filling her whole being with alarm.

"Do you think they noticed that?" asked Charles in a whisper.

CRASH! An apparition slammed into the mesh wall, right beside her, bending the metal on impact. She screamed and flung her arms up over her face.

"MILLIE!" Ander spun around and threw his lantern into the mesh wall. The lantern shattered, throwing burning oil up the wall. The apparition recoiled. In a flash, he grabbed her hand and pulled her away.

The group scrambled down the stairs, heedless now of the noise they made. The apparition followed them, raking its claws against the metal lattice, grasping for them.

They reached the landing for the next level. *CRASH!* Another apparition smashed into the mesh in front of them. Amelia screamed again, and buried her face in Ander's arm as they turned the corner and barreled down another series of steps.

Axel roared above them, firing his flamethrower through the mesh walls. The apparitions skittered away from the intense light of his flames, only to come swinging back at the cage from other directions.

They reached another level and turned.

"Almost there!" shouted Ander. Below them was a tunnel

CRAIG & JALEESA SNOW

opening, just one more level down. On the mesh wall of the same level was another apparition, banging against the scaffolding with such intensity the metal was bending and groaning. The edges of one side were already beginning to peel off.

Amelia gasped. "Ander!"

"I see it," he said. "Imminent breach!" As soon as they reached the landing, he pushed her into the cave and shouted, "GO!"

"What?!" She stopped to the side of the opening and watched him urge the group past. They did so without any hesitation. Then he drew the Everblade. The apparition now had its claws into a gash in the mesh and was yanking it open.

"Are you INSANE?!" It was her turn to rush over and yank his arm.

"Millie!" His face was a mask of shock. "What are you doing? You need to run!"

"JUST SHUT UP AND STOP BEING A HERO!" She dropped a flash bang at his feet.

That got him moving. They scrambled into the tunnel entrance as the explosive went off. She didn't look back to see what effect it had. Her entire focus was on sprinting now. That and making sure Ander didn't turn back.

"I could have held them off!" he said between breaths. "I could sense something stirring in the blade."

They dodged past a ladder leaning against a wall.

"Held them off?" she repeated with heat. "You *can't* get the blade to work, remember? Or did that somehow slip through your *dense* head?"

SCREEECH CLANG! Cold air flooded past them, silencing their argument. The sound of skittering claws on stone followed.

"Take my lantern," she said, shoving it into his hands. She ripped out a flare and threw it behind them. Then another.

"What are you doing?" he asked.

"Slowing them down, you idiot." She threw another flare. The plan seemed to work because the skittering paused.

Lights grew ahead. Then the rest of the group appeared. They stood at the edge of where the tunnel dipped downward into water.

"Is this the right way?" asked Garret hurriedly.

Amelia checked the map and frowned. "We're supposed to follow this path to a room with pillars. And we climb the farthest pillar. But it says nothing about water!"

"Did we missed a turn?" asked Ander, looking back.

The skittering resumed, coming closer before pausing again. They were running out of time.

"I'm not waiting to find out if it's the right way," said Axel. He began sloshing through the water. The rest of the group followed.

Amelia hung back to pack her journal in her magpack, shoving it where it would stay dry. Another of the flares behind flickered out. She threw her magpack back on and raced after the others.

The water in the tunnel grew deeper until it was up to her waist. The flares behind continued to flicker out one by one until finally, the cave behind her went dark.

"Hurry!" called Ander from just ahead of her.

She waded as fast as she could, but it felt like moving through molasses. This was compounded by the fact that the water level was rising.

Splash! The sound came from behind her, and maybe it was in her head, but it felt like the water suddenly grew colder.

Fear coursed through her again, pushing her to go faster.

Frantically, she used her hands to pull herself forward in addition to pushing off with her feet. She looked back and saw a dark form swimming toward her.

She gasped. *Faster! Come on!* The water was to her chin now and steadily rising.

She dove into the water. She could feel the others ahead of her, sending ripples with their powerful strokes. She followed as best as she could.

Everything was submerged now up to the ceiling, and she prayed the tunnel wouldn't end in a collapse or continue underwater forever. With the apparition behind them, there was no turning back now.

Her lungs throbbed, screaming for air. This was made even worse by the suffocating feeling of the apparition closing in from her rear. Desperation grew inside her, tightening inside her chest like a vise. Then the tunnel opened out.

She swam up and out, surfacing. She gulped in air as she quickly took in the room. They were in an underground aquifer with large stalactites and stalagmites that, over the years, had joined together.

Like pillars! This is the right way! She spotted the rest of the group heading to the farthest pillar.

Energy surged into her, fueling her arms to slice through the waters in quick strokes.

BOOSH! Something large surfaced right behind her.

Her heart raced, thumping in her chest as her strokes became increasingly frantic. With each passing second, her arms grew more and more tired. She could feel herself flagging, and the distance between herself and the others grew. Even Eugene, who was the slowest swimmer of the bunch, had a lead on her.

Come on! COME ON! The heavy magpack on her back was

weighing her down. But the map was in there. If they lost that, they were as good as dead.

She heard splashes as some of the others reached the natural pillar and were climbing up it. It was just twenty feet away now.

She pushed her deadened limbs faster as the sickening, wet sloshing of claws against water grew louder and louder in her ears. Her mind whirred, calculating the time it'd take her to reach the pillar versus the time it'd take before the apparition would reach her.

Cold realization washed through her.

I'm not going to make it! she thought.

NO! She couldn't let that happen, not after everything she had gone through to get here. The rest of the group was counting on her. If she was caught, they were all dead too.

She groaned as she forced her body to push harder than she ever had in her life. Her eyes burned and tears grew at the sides of her eyes from the effort. The edges of her vision grew fuzzy from the exertion, but none of that mattered to her. She didn't care that her limbs screamed for her to stop. She didn't care that her vision was going black. All that mattered was reaching the pillar before the apparition got to her.

Slowly, she pulled away from the apparition and drew close to the pillar. The whole group was on the pillar's side now. Some were even entering some sort of cavity at the top. At the bottom was Ander, shouting something at her she couldn't understand. He threw something that splashed behind her and flared brightly. All of this she barely registered.

I'm going to make it! she told herself. *I'm going to make it!* The words flooded through her like a drumbeat, helping her to keep tempo. The sight of Ander grew closer, his arm outstretched toward her.

The edges of her vision grew darker. Her head was growing foggy. He was so close, so close!

She reached the pillar and threw her hand toward him. Right before he could clasp it, something grabbed her leg from behind. Before either of them could respond, she was dragged straight under the water.

Bubbles flew from her mouth as she screamed and kicked against the claws clutching her leg. The apparition pulled her downward into its cloud of dark murk.

Her heart stopped as she looked into two pupilless amber eyes, which glowed malevolently from an amorphous body. Limbs twisted randomly out of its mass, each ending in long white claws. All over its body, darkness coiled off like ink in water, rising above to close off any light that permeated through the water above.

Its claws dug through her pant leg, biting into her flesh. She thrashed again, but the creature held firm. It pulled her close so she was level with its glowing, horrifying eyes. Shadow pulsated from the creature, somehow solid and like smoke at the same time. She sensed the same malevolent darkness that had been around the Nardoowe beast. But this creature looked like it had been so consumed by darkness that it had *become* it.

Tendrils of shadow reached out to her, wrapping around her body. Everywhere it touched, her skin seared with frigid chill. Bubbles flew out of her mouth as she screamed again, releasing the last of her air.

BOOM! Blinding light exploded from above her. She was released and the inky tendrils scurried away. Amelia clawed her way up to light as her head pounded and her vision faded.

Hands grabbed her as soon as her head broke the surface. She gasped for air and coughed out water.

"Get her up!" shouted Ander. "It's not going to hold for long!"

Hammer threw her over his shoulder and began climbing up the pillar. She clung to him like a lifeline, still gasping for air. Her whole body shook with chills.

Ander dropped another flare down for good measure before following them. They reached the top and climbed into a small alcove that turned out to be a natural water shoot of some kind. Once there, Hammer set her down on the smoothed stone floor.

She scooted deeper into the water shoot before laying back and catching her breath. Her heart hurt from how hard it was pounding, and her head buzzed with pressure. Eugene knelt next to her and checked her pulse. Then he took a hard biscuit from his pack and handed it to her.

"Take this," he said. "You'll feel better afterward."

She took it with her shaky hands and waited a full minute before taking a bite. The dark image of the apparition reappeared in her mind every time she blinked. Still, the food helped clear her mind and calm her trembling limbs.

Why did I choose to come here? she wondered. *This place is worse than a nightmare.*

Ander crouched down next to her. "How are you feeling?"

She didn't answer at first. Then she blinked. "When we get back... I think I'm going to slap Rasharr Voh's dead corpse. What kind of sick lunatic hides a treasure in a place like this?"

He shook his head and tried, unsuccessfully, to stifle a relieved grin. "You had me scared back there. Those couple seconds you were under water—"

"Couple seconds?!" she said, cutting him off. "I was under for only a couple seconds?!"

"We need to keep moving," said Garret near the opening to the alcove. "It's not coming up, but I get the sense it might know where we are going next."

"Are you good to keep going?" Ander asked.

She huffed. "Of course I'm not, but what choice do we have?" He reached down a hand, and she took it, letting him help her up. Then she retrieved the map. "It looks like we follow this water shoot until it branches downward."

"Alright," said Ander. "Let's keep moving."

They climbed deeper into the water shoot, using the sides to steady themselves as the angle became more pitched. As they walked, the tunnel grew narrower and narrower. Soon, they were scooting forward on their hands and knees.

Axel and Hammer had the worst of it, being the largest of the group. At points, they had to be pulled through to keep going. Finally, they found a branch. One part of the tunnel went directly up while the other arced steeply down.

They took the downward path, shifting their positions so they were scooting rather than crawling head first. The sides were smooth from years of erosion, but it was clear there hadn't been any water down this shoot for a long time. The passage was slick, but thankfully, the stone offered enough traction to control their descent.

They followed down the shoot for a much longer span than they had traveled up before squeezing through into a wider tunnel.

The tunnel looked to have once been a major throughway. There were even two rusted wheelbarrows, left abandoned with their loads still gleaming in the light. The way to the left was blocked from a cave-in, while the way to the right continued until it opened into thick darkness. Amelia shivered, knowing what that meant. More apparitions.

She referenced the map again and swallowed. "The path goes back into the Heart again." Her words were barely a whisper. "This time, we're much deeper than before."

Several soldiers cursed.

Ander hovered over her shoulder. "It looks like we cross to the center of a bridge? And then, what's that in the center?"

She shrugged. It looked like a rock was drawn on the bridge and there was a note in ancient writing she couldn't read. There was something they needed to do, and then the path continued until they could drop down.

Garret slowly moved toward the opening and peaked out. Then he retreated backward. "There's no cage over this bridge. It's completely exposed."

Fear ran down Amelia in a torrent of chills. "We can't go back out there," she said. "Maybe we're missing something?" She checked the map again, and sure enough, it specified for them to cross to the center of the bridge.

"Going out there is a death trap!" hissed Charles.

"We can't return the way we came," said Freya, pointing to the water shoot they exited. "Even if we could get through the flooded cavern, the scaffolding is now breached."

Amelia leaned into the cavern wall, feeling nausea fill her stomach. They were trapped.

"I think we're all asking the wrong question," said Blaze. "We should be asking, *what would Beef Jerky do?*"

Several people groaned.

"Maybe," said Axel, "we throw you out there, Blaze, and while they're eating you, the rest of us get out of here."

"I support that," said Eugene.

"Shh," said Hammer. He pointed to the opening. "Not safe."

He was right. The opening to this cave was easily large enough to let in the nightmarish apparitions.

Ander pointed to Freya and Garret and signaled for them to take watch at the entrance. Then he turned to the group. "Blaze is right. We need to figure out how Rasharr Voh got through."

"He had the Wayfinder," said Eugene. "Clearly that was more helpful than the shriveled-up tattoo map we're working with."

Blaze lifted a silver, metallic rock from one of the decrepit wheelbarrows. "Maybe he built a cage with all this iron?"

Axel's eyes widened. "Blaze, you might want to move your lantern away from that."

Blaze frowned. "Why?"

Amelia broke into a smile. "That's magnesium!" She hurried over and looked into the wheelbarrows. They were filled with magnesium.

"Does anyone mind explaining why this is significant?" asked Eugene.

Amelia picked one up and showed the group. "Magnesium burns hot and bright. We use a powdered form of it in our flashbangs."

Axel pointed to the floor. "There are traces of it on the floor. Do you see this white powder? It's definitely been used here before."

She grinned at Axel. "This *has* to be how Rasharr Voh did it before."

Charles stepped in. "You mean this could burn bright enough to keep the monsters away?"

Amelia put a finger on her lips. "We'd need to crush a lot of it to keep it sustained."

Axel shook his head. "It'll burn longer if we light it raw."

"But won't that diminish the intensity?"

He shrugged. "We've got enough here to make everyone a magnesium torch." They both looked at Ander.

He took a deep breath. "Alright. Let's do it."

Axel took charge, helping the group rig torches. Once they were finished, they each took more magnesium, just in case.

"We've got movement," said Garret from the entrance, "heading this way."

"Quick," said Ander. "Light them up!"

The torches flared to life, burning so brightly they were blinding. The heat was so intense, Amelia stretched her torch out as far away from herself as possible. The cave glowed brighter than broad daylight.

"Whatever was coming is scattering now," said Garret.

"Perfect," said Ander. "Let's cross this bridge."

They stepped into the cavern, amazed at how much the magnesium did to press back the thick shadows. The bridge was rotted and warped just like the others, with holes and chunks missing. The whole structure looked precarious enough that if it weren't for the thick suspension chains that supported it from the walls, it would have collapsed long ago.

"We need to go quick," said Axel. "These won't last forever."

They started across the bridge quickly and carefully. Each creak and groan set Amelia's teeth on edge. The last thing she wanted was to break through another step like earlier.

Scrapes started coming from the dark depths above and below them, edging closer to where they were walking, growing more confident. Her pulse quickened, along with her pace.

"Is it getting darker?" whispered Charles.

The thick darkness of the cavern seemed to press in on their light, compressing it in the most unnatural way possible.

Amelia's mouth parted. *Shadow wasn't supposed to do that. It was the absence of light. How could it block it?*

The craggy walls disappeared behind them, obscuring their only path of escape. Her stomach twisted again, growing with unease.

"Come on," she whimpered.

The sounds of sharp claws grinding on rock grew louder. From the quantity of the sounds, there must have been dozens of the apparitions closing in.

Pressure filled her chest, pressing against her ribs and making it hard to breathe.

Don't blink. Don't blink. She did and flinched as she imagined clawed abominations coming for them. She clenched her free hand into a fist, digging her fingertips into her palm, and hurried to Ander. He glanced at her as she took his side, eyeing her with a steely calm, the same calm he usually had when danger was about.

They reached the center of the bridge, where a large contraption rested. The outside frame of it was made entirely of metal and housed a single crystal half the size of her wingspan. Light from their torches reflected off the cut edges.

"What is that?" asked Charles.

Amelia didn't have an answer. Whatever it was, it looked like it had once been suspended in the air by chains. Time or something else had dropped it down to the bridge.

"This is the center of the bridge," said Ander, coming to a stop. "Now what?"

The chains of the bridge jangled violently on either side. This was followed by the *thunks* of things dropping onto the bridge on both ends.

"Uh! They're coming closer!" Axel squeaked. The darkness moved toward them, compressing their collective light into a shrinking island. It was slow but progressively moving toward them.

"Quick!" said Ander. "Garret, Eugene, Freya! Look at the crystal and see if we're supposed to do something with it. The rest of you, raise your torches and try to keep the apparitions away."

Amelia turned her back to the crystal and faced the darkness. It seemed to grow thicker at the edges of the light. At the same time, her torch seemed to grow *dimmer*, even though it was still burning just fine.

This isn't natural at all!

A clawed hand stretched toward them from the darkness and immediately retreated.

"How's it coming back there?" she said nervously out of the corner of her mouth.

"It looks like a... chandelier of some type," said Garret. "But I can't see how to get it to work."

Hammer's torch went out, letting in a wave of paralyzing cold. Another clawed limb reached out from the darkness, pushing more of its amorphous body into the light before retreating.

"You better figure it out quickly," said Axel, "or we'll all be dead soon!"

Ander's torch dimmed before winking out, and then Axel's torch went out next. Axel tried to relight it with his flamethrower, but the barrel wouldn't spark.

Blood drained from Amelia's face. *We are going to die.*

She must have spoken the thought out loud because Ander shook his head. "No, we aren't. There has to be something we're missing."

"Like what?!" she asked. "Why did Rasharr Voh bring us here if it leads to nothing?"

"We must be missing something."

The group backed closer to where Garret, Eugene, and Freya were still studying the crystal chandelier. Amelia turned, her eyes roaming over the chandelier. She looked for anything—a clue, instructions, a special facet.

"You'd think there would be an oil pan or something underneath," said Eugene.

"Or maybe they used magic to light it?" said Freya.

She could tell from the way the chandelier was designed, nothing ever existed underneath it. Maybe anciently they *had* used magic. Yet, it almost looked like there was something *inside* the chandelier. Near the top were perforations. Had something been poured inside it through the holes?

The soldiers were now firing their weapons into the dark. Axel had somehow gotten his flamethrower to work as well and was using that, but they were losing ground.

Come on, Amelia, come on. There had to be something here!

Then she saw it. The top of the crystal had a subtle grove in it, so subtle it looked like it was part of the facets, but it was actually a way to twist the top open. She wrenched it open and inside was white powder.

"Magnesium!" She looked up and saw that her torch was the only one left burning. All the rest had gone out. In fact, everyone was now crowded around her as the shadows pressed dangerously close to them. If she put her torch in the crystal, they'd have no other light.

She took a deep breath and prayed this would work. If not, they were about to die.

She shoved her torch into the hole.

The light went out, throwing the cavern into darkness and shadow. The apparitions pounded toward them in a frenzy. Then suddenly, brilliant light blared through the crystal. The light stabbed into the amorphous nightmares, sending them reeling backward.

"More magnesium!" she called to the others.

Magnesium was handed to her, and she stuffed them into the crystal. The light grew brighter and brighter, throwing every inch of the cavern into high relief. The apparitions were skittering up the walls now, taking any cave opening they could to get away from the light. Soon, their group was alone.

"We did it!" said Eugene.

"Millie did it," said Ander. He gave her a crushing hug.

The others celebrated along with them, whooping and hollering.

Smiling, Amelia checked the map.

"It looks like the Wayfinder is in a cave just below us," Amelia said. She looked down, pointing to a hole in the cavern wall. "It should be that one. We just need to climb down."

"There's some scaffolding over there," Charles said, peering down at an old, caged scaffolding attached to the opposite wall of the cavern they had come from.

"Well done," said a raspy voice.

The group all turned to see the ragged stowaway standing at the tunnel they had just come from.

"Cid?" said Amelia. "Wha... what are *you* doing here?"

The stowaway raised his arms. Thick tendrils of darkness poured from his hands, curling around the chains of the bridge.

"You've done well," he said. "I'll take it from here."

Realization of what was happening dawned on her. "NO!" she screamed. She stepped forward right as the darkness cut the chains.

The bridge groaned and dropped, plunging everyone into the pit below. She screamed, grabbing the railing as her stomach rose to her throat. The floor of the bridge crumbled as they fell, separating into pieces. Then they hit the ground abruptly. The impact threw her violently over the railing across the uneven, rocky floor. At the same time, the crystal chandelier shattered with a brilliant flash of light before throwing the Heart into complete darkness.

She sucked in a painful breath and froze. From the darkness high above, a cascade of skittering claws descended toward them. The apparitions were coming for them.

Chapter 39: Wayfinder

Ander

Ander swayed slightly as he pushed himself to his feet. The side of his head was sticky with blood, but that was the least of his worries. The bridge had twisted as it fell, flinging him away from the rest of the group. The Everblade was gone from his grasp, but he could sense it nearby. He could sense the apparitions too, scrambling down the walls and dropping from platform to platform. He couldn't discern the apparitions clearly before, but now in the total darkness, he could detect their aura plainly, which glowed dark violet in his mind. In fact, the Heart was tainted with their power, flowing all around them like a poisonous fog.

He sensed the Everblade feet from him and scrambled for it. In a flash, he had it in his grasp again. Now he just needed to find the others. He could hear them, but he couldn't tell exactly where they were with how their voices bounced off the rocky surfaces of the cavern. They were invisible to him since none of them had any Gifted power. Cid, wherever he was, was also invisible—which was strange. How had the stowaway hidden his abilities all this time? Surely Ander would have noticed if he had Gifted power?

That was a question for another time. In less than a minute, the apparitions would reach the ground and charge at them. Unless they could figure out a way to fight them, their odds of survival were close to zero.

He looked down at the glowing shape of the Everblade in his mind's eye. In the actual world, it was lifeless in his grasp. No flames spread across its length.

Come on, light!

Nothing happened.

I command you to light!

Still nothing. His frustration grew. He could sense the power within the blade. Why wasn't it working for him like it had briefly near the mesa village?

He was running out of time. The skittering of claws was growing nearer, echoing through the Heart like an incoming avalanche. There wasn't time to make the blade work. Maybe he was stupid to think that he could.

Time for Plan B. He needed to rejoin the rest of the team as quickly as possible. Their first priority was to survive. The second was their objective: the Wayfinder. He ripped off his last flare and expected it to come to life. It sparked briefly and then went dead.

What?!

He threw the flare and searched frantically for the team. *There!* Sparks. Someone was trying to bring back the light. *Multiple* someones by the dim outlines their light created.

Quickly, he stumbled toward the light. The floor beneath him was rough and uneven, but the crescendo of incoming apparitions urged him to hurry. Soon, the apparitions reached the bottom of the Heart, spilling across the floor like running water.

"Incoming!" he shouted. A scream sounded somewhere to his left. His blood ran cold. Was that Frederick or Percival? He couldn't tell. He pivoted, racing toward the sound and hoping against hope to rescue the soldier. The violet glows converged on the spot where the scream came from, overrunning the point and attacking it with a frenzy. Then the scream ended abruptly.

Bile rose up Ander's throat, but he swallowed it down. Now wasn't the time for shock. He needed to get to the rest of the team before there were any more casualties. Just as he was pivoting, the apparitions charged toward him next.

He cursed and sprinted, keeping his body low to the ground so he could recover quickly each time he stumbled. The apparitions' claws screeched behind him in their mad, bloodlust haste to get to him. Other apparitions were converging on him from the sides as well. Soon, he'd be closed off.

He gripped the Everblade harder as he ran. *Work, you stupid thing! Work!*

Ahead, where he had last seen sparks, light flared up like a lighthouse in a dark storm. Axel's flamethrower was outstretched and pointed at the flaming pile of raw magnesium. All the team were there, fanning the flames while looking frantically into the pressing darkness.

A tiny measure of relief filled him to see Millie's face there, too. She was safe, or at least as safe as she could be, considering they were all trapped in the middle of an abandoned mine surrounded by

CRAIG & JALEESA SNOW

freakish monsters and very far away from the exit.

His thoughts were interrupted by swiping claws coming in from his left. He barely registered the incoming strike before ducking below the swing and slashing up with the Everblade. The sword met no resistance as it passed through the dark violet aura. In a flash, he was dodging and weaving through more strikes as additional dark apparitions converged on all sides. It was like being in the Everblade vault again, moving blindly while deadly blades of all sizes sought to cut him in two. This time, however, there was no mechanism he could jam to make it all stop.

Instinct took over completely as he continued to press his way toward the light. Just like with his encounter with Gifted soldiers, the apparitions' energy telegraphed their movements milliseconds before they transpired, giving him a hairbreadth warning to move. But there were too many.

As he neared the light, claws snagged him from behind and yanked his feet out. He shouted out as he crashed to the ground. In an instant, the beasts were on top of him, slashing into his magpack as he covered his head with his hands and arms.

"Ander!" The voice was Amelia's. He heard her footsteps pound toward him.

"No!" he shouted. "Don't!" He gasped as one of the claws cut into his leg. He pulled his legs in further and let the magpack take the brunt of the assault. He could feel the pack being mangled beyond belief. Once it was gone, they'd go for his armor underneath.

Light broke out around him, blindingly bright. The apparitions scrambled away, leaving him alone as a slim figure reached him. Amelia dropped beside him and shook him frantically. "Ander! Get up!"

He raised his head level with her deathly pale face. There were tears brimming at the edges of her terror-filled eyes. She threw her arms around him. "You're okay." Then she pulled away and punched him in the arm. "I couldn't find you anywhere! I thought you were dead!"

A scuffle caught Ander's ear. He turned to see the apparitions creeping back, pressing at the edges of the light. He and Amelia rose, back-to-back. They were surrounded.

"This light isn't going to last forever," he said.

She shook her head. "If we're going after the Wayfinder, it's got to be now."

"The Wayfinder?" He would have run a hand through his hair if he wasn't worried about it being clawed off in the process. "What about the rest of the group?"

"Everyone but Frederick made it to the light. It should hold temporarily, but we can't move it without rigging something together. Axel's working on it, but it's going to take time."

Ander swallowed. "We don't have time. Not with Cid and his powers. Somehow, he followed us this far, which tells me he might have a way of avoiding these creatures." He took a deep breath and composed himself. "Alright, let's find that cave."

They moved together, keeping close so that both of them always remained in the center of the light. Even so, the light from their torch shrank again, straining under the weight of the nightmarish fiends pressing toward them.

They hurried into the dark until they found the wall of the Heart. Quickly, they followed along its edge until it opened into a dark tunnel. Ander focused his senses. He sensed nothing down the tunnel, but he *could* sense something to their left. It hummed gently in the back of his mind, a subtle tone underneath the pressure of so much violet power all around.

"This way," he said. They continued on around the Heart, passing another tunnel without bothering to stop, until they reached a third tunnel that hummed with the power.

"Here," said Ander. "I can sense something up ahead."

"More apparitions?" she asked.

He shook his head and closed his eyes to concentrate. "No. This feels like...." He caught hold of the sensation in his mind. It was familiar.

He opened his eyes. "It feels like the Everblade."

They shared an excited glance and saw their torch dim further. It wasn't the apparitions this time. The magnesium was running out.

They dashed into the tunnel. The apparitions followed, their claws echoing more loudly now in the confined space. The light continued to diminish in their hands, shrinking their island of safety, but the power ahead grew stronger. When the tunnel straightened out, something blue dimly glowed ahead.

"There!" said Ander. He felt the power radiating from it.

Their torch went out. As it did, a frigid chill blew past them.

"RUN!" said Amelia. They bolted toward the blue light as the apparitions' chase turned frenetic. Terror clawed at Ander's chest, making each breath harder than the last.

Amelia gasped and pitched forward on the uneven ground. He caught her arm and helped her recover quickly. The violet glows were at their heels now.

"Keep running!" he breathed, panic filling his words. The last ten steps felt like an eternity before they burst into the cavern.

A rotting gangplank stretched to an island of rock where an

object glowed blue on a lone pedestal. They sprinted halfway across the gangplank before Amelia pulled his arm.

"Ander, they've stopped!" They slowed down and turned. The apparitions remained, clawing at the entrance to the cavern. None of them entered the room.

They leaned over and took in gasping breaths.

"That was close," he said.

Amelia drew in a sharp breath and pointed below the gangplank. The dim light showed treasure below them. He stared at it, seeing more details appear as his eyes adjusted. There were mounds upon mounds of coins, gold bars, glittering jewelry, rare stones, exquisitely carved statues, faded paintings, fine weapons and armor, silver goblets and plates, and so much more. There was even a golden throne stashed on top of the largest pile. The diversity of the treasure was breathtaking.

"There has to be loot here from hundreds of raids," said Amelia. "There's treasure from more civilizations here than I could count. And look, it stretches all around us!"

They rotated around, surveying the rest of the room. Then their eyes landed on the glowing object on the center island, rising above everything else.

"Is that what I think it is?" she asked with an excited gleam in her eye.

He nodded. "The Wayfinder." The emanation of power from it was unmistakable. "We found it."

They approached slowly, reaching the island and stepping up to the pedestal. On top was a glass lens with a gold frame like sea serpents circling around it, with their tails weaving together to make a handle at the bottom.

He picked it up. It was remarkably light in his hands and he marveled at the intricate details.

Amelia leaned over his shoulder. "It's incredible," she breathed, touching a single finger to the carvings of the sea serpents. She yelped and pulled away. Ander wheeled around to see Cid a few paces away, holding a knife to Amelia's throat. Tendrils of darkness coiled around her like rope, binding her arms to her sides.

"Give me the Wayfinder, Blackwell, or Miss Steam will be as dead as Bragg," he rasped. Cid no longer stood hunched over. Instead, he stood erect and confident, his movements mirroring his tone.

Ander's mouth opened, but he made no move to hand over the artifact.

Amelia struggled against the dark restraints. "Ander, you can't!"

Cid pushed the knife closer to her neck and drew blood.

Ander put his hands up. "Whoa, okay. I'll give it to you." He slowly stepped toward them.

"Stop," said Cid. "Toss it to me."

Ander gently threw it, and Cid snatched it with one hand, keeping his other at Amelia's throat. He lifted the Wayfinder up and stared into it.

Power surged from the artifact as the glassy center of it glowed with dazzling blue light. An image grew into focus, showing an aerial view of where they stood. Then the image changed, flying away down the tunnel they came through. It zigzagged through the Heart, moving upward through a series of scaffolding and ladders until it zipped out through the tunnel and up the lift shaft. As the image exited the mine, it flew even faster, flying over blurred landscapes and ocean until it came to a city full of smoke and steam, with factories and workshops. It zoomed straight into the center of the city and nosedived into the ground. Levels of gears and cogs passed until the picture slowed to a room glowing with golden light. In the center was a brass machine with an amulet attached to the top.

Amelia took in a sharp breath.

Cid chuckled. "So that's where you put it." The image went out immediately.

"You've got what you want," said Ander. "Now let her go."

Cid gave him a cruel, dark smile. "Give me the Everblade."

Ander hesitated. Who was Cid? Clearly, he wasn't an accidental stowaway or merely just a thief.

Cid pressed his knife harder against her throat. "Do it!" Amelia gasped in pain as a trickle of blood ran from the blade down her white throat.

Ander took the Everblade and flipped it point down. Slowly, he approached Cid, staring into the stowaway's cold eyes while assessing the angle of the knife from his peripheral vision. Then he tossed the Everblade just barely off so that the stowaway had to lean away to catch it.

In a blink, Ander wrenched the knife free and slammed into Cid's gut.

Cid dropped the Everblade and stumbled back. Ander grabbed the blade and pulled Amelia behind him, aiming the point of his sword to the traitorous stowaway.

Cid's face transformed suddenly. Burn scars melted away into pale, wrinkled, and skeletally thin skin. His cheekbones became sharp and angular, almost predatory. His lips shrunk and his eyes turned dark and hollow. All of it radiated an aged, intelligent malevolence.

In an instant, the aged face was gone, replaced by the much younger version of Cid, covered with burn scars. The transformation

CRAIG & JALEESA SNOW

happened so suddenly that Ander wondered if he had imagined it all.

Cid looked at the knife in his gut and pulled it out. The blade was clean rather than covered in blood. Then tendrils of darkness flowed out of the wound and knitted it back together.

A freezing shiver passed through Ander. He had only seen this happen once before, and it was with the Nardoowe beast. Something was wrong about Cid, deadly wrong, and so far out of his understanding. He took a step back, keeping Amelia behind him.

"How. Dare. You." Cid's words were no longer raspy, but oily and smooth. "You *will* give me the blade!" Dark tendrils of power sprouted from his hands and launched straight into Ander. It punched holes straight through his breastplate and entered inside him.

He screamed and doubled over as the tendrils ran into his chest and spread through his body. The darkness was frigid, like ice running through his veins, while simultaneously pulling and twisting inside him in the most nauseating way. His body begged to fall to the ground and curl up into a ball. He wanted it to stop.

Amelia gave a strangled cry. "Ander!" She clung to his arm, but he could barely feel her warmth. He could barely hear the pleading fear in her voice as she repeated his name again and again.

All at once, the tendrils retreated out of him, returning to Cid's fingers. Ander fell to a knee and sucked in ragged breaths.

"Lay down the blade!" commanded Cid. "Yield to me!"

Ander closed his eyes, knowing full well how this would go. If he gave over the sword, Cid would take it and the Wayfinder, leaving them in the dark. With how many violet glows lined the edge of the cavern entrance, he had little hope of them surviving longer than a couple of seconds. Then the Enchantrans would have two of the four keys to the Source. That, and an insane stowaway.

No. There was only one way they'd get through this alive. One way that would keep the Republic safe.

He gripped the Everblade tighter and, against his protesting body, launched himself at Cid. As he leapt, Cid blasted him with a shockwave of darkness. It slammed into him and Amelia both, throwing them flying off the island into the pit below. They crashed into piles of treasure, items jabbing them, before they rolled to a stop.

Cid stalked to edge of the island and looked down as they rose to their feet. "I will get that blade," he said contemptuously. "One way or another." He raised the Wayfinder and then tucked it away into his cloak.

Darkness fell across the room, bringing with it a horrible chill. Violet glows began crawling from the tunnel entrance down into the pit.

Amelia ripped out a flare. "How many are there?" she asked.

"Too many," he answered in a calm he didn't feel. The flood kept coming down into the chamber, creeping toward them now as if the fiends knew there was no other way of escape.

They backed up, trying to put more distance between themselves and the approaching monsters.

"There's got to be a way out," said Amelia with fear rising in her voice. "Maybe there's something we missed? An alternative tunnel? Something incredibly flammable? Anything?"

They backed into the cavern wall.

"I don't see any way out!" she said.

There was no other way out, but he couldn't voice the words. Not with how much the waver in her voice ripped at his heart.

He did the only thing he could think to do. He reached out his hand, and she took it, lacing her fingers through his. It warmed him despite the frigid cold and dread building all around.

"Is this where our journey ends?" she asked.

He met her eyes, which were wide with terror and brimming with tears. In that moment, as the light of their flare was dying, he realized a truth that he'd been all but blind to. He *cared* about her. Not like a teammate or as a coworker. What he felt for her was much deeper.

The realization flowed through him like the rising dawn, bringing detail to the thousands of unspoken moments between them. All the times he had felt so protective of her. All the times she had made him want to be a better man. All the times she had completely taken his breath away. He should have realized it before.

Regret poured into him now. He'd been so focused as a soldier, so focused on his mission, that he had been totally oblivious to his own feelings. Now, everything was ending. They were about to die, and his greatest regret was that he'd never be able to see if she felt the same way.

The flare flickered out, leaving the image of her face as the last impression in his mind.

No! He thought. There had to be something to change this. This wasn't how their story would end.

He felt the handle of the Everblade in his other hand. If only *that* would work, they'd have a way out. But he had tried, multiple times. All at desperate moments. Each time, it didn't work because he didn't have power.

The apparitions moved more swiftly now, closing the gap to them quickly. Thick darkness billowed out from them, filled with energy.

Energy! Realization struck him like lightning. There wasn't power inside himself, but there was power all around him. It filled this chamber to the brim. Granted, what controlled the energy was vile and evil, but the energy itself was just that—energy.

That was how he had used the Everblade when first fighting the Mirage. He had tapped into the energy in the room.

The apparitions launched at them, flying through the air with their claws outstretched. In the same second, Ander reached his mind out to the swirling cloud of power and mentally connected it to the Everblade like he would a wire to a battery.

Whoosh! Flames ran down the Everblade like dripping, burning oil, coating its steel edge with blazing light. Then the energy surged into him, making time slow down.

He let go of Amelia's hand and slashed through the incoming apparitions. This time, instead of just passing through the creatures, the blade ripped through their dark forms and set them ablaze. They crashed to the ground and convulsed as the fire consumed them. More dove from the sides. He pivoted and struck out at these as well, sending them away in flames.

The rest of the dark creatures reeled back from the blazing light of the Everblade. Gone was the bone piercing chill and terrifying paralysis. In its place was warmth and light.

"Impossible," said Cid from above. "KILL HIM!"

The apparitions flung themselves back at them. Ander met their charge, easily slicing off clawed arms and cutting through amorphous bodies. Wherever the Everblade struck, flames erupted against the darkness and released the energy controlling it—generating more fuel for the blade to consume.

Cid growled and shot tendrils down at Ander with startling ferocity, nearly spearing him before he twisted at the last second.

Another one lanced straight toward Amelia. He leapt in the air and cut through it before it could reach her.

Flames consumed the tendril, racing up toward Cid. He roared, cutting the stream of power before the flames could reach him. Then he turned and ran. A beat later, the remaining apparitions followed.

Ander glanced at Amelia and immediately felt his strength weaken. Flames flickered here and there where some of the plundered treasure had been caught alight by the Everblade.

"Go!" Amelia said, pushing him forward. "He's getting away with the Wayfinder!"

"But you—"

"Go!" She picked up a burning pole and blew to stoke its flame. "I'll be fine!"

He sprinted toward the other side of the cavern and leapt to the entrance in one jump. At the top, he hesitated and looked back. He didn't like leaving her behind, but she had plenty of light.

"Go!" she urged again.

He turned and sprinted down the tunnel in quick, long strides. Apparitions leapt at him from behind large boulders, trying to catch him off guard. He dispatched each easily, finally making his way back into the Heart itself.

Dozens of apparitions assaulted a dimming island of light, where his soldiers fought desperately to keep the light burning. Nearby, Cid reached the base of a set of scaffolding.

They're eyes met, and immediately Ander surged toward him. Cid threw a hurried hand toward the team and shot a dark tendril of power. It slammed into their dying light and extinguished it in an instant.

Ander cursed and pivoted to where his team was now shouting

and screaming. In a flash, he was slicing through apparitions left and right, pushing his way to them. All the while, he could sense the power of the Wayfinder, ascending quickly up the Heart.

He redoubled his speed, ignoring the weariness growing inside. He had to save the team and get Cid before his strength gave out.

One by one, he dispatched the apparitions, freeing each person from their grasp. Each reacted in their own characteristic way— Garret breathing a thanks, Hammer grinning, Eugene saying it was about time, Blaze asking for his turn, and Axel blinking and saying, "Where was this the whole time?" Charles stared at him wide-eyed while Freya, who was being dragged by the apparition when Ander had rescued her, said nothing but took his hand to pull herself back to her feet.

Ander attacked with such ferocity, the remaining fiends turned and fled, scrambling up into the cavern. Whatever influence Cid had over them was now gone, replaced with fear of the Everblade.

Seeing the creatures on the run, Ander didn't waste any time. He raced up the scaffolding Cid took. Then he leaped up from platform to platform. He could barely sense the power of the Wayfinder, high above him. The strength inside him was fading faster now too, and he could feel throbbing dizziness growing inside his head. But he couldn't let Cid get away.

By the time he reached the top, his arms and legs were shaking. He swayed on his feet as the world blurred for moment. Then his vision cleared, and he was sprinting down the tunnel, following its windy course back to the cavern with the chasm and sinister bridge. He vaulted over both in one leap and hit the other side hard.

The impact knocked the breath out of him, and he staggered to his hands and knees. The flames of the Everblade were shrinking now that it had no more power to syphon away.

No! He pushed himself to his feet and stumbled onward, reaching out with his mind for the familiar sensation of the Wayfinder. Its power was ahead, but terribly faint. His legs grew weaker with each step, but that didn't stop him from reaching the lift chamber.

The cable was cut, leaving an unattached platform at the bottom. He cursed and looked up. The Wayfinder was somewhere up there, but its impression was so faint he could have been imagining it.

He jumped and grabbed the dangling cable with one hand. Then he reached up the hand holding the blade, intending to climb the rope when the fire went out. His strength gave out and before he knew it, he crashed to the floor in total darkness.

"No!" he screamed. *I have to get it back! We can't lose it!* These were his last thoughts before his mind grew dark.

It was hours before the team reached him and revived him. It was hours more before they were able to repair the lift and exit. By the time they got out, Cid, the Wayfinder, and the *Firelancer* were all gone.

Chapter 40: Gifted

Amelia

A tear dropped onto the parchment paper in front of Amelia. She didn't stop to wipe it off. It would only smear the ink if she did, and it was hard enough writing the words she needed to say as many times as she needed to say them. Rather, she took a deep breath and finished the apology, ending by signing her name with the decorative flourish her tutors taught her years ago.

There. She let out a deep sigh and waited for the ink to dry. As she did, her gaze drifted to the window, where the silvery glow of the moon showed through. They'd be seeing the grey smog of the Republic soon.

The thought of returning back should have made her feel excited. Instead, her stomach churned with nervous energy. They lost the Wayfinder to the Enchantrans. Sure, they had the Everblade, but how long would that last now that the enemy had the power to find the path to anything they desired?

Losing the Wayfinder wasn't the only troubling news. Cid's betrayal was also on her mind—if Cid was even his name—and the terrifying dark power he somehow wielded. She shuddered to think about the influence he had over the apparitions in the Silent Shaft. If the Enchantrans wielded that kind of power, what would happen if they got hold of the Source?

A knock sounded on her cabin door. She wiped her eyes with her sleeve and cleared her throat. "Come in."

Ander opened the door and poked his head through. "We're getting close."

Her stomach rolled over. "Okay," she said in a small voice.

He gave her a gentle smile. "You doing all right?"

She shrugged. "I finished writing my last letter." She pointed at the parchment, now dried. "I just need to put it into an envelope and seal it."

"Here, I can help." He took the parchment and folded it into thirds. Then he slid it into an envelope and offered it back to her. She took it and slid in two Valeran gold coins. The gold was no small gift, but to her it didn't even come close to compensating for the loss of those who perished in the Steam Invention Company fire years ago. She closed the envelope and poured hot wax onto it. Then she pressed a stamp of an airship—her family seal.

"There," she said. "Now I'm done." She set it next to the stack of the other hundred and twenty-six envelopes. The fortune she was giving away was staggering, but she didn't want it anyway. How could she when there were so many people who needed it more than she did? Granted, there were still a couple handfuls of coins left for herself, enough to begin rebuilding her father's company when the time was right.

He put an arm around her shoulders. "You're doing the right thing."

Her throat suddenly felt thick, and she didn't trust herself to respond. So instead, she nodded. This was the right thing. The peaceful feeling she felt inside confirmed it, even though writing the apologies was emotionally straining. After a moment, she cleared her throat again. "Well, I suppose we should probably be on deck when we arrive."

She rose and slipped on her pilot's overcoat, which was now torn and worn since their trip into the Silent Shaft. But it was the warmest thing she owned, and she could use all the comfort she could get.

They exited the cabin together. The sailors and soldiers on duty turned their heads, eyes on Ander and the sword on his hip. Everyone knew he could use the Everblade now. It was impossible to hide that news after their adventure in the Silent Shaft. All the same, it was strange to have the secret out. Stranger still was that no one had said anything after the fact either. She suspected no one knew what to say, considering how many people he saved because of the blade. They couldn't claim him to be a traitor after what he did.

"Oi," said Veronica, "we've got two warships on approach, cap. Just off the bow."

"Do we have identification?" she asked, moving to the railing with Ander.

"Not yet. Neither are the *Firelancer* though."

Amelia studied the warships through her spyglass. Both were turned directly toward them, which made it impossible to identify the names that'd be printed on the sides. Regardless, both were clearly Republic military airships.

"Looks like we've got a welcome party?" asked Amelia.

Ander shrugged. "I asked Charles to telegraph the Republic, so they know we are en route."

She eyed the Everblade. "I suppose with the cargo we're carrying, and with the *Firelancer* still at large, it makes sense."

They moved to the captain's helm, though she made no move to relieve Veronica. Her first mate was plenty capable of taking the *Legacy* into the Republic harbor, and there was way too much on her mind to take the wheel, anyway.

They waited there in silence as the warships approached. When they neared, one of them signaled them with a blinking lantern. Amelia read the pattern and then interpreted.

"We're to dock in the military sector. They'll escort us in."

She took a lantern hanging by the helm and blinked back a confirmation. The warships pivoted to flank them on both sides. Steam soldiers covered the decks of the warships, all armed and ready for battle. Even the porthole covers of the artillery decks were opened up, with ballista bolts protruding out. The sight gave her a sense of comfort. If the *Firelancer* appeared, they'd have to fight hard to get the Everblade.

A grey haze grew ahead. Then the Isle of Forge appeared, complete with orange lights, factories, workshops, and rising buildings belching smog. Even now, she could faintly taste the smog in the air. They were finally coming back.

They angled their approach toward the Forge Military Quarter. Lamplight signaled them from the docks on where to land. Veronica called down to the engine deck to accelerate their descent. Then they drifted down to where a detachment of soldiers waited at an empty pier.

Splash! The airship landed into the water and coasted the last few feet before coming to a stop.

"Lower the gangplank!" shouted Amelia. The sailors complied, dropping the boards down.

"Permission to board?" called up the familiar voice of Secretary Drake.

"Permission granted," she replied. She and Ander climbed down from the helm and waited for the tall, grey-haired Secretary of External Affairs to limp up the gangplank.

The secretary reached the top and leaned heavily on his silver tipped cane. His soldiers followed afterward, taking positions on either side of him. He gave Ander and Amelia both a nod. "Good to see you both safe and sound."

Amelia closed the distance between them and shook his hand. The secretary may have been getting on with his years, but his grip was still firm. "We're glad to be back safe as well."

He nodded and shook Ander's hand. Then his expression turned serious and businesslike. "I suspect we have much to discuss, and I want to hear all of it. Right now, however, there are a few pressing issues. Miss Steam, would you mind if we met in your captain's office?"

She nodded and led the way.

"I received your telegraph about the Wayfinder," said the secretary when the office door was closed. "I regret our warning about the traitor didn't reach you in time."

"We had suspicions before that," said Ander. "But Cid covered his tracks well."

Secretary Drake nodded. "That he did. But you aren't here bearing only bad news. My understanding is you recovered the

Everblade?"

They nodded.

"May I see it?"

Ander drew the sword and laid it down on the table. The secretary leaned over and studied it. "Fascinating. I know the Wayfinder was a loss, but you both did well in recovering this."

"Sir," said Ander, "now that the Enchantrans have the Wayfinder, they'll be able to locate the other talismans to the Source."

The secretary pursed his lips in thought. Then he said, "True, but do you know how many talismans it takes to keep the Enchantrans from reaching the Source?"

Ander frowned.

"Just one," said the secretary. "They may have the power to discover where we lock this up, but they will still have to go through our security."

Ander didn't look convinced that would be enough. She wasn't either, for that matter—she saw the raw power Cid wielded.

The memory sparked another thought. "Secretary... when Cid used the Wayfinder, we saw a glimpse to where the Amulet of Power was hidden."

His eyes widened. "Really?"

Amelia nodded. "It's here in the Republic."

"Do you know where?"

She shook her head. "Only that it's underground."

He took a deep breath. "Of all the talismans, the Amulet of Power is the one I worry about most. It was once wielded by the emperors of Enchantra, augmenting their power tenfold. The only reason our founders succeeded in a steam revolution was because your grandfather, Miss Steam, bested Emperor Magnusson and took it away. If the Enchantrans recovered the Amulet, they would wield a power much greater than we could match."

"Now that the Enchantrans have the Wayfinder," said Amelia, "they know exactly where it is."

Ander folded his arms. "Sounds like we need to find the Amulet first and secure it immediately."

The secretary nodded in agreement. "This needs to be your top priority. I can't stress more the importance of success from a national security standpoint. I'll contact Secretary Dagworth tomorrow morning and enlist the resources of the enforcers to help you in your search."

He nodded in finality. "Now, let's secure this relic." He called for his guards, and they appeared a few seconds later, carrying a long black case. They set the case on the table and flipped it open. Inside was a velvet lining.

"The sword please," said Secretary Drake.

Ander picked up the blade and hesitated. She could sense the thought whirling through his head, how he felt a purpose and connection to the blade. She hadn't fully understood his feelings until he had wielded the blade again in the Silent Shaft. In that moment, it was as if a whole other part of him had opened up before her. All of his passions and drive to protect were unleashed to their full potential. He was an incredible force for good with it in his hands. She was alive today because of him and that blade.

Ander handed the sword to the soldiers, who then lightly set it into the box and snapped the lid tight.

Ander watched the soldiers carry it from the room, lifting an unconscious hand out to them. Amelia took his hand in her own and gave it a squeeze.

"It'll be alright," she said.

"I know." He curled his fingers around hers. Warm tingles shot through her whole body at the contact. A smile grew across her face as their eyes met. Together, they walked out the door.

As they stepped over the threshold, Steam soldiers appeared and ripped Ander away from her faster than she could blink. They shoved him to the deck and yanked his arms behind his back.

She screamed and darted toward him, only to be grabbed on both sides by soldiers and pulled away. Only then did she notice the sheer quantity of soldiers all around. They lined the deck and the helm behind her, each with their crossbows aimed at Ander. Even the two warships were now lowered so that ballistae were pointed toward Ander. In the center of it all, Major General Hawkes stood with his sword drawn.

"Reginald!" shouted Secretary Drake, limping out of the captain's cabin. "What's this all about?"

General Hawkes ignored him, focusing on Ander. "Lieutenant Ander Blackwell, you are under arrest for treason."

Amelia's heart fell.

"Treason?!" repeated Secretary Drake. "Under what charges?"

"For Gifted blood status," said the general.

"Blood status," breathed Amelia. She glanced toward where the crew stood assembled just beyond the soldiers. Her eyes locked on Charles, who stared at the ground.

He did this?! she thought. Anger rose inside her in a torrent. *Of course he did! It was in the regulations to report anyone who manifested Gifted power.* If she wasn't pinned back, she would have grabbed him by the collar and slapped him right then and there.

"Reginald, this is ridiculous!" said the secretary, his voice rising.

"If he was Gifted, how did that slip past enlistment? How did that slip past every check at the gates into the military district? Do you not see how ludicrous this is?"

General Hawkes' eyes narrowed.

An idea struck Amelia. "Give him an electrodetectualizer. Then you'll know for sure."

General Hawkes paused a moment before waving a hand. A soldier appeared with a meter and approached Ander. Amelia held her breath as they took one of Ander's hands and placed it onto the metal rod.

The needle on the gauge rose ever so slightly. Her eyes widened.

"We've got a weak positive," said the soldier.

No! No no no no no!

"Take him to a holding cell," commanded General Hawkes.

"No!" screamed Amelia. "He's not Gifted! He's a hero! You can't take him away! You can't!"

Tears streamed down her face, blurring her vision. They were pulling him away, escorting him off the airship. She barely caught his eye and saw the pain in them. This was everything he had feared would happen.

"ANDER!"

Her arms slipped free from the soldiers holding her, and she sprinted after him. She only made it a few steps before they seized her again, pulling her back. She struggled against them, fighting to get to Ander.

A thousand thoughts flew through her mind. What was she going to do without him? How were they going to beat the Enchantrans? What would she do without her best friend?

Garret appeared and put a hand on her shoulder. His eyes were full of emotion.

"Garret! What are we going to do?" she pleaded.

"I don't know," Garret responded, "but we'll figure something out."

Need to know what happens next?

Join our newsletter to unlock sneak peeks, surprise bonuses, and the first word when Book Three releases.

Acknowledgements

W ell, are you curious what comes next? We can't wait to share the next installment of the *Republic of Steam Chronicles*. We've been building up to this next book, which we have been looking forward to for years.

This next part of Ander and Amelia's journey will change everything. Dark forces are on the move, and their sights are set on the Amulet of Power, hidden deep within the Republic of Steam. There's a reason the talisman was concealed—it has the ability to amplify power tenfold. In the wrong hands, it could bring catastrophic destruction. It's the worst possible time for Ander to be taken away and Amelia to be the most hated person in the Republic. The Republic will need them now more than ever.

Stay tuned because the adventure is about to get even bigger.

Well, there are many people we want to thank for their enormous support with *Wayfinder*. First, we want to thank our editors, Valerie and Jamie. They were *amazing!* Their attention to detail and critical eye helped us to polish this adventure. We are so grateful for you both!

We also want to thank our beta readers, Amy, Spencer, and Shawn. Your feedback was so rewarding after spending hundreds of hours writing this adventure. Thank you for putting wind behind our sails.

Julie, the cover artwork is breathtaking! The fact that you can take our stick figure drawings and turn it into *that* is proof that magic is real. Thank you for painting this world for our readers!

We are in love with the maps, schematics, and chapter graphics Camilla drew for us. She poured in so much detail to make these feel authentic, even so far as to put stains and fold lines on the maps. We look at them, and it feels like we are seeing exactly the same maps our characters are holding.

Jeana, thank you for designing our cover layout and graphics! Your patience and expertise have helped elevate our series brand to the next level. We are truly grateful for you!

And finally, thank you to our readers. Hearing how much you've enjoyed following Ander and Amelia's journey has made every moment of writing and editing worthwhile. You are the reason we write.

We'll see you soon in the next adventure, *Amulet*. Until then, stay connected with us on social media and visit our website for updates, additional content, and more.

ABOUT THE AUTHORS

Craig and Jaleesa were born and raised near the Rocky Mountains in the United States of America. Together, they have three kids who have brought fun and adventure to their lives. They enjoy spending their time reading books, camping in the mountains, and hiking.

Made in the USA
Monee, IL
20 January 2026